D0887832

The Heart of Karameikos

Altan Tepes Mountains

Castellan Keep

Duke's Road Keep

Castellan River

Wulfholde Hills

Threshold

Castle of the Three Suns

Highreach River

Hillfollow River

Penhaligon

Verge

High Forge

Kelvin

Ford

Ford

Riffian

Windrush River

The Moor

Bywater Village

Lake of Lost Dreams

Rugalov River

Duke's Road

Dymrak Forest

Ruins of Krakatos

Rugalov Village

Specularum

Rugalov Key

40 miles

N

Gulf of Marilenev

Sea of Dread

Village of Bywater

Castellan River

Town Hall

Will 'o
the Wisp

Winery

Menton
Smithy

Baildon's
Mercantile

Garaman's
Pottery

Inn
of the
Wyvern

Dale
Livery

N

Penhaligon Region

Hillfollow River

Castellan River

Rooster's tribe

Karleah Kunzay's home

Greasetongue's tribe

Braddoc's home

Broken Arch

Castle of the Three Suns

Abelaat's valley

Orc attack

Highreach River

Abelaat attack

Flinn's home

Ford

Ford

Bywater

N

16 miles

"Tell me why your tribe's on the move," Flinn said calmly. He flicked a small piece of meat at Kushik, the bound orc. The tidbit landed in the creature's lanky hair by his ear. Jo watched the orc's snout wrinkle, and the monster suddenly writhed in his bindings.

The orc hissed, and his tiny eyes darted above him in terror. "To attack village-by-the-water." He struggled against the ropes that bound him.

"By-the-water?" Jo exclaimed, leaning forward. "Flinn, the orcs are attacking the village of Bywater!"

"*Fliiiin?*" the orc hissed again, this time his terror self-evident. "Flinn has caught Kushik! Flinn will kill Kushik!"

Kushik was right.

BOOKS

The Penhaligon Trilogy
D.J. Heinrich

Book One
The Tainted Sword
October 1992

Book Two
The Dragon's Tomb
April 1993

Book Three
The Death of Magic
October 1993

DUNGEONS & DRAGONS™ BOOKS

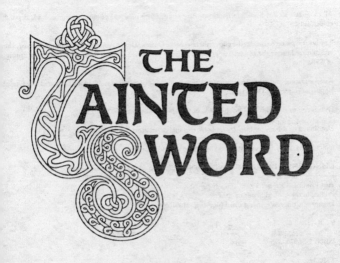

THE TAINTED SWORD

D.J. Heinrich

TSR Inc.

THE TAINTED SWORD

Random House and its affiliate companies have worldwide distribution rights in the book trade for English language products of TSR, Inc.

Distributed to the book and hobby trade in the United Kingdom by TSR Ltd.

Distributed to the toy and hobby trade by regional distributors.

Color art by Larry Elmore. Mapping by David C. Sutherland III.

DUNGEONS & DRAGONS, D&D, and the TSR logo are trademarks owned by TSR, Inc.

First Printing: October 1992
Printed in the United States of America
Library of Congress Catalog Card Number: 91-67659

9 8 7 6 5 4 3 2 1

ISBN: 1-56076-395-7

TSR, Inc.
P.O. Box 756
Lake Geneva, WI 53147
United States of America

TSR Ltd.
120 Church End, Cherry Hinton
Cambridge CB1 3LB
United Kingdom

About the Author

D. J. Heinrich is TSR's pseudonym for an author who resides in Wisconsin. In addition to writing fantasy, science-fiction, and Gothic romance, she prides herself on her "really bad" poetry. Her passion in life, however, is the creation of costumes.

For Jim,
without whom this book would never have been.

Chapter I

linn the Fallen! Flinn the Fool!"

The taunts ripped loudly through the cold winter air. Children raced about the man on the griffon and continued their chant, their words growing more bold and cruel when nearby adults did not chastise them. One man—a baker by the looks of his flour-covered apron—even cheered his son's viciousness. He made a wicked gesture with his hands, then turned toward his companions and laughed. "Flinn the *Fool*! Flinn the Mighty is no more!" the baker shouted spitefully.

A young woman edged closer, her tall, lanky frame moving gracefully through the onlookers. A gust of wind blew her braided hair into her face, and she tossed the reddish plait to her back. Her clean, calloused hands gripped her leather belt, which bound a shift to her thin waist. Johauna Menhir had yet to see her twentieth year, but her clear gray eyes held wisdom—wisdom gleaned from thirteen years spent as an orphan on the streets of Specularum. Jo had lived in the southern seaport city until recently, when she journeyed north and found herself in the tiny village of Bywater.

Jo's gaze slid from the baker to the man surrounded by the

1

growing mob of children. She scanned his rough, leather and fur attire and noted that he wore no armor. He wore no hat, and iron-gray streaks filled his once-black hair. Wind and sun had deeply tanned his face, which was marked by scars and wrinkles. He looked neither right nor left, one hand casually gripping the griffon's reins and the other holding the lead to a pack mule that followed close behind. His breath formed white puffs in the early winter air.

The man's griffon appeared to have abnormally short wings, but Jo thought that might be because they were tucked close to the beast's body. She stared at the creature's front legs. Why are his claws gripping those strange leather balls? she wondered. After the griffon paced forward she saw why: The bird-lion's talons weren't made for walking long distances, and the leather bags cushioned the impact between the beast's claws and the ground.

Johauna searched the rider's face again. His stern, straight lips were partially hidden by a drooping moustache. His eyes betrayed no emotion. He seemed unaware of the taunting children, the stares from the adults, and the unease that spread from him in waves. Could this old man really be Flinn the Mighty?

Bad fortune had tossed Jo off the path to the Castle of the Three Suns, the home of Baroness Arteris Penhaligon, whom Jo hoped to petition for knighthood. Now she was stranded in the little village of Bywater, some sixty miles southeast of the castle, or so the village blacksmith had told her. Jo had never expected to come across Fain Flinn, the knight who had fallen from grace seven years ago. Like most everyone back in far-off Specularum, Jo assumed he had died shortly after his disgrace.

Yet if Flinn the Mighty still lives, surely he would be treated with respect and reverence and not this . . . this insolence, Jo thought. She sidled her way through the crowd to get closer to the warrior. For nineteen years she had listened to tales of Flinn the Mighty and had developed a fascination for the man of legend. He, if anyone, could advise her on petitioning Baroness Arteris.

Intently, Jo watched the man called Flinn pull his griffon to a halt and dismount before Bywater's only supply store. The white walls and brass sconces of Baildon's Mercantile gleamed in the morning sun. A large, ornately painted sign swung overhead, proclaiming the establishment's name. Double doors with a window to either side marked the center of the building. Half a dozen hitching posts, each with two brass rings, fronted the shop. A single wooden bench, painted bright red, stood to the left of the door. The shop's air of tidy prosperity contrasted sharply with the disrepair of an abandoned winery to its left and the ramshackle look of Garaman's Pottery to its right.

The griffon screeched a shrill, eaglelike scream and reared. Jo's attention turned toward the mount. His golden eyes were swirling in terror. The crowd's jeers clearly made the animal skittish. His claws released the balls as he reared again, and the pads dangled from thin chains attached to the creature's ankles. The rider stroked the silky feathers of the griffon's neck and calmly urged him back to the ground.

Jo watched Flinn tie his mount and pack mule to a hitching ring. His jaw clenched as he shouldered the crowd out of his way. The griffon snapped at the children, sending them scurrying back. A slight smile formed on Flinn's lips. The warrior then muzzled the skittish griffon, which nipped once or twice before submitting.

The children, seeing the griffon's muzzle, grew bolder. Their chants rang louder, and more joined in. One or two of them even poked the griffon's haunches with sticks, but backed away after being struck by his thick, lionlike tail. Flinn resolutely ignored the children and began unloading the mule.

Why isn't he putting the brats in their place? Jo wondered. The children reminded her of the gangs infesting Specularum. They lay in wait and attacked passersby. Rich victims were robbed; poor victims were tormented. Jo had witnessed enough gangs to know that the one centered on Flinn verged on violence.

From the corner of her eye, Jo saw a boy pick up a rock from the muddy, partially frozen road. He was a big youth, easily as tall as Jo. His eyes were puffy slits, and he wore a deeply lined pout. Just the sort of boy to spark a riot, Jo thought.

She touched a brown, furry tail hanging from her belt and spoke a magical phrase that sounded like a growl. She blinked out of existence and reappeared before the boy, who had been at least twenty paces away. Jo struck the youth's hand, knocking the rock from it. The boy gasped as she knelt, emitted her low growl again, and touched the tail at her belt. She reappeared in the thick of the crowd and slowly rose from her crouch. In the bustle of the street, her sudden appearance went unnoticed.

Cautiously Jo looked toward the youth, taking care to keep a person or two between her and the boy. He was looking around, befuddled, trying to find his attacker. At last he shook his head and faded into the crowd. Jo turned back to the man with the griffon, a smirk crossing her lips.

She froze. Flinn's dark eyes were on her. Had he seen her use her blink dog's tail? His cold gaze remained inscrutable. Turning, he continued unloading the mule. Jo rubbed her hands, then stepped forward boldly, leaving the crowd of adults and breaking the line of children circling Flinn.

"You've trained your griffon well, Sir Flinn," Jo said, nodding toward the mule and horse tied together. "Either him or your mule. Not many griffons would pass up a meal of horseflesh."

The man looked down at Johauna. He was very tall, a head taller than Jo. A fiercely curving scar sliced along his left jawline and just nicked his throat; a second scar cut through his left eyebrow. His eyes were deep brown, nearly black. Jo caught the briefest twitch of his moustache, and she wondered whether he were amused or angered . . . or both.

"I'm no longer a knight, so don't address me as such," he said coldly. He gestured toward the animals and added, grudgingly, "They're both well-trained. Ariac—the griffon— hasn't had horseflesh in years."

"What does he eat if not horseflesh?" Jo asked, interested. "When I worked for a hostler, the griffons almost always attacked the horses."

The warrior paused at the knot he was unraveling and flicked his gaze at Johauna, then turned back to the mule. "He's happy enough with fox or bear—whatever I trap. It helps that he's crippled and can't fly," Flinn replied, hefting the last bundle off the mule. He turned toward the shop. "You might pack that fly swatter of yours away. It'll get you in trouble."

Surprised, Jo touched the blink dog's tail and stroked the thin, bristly fur. So he had noticed! Johauna grimaced, then hurriedly tucked the tail inside her bag. Glancing at the shop, she followed Flinn.

"Enough!" someone roared. "Enough of this badgering, you pups!" A burly man burst through the shop's double doors, throwing both open at once. "I'll not have you pestering my customers! Now get along, all of you, or I'll—" The merchant cuffed one child on the ears when she didn't flee fast enough to please him. Jo glanced at the sign above the man's head. This must be Baildon, she thought.

"Ah, Flinn!" the merchant said, beaming. His tanned, shiny face was framed by huge sideburns that covered much of his cheeks, perhaps to compensate for the lack of hair above. One or two extra chins graced the shopkeeper's neck. His bloodied butcher's apron draped over a sleeveless, dirty gray tunic and a pair of even dirtier brown breeches. He wore sandals despite the cold, and Jo saw bright spots of blood spattered on them. The merchant stepped forward, and he and Flinn clasped each other's wrists.

"Come in, Flinn! Have you anything worth my money this year?" Baildon laughed and returned to his shop, Flinn following with his load of furs. Discreetly Jo followed, too, bent on discovering more about the man who had always been legend to her. She eagerly passed through the doors of the mercantile.

Bywater's only supply store was a two-story building crammed to the rafters with all things imaginable. Fantastic wares such as magical daggers and rings lay casually beside such common items as bits and bridles.

Jo halted just inside the door. The fragrant smell of fresh baked goods filled her nose. She drew a deep breath, watching Flinn and Baildon meander through the cluttered store to the counter at the back. Her mouth watered. She hadn't eaten in more than a day. Although she had no money, the smell of the bread was irresistible. She drifted into the mercantile, hoping to find the foodstuffs and feast her eyes, if not her stomach. As she passed among crates and stacks of merchandise, the flash of metal caught her eye.

Shiny armor stood near the windows, glowing with light from lanterns both magical and mundane. Beside the armor ran a counter that held new and used weapons, some with elaborate runes. One well-crafted morning star rested behind glass. Its spikes were formed of a black metal Jo hadn't seen before. At the end of the counter lay a pile of battered armor, scarred with much use. Ordinarily Jo would have been intrigued, but the smell of bread grew stronger. Sniffing, she turned toward a table laden with bolts of cloth. As she followed the scent, her fingers glided over burlap, fine silk, and even an exotic weave that faintly glowed. Beyond the table lay bags of oats, clustered about a ceiling post. A pair of boots dangled from the post by their bootstraps. On a peg above the boots hung a cloak that blended so well with its surroundings that Jo nearly missed it. New tools, spare harness parts, and saddles cluttered one corner as she walked on, still following the teasing aroma of bread.

Jo moved to the center of the store, her gaze drifting upward. From the tall rafters dangled lengths of rope and chains and drying herbs. Beside the ropes, two ripening deer carcasses hung. As she passed beneath them, their smell masked the scent she had been following. Spying a glass case, she moved forward, hoping it would hold the bread. Instead, she found gems and stones, some bathed in colorful auras of magic, some chased in metal, and others loose.

In an adjacent case lay elvish candy—spun sugar creations of breathtaking beauty and taste. A sheet of glass guarded the confections. Jo licked her lips. Across the top of the case lay slices of spiced beef, aging and drying, nearly obscuring the treasures below.

Johauna stopped—she had found the baked goods, in a nearby cupboard. She stood in awe. Shelf after shelf brimmed with golden loaves. Jo saw currant buns, loaves made of brown wheat, and delicate pastries. Briefly she toyed with the idea of stealing a popover since the merchant was clearly busy with Flinn, but she drove the thought from her mind.

Knights are not bread stealers, she decided. After a heady breath, she realized that her resolution would not endure for long, and she wandered to the back of the store.

Flinn and the merchant stood at the rear counter. As Jo approached, Baildon used a cleaver to sweep the remains of the goose he had been quartering onto the floor. With the heavy blade, he gestured for Flinn to put down his bundle.

"The furs are fine ones, Flinn, fine indeed," the merchant was saying. "But fox and owlbear just aren't fetching the price they once did, not with the rich cloths coming from the South. No one wants fur when they can have silk. The best I can give you is thirty gold." The merchant smiled apologetically and crossed his arms.

"I need forty, Baildon, no less." Flinn, too, crossed his arms. His mouth formed a mulish frown.

"Excuse me, sirs," Jo interrupted as she moved closer to the counter. The merchant spat tobacco juice onto the dirt floor. Jo ignored the gesture. "I worked for Tauntom, master of the Tanner's Guild in Specularum."

"Yes, yes, girl, that's all well and good," the merchant snapped, "but what has that to do with us?"

Jo's gray eyes flashed in anger, but she glanced away immediately. She had learned the art of negotiation and did not want to rile Baildon. If she could get Flinn his forty coins—his beautiful pelts would be worth twice that in Specularum—Flinn might give her a moment of his time.

"It has everything to do with you," Jo said smoothly. "You see, Tauntom recently received an order for all the furs he can provide. It seems a lord of Specularum has planned a gala for his son's wedding next spring." Johauna leaned toward the merchant with a conspiratorial air, aware of the suspicion in Flinn's keen eyes. The merchant leaned forward. "Tauntom is panicked—he can't supply all the pelts. The lands around Specularum have been hunted to exhaustion," Jo paused for effect. "Tauntom will pay you eighty gold for these furs."

She backed off and shrugged. "If you can't meet Master Flinn's asking price, then I'd suggest he take them to someone else. Someone who would benefit from your shy purse." She smiled politely at the round-bellied man before her but averted her eyes from Flinn's. The tall warrior still regarded her with suspicion.

The merchant stroked the stubble of his beard. His beady brown eyes dimmed a little, then he turned to Flinn and jerked his thumb toward Jo. "Do you trust her, Flinn? Seems like she's trying to hoodwink me."

Flinn looked down at his splayed hands. "I've no reason not to believe her, Baildon. The decision is yours." Flinn looked at Jo. "She did, however, do me a good turn earlier."

Baildon nodded toward Flinn. "That's good enough for me. A friend of yours is a friend of mine," the merchant said briskly. Baildon tied the furs back into a bundle and put them on the crowded floor behind the counter. "I'll have that list of supplies in two shakes of a wyvern's tail." The merchant grabbed some burlap sacks and headed down a crowded walkway.

Flinn crossed his arms again and looked at Jo. She consciously returned the gesture, and the two of them stared at each other. Finally Flinn broke the silence.

"You were lying, weren't you?"

"I was not," Jo countered coolly.

Flinn's eyebrows rose. "Earlier you said you were a stablehand. Now you're a tanner's helper?"

"I've been both. I've also worked at an armory and for a weaponsmith, fletching arrows," she said proudly. She hoped Flinn was impressed with her credentials, all of which would prove useful to a potential knight.

He wasn't. One brow arched higher, and he said, "Being unable to hold a job is nothing to be smug about."

"Nevertheless, the tale is true," Johauna interjected sharply, stung by Flinn's derision. "Tauntom the tanner will be needing extra furs by spring. I didn't lie." Jo put her hands on her hips.

Before Flinn could respond, Baildon returned with several large bundles. "Here you be, Flinn, all the supplies you asked for and the remainder of your gold." The merchant's eyes fairly gleamed at the prospect Flinn's furs presented to him. Feeling benevolent, he nodded to Jo and said, "There's a loaf of pumpkin bread that's two days' old over in the cupboard, to the left. You're welcome to it if you want. I appreciate the tip."

Jo murmured thanks and hurried to the nearby cabinet. After a moment of searching, she found the small, dark orange loaf Baildon had mentioned. She picked up the bread and sniffed the aroma of cinnamon, cloves, and exotic spices. Hungrily she began eating it there in the store. Bits of conversation between Flinn and the merchant floated toward her, and she turned to watch the two men.

". . . Verdilith. That wyrm is back in the territory, Flinn! You've got to do something," the merchant pleaded. "Won't you—"

"You know I can't do that, Baildon. Don't hope—"

"I can hope all I want!"

"Well, hope away then. I won't go after Verdilith, and that's final."

"Is it because of the prophecy? Is that it? Karleah Kunzay's crazy, Flinn! She—"

"Enough!" Flinn shouted, his fist hammering the shopkeeper's counter. "It is not the prophecy! It's because

I'm no longer a knight! I'm not—!" The words were strangled short. "Baildon, you should know that!"

Jo's curiosity was piqued. She edged nearer only to have Flinn abruptly brush past her, his supplies draped over his shoulder. The warrior stomped out of the shop, his face grim. He didn't glance at Jo, though she watched him go. She wondered if she had the time to pry information from the merchant but decided she didn't. Holding up the loaf, she mumbled her thanks to Baildon and followed Flinn.

She stopped outside the shop's doors and eyed the warrior. He was trying to goad the griffon into a standing position so he could mount. The recalcitrant beast merely pecked at Flinn with his muzzled beak. Jo sauntered over.

"Try cupping your hands around his eyes," she said when Flinn's latest efforts proved futile. "It's a trick I learned from the hostler. The griffon'll stand up and try to fly because he's scared. Try it."

The man cast an indignant glance toward Jo. "That doesn't work with Ariac," he said in rebuke. Jo grimaced and bit her lip. Obviously Flinn knew the trick.

Flinn coaxed the bird-lion once more, this time pulling on the feathers surrounding one tender ear opening. Ariac stood immediately. The griffon's lion feet nervously scratched the mud and ice of Bywater's only road, and his front claws reluctantly closed upon the leather balls. Flinn leaped into the saddle. He reached forward, tore the muzzle off, and grabbed the mule's lead rein all in one smooth motion.

He turned to Jo and nodded once, curtly. "My thanks, girl."

"The name's Jo—" The rest of her name went unspoken. The man of legend had turned his animals around without a second glance.

Dejected, Jo sat down on the bench outside Baildon's

Mercantile. Flinn's tall form slowly disappeared down the street. Sighing, Jo nibbled a little more from her loaf, looked at the remaining half, and then prudently packed it away in her bag. She looked down the muddy road once more, listening to horses break pockets of ice to find the water below.

Well, Johauna, she thought, what's it to be? You have one meal—maybe two if you stretch it. Is it back to Specularum? Her thoughts grew grim at that prospect, and she shook her head. No, no, that won't do. You set out to do something, and it's time you did it. And it's no use to stay here and drum up work, either. No. On to the Castle of the Three Suns. Flinn the Mighty seems to be heading in that general direction. Perhaps he will answer some questions if you catch him.

Jo slung her bag across her shoulder and proceeded down Bywater's only street. Opposite the mercantile stood a livery, with a narrow inn on one side and a blacksmith's shop on the other. The smith looked up from the draft horse he was shoeing as Johauna went by. He nodded cordially, his hands holding a tong and a hammer. Not a bad little village, Jo thought, remembering the farrier's kindness last night in letting her sleep inside his shop in return for a little cleaning.

Next she passed ten or so houses, each with identical thatched roofs and limed walls. Near the edge of the village stood a stone-walled church dedicated to the worship of any Immortal. Jo was tempted to stop and pray, but Odin would understand if she pressed on after Flinn. Odin would be the first to follow his dreams rather than pray about them.

Sharp rocks and jags of ice poked Johauna's feet through the shoes she wore, and she slowed her pace a little. She came to a stop altogether at the outskirts of the village, where a red and purple tavern proclaimed itself the Will-o'-the-Wisp. In front of the tavern, a smartly armored elf maiden was cautiously approaching her hippogriff, trying to calm the steed.

Jo had handled such creatures before at the hostler's. This particular hippogriff was of excellent conformation and unusual coloration. Jo stepped forward, her eyes locked on the creature. The feathers of its forequarters glistened whitely in the midmorning sun. Just behind the forelegs, the feathers slowly transformed into a thick coat of roan hair. The merging of feather and hair produced a wide, solid band of fiber, which served as a protective blanket under the saddle and rider.

Suddenly a hand clamped on Jo's shoulder. Jo reached for the tail at her belt, a low growl instantly on her lips. But the tail was in her bag, and she landed flat on her back in the icy mud.

"It was you! You!" The surly, puffy-eyed youth straddled her, slapping her face hard. "What magic did you pull, coward? I'll show you!"

Jo had learned a thing or two about brawling during her years in Specularum. She crossed one arm over her face to protect it, then punched the youth's loins. The boy screamed and scrambled off Jo. He doubled over in pain and lay in the mud, tears in his eyes and curses on his breath. Jo stood up, brushing the cold mud off her clothes.

"That's hardly fair fighting, miss," came a lilting, melodic voice. Startled, Jo turned around to see the warrior elf astride her hippogriff. Sunlight glinted off her silvery armor, pale white hair, and violet eyes. On her polished breastplate lay an amulet radiating a faint green aura. The maid saluted Jo with a mailed hand and smiled serenely.

Jo found it impossible not to smile in return. She had always loved the elven race, thinking it by far the loveliest to inhabit her world. Specularum catered primarily to humans, but a few elves had crossed her path before. She counted herself lucky anytime they actually spoke to her.

"No, it's not fair, good warrior," Jo said as graciously as she could. "But he deserved nothing less." Jo glowered at the boy, who could only grimace in return.

The elf maid laughed. "You are quite right. I saw his churlish attack." The maid saluted once more and said, "May the Immortals favor you with good fortune. Good day."

"Go with joy," Jo replied. She waved when the elf lightly tapped her steed and it leaped into the air.

Jo turned to the youth, who was on his knees. She pointed at him with two fingers. "You!" she barked. "If you follow me any more you'll get more of the same! Got it?" She stomped past him, splashing icy water from a mud puddle onto him.

Jo shook her head and continued out of town, forgetting the youth completely. Her mind was intent on catching Flinn. She didn't think he could travel fast with the griffon and the heavily laden mule, and she was confident she could catch up soon. When she did, she would find out from Flinn the Mighty himself just how to become a knight at the Castle of the Three Suns. She headed toward the foothills surrounding Bywater.

After almost an hour's climb, Johauna began to doubt whether she could overtake Flinn. The mountainous terrain had become dry, hard, and rocky. Although the hostler had taught her the rudiments of tracking on the rare occasions when an animal escaped, the ground yielded not even the slightest clue to follow. Even the snow had thinned away to nothing. Jagged stones bit into the soles of her feet. Twice she had slipped and fallen on loose shale, scraping her hands and knees. The second time it happened, Jo contemplated using her blink dog's tail to make multiple jumps and cover more ground. But continuous blinking tended to make her ill, and she wasn't at all sure which direction to proceed.

The foothills grew steeper and harder to traverse, and the shale-strewn ground gave way to soft soil and snow. Jo soon found sign of Flinn's passage, and she doggedly followed the trail. Ahead, thorny bushes covered the land in thick clumps. Jo lost time trying to walk around the copses rather than through them. At last, she resigned herself to following the animals' trail, hoping they had broken through the growth so she wouldn't have to. But the brush still clawed and bit at her.

High noon came and went without Flinn resting the animals or setting up a midday camp. She had hoped to overtake them at lunch so she could charm her way into a bit of food. She had already eaten the last of the flattened pumpkin loaf, and she was still famished. Her thoughts drifted off to the last real meal she had eaten.

Jo had stowed away on a river caravan heading north from Specularum. All had gone well until the day before yesterday, when the captain discovered her in the cargo hold—two hungry, cramped days into the journey. He tossed her overboard into the icy river. Cursing her ill fortune, Johauna swam to shore and hastily built a fire to dry her clothes and warm her blue skin. Afterward, she wandered into the wilderness, intent on reaching the Castle of the Three Suns, even on foot.

She spent two hungry days walking along the wooded banks of the Castellan River. Then she smelled what was surely the world's most delicious cooking. She stopped to investigate.

One hundred paces from the river lay a deserted camp. In the center of the camp, a fire burned beneath a bubbling cookpot. Jo crept up behind a nearby lean-to and gazed into the pot. Pieces of chicken boiled merrily away in a thick, creamy sauce, along with vegetables and dumplings. A golden loaf of bread sat warming on a rock by the fire. Jo approached the camp warily. No one was in sight, but still she remained hidden.

Her lips wetted in anticipation. She had never stolen before, not even when the temptation had been strong and the moment opportune, like when the drunken lord had accosted her and she bit off his ear instead of taking his purse. But hunger softened her scruples. She couldn't wait for the cook to return to beg a bite, so she used her blink dog's tail to appear by the fire. She eagerly spooned the stew onto the waiting plate and tore a chunk from the loaf before blinking away.

The meal was delicious, though she was sure that hunger had flavored it well. Briefly she wondered why someone should leave a camp so unguarded, but she gave it no further thought. Jo wolfed down the food in moments and then debated whether to return the plate and spoon. She told herself she wasn't a true thief, licked the plate and spoon as clean as she could, and blinked back to the campfire. With any luck, the owner might not even notice the missing stew. Of course, she thought, eyeing the missing chunk of bread, she could only get so lucky.

The next day, when she expected to reach the castle, she stumbled instead into Bywater. At the time, she considered the sidetrack to be ill fortune. Now, after meeting Fain Flinn, she believed it was fate.

Jo sighed, her thoughts returning to the present. Absently, she looked up. With a start she saw she was out of the brushy foothills and into true forest. Spruce and pine grew in tight stands, blocking out the gray winter sun. The dead branches of the trees clawed her even more viciously than had the thorny bushes of the foothills. The undergrowth was so dense that Jo could clearly see where Flinn and his mounts had passed. Wearily she realized darkness would soon fall on these woods; she would need to overtake Flinn soon to claim pilgrim's rights from him. She thought forlornly, I wonder if he'll even offer me food and lodging, no matter how hard I work. She gritted her teeth and pressed on, rethinking her decision to use the blink dog's tail. Maybe, she thought, if I just use it to go ten paces at a time—

For the second time that day a hand came down on her shoulder. This time Jo dropped to the ground in a defensive move, prepared to roll away and onto her feet for flight. But the underbrush hemmed her in, preventing the roll. She fell in an undignified heap and stared up at her attacker—Flinn the Fallen.

🙞 🙞 🙞 🙞 🙞

Flinn put his hands on his hips and glared down at the girl. "Just what do you think you're doing?" he snapped. He was surprised by the anger in his own voice, but he had dodged and evaded this girl long enough. Besides, Baildon's insistence about hunting the dragon still rang irritatingly in his head. He was no longer a knight, yet people still expected him to act like one. They heaped insults on him, then expected his protection!

The girl blinked her gray eyes and Flinn realized they matched the eyes of the Immortal Diulanna, as did the girl's reddish hair. Flinn prayed to Diulanna often, for she inspired willpower and discipline. The Immortal had appeared to Flinn twice in the past, and he found the physical resemblance between Diulanna and this girl disconcerting. She blinked again, then said, "I want to talk to you, Master Flinn."

Flinn snorted. "Don't stand on ceremony with me, girl. I am not your master." Grudgingly he extended his hand to her lithe form and pulled her to her feet. "Stop following me and go back to where you came from."

She tried vainly to brush a few of the pine needles out of her clothing. "My name's—" she began.

"I don't care what your name is or who you are," Flinn interrupted brutally. "Just go back, or else I'll tie you up here and leave you to the wolves. You've invaded my forest and now you want to invade my home?!" Flinn gestured to the woods surrounding them. "Leave me alone."

The young woman's expression became quizzical, then thoughtful. Flinn felt an inexplicable urge to turn away under the girl's gaze, but instead he repeated angrily, "Leave me!"

Still she stared at him. Then came words that would haunt Flinn, said simply and with trust, "But you're Flinn the Mighty. My father told me all the tales of you when I was a child. I want to become a knight in the Order of the Three Suns at the castle. You can help me become a knight like you."

Flinn half-turned away but kept his eyes locked on the girl's. She had pried into his business affairs in town, followed him through the woods almost to his very doorstep, and was now idolizing him. Most damnable of all the transgressions was the last—a painful reminder of all that he had been. His eyes narrowed and his lips tightened. The longer he looked into the girl's innocent gray eyes, the more he saw the worship there. He could almost hear the tales she had been told of him, hear the songs that had been sung of Flinn the Mighty. He could hear the story of his fight with Verdilith the great green, his single-handed defeat of two giants, his lonely sojourn to the Lost Valley of Hutaaka to recover his baron's stolen scepter. He could see the depth of her adoration. And the more he glimpsed her absolute faith, the greater grew his anger and rage and pain.

He slapped her.

The blow knocked the girl off her feet. Flinn stepped over her. "Leave me be!" He strode off to where he had tethered the griffon and mule. He yanked once on Ariac's lead rein, and the bird-lion screeched its disapproval. Flinn took no notice and began leading the mounts through the thick undergrowth.

His way was blocked suddenly by the girl, her hand holding the tail he had noticed earlier.

"What kind of knight are you? What *right* have you to hit me when all I want is to ask you a few questions?" she shouted, her eyes flashing. She held one hand to her cheek, and he saw a faint trickle of blood at her lip. He quelled the feeling of remorse that tried to rise.

"I am no longer a knight, girl, and *you* have no right to question me! Leave me be!" With that he tried to brush her aside, but she was stronger than she looked and stood her ground. She had the effrontery to put her hands on his arms to stop him.

"But you're a legend—you're Flinn the Mighty!" she cried.

He grimaced and then savagely pushed her away. The undergrowth caught her fall this time. Through clenched teeth he spat, "The man you're looking for is dead. Dead. There is no more 'Flinn the Mighty.'" The words were bitter on his tongue.

Amazed, the girl stared at him. Flinn shook his head in disbelief and walked into the undergrowth, leading Ariac and Fernlover, his mule.

Deliberately, he closed his mind to what had just transpired.

He quelled the small voice that prompted him to turn around and ask for her forgiveness. The matter was settled. He wondered how the child could be so foolish as to search for Flinn the Mighty. His thoughts threatened to grow darker yet, and deftly he cut them off, dismissing the girl from his mind completely. The last seven years had taught him how to ward off painful thoughts.

Flinn pushed through the brush and hurried Ariac along. The home trail lay just ahead; if he could reach it in the next hour, he would be back to the lodge by true dark. He suddenly longed for the comfort and safety of his little home, a crudely built house of logs. "Some warrior," he muttered to himself. "I didn't used to need a haven." All at once he felt weary and indescribably old.

Always before, Flinn had called a campfire his home. Whether he was on the trail of an orc troop as a knight or hunting bear as a trapper, Flinn had spent more than two decades by a fire. Now, he only wanted the safety and privacy that his own hearth could provide. That longing disturbed him. After thirty-seven winters, he was content with a lap-robe and a fire and a good pipe?

He glanced behind him to make sure the girl wasn't following. Nothing but dark tree branches met his gaze.

His mind wandered back to the morning's events. For some reason he had dreaded entering the village, even more so than usual. Flinn's semiannual sojourns into Bywater— every spring and fall—accounted for all of his social contact. His long solitude made these contacts more painful over the years. He couldn't help feeling a superstitious twinge at how this particular trip could have turned out, and he dreaded what the next might hold.

As always, the children of the village had come out to taunt him. He had grown inured to their words, though, and hadn't given them any notice. The boy with the rock had been a different matter, however. Never before had one of the children threatened to stone him. Flinn wondered what would have happened had the girl not intervened. Then he wondered why she had. He thought about trading his furs elsewhere, but the nearest place was the castle he had once called home. Flinn snorted. He would never return to the Castle of the Three Suns again. No, Bywater had proved ideal: one day's ride from his home, small, but with a large enough mercantile to supply most of his wants and a merchant whom Flinn trusted as much as he could. In a larger town, he might encounter someone from the order, and that he couldn't abide.

The mule brayed eagerly, and Flinn saw the scraggy pine that marked the clearing where his cabin stood. His thoughts turned to the business at hand. As always after having been away, he approached his camp warily. On the little crest overlooking his place he stopped, his eyes straining in the dark.

Nothing seemed amiss. On the right stood the cabin, dark and undisturbed. On the left loomed the barn, home to Ariac and Fernlover. Along one side of the barn rested a stone cellar with heavy wooden doors, doubly barred. Flinn kept Ariac's meat there. The smell often drew wolves at night, but the stone walls and stout wood had kept them at bay in the past. Thankfully, no wolves nosed about the camp now. A divided corral abutted the back of the stables. He sensed rather than saw that the top bar of the gate was down. "Perhaps it was the wind," Flinn murmured.

Something appeared next to him. "What's wrong?"

Flinn jumped violently, his hand reaching in reflex for his sword. He could just make out the girl's form in the gloom. "What in Thor's Thunder are you doing here?" he demanded angrily. He hadn't thought of her during the last hour of the trip and was badly startled by her sudden appearance. My reflexes are rusty, he thought.

She pointed down the hill toward the camp. "Is something wrong?"

"No," he said gruffly. "I always check out the camp before I go in." He blinked, realizing he had volunteered information.

The girl shrugged. "It's too dark for me to go back to Bywater tonight. I'll clean your barn for a night's lodging and supper."

"You're claiming pilgrim's rights, I take it?"

The girl nodded. "You bet I am. It's too cold to bed down under the trees."

"One night's worth—that's it," Flinn replied.

She nodded again, then took a deep breath, her eyes scanning the treetops. "Think you'd answer just a few questions about how to become a knight at the Castle of the Three Suns?" the girl ventured, one hand touching the cheek he had slapped. Her tone carried a faint suggestion of hurt.

Flinn stared at the girl. By Diulanna, he thought, I am guilty! I had no right to hit her! He pursed his lips and then said curtly, "Too late for questions tonight. In the morning, perhaps." Then he led the griffon and mule down to the stable, resolutely ignoring the girl who followed him. Briefly Flinn checked out the fallen rail and decided the wind did indeed blow it over; he resolved to find a longer pole in the morning. Opening the shed doors, he let the animals loose while seeking the lantern that hung inside the doorway. With practiced ease, he grabbed the tinderbox next to it and sparked the light.

Ariac and Fernlover eagerly sought their respective stalls.

The griffon made mewling noises and clawed his bedding as he sniffed the warm and familiar odors of home. The mule grazed his head along a rough-hewn log, scratching an itch against a familiar burl in the post. Flinn carried the lantern over to the griffon's stall and hung it on a nearby wooden peg.

"You can start by seeing to the mule," Flinn said gruffly, then entered Ariac's stall and began loosening the saddle on his back. He removed the saddle, blanket, and bridle, taking care to gently remove the bit from the griffon's sensitive beak. He went outside, his eyes adjusting quickly to the lack of light, and retrieved a frozen rabbit carcass from the meat cellar. Ariac clicked his beak eagerly when the carcass landed in his food trough. Picking up a coarse brush, Flinn began to rub down the griffon's lion hair.

The girl had entered the mule's stall and was worrying at the knots that held the supplies to Fernlover's back. But the knots were of Flinn's own design—he was certain the girl couldn't loose them.

"Best leave them to me," he stated briskly, appearing at the front of the stall. He realized he had said more words today than he had spoken in the last year. "The knots are—"

A sudden *whump* announced that the pack had fallen to the stable floor. The girl was watching Flinn expectantly.

"Let me guess," he said sarcastically, "you worked as a sailor's mate."

The girl grinned. "Close. I knew an old man who mended nets down by the wharfs of Specularum. He taught me a trick or two."

Fernlover sniffed the pack delicately, then gave the bundle a tentative nibble.

"Ssst!" Flinn leaped across the barn floor and swatted the

mule. The animal jerked his head and backed away. After pulling the pack out of the stall, the warrior returned to finish Ariac's grooming. The girl began removing Fernlover's tack and preparing him for the night.

Idly, Flinn rubbed Ariac's skin, unconsciously checking the griffon's eaglelike legs for strains. As usual there were none. The leather balls he had made for the griffon to clutch while walking were working perfectly. He didn't mind that this was the third set he had made in the last year—Ariac had avoided a sprain the entire time. Flinn was relieved. A flightless griffon prone to sprains would have to be put down. But Ariac had twice journeyed to Bywater and back in one day without injury. He patted the bird-lion's neck and turned to check on the girl's progress with the mule.

On the ground outside Fernlover's stall lay the girl. She was curled up between his bundle of supplies and the chest that held the animals' tack. She was sound asleep. Lines of exhaustion traced her lips and dark patches shadowed her eyes. Flinn wondered if she suffered nightmares, like he did. Her reddish brown hair—once neatly plaited down her back—was disheveled and matted. Its very disarray lent a vulnerable look to her. . . .

The child, for so she seemed to him in the feeble light of the lantern, was dirty, thin, and obviously poor. The thorn bushes had torn her clothing to tatters. The girl shifted in her exhaustion and whimpered, her hand clutching the blink dog's tail. He wondered whether she ever blinked in and out during her sleep.

Quietly he entered Fernlover's stall and checked over the mule. Every now and then he glanced down at the sleeping girl. The mule was perfectly tended; the girl mustn't have been lying about having worked for a hostler. Even Fernlover's hooves had been checked, for no mud encased the tender frogs.

Flinn wondered if he should wake her for the supper that was part of her recompense, but decided not to. "No need to encourage her," he muttered. If in the morning the girl fulfilled her promise to clean the barn, then he would give her a meal. Not before.

That's it, he said to himself. I'll leave her here and hope she's gone in the morning. Like as not she will be. Flinn's lips tightened and grew bitter, the scar across his brow whitening. He looked down again at the girl. Without really thinking, he pulled Ariac's blanket off the rail and covered her. He took the lantern and looked about the stable, taking in the familiar sound of Fernlover chomping his hay and Ariac whistling in his sleep. To those sounds was added the rhythmic breathing of the girl.

"By Tarastia and Thor and Diulanna," Flinn said, calling on the Immortals he honored, "I don't even know your name."

Chapter II

orning dawned cold and gray. Flinn awoke early, as was his wont, and glanced out one of the two windows of his cabin. Snow loomed in the low clouds. With a muffled groan, he threw back the pile of blemished furs on the bed and swung his legs out. The leather thongs strung across the bed frame were stretched beyond the point of support. Flinn's weight made him sink nearly to the floor. He needed to replace them before his back gave out.

He sighed, wondering if he should just make a proper mattress and be done with it. His hand idly smoothed the rough hair of an owlbear's pelt on the bed. *I am a warrior,* Flinn thought, *and by all that is holy, I don't need a mattress. It's sorry enough I don't sleep on the floor.*

Flinn threw back the furs and stood. He stretched his arms overhead and felt the old bones along his spine shift into place. Then he remembered the girl and his eyes narrowed. "Is she still here?" he wondered aloud. In two strides, Flinn reached the cupboard standing against the opposite wall. He pulled his breeches off a peg on the cupboard's door and hurriedly dressed in the cold morning air. Then he glanced at the hearth; the fire was almost out. Three quick paces brought him to the fireplace, which stood between the bed and the shelves where he kept his foodstuffs. Flinn quickly coaxed the embers into flames.

"If she's still here and has cleaned the barn, I'll have to feed her," Flinn muttered. He glanced at his fresh supplies from Bywater. Flinn detested cooking. He turned away from the cabinet and peered out the window. The girl's probably gone, and with a good pelt or two, he thought caustically. The warrior pulled his warm, gray woolen tunic over his head, then opened the rough-hewn door and strode to the barn, twenty paces away.

At the stable door he halted, his hand stopping as it reached for the bar. Is she in there? he thought suddenly. Does it matter if she isn't? his mind countered. He ignored the questions and opened the stable door. Ariac let out a shrill squeal at the sight of his master, and even Fernlover gave a little snort of recognition. Ariac's red-and-black blanket was hung neatly on the rail by the griffon's stall. The girl was nowhere in sight.

Flinn opened Ariac's stall gate and led the creature out the side door to his half of the corral. The griffon nibbled his shirt, looking for dried meat treats. The warrior gave Ariac a gentle tap, then watched the animal pace once around the pen, settle onto his haunches, and fluff his wings. Flinn went back for Fernlover.

The girl was standing in the barn, her arms filled with dried bracken. Her gray eyes were wary in the wan morning light, and he could see the beginnings of a bruise marking her left cheek. When he didn't speak, she gestured toward Fernlover's stall. "The mule needed fresh bedding."

Flinn merely nodded. "You missed supper last night, so breakfast will have to do." He paused, fighting down the desire to make amends for bruising her. "Thank you, by the way, for staying to clean the barn. I thought you'd left."

"I'm not in the habit of breaking my pacts," the girl said, dropping the bracken to one side of the stall. She cocked her head and then added, "My name's Johauna, Johauna Menhir. Or Jo for short—I answer to both." She inhaled, glancing up at him. "I appreciate the opportunity you're giving me."

Flinn pulled up short. He fixed his eyes on hers, intent on putting her in her place. "Don't think I'm going to any great lengths for you, girl. A few questions are all I'm answering."

He took hold of Fernlover's halter and led the mule through the side door. After letting him loose in his corral, Flinn returned to the barn. He grabbed the pitchfork and moved toward Jo, who was standing in the center of the barn. She ran the back of her hand over her bruised mouth and cheek. His eyes met hers, but he refused to acknowledge the hurt accusation there. "Look," he said, holding the pitchfork out to the girl. "You clean the stalls, and I'll get some breakfast ready. Come in when you're finished." He stalked out of the barn and into the open air.

Snow had begun falling. The early morning sunlight dwindled away to a blanket of gray. The air felt heavy, still, and silent. Flinn stopped abruptly near the door to his cabin. The quiet was palpable, unnatural. He could almost hear the snowflakes fall. He sucked in his breath and sank to a crouch, his knife in hand.

Something's out there, Flinn thought. Warily, he scanned the black lengths of trees surrounding him. Nearly all of the foliage had fallen by now, and the utter white of the falling snow filled the air. Flinn couldn't see beyond the perimeter of the camp. Nothing moved, nothing but the steadily falling flakes.

Slowly, carefully, he turned to eye the animals. Fernlover, as usual, was lying on the ground, resting. Ariac, however, was watching his master. The griffon's ivory beak was pointed directly at Flinn. He saw one feathery ear-tuft, then the other, flick toward him. The bird–lion's beak snapped once or twice, but otherwise the creature seemed at ease.

Flinn felt his muscles loosen. Ariac's senses had always proved reliable in the past, and Flinn had no reason to doubt his mount now. Perhaps the wildboy's out there, he thought to himself. Perhaps he knows the girl's here and is spooked. Flinn entered the cabin, shrugging off the strangeness of the moment. He paused at the hearth to add some small pieces of wood, then the lone chair caught his attention. The girl would have to sit on an upended piece of firewood or else the floor. He set aside a likely looking log.

The warrior pulled the cookpot away from the flames and peered inside. He scraped the pot's bottom with a thick wooden paddle. When only a little muck came away, he smiled. Clean enough, he thought.

He poured in a little water from the nearby bucket and added two handfuls of grain from one of the burlap bags beside the cupboard. He looked into the pot and then added half a handful more. Checking a small wooden canister for salt, he frowned. Not much left, he thought. It's a shame I couldn't afford any yesterday, and this certainly won't last until spring. Shrugging, he added a pinch of the white grains to the gruel. The girl looks peaked, he rationalized. A little salt will help her back to Bywater.

The grain was boiling away by the time the girl came through the door. Flinn knelt at the hearth, stirring the mush. He watched her as she closed the door.

She had obviously found the stream nearby, for much of the grime was gone from her face and hands and legs. She'd also removed the brambles from her hair, combed it— apparently with her fingers—and rebraided it. The bits of hay had been brushed from the shapeless shift she wore. From her leather belt hung the blink dog's tail. He nodded in approval. In the wilderness she was sensible to keep the magical item close at hand. Her shoes—what was left of them—had obviously once been quite finely crafted, and he wondered if she had stolen them. She had wrapped a shawl over her shoulders and across her chest, and tied it at her back—a shawl so old its pattern was indistinguishable.

"The barn's cleaned, Flinn," the girl said quietly, setting her knapsack beside the door. Her eyes were fixed hungrily on the pot before Flinn, and he wondered how long it had been since she'd eaten.

He gestured silently to the table, and she sat down on the only chair. Grunting, he pointed to the piece of wood standing by the hearth, and she changed her seat. The warrior paddled porridge into his only two bowls—a large wooden mixing bowl and a small clay serving bowl. He pushed the second bowl toward the girl and gave her the only spoon he owned.

She ate greedily, apparently unconcerned by the heat of the food. Flinn ate more slowly, trying to get the thick gruel to pour from the bowl into his mouth. He was marginally successful, and what little fell to his cheek or beyond he smeared away with his hand. The girl was beginning to slow now as the first pangs of hunger were satisfied. Turning to the cupboard behind him, Flinn pulled out a small loaf of bread. He tore it in half and handed part to her.

"Here," he said gruffly. "It's flat and bland, but edible." He used the bread to ladle up the gruel from his bowl.

She tried a bite and chewed thoughtfully. "Did you make this?"

He nodded and dipped his only drinking mug into the bucket of water, placing it on the table between them. They finished their meal in companionable silence.

When they finished and she had drunk the last of the water, Flinn sat back and folded his arms. "All right, girl," he said. "Your pilgrim's right is up. You've cleaned my barn; I've sheltered and fed you. Because my hitting you was uncalled for, I'd like to make amends. Now ask your questions—I'll give you only three—and then be off with you."

The girl looked up, her eyes startled like a doe's. She glanced down toward her lap, and then up again, obviously formulating her questions. "What's it like to be a knight of the Order of the Three Suns at the castle? Is it as grand as I've heard? Is it?"

Flinn found himself smiling, albeit grudgingly. "Is that one or all three?"

She held out her hand. "Oh, only one! Only one. The other two I want to ask after you've answered the first."

Flinn's eyes met hers, and then he began. "To be a knight of the Three Suns is the greatest thing a man—" he nodded to Jo "—or woman—can be. First and foremost, it is a way of life. By the way, do you know why it's called the Castle of the Three Suns?"

She shook her head.

"I'll tell you. It'll be a free question for you," Flinn smiled with less hesitation this time. "The Castle of the Three Suns is so called because, for much of the year, the sun rises behind two peaks to the east of the castle. These peaks are the Craven Sisters, named after two witches whose spirits are said to inhabit them.

"Anyway, the rising sun is split by the hills into three parts, or three suns. That's how the castle was named. The Order of the Three Suns was formed by the first baron of Penhaligon in honor of the three suns," Flinn finished.

"How interesting!" Jo exclaimed, her voice enthused. "In all the tales I'd heard of you as a knight of Penhaligon, none ever mentioned how the castle got its name!"

Flinn felt a familiar dread wash over him at the mention of his past deeds. He averted his gaze. His mouth tightened, and for a moment he was lost in the memory of his past disgrace. But he felt the girl's eyes still on him, and he turned back to her, an unsteady smile on his lips.

"You asked what it's like to be a knight at the castle," he said slowly, turning back to the matter at hand. "I'll tell you. It's hard work, daily drilling—regardless of the weather—constant tutelage, not only of you but by you. You see, you're taught by those who are your betters, and in turn you teach those less skilled than you."

"What could I teach anyone?" Jo interrupted. She added hastily, "That's not my second question. I just want to know what you mean."

Flinn nodded. "You wouldn't be in a position to teach anyone for quite a while. You start out as a squire before you advance to knighthood, and squires aren't expected to know too much—though you could probably teach the other squires about caring for their mounts!" He smiled at the girl again, then his expression sobered. "The point I was trying to make is this: It's hard work to become a knight. The demands are strenuous, and only a few squires meet them well enough to actually become knights. I knew one boy who was a squire for six years before he was finally ready to be promoted. It isn't all glory and pomp. No, the path to knighthood is fraught with difficulty and requires much dedication."

"Dedication?" Jo repeated. "Do you mean like priests who take vows of silence or celibacy?"

"Not quite," Flinn replied, "though knights do take

certain vows. By dedication I mean that becoming a knight
is not something to be considered lightly. The ruling council
appoints only a limited number of squires every year, and it
chooses only those who can prove themselves responsible,
those who are dedicated to furthering good in Penhaligon."

"I'm dedicated. I'm responsible," Jo offered.

Flinn looked at her intently. "How old are you, Jo?"

Jo rubbed her calloused hands together nervously, then
responded, "Nineteen. This will be my twentieth midwinter."

"And you've held—what?—four jobs already?" Flinn
queried.

Jo squirmed. "Er, five if you count my work at the
shoemaker's." She held a foot out from underneath the table.
"That's how I got these."

The warrior looked at the girl for a long, steady moment.
"Jo," he said at last, trying to gentle his gruff voice, "the
council doesn't want flibbertigibbets, people who can't take
their responsibilities seriously—"

"But I do take my responsibilities seriously!"

"Perhaps, but not the responsibility you owe to a master!
Think how the council is going to view you: a nineteen-
year-old vagabond seeking her sixth master in probably as
many years! Forget about this nonsense and go back to
Specularum, perhaps back to one of your former masters. Or
go back to Bywater and see what the village can offer." Flinn
settled back in his chair, hoping he had gotten through to the
girl.

Jo crossed her arms, a determined look settling about her
mouth. "Flinn," she hesitated, then proceeded boldly, "Flinn,
it's true I'm a . . . a 'flibbertigibbet,' but I do have solid
experience that will hold me in good stead as a knight. If *you*
took me on as your squire and trained me, the council would
be sure to accept—"

Flinn jumped to his feet, his chair scraping across the rough pine board floor and crashing into the wall behind him. "You've got too much brass, girl, and I won't stand for it! I've answered more than enough questions, now get!" The warrior strode to the door and tore it open, his eyes flashing and his mouth mulish.

Jo coolly crossed her arms in return and sat back, her eyes focused upon a corner of the room. In battles, Flinn watched his opponents' eyes, looking for clues to their next action. Flinn cocked an eyebrow as he studied her blank expression. She would make quite an opponent, he thought.

Fully ten heartbeats passed before the girl spoke. "Did you really slay two giants with only one stroke?" she asked.

Flinn was taken aback. "What?"

"As my second question of you—" she looked at him sharply, as if daring him to take away the other questions he had promised her "—I'd like to know if you really killed two giants with a single stroke. It's my favorite story," the girl added.

Flinn grunted. "They were hill giants." Noting the veil of snow forming on the floor, he closed the door.

"What's that got to do with it? Giants are giants."

"It has everything to do with it! Hill giants are stupid."

"Are they so stupid that they lined up, waiting for you to kill them with a single swipe of your sword?" Jo inquired.

"Almost," Flinn said with scorn. "Besides, they were father and son. Stupidity ran in their blood, even more so than with most hill giants."

The girl uncrossed her arms and leaned toward him, pushing the dirty dishes aside. "Well?" she asked eagerly. "Won't you sit down and tell me what really happened?"

"Tell me the tale as you know it," Flinn countered, slowly returning to his chair. Despite his irritation with the girl, her refusal to flee the cabin had won his grudging respect. Flinn sat down at the table, feeling an awkward interest in what she had to say.

Johauna leaned back, and for a moment he thought she might not speak, for her lips quivered and her eyes looked past him. "The tale begins with a time of woe," she began, her voice husky and low.

"The baron of Penhaligon—Arturus was his name—had died that very winter. His body lay upon the dried boughs of the pyre, his only comfort the wind and the rain and the snow. His mourners had all deserted him after the one day's observance of grief, all save one—his niece's husband, the Mighty Flinn.

"Flinn deeply mourned the loss of his baron, the man who had believed in him, the man who had fostered all that was good and brave in him. And so Flinn waited by the pyre for ten days and ten nights—"

"It was only four," Flinn interrupted.

The girl shushed him, as if he had disturbed an invisible audience. "—as was the old custom," she continued. "Now the baron had admired the old customs and had oft lamented their passing. Flinn's vigil was the last honor Arturus would receive.

"And so for those *four* days and *four* nights Flinn kept vigil over the baron's body until the day of burning. In all this time he stood straight and tall at his post, his sword shining bright in his hands. Never once did he lay upon the ground and rest. He stayed ever awake while the soul of the departed baron journeyed home." Outside a gust of wind whistled mournfully.

"Arturus was known throughout Penhaligon for the terrible battles he had waged against monsters of the land. Many of these monsters' kin came to the pyre. They thought to pay their last respects by defiling the boughs of aspen and apple that made up the baron's final bed. Worse yet, they sought to fling offal at the baron's midnight raiment."

The girl paused, her eyes lingering on Flinn's, perhaps seeking to appease him with her story. His lips pursed, but he said nothing.

"It is said that when the monsters saw the Mighty Flinn standing vigil over the baron of Penhaligon, the sensible ones turned away and brooded on vengeance for another day. But the foolish ones—aye, the ones corrupted by anger and hatred for the noble baron—one by one came down from the hills. And one by one Flinn slew them all.

"It is said that none have recorded how many monsters fell those ten—er, four—days. It is said that even Flinn himself knew not how many monsters came upon him, again and again."

"It was seven," Flinn interrupted.

"Seven?" Jo's voice rose to nearly a shriek. "Is that all?"

Flinn nodded. "Two hill giants, a trio of bugbears, one ogre, and one very foolish goblin."

"Oh," the girl responded. Flinn smiled inwardly. He could see her struggle to reconcile fact with legend.

Johauna continued after a moment, apparently chagrined at the flaws in her story. "But the tale that is to be told here, the tale of how Flinn slew two giants with a single blow, recounts the fourth and final day of Flinn's vigil. The lords and ladies of Penhaligon rode out on that last day, carrying the torches with which they would light their beloved baron's pyre. There, they beheld Flinn's final battle for his baron.

"Two fearsome giants from the northern Wulfholde Hills approached Flinn on foot. Flinn swayed a little in the cold wind that rose then, and in his fatigue he fell to one knee. His exhaustion was complete, but he did not yield to the temptation to sleep or flee, for soon his master's body would be burned and his soul at rest. Flinn forced himself to stand once more as the giants approached.

"One giant carried an oak tree whose girth was thrice that of a barrel-chested man. The club, for such was the tree to the giant, was twice as tall as its bearer. The giant used the tree with its trunk still whole and sound, its branches still green, and its roots still quivering with fresh loam. The second giant was even more fierce! In his brawny arms lay a mountain's babe of a rock, a granite waiting to take root in the ground and grow. This giant was even taller and broader than the first. Surely Flinn, in his exhaustion, could not hope to defeat these two behemoths.

"As the lords and ladies of Penhaligon drew near on their brightly liveried chargers, they saw a titanic struggle. The giants' might proved a powerful match for Flinn's skill with his blade, Wyrmblight. Although Wyrmblight was christened for shedding dragon's blood, the blade sank deep and true that day into giant flesh, too.

"The lords and ladies of Penhaligon, hearing the clang of steel, spurred on their steeds, desperate to help a loyal member of their court. But they arrived in time only to see Flinn draw back Wyrmblight with both hands. He swung that shining blade in a noble arc, an arc that sliced clear through one giant's neck, and then through the other's.

"And in one blow—in but *one* blow—did Flinn the Mighty slay two giants." Johauna sighed, her cheeks flushed.

Flinn said nothing for several moments, contenting himself to watch the emotions flitter across the girl's expressive face. Finally he forced himself to say, "You're quite a storyteller, Jo." It was feeble praise indeed—her telling had equalled any he had heard.

Johauna only smiled in return.

"Now," said Flinn, leaning forward and locking his eyes on the girl, "ask your third question, and let's be done with this." He balled one hand into a fist and wrapped the other around it.

She returned his look steadily. "I want to know about the Quadrivial. I've heard it mentioned in legends about the knights of the Order of the Three Suns, but I don't know what it is. Tell me about it, then point the way to the castle and I will leave you." Her lips tightened.

Flinn's face clouded, and he looked away. "The Quadrivial is the path to true knighthood, a path that turns Four Corners: honor, courage, faith, and glory. Knights who don't attain—and then retain—the four points of the Quadrivial aren't really true knights." He looked at Jo. "There's nothing more to say."

The girl looked down at her hands and then about the room. "You are out of water and wood. May I fetch you some?"

"Why?" Flinn asked abruptly, disconcerted by the offer.

Jo stared at him intently, chewing her lower lip. "Because I want more than anything to be a knight of the Order of the Three Suns. If I fetch the wood and the water, perhaps you'll tell me what the Quadrivial is really about. Perhaps you'll tell me how to get the council to accept my petition."

Flinn saw the girl's cheek pulse, and he realized she was grinding her teeth—something he did every night in his sleep. He saw, too, that the bruise on her face had darkened. Again a pang of shame rose in him, and again he found himself relinquishing. He nodded slowly.

"All right, girl. If that's what you wish." Standing, he grabbed the water pail and set it on the table. "You know where the stream is—wade out into it and fill the bucket at the deepest part. The water's cleanest there. The wood pile's beside the barn, but I'm out of small kindling. I think you'll find some dead wood not too far west from here. I'm going to tether the animals in the high pasture."

Flinn's long legs carried him the two short strides to his weapon cupboard, which stood beside the door. He strapped his sword to his wide belt. The blade certainly wasn't the quality of the accursed Wyrmblight, which he'd deliberately lost in a dice game, but it was serviceable nonetheless. Opening the cupboard doors, he took out a ragged fur vest and threw it at the girl. "This'll keep you a bit warmer." With another stride he was out the door.

🖎 🖎 🖎 🖎 🖎

Jo waited for Flinn to leave the cabin before she let out the breath she'd been subconsciously holding. She was bemused. Today, more clearly than ever, she realized just how important her lifelong dream of knighthood was. True, she had enthusiastically pursued other positions, only to lose interest in them in time. Somehow, she felt sure her desire for knighthood was different. She really did want to be a knight—and not for only a year or two. Just thinking about it made her hands tremble as she put on the fur vest. She grabbed the bucket by its willow-wrapped handle and headed out the door.

Outside, snow was falling in silent, fat flakes. Jo stopped just beyond the shelter of the buildings and looked around. Having lived in the bustling city of Specularum for the last thirteen years, she was unnerved by the strange silence of the wilderness. She turned to the path that led to the stream, taking care to keep the snow out of her torn shoes. The path was frozen and icy. As she made her way along, Jo grabbed at branches to keep from falling. Once the bucket fell from her hands and slid down the slope, but she quickly retrieved it.

The bank of the stream was surrounded by scrubby bushes and water-loving birch and willow. A few twisted river oaks stood nearby, their leaves still clinging to the branches. The stream's bank was wet with snow and water and Jo wrinkled her nose. She hated getting wet—the morning's ablutions had been torture enough. Still, Flinn told her to draw water at the deepest part of the stream, and Jo saw no way to reach that point without wading.

Toward the middle of the stream, she spied a large, flat rock standing about a foot above the waterline. Gingerly she fingered the blink dog's tail dangling at her waist. She could easily blink that distance, but the landing could prove tricky. The flowing water that broke against the rock and splashed over it had coated it with ice. She looked again at the icy water of the river and made her choice.

With a low growl and a shake of the tail, she blinked onto the rock. Jo struggled to retain her footing on the icy stone. Abruptly she slipped to her knees, her hands groping for the sides of the rock. She had the sense to hold on to the handle of the bucket so it wouldn't be swept downstream. Her fingers tightened upon the rock's edges and she stopped sliding. Ignoring the pain in her knees, she lowered her bucket into the waiting water.

Jo looked back to shore. She didn't dare try standing before she blinked back, for fear of slipping off the stone. She touched the tail and growled. A moment later she was back on the bank, kneeling in the sloppy, wet snow. Then, above the sound of rushing water, she heard the quick intake of breath. She jerked her head up and screamed.

The round white face of a young boy peered back at her through the brush. One dirty hand held thin branches aside.

His pale blue eyes flared in fear at her outcry, then shifted up the pathway.

Something was crashing down the path.

The boy turned back to Jo, gave a shy, sweet smile, and vanished. Jo stared dazedly at the spot where he had been. She could hardly believe what she had seen. The rumbling footfalls on the trail neared. Jo leaped to her feet, clutching a thick branch in her hand.

It was Flinn. He leaped over a log and landed precariously on the icy ground. His wide eyes searched the woodlands around Jo, his sword drawn and ready.

"I'm sorry I screamed," she said, pointing the way she imagined the boy must have gone. "There was this child—"

Flinn rolled his eyes and returned his sword to its scabbard. "I might have known," he said, shaking his head.

"Might have known what?" Jo asked. "He just appeared in front of me. I looked up and there he was. What's a little boy doing out here? Do you know him?"

Flinn shrugged. "I know of him. I first saw him about a year and a half ago. He never says anything, and I doubt he'd ever harm you."

"No, I doubt he'd harm me, either." Jo shook her head. "He smiled at me."

Flinn cocked an eyebrow. "Usually he disappears the moment I make eye contact with him."

"Does he have kin around here?" Jo asked, her curiosity aroused.

Flinn made for the path. "Not that I know of," he said casually. Jo watched him go, shaking her head. Flinn showed little concern for the boy, who couldn't have been more than ten winters old. Frowning, she picked up the bucket and followed Flinn up the steep path.

The path to the cabin was slippery, and Jo walked cautiously to keep the bucket from spilling. She left the water in the cabin by the hearth, then went back outside to gather firewood. Flinn came out of the barn, carrying a yoke dangling two more water buckets. He pointed off to the west and shouted, "Kindling," then headed for the second time down the path to the stream. Jo smiled, grateful he hadn't asked her to fetch the water for the animals, too.

Walking through the silent woods of larch and beech, Johauna felt the weight of the winter day close in on her. The silence seemed almost palpable. Everywhere she looked, she saw only the still woods, bare trunks of strange and twisted trees. A dark red oak leaf or two waved feebly at her passing, as did one brave clutch of golden aspen leaves. Their colors were dimmed beneath the looming clouds. Jo cast her eyes toward the leaden sky: thankfully, the snow had stopped.

The silence began to gnaw at her. The forest itself seemed to be watching, holding its breath. Where are the sparrows? she thought. Or the chipmunks or ground-squirrels? She chided herself and tried to ignore the eerie sensations. She began to whistle her favorite tune as she gathered small twigs. But the whistled notes sounded loud and conspicuous in the silence. The tune trailed off and stopped. She looked up. Aspens stood in a cautious ring around her, as though warning her not to disturb the hush. Alarmed, she stooped, picking up the branches as quickly and quietly as she could.

Johauna tried to discriminate between dead wood and branches that had merely lost their leaves. The trees here were sparse, with little underbrush. Kindling was slim. She wandered from tree to tree, snapping twigs to see if they were brown or green inside. Little by little, her bundle grew.

Jo's exertions made her warm, so she took off the vest and piled her kindling inside it. A few paces ahead an oak tree towered, sporting a large lower branch that was clearly dead. Jo approached the branch and tugged at it. She heard the bark tear, but the branch still held. Jo pulled harder, straining her young muscles against the wiry might of the oak. She grunted in her effort, finally hanging on the branch. It gave way slowly, but she was sure with a little more work the branch would work loose. Then she could drag the whole thing back to the cabin and have all the kindling Flinn could need.

A strange odor passed her nose. Jo paused, quieting her loud breaths. She sniffed the air. Where is that fetid odor coming from? "Smells like dead cats," she muttered. She smelled her hands, red from the rough bark, thinking the wood sap might be causing the stench. Nothing but the clean smell of wood there, she thought. She dismissed the odor and gave one last tug. The branch pulled free, jerking past and behind her body.

Something screeched in rage. Jo fell to the ground, touched her tail, and growled. But the creature was quicker than even the magical tail. Searing pain tore through her shoulder. Then came blackness, and she reappeared twenty paces away. Clutching her lacerated shoulder, she stumbled to her feet. Red wetness ran down her hand. Spinning about, she glimpsed her attacker: dark and twisted and humanlike in shape, it hurtled toward her. The creature's long, brittle fingers raked at her, catching threads of cloth and strands of hair as she jumped backward. She blinked again, only narrowly escaping the darting jaws and tobacco-colored fangs that gleamed dully with spittle.

Jo reappeared a heartbeat later, only fifteen paces away. She dropped to the ground and lay crouched very still. The creature's ten-foot-tall body faced away from her. Its bony spine bristled as it slowly turned around. It had brittle-

looking legs and arms, which ended in sharp talons. Jo gasped
as the gaunt creature stretched to its full height, its long arms
arching outward at its sides. It sniffed the air, the wiry hair on
its dry skin prickling. Jo cautiously exhaled, then filled her
lungs with much-needed air. Blinking continuously was
hard work, and she was dizzy from both that and the wound
to her shoulder.

Jo stiffened. The creature's small, roundish ears flattened
her way. Its tiny black eyes glinted. It whirled and leaped, a
single, gigantic bound. One more such leap and it would be
on her. Jo blinked again, hoping not to lose herself in travel.

Two heartbeats sounded before she reappeared. The
thought fled through her mind that another use might trap
her in the spatial dimension through which the blink dog's
tail transported her. She remembered her father giving her
the tail on her sixth birthday, telling her not to abuse it. He
had warned that too much use of it would shorten the
distance traveled and lengthen the time in the void.

She reappeared now only ten paces from the creature, and
directly in front of it. Daring not to blink again, she turned
to run.

Jo's experience at dodging authorities in Specularum and
leaping carts in the marketplace now proved invaluable. She
vaulted branches and fallen trees with a speed she had never
shown in the city. But the branches didn't hinder the beast
behind her, either. She stumbled blindly on, her feet twisting
on the icy roots. She had no idea how long she ran, knowing
only that the monster still panted relentlessly behind her.

Her breathing came in ragged gasps—she had no breath to
spare in shouting for Flinn. Jo could only pray that she was
running toward the cabin and not farther away. The creature's
panting moans filled her ears. Twice, razor claws raked her
hair, almost snagging her braid. Both times she ducked and

scrambled out of the way. The beast followed close on her heels. Her heart felt near bursting.

The beast's bone claws flew again. This time the nails sunk deep into Jo's tattered shift. With a swift yank, the creature pulled Johauna off her feet and onto her back. The impact knocked the wind from her body, and a scream of terror escaped her lips. The creature tumbled onto her, its claws—both fore and rear—raking at her. They tore away her shift and ripped into the skin beneath.

Jo reached for her magical tail, determined to make one more blink despite where it might leave her. The tail was gone; it had dropped from her belt as she ran. She panicked. The heavy creature on her chest squeezed the breath out of her, pinning her arm. The monster's maw opened wide, its eight stained fangs gaping and drooling rusty spittle.

She screamed. Pain ripped through her shoulder, a pain so great it drove all thoughts from her mind and thrust her into a brown void of noise. The creature was devouring her. Its saliva seared into her blood. Nausea washed over her, but still she pushed against the dry, papery skin of the brutal hulk covering her.

Jo screamed again, or so she thought. But the scream was deeper, yet strangely higher-pitched than her own. In the dark red haze that was falling across her vision, she saw Flinn the Mighty and the deadly creature circle one another, as if dancing.

Johauna was reminded of the tale of the two giants, and she wondered if they, too, had danced with Flinn. From somewhere far off she laughed, and the haze washed down in a wave over her. She was at the port at Specularum, waiting for her ship to come in because her parents were on board. They never came. She was only six years old.

The blood-red haze turned to black.

৯৫ ৯৫ ৯৫ ৯৫ ৯৫

Flinn stood beside the stable, stretching a green hide across a frame, when he heard the scream. His gaze shot to the west, and his hand leaped to the sword at his side.

"Jo!" he shouted, unaware that he did. He jumped toward the woods and ran up the slight hill as fast as he could. Branches tore at him, but he gave them no heed.

Jo! his mind cried. What's wrong? Has she run into the wildboy again? No—this is a scream of terror. Something's attacked her. He thought of the mountain lion tracks he had recently seen and his pace quickened.

Flinn crested a slight rise and heard Jo scream again, a scream that cut Flinn to the quick. Before him, not more than three paces away, lay Jo, thrashing beneath some strange creature. Blood spotted the dirty, trampled snow. The monster was atop the girl, gnawing at her shoulder. With a cry, Flinn drew his blade in an upward arc and leaped forward. He brought the sword singing down upon the back of the beast.

The creature screamed and leaped aside. Clawing the icy branches, it rose to its full height, towering over the aging warrior. Flinn gritted his teeth and took a swing at the beast. It dodged the blade, lunging for Flinn's open side. He battered it back, the sword's edge biting into the bone claws. The beast drew back and they circled each other, warily gauging the other's strength. Blood dripped from the creature's knobby back, forming rivulets in the snow. It hissed once, and its eight-fanged jaw confirmed the warrior's suspicions. The creature was an abelaat, a fiend from the blackest planes of creation. Abelaats were powerful servants, and Flinn wondered if more such beasts roamed the wood—or if the creature's master was nearby. The warrior's skin crawled.

The abelaat crouched, its bony claws clicking against its palms. Flinn readied himself, sure the creature would attack.

The creature sprang toward him, slashing out with its claws. Flinn leaped to the side, countering with a backhand arc of his sword. But the abelaat pulled back, its attack merely a feint. Turning, it sprinted off into the murky woods. Flinn took a single step after it, wondering why it had chosen to run. Then he heard the girl moan. He watched a moment longer, making sure the creature had truly fled, then dropped to his knee beside Johauna.

"Jo? Jo?" He gazed at the bloodied flesh of the girl's left shoulder.

Sluggishly Jo opened her eyes and looked up at him, a tiny smile on her lips. "My Da's coming home," she whispered, then her eyes rolled up in their sockets and her eyelids flickered shut.

Flinn studied the wound apprehensively. The flow of blood hadn't stopped. He thought to staunch it, but hesitated. "Abelaats are poisonous," he muttered to himself, sighing deeply. Cautiously, the warrior lifted the girl and headed for the cabin. He had medications there that might help her. In the meantime, letting the wound bleed could drain away much of the poison.

"Hang on, Jo," he murmured. "Hang on."

Chapter III

linn kicked open the door, his breath ragged. He had carried Johauna's body through the icy woods, struggling to hold onto the girl during her sudden convulsions. But she was in the cabin now, and here they would be safe.

Flinn gently placed the girl on the bed's furs. She lay still and lifeless; her spasms of pain had stopped nearly fifty paces ago. At the time he'd been relieved because she was easier to carry, but now her stillness scared him. Jo's skin, once the color of clear honey, was flushed crimson. She was sweating and fevered to the touch.

Flinn pulled off her shift and threw it on the fire, hoping the stench of the creature would be consumed with the fabric. He drew his softest fur over her. Then he turned to the mawed shoulder. The girl had lost a considerable amount of blood—more than he thought she would. Clearly some of the abelaat's poison remained in her body. The fever was proof of that.

Carefully, Flinn cleaned the wound. A circle of eight fang marks ringed Jo's shoulder, each still pulsing blood, albeit slowly. Flinn washed out what debris he could find, grimacing at the strange chunks of rusty crystal he removed. As he withdrew the last chunk from the eighth hole, he stopped to looked at the granular substance more closely. The creature's poisonous saliva must have solidified in Jo's wounds, he thought. He put the chunks in a bowl, set them aside, and searched the flesh one last time for anything he may have missed.

The girl had turned deathly pale, but her sweating had stopped. Her shallow breathing filled the cabin with its irregular rhythm. For a moment, Flinn stroked the damp tendrils of hair on her brow. He knew he couldn't take her to Bywater for a cleric's ministrations—she wouldn't survive a day's ride.

He went to his cupboard and sifted through the few herbs he had. He pulled out a dried bouquet of yellow flowers. "Feverfew," he murmured, gazing at the petals, "But her fever is down." He set the bouquet beside a batch of bloodwort, which could have stanched the blood flow, but Jo's punctures had stopped bleeding. The other herbs were useful in times of tainted water or spoiled food, bee sting, or nettle itch. None would help the girl now.

Shutting the cabinet door, Flinn spied movement outside the cabin. "The abelaat," Flinn whispered. He drew his sword and, in one swift leap, positioned himself before the door. He yanked the door nearly off its wood-and-leather hinges, his sword arcing through the air at the same time. The wildboy stood in the doorway. Flinn grunted and twisted the whirling blade away from the ducking boy. The sword's tip whistled past the wildboy's ear and struck the doorjamb, biting deep.

The wildboy huddled on the step, paralyzed with fear. He looked up as Flinn yanked on his sword, struggling to free it from the wood. Seeing that he was safe, the boy turned his attention to the crudely made willow basket he held. His furtive hands darted in and out of the basket, arranging its contents. Then, standing, the boy gestured for the warrior to take it. Flinn stopped yanking on the sword and turned a dumbfounded gaze on the boy. He took the basket, slowly examining its contents.

"I saw the fight with the abelaat and brought these herbs to heal the pretty one. Use all but the narrow-leaved ones in a poultice," the child's voice was barely more than a whisper. Flinn looked sharply at the boy, surprised that he could speak at all, let alone in complete sentences. The boy continued, "Use the narrow-leaved ones in a tea. You may have to force her to drink it." Before Flinn could speak, either in thanks or protest, the wildboy disappeared into the gloom surrounding the cabin.

Flinn shook his head, struggling to believe the incident even occurred. He stared, befuddled, at the basket in his hands and then back at the girl lying in the bed. He kicked at the side of his blade and knocked it loose from the wood, taking a sizable chunk from the doorjamb. This time he barred the door after closing it.

The warrior set two pots over the fire and added a few more pieces of wood. Sitting at the hearth, he leaned forward, his elbows on his knees. He glanced once at the girl, who now lay strangely motionless, as if paralyzed. Listening closely, he heard Jo's quick, irregular breath, and he thanked the Immortal Thor.

Flinn turned to watch the flames lick at the bottoms of the black iron pots, unaware that his lips had pulled into a grimace. The girl would likely die here in his cabin tonight, for he didn't have the knowledge to heal her himself. "She is so young," he murmured, shaking his head sadly. And the death of this innocent girl would be another stain on his honor as a former knight. It was he who had sent her off into the forest, he who had come too late to save her life, he whose lack of healing knowledge left her to die. But something else bothered him. The aging warrior rubbed his chin with one hand, then gazed past his fingers and thought about the girl. Her persistent questions about knighthood, her childlike trust in Flinn the Mighty—both had reminded him of what being a knight had meant to him. Her quest for knighthood reminded him of his own need to be a good and honorable man.

She couldn't die now, he thought, not when she has awakened these feelings in me.

Flinn sighed and began crumbling the herbs into their appropriate pots, adding grain to the poultice pot to thicken it. He hesitated a moment, the crumpled leaves sticking to his hand. "What if this is poison?" he asked himself. Glancing at the lifeless Jo, he realized she would die if not treated, and any chance was better than none. Brushing off his hand, he leaned back and let the potions brew for a few minutes. Then he stirred the paste once more and removed the tea from the heat.

Rifling through the cupboard where he kept his weapons and personal effects, Flinn searched for something suitable to bind the poultice in place. Grunting in annoyance, he discovered he had no clothes left except for those on his back and the ceremonial tunic he had worn in the knightly Order of the Three Suns. He pulled out the silky, midnight-blue cloth and held it up, looking at the brilliance of the three embroidered suns on the front. In the murky light of the cabin the tunic shimmered; the golden threads in the cloth were enchanted, radiating a faint, continual light. Even after all these years, the tunic's three suns still glowed.

Flinn looked at the garment and then looked at the girl lying helpless on his bed of furs. Biting a notch in the hem, he ripped the tunic, pulling it into long, usable strands. The cloth was old and tore easily, the metallic strands of gold breaking away and falling into the cracks of the pine board floor.

Seeing that the poultice had thickened properly, the warrior pulled the kettle off the fire, and then scooped some into a bowl to let it cool. Flinn checked Jo's punctures one more time, wiping away both fresh and dried blood. The wounds would receive the poultice best if they hadn't closed over.

He gathered a tankard of the tea and the remaining things he would need and settled himself on the bed. He drew the girl into his arms. Applying the poultice to the injured shoulder, he gently pressed the skin surrounding the wounds, noting that red streaks of infection radiated from the fang marks. He hoped the poultice would draw out the pus. Jo gasped at the heat of the grain-herb paste but gave no other sign of wakefulness. Flinn bound the poultice in place with the strands he had torn from his knight's tunic, wrapping the cloth around her neck and under both arms to anchor the paste to the torn shoulder.

Flinn pulled the furs around the girl to keep her warm and leaned her against him. He picked up the tea and tested it for warmth. "Just about right," he murmured. He set the mug to her lips, holding her head, and tried to get her to drink a little. She did swallow some, but then convulsed and spat out the rest. Flinn held her nose shut and tilted her head back, pouring the tea as fast she could reflexively swallow. Once or twice she tried to turn her head, but Flinn's grip was firm. He stroked her throat to force her to swallow the last of the liquid, and then he wrapped his arms about her.

"You'll be all right," he whispered, hoping the words would penetrate her haze of pain. "Hold on, Jo. Don't die," he added gruffly. His arms tightened briefly about her. Then he laid her back into the waiting furs. He loosened the hair still bound in her braid and covered her with yet another fur, then rose from the warm bed.

Her breathing had become deeper and more regular. Although her arms were still blanched and clammy, Flinn fancied he saw a little color returning to the girl's cheeks. He tucked the skins more closely about her neck, noting the moist sheen of her lips.

"Better tend to Ariac and Fernlover, what with that abelaat around . . ." the words trailed off. He peered at Jo, thinking she should be safe alone for a few minutes. Flinn unbarred the cabin door and went outside, taking his sword with him. Warily he looked about, but the afternoon light had faded already and he could see little. He listened to the wind and was reassured by its quiet chatter. Flinn broke into a lope up the path behind the barn, heading toward the northern meadow where the beasts were hobbled.

The bird-lion and mule stood waiting for him when he crested the rise, for they had heard his approach. Flinn removed the hobbles and took hold of the braided leather halter he kept on Ariac whenever the griffon wasn't wearing a bridle. He did not take hold of Fernlover—the mule would follow Ariac back to the stable readily enough. Together they retraced the trail to their home.

Flinn quickly settled the animals in for the night, foregoing care of the griffon to return and tend Jo. Before he left the barn, he retrieved some tanned hides from a chest to make her a new shift.

The girl had grown restless in his absence. She had thrown back the covers and curled into a tight ball, her good arm stretched over her furrowed brow. Flinn wondered if she were dreaming about the attack and trying to defend herself. Carefully he returned her to a more comfortable position.

Johauna moaned in protest and pulled her good arm closer across her face.

An hour or so later Flinn felt the poultice; it had grown cold and needed to be replaced. He sat before the fire and returned both pots to the flames. As Flinn waited for the concoction to heat, he wondered about the abelaat. Why is it here? Did it attack Jo deliberately? Or is it after me? Flinn's thoughts whirled. Who had released it into these woods? Johauna's wounds bore testimony to the strangeness of the creature; the abelaat's bite yielded a puncture wound from each of its eight canine teeth.

The mixture had grown suitably hot as had the tea, and Flinn repeated his ministrations. This time the girl seemed nearer consciousness; she struggled as he applied the steaming poultice. Flinn set his jaw, restraining her clawing hands as he fixed the new poultice and administered another cup of the tea.

Jo fell into a deep slumber, exhaustion written across her pale face. Rubbing the scratches Jo had left on his arm, Flinn began pacing the narrow confines of the cabin.

What am I supposed to do with this girl? he thought suddenly. Because I gave her pilgrim's right, I'm now responsible for her? Then he remembered that it was he who had sent her after kindling. He sighed, dropping into his chair. The girl was awakening in him the old honorable principles he had once championed. Those selfless impulses ran counter to the baser instincts he had developed during his seclusion.

The girl stirred and moaned in her sleep then, her eyes fluttering in an effort to open. At last they did open, and her gray irises struggled to focus on him. She whispered a word, but her voice was too frail to hear. Approaching the bed, he leaned over her and coaxed her to speak a second time.

"Water," came the hoarse whisper.

Flinn poured water into the tankard he had used for tea. Returning to the bed, he pulled Johauna into a sitting position and set the tankard to her lips. She drank thirstily. Jo sighed and fell asleep in his arms. He laid her back on the furs and then touched her throat gently. The fever had returned. He fetched a bowl of water and a soft rag and began sponging her body, taking special care around the injured shoulder. In the flickering firelight, he saw that the angry red streaks had spread farther across her skin.

Flinn pulled a few of the lighter furs over Jo, then wet the rag and wrung it out one more time. He draped it across Johauna's throat in an attempt to cool her. Standing, he stretched his weary muscles, feeling the bones along his spine shift into place. Then he moved to the chair before the fire and began his lonely night's vigil. He prayed to the Immortal Diulanna that the girl would live until morning.

    🙚 🙚 🙚 🙚 🙚

The next day, Flinn stoked the fire in the cabin and looked at the girl lying in his bed. She still breathed, and in time her eyes opened.

"Flinn," Jo said, her voice frail and labored, "tell me about the Quadrivial. . . ."

Flinn hesitated; the Quadrivial was a code he had failed, a way of life to which he was exiled. Still, he couldn't refuse her request, not when he had—however indirectly—caused her pain. He didn't know how much she knew of his fall from grace and his banishment from the Order of the Three Suns, but perhaps he could tell her about the Quadrivial without going into either of those. He fervently hoped so.

Flinn settled himself on the side of the bed and looked

down at the pale face before him. Jo's gray eyes were luminous in the light, and dark shadows of pain circled them.

"As I told you," Flinn began wearily, "the Quadrivial is the path to righteousness. All knights who are true and noble, good and virtuous, follow the Quadrivial. The path of the Quadrivial leads to four corners—four points of truth. The path is never-ending, and not all knights reach every corner. But these are the goals all true knights strive for. The first point is honor; without honor a knight can never attain the other three points of truth."

"You fell from honor, didn't you? The 'Fall of Flinn' says you did." The quiet words cut into Flinn's heart.

His voice was husky and hesitant. "Aye, I fell from honor, Jo. But the story as you know it is wrong."

Jo's breath caught short. "I never believed it. Not for one moment. You wouldn't deny mercy on the battlefield, not even to an ogre! Surely the baron's court was wrong, and the people, too!" She gasped for breath and her eyes clenched tight.

Flinn's heart contracted in pain. For the first time in seven years, he opened his mouth in his own defense.

"The ogre never sought mercy, and I killed him as a matter of course. But a knight who wanted to tarnish my reputation accused me upon our return to the castle, claiming I had denied mercy. Unfortunately, some people chose to believe him—" most notably Yvaughan, Flinn thought bitterly "—and I left the order in disgrace."

"Why didn't they believe you when you told them the truth?"

"I—" Flinn swallowed his words. I don't need to tell her anything, he thought suddenly. But some impulse drove him on. "I didn't argue my case strongly enough for two reasons. The first, I'll admit, was pride. I didn't think the court would believe the other knight over my reputation—I was near to attaining the fourth point of righteousness. The council wouldn't have believed the knight, either, if it hadn't been for someone else's testimony."

"Whose?"

Flinn paused, gall sharp and bitter on his tongue. "My wife's." He swallowed hard. "The second reason why I didn't tell the truth was because Yvaughan, my wife, sided with the other knight. My telling the truth would have harmed the people's respect in her, for she is niece to old Baron Arturus Penhaligon. I . . . I didn't want that on my conscience." Flinn shifted his gaze to the floor, then turned back to the girl. *Jo doesn't need to know I held my tongue out of love for Yvaughan,* he thought.

The girl's eyes regarded him thoughtfully, but he couldn't tell what she was thinking. At last she spoke, her words hushed, "I believe you, Flinn."

"Yes. Well," Flinn faltered, gratitude a long-forgotten emotion to him. "The . . . ah . . . second point of righteousness that a knight must attain is courage. Without courage, a knight can't battle evil in the world. Without courage, he can't prove himself worthy of the other two points of the Quadrivial."

"Have you always had courage, Flinn?" The girl struggled to keep her eyes open. Flinn planned to stop talking the moment they closed.

"Always, except for once," Flinn responded, then grimaced at his immodesty. All his life he had been courageous, knowing what needed to be done and doing it. *Until the day of your fall,* his inner voice mocked him. *You couldn't face Yvaughan.* He quelled the voice. "Only once did I fear a beast so much as to flinch from challenging it. But I did confront Verdilith."

"Verdilith?" The name caught the girl's attention. "The great green dragon who's back in the territory? The same one from the tale?"

"Yes, the same," Flinn said wryly. "I was much younger when I faced Verdilith, and I was scared. But following the path to courage doesn't mean a knight can't be afraid—only that he must overcome that fear, as I did." Flinn touched the scars on his face. "This is my badge of courage, the result of confronting my fears and facing Verdilith."

Jo said slowly, "The merchant in Bywater spoke of a prophecy . . ."

Flinn looked away for a moment and closed his eyes. He blinked, breathing deeply. "There's a mad wizardess who lives in the hills near the Castle of the Three Suns. Karleah Kunzay, the wizardess, says she dreamed of the fight between Verdilith and me. She prophesied that the next time we meet, one of us will die."

"Is that why you never fought Verdilith again?" Jo asked slowly, her voice trembling. Flinn studied her face, knowing she feared his response. His answer could shatter her image of him. He felt strangely humbled.

"No. To be quite honest, no," Flinn answered. "I don't believe the prophecy. I never have. Verdilith was badly injured in our fight, and he flew off. I thought he was mortally wounded, but he's returned to Penhaligon in the last year. Green dragons are notoriously slow to heal." Flinn smiled at Jo, unconsciously seeking her belief in him again. "No, Jo, I fought Verdilith only once, and only once it will be, but not because of the prophecy."

"Why don't you go after the green? Like Baildon asked you to?"

Flinn shook his head. "Hunting dragons is a job for knights, not hermits. It's the order's duty to protect Bywater—

not mine."

"But the prophecy implies that the two of you will meet again—"

"I told you, I don't believe the prophecy. I won't hunt Verdilith again," he said bitterly. "They've stripped me of my knighthood, they've spit on me and reviled me, they've set my name with villains and traitors, yet still they expect me to slay the dragon. That's their job, not mine," Flinn finished, pacing stiffly toward the fireplace.

The girl stared at him, her eyes shining once more. "I understand, Flinn, I really do. When I'm better and I become a squire at the castle, I'll tell the knights what you've said— I'll get them to hunt that dragon and kill it like they should. Maybe I'll hunt Verdilith, just as you did." Wishful longing showed on her face as her words trailed off.

For one moment, Flinn envisioned himself as a knight in her company. He thought of long, tiring days in the saddle and the easy camaraderie of the shared campfire. His heart ached. Flinn braced himself against the mantle. Abruptly, he realized he was lonely. His self-imposed exile seemed suddenly pointless and childish. He wanted to whirl around and propose an expedition to slay the dragon with Jo by his side. Then his eyes shifted to the mantle, where his calloused and scarred hands lay. You are a hermit, not a knight, he thought.

"The . . . third point of the Quadrivial," he said slowly, trying to remember the injunctions he had learned in the past, "is that of faith. A knight must have faith in himself and must deserve the faith of the people. The true measure of a knight's worth is the faith placed in him by his fellow knights and the world around.

"Without faith," Flinn continued, "a knight can never achieve glory—the fourth and final corner on the path to righteousness. The first baron of Penhaligon, who established

the Order of the Three Suns, decreed that a knight of renown is equal to his deeds. Acts of righteousness should be
sung as a testimony to all folk everywhere."

Jo was silent for several heartbeats before she spoke. "Did
it . . . did it hurt much when the people at the castle lost their
faith in you, Flinn?"

Flinn flinched and released a long sigh. "Yes," he said
raggedly, "yes." Anger rose like a sudden flame around his
heart. He turned from the fireplace, averting his eyes. In two
quick strides, he reached the door and stalked out into the
gathering dusk.

He could feel the blood pounding in his ears. Part of him
longed to return to the cabin and rage at the girl, to take out
his bitterness on her. He stomped toward the stable, muttering
imprecations about Jo. But he knew that he couldn't blame
her, that he had brought about his own hurt. He should have
defended himself against the accusations of Yvaughan and Sir
Brisbois. His fall was his own doing, and no one could ever
change that. Not he, not Johauna Menhir.

　　　　　　　🙢 🙢 🙢 🙢 🙢

Three days later Jo had recovered enough to leave the
stuffy cabin and walk about outside, exercising her cramped
muscles. She paused in the knee-deep snow, pulling the fur
tighter about her shoulders. Even the new leather shift Flinn
had made for her didn't stop the cold. Slush trickled into her
worn shoes. She sighed heavily, watching the breath whirl
away like a ghost before her. Turning, she trudged tiredly
back toward the cabin door.

Some instinct made her stop in the act of opening the
door, and she looked into the surrounding woods. The
barren trees formed a black lace against the overcast sky.

Movement along the cabin wall caught Jo's eye. She peered closer at the bushes near the cabin, then realized with a start that she was staring directly at the wildboy. His scraggly blond hair, smudged face, and ragged clothing blended well with the surroundings. Jo waved at the child.

The boy gave a shy nod in return and said, "My name's Dayin. What's yours?" Despite his rough clothes, the boy's voice was surprisingly sweet and clear.

"It's Jo. My name is Jo," Johauna smiled reassuringly. The boy nodded and then vanished. Jo scanned the wall of the cabin and the woods that lay beyond. She saw no trace of him. Shrugging, she entered the cabin.

Flinn was kneeling by the fire, stirring gruel. Jo stomped her feet at the door, trying to shake off the snow. As she removed her shoes, she noticed that Flinn was watching her. He shifted away from the pot of gruel and began to rise.

"I can take off my shoes, Flinn," she said a little breathlessly. "I made it all the way to the privy, and I can remove—" her struggles got the better of her, and she stopped talking. Flinn turned back to the porridge, taking it off the fire and ladling it into the bowls. He pulled a loaf of bread from the cupboard and filled the tankard with water. By the time he had put all the food on the table, Jo had donned the warm fur slippers Flinn had fashioned for her yesterday. She sat on her log beside the table.

"I saw the wildboy just now," Jo said, between alternating bites of gruel and bread. "He says his name is Dayin. I wonder if he knows about the attack."

"He does," Flinn answered brusquely. "Dayin, huh? That scamp saved your life. He concocted the herbs that drew out the poison."

"What do you know about him, Flinn?" Jo asked, chewing a piece of the flat bread. Her appetite was slowly returning, and this was the first regular meal Flinn had fed her since the attack.

Flinn shrugged, disinterested. "He doesn't bother me and I don't bother him. What more can I say?"

"But why's he all alone in these woods?" Jo persisted.

Flinn looked up from his bowl, his left eyebrow arching deeply. "Why are you all alone out here in the woods? Why am I?"

"But that's different, Flinn, and you know it. I'm here because I wanted to find you—"

Flinn interrupted, his voice mocking and bitter, "You wanted to find Flinn the Mighty, not me."

Johauna ignored him. "And you're here because this is where you want to be. But that doesn't explain why . . ." Her voice trailed off as a scowl deepened across Flinn's face and his cheek pulsed.

"Sometimes you have no idea what you babble about," he spat out, standing up. He strode about the cabin, collecting gear and cooking supplies. Jo watched him in shock as he packed the items into a backpack. "I have trap lines to tend, and this—" he waved his hand about the room "—is only keeping me from them. You're well enough to fend for yourself here in the cabin."

"You're leaving, Flinn?" she asked, her voice unexpectedly small and pained. For a moment Flinn's eyes caught hers, and she thought she saw some emotion flicker there, but he averted his gaze.

"I'll be gone a week, maybe ten days, to check the trap lines. I'm a trapper, remember. The griffon and mule will be with me, so you won't need to worry about tending either of them." He was backing out the door, finally turning his stony face toward her. He pivoted and began walking toward the barn, leaving Jo at the doorway.

"What will I do while you're gone?"

Flinn stopped in the yard, then turned about slowly. "If—" he stressed the word "—you're still here when I return, we will see." His eyes caught hers again. "We will see."

He turned and left.

🙚 🙚 🙚 🙚 🙚

A week passed, then a fortnight before Flinn finished his trapping and returned to the cabin in the woods. Snow had fallen recently, and in some parts of the woods it reached his waist; he had had to dismount from Ariac and lead the animals through snow-blocked passages. Now Flinn peered down at his cabin, studying the few tracks surrounding the buildings. He wondered if Johauna had indeed left. Then he saw smoke curling lazily away toward the blue, afternoon sky. He sighed.

The girl is still here, he thought. She is still here. Praise the Immortals.

Giving Ariac's flanks a light tap, Flinn pressed onward. Fernlover brayed in anticipation of the comforts the barn promised. Flinn wasn't surprised to see the barn door swing open and the girl emerge. He nodded at her but said nothing, not even after she broke into a wide smile.

"Flinn!" she shouted and raced to meet him. "You're back!"

"Obviously."

"I expected you a week ago."

"I told you I might be longer than a week."

"You said ten days, outside. It's been two weeks." She took Fernlover's lead from him and led the pack animal into his own stall. "I was beginning to worry."

Flinn halted his dismount in midstep to look at her, his

eyebrow arching in amusement. "I find it unlikely you'd ever worry, girl, save perhaps when your next meal is postponed." He finished swinging off the griffon. "Besides, I left plenty of food, and you obviously didn't starve."

She faced him squarely. "No, I didn't starve."

He eyed her slowly, noting that she had fashioned herself some breeches from the damaged hides he couldn't take to market. She was wearing the shift he had made her, and she also had a new fur vest. Her damaged shoes, he noticed, had been repaired with some leather.

"You also didn't leave."

The words hung in the air between them. She moved her hand and pursed her lips, as if words threatened to spill forth that she couldn't give voice to. At last she said, "I didn't want to leave, Flinn."

Without taking his eyes off Jo, Flinn opened the saddlebag next to him. He pulled out the blink dog's tail and threw it at her. "Good. I'm glad."

Jo caught the tail and cried, "Flinn! You found my tail! How? When? I thought too much snow had fallen! I thought I was never going to see this again."

"I brought Ariac over to the scene of the fight. He's got a keen nose—he found the tail without much trouble." The warrior turned to the griffon and began undoing Ariac's tack.

Jo stepped into the stall's doorway. "Flinn," she said tentatively.

"Yes?" he drawled, his back to her.

"Flinn," she repeated, "why were you glad I hadn't left?"

The warrior paused, then continued undoing the buckles of the griffon's girth strap. Still, he wouldn't turn to her, but said instead, "How's your shoulder? Any pain?"

"A little—not much. It itches," Jo replied.

"Good. That means you're healing."

"Flinn? You were saying . . ."

"Saying what?"

Jo sighed in exasperation. "Unless my ears tricked me, you were saying you were glad I hadn't left. Why?"

Flinn ground his teeth, then shook his head. He turned around, his expression serious. I can't tease her any more, he thought. I must tell her what's on my mind. "I've decided to teach you a few things you'll need to know to petition as squire."

"Flinn!" the girl cried, her voice breaking an octave. She looked positively stunned. Jo took a step forward, her hands out to embrace him, but she stopped short. Flinn felt a wave of both relief and disappointment wash over him.

"Oh, Flinn!" Jo said again. Suddenly she looked out the barn door. "I've got something on the fire that needs watching, Flinn. I hope you like it! Hurry in!" The girl whirled out the stable and raced toward the cabin.

Flinn shook his head ruefully as she ran off. "What have I done," he muttered to himself. Turning, he stabled the animals, tending to their ice-crusted hooves and pads. Then Flinn walked to the cabin. A savory smell wafted from the pot Jo was stirring.

"That smells good," he said, putting some of his belongings in the cupboard by the door. "What is it?"

"Rabbit stew." Delicately she blew on the ladle and tentatively tasted the sauce.

"Rabbit?" Flinn asked over his shoulder. "I know I had some stored vegetables, but where'd you get rabbit?"

"I trapped them yesterday."

Flinn was dumbfounded. "You—a city girl—trapped them?"

Exasperated, she glared at him. "Don't look so surprised,

Flinn. Not all city girls are helpless, you know. Some of us do know how to hunt. There's really no difference between trapping rabbit for the pot and wharf rat for the spit." She turned away and began ladling the stew into bowls.

"Wharf rat?" Flinn's voice rose. "You ate wharf rat?"

Johauna nodded. "It wasn't bad, really. You have to eat something, so when you've got no money, you hunt whatever's around. At the wharfs in Specularum you hunt wharf rat. There are worse ways of surviving. The sailors would've paid handsomely for . . . favors, but . . ." her voice trailed off and she was suddenly still.

Silently Flinn's hand reached out to touch the glossy braid down her back. She moved briskly away, fetching the bread and water. He drew back his hand.

Jo faced him across the table as they sat down to the meal. "What made you decide to teach me how to be a squire?" she asked awkwardly.

Flinn shrugged, then sniffed happily. He didn't cook very well, and the rabbit stew smelled excellent. "I . . . I'm not sure I know why. Suffice to say that I think you'd be a good squire, and that I think I could teach you a few pointers."

Jo said nothing, only looking at him inquiringly.

"In a few weeks I'll find out your ability to learn—your strengths and weaknesses. I'll also know how the council's likely to react to you. You won't have a formal sponsor—that is, a knight or a noble to vouch for you," Flinn added.

Jo's eyes were wide and unblinking. "Must I have a sponsor, Flinn? And—" she hesitated "—can't you sponsor me?"

Flinn returned her gaze, a strange pain in his chest. "No. I can't sponsor you. I'm no longer a knight," he said heavily. "As to whether you need a sponsor, the answer is no, but you'd be better off to have one. Still, we can get around it."

Jo nodded, her gaze intent. "Fair enough, Flinn, fair enough." She smiled quickly, handing him the plate of bread. "Now, let's eat. You've had a long journey. Time enough to talk about this later." Her eyes were shining, and he sensed a terrible tension in her. "Flinn," the girl's voice was barely more than a whisper, "thank you."

"The rabbit stew's excellent, Jo," Flinn said after a few swallows. "Tell me more about Specularum, and . . . tell me about you," he added after a moment's consideration.

The girl looked at him abruptly, as if unsure what to make of his last remark. She looked down at her bowl and finished chewing a bit of food.

"It's true that I did hunt wharf rat for food. I learned how from a crippled fisherman who lived by repairing nets. Pauli taught me how to make a thin, strong twine from unsalvageable netting. He showed me how to place a loop trap where the rats'd run." She shrugged. "I had a choice: I could hunt wharf rats, scavenge rotten fish, or steal marketplace food." The girl leaned toward him. "I chose to hunt."

"Tell me about the city," Flinn requested.

"Specularum? It's crowded, filthy, and unwelcoming. What would you expect from the largest seaport around? The stench is unbelievable. Even a week after I left the city I couldn't smell anything."

"Why did you leave the city? Really?" Flinn asked suddenly.

Jo looked at him for a moment, then her eyes crinkled and she laughed. "I left because a drunken lord tried to get frisky with me in an alley—he must've stumbled down the wrong way in the dark, for no lord had ever been down that street before, I'll warrant. Anyway, I bit his ear off."

Flinn snorted derisively.

"The next day there were warrants out for the arrest of the

'fiend who had accosted Lord Arston.' It seemed a good reason to leave Specularum. I stowed away on a river caravan heading north for the Castle of the Three Suns, but the captain found me and threw me overboard. I followed the river north, but somehow I ended up in Bywater instead of at the castle."

Flinn smiled at her, freshly amused at the girl. "You came up the Castellan instead of the Hillfollow. The Hillfollow would've taken you straight past the castle."

Jo smiled back and shrugged, then she said, "There's something I want to show you." She went to the bed, reached under a soft fur, withdrew a foot-wide square of blue silk, and handed it to him. "I found what was left of your tunic and did what I could to salvage it."

Flinn fingered the square of cloth in his hands. The girl had skillfully taken apart the embroidery of the suns and used the thin yellow strands to sew the midnight blue cloth together. From a distance the contrasting stitches were hardly noticeable, but close up they created a pleasing mosaic pattern. The three suns, though now much smaller, were still situated on the front of cloth. Flinn touched the frail golden threads that ran through the yellow threads, surprised to see the strands shimmer.

"The gold threads are still enchanted, Flinn," the girl said. "When I pieced them together they glowed, though only faintly. Whoever cast the spell must have been a powerful wizard."

"Camlet the seamstress took great pride in her work. I'm not surprised the threads still glow."

He looked up at Jo standing beside him. Her cheeks were flushed and her eyes bright. "It's beautiful, Johauna," he said simply. "Thank you for saving as much as you could."

Her voice was breathless. "You're more than welcome,

Flinn." She stroked the three suns briefly. "I know this square can't replace the tunic, but perhaps you can keep this as a . . . a favor, I think the knights call them."

"They do." Flinn pointed at one of the sacks he had brought in. "I have a present for you, too. Take a look in there."

Johauna looked in a long, narrow bag and pulled out a wooden sword. The dull gray wood that formed the blade had a fine, tight grain. Although the sword was thicker than a normal steel sword, its beveled edge was very sharp. The leather-wrapped hilt and fitted, wooden guard fit perfectly in Jo's hand. She said nothing, her eyes searching his inquiringly.

"I didn't give it to you earlier because—" Flinn paused, rubbing his neck uncomfortably, "—I didn't know if you were serious enough." He gazed toward her, his face reddening. He continued, "It'll do for us to parry with. I figured I would teach you first how to defend yourself." He took the sword from her and gave it a few swings. "I made it from a piece of ironwood. It's virtually indestructible and almost as heavy as steel." He shrugged. "It'll make a good practice blade for you. It doesn't have the bite of metal, of course, but it'll dent just about anything you'll find in these woods."

A shadow crossed the girl's face. "Even the creature that attacked me?"

Flinn considered his words, then nodded slowly. "Even the creature that attacked you."

❧ ❧ ❧ ❧ ❧

"I don't understand!" Johauna shouted at Flinn, one week later. She was lying flat on the now-packed snow of the commons between the cabin and the barn. The tip of Flinn's blade rested squarely on her chest.

"That's because you're not trying!" Flinn shouted back. He abruptly stuck his sword into the ground and jerked her to her feet. "You're not listening! You've *got* to learn defense before you can think about attacking!"

"What do you think I was trying to do? I had my sword out! I tried to stop you!"

Flinn's hands clamped firmly on his waist. "Well, it didn't work, did it?"

"I did everything you said!" Jo mimicked Flinn's posture. "You're not teaching me right!"

"Hah!" Flinn snorted. "You've got another think coming there, you thick-headed girl!" Angrily he picked up Jo's sword where it had fallen in the snow and then grabbed his own. He threw the wooden blade at Jo, who caught it handily this time. Flinn grunted his approval. "That's better," he snorted again and went into a crouching position. "This time, let *me* attack and *you* defend," he said.

Johauna, too, crouched in the ready position and held her sword like a bar before her. "I don't know why you won't let me have a shield, Flinn," Jo said as she blocked Flinn's initial move.

"I told you!" Flinn whirled his blade in a fast, low arc. Jo barely jumped in time. "You don't need a shield. Your sword's everything you need to stay alive. The shield might protect you, but it won't save your hide like a sword will." He swung his blade overhead, letting it come crashing down on Jo's wooden blade. She winced at the force of the stroke and fell to one knee, but she didn't release the blade.

"Good girl," Flinn said quickly and backed away, preparing his next move.

"What if I lose the sword? Then I'll need the shield," she

said. She blocked his next move easily and smiled, only to find his sword at her stomach.

Flinn sighed in exasperation, backing away. "If you lose your sword, Jo, you're dead! Think! Hold onto your sword as though your life depends on it—because it does. A shield is expendable; you haven't time to worry about expendable distractions. Devote your attention to what is necessary. Now—prepare yourself!"

Flinn advanced toward her again, his blade swinging out in faster strokes. His gaze passed over the spot on her calf where one of his strokes had nicked her. He had taken extra care since then. Jo fended the first few strokes well enough, but then Flinn's sword flashed faster. She stepped back, fumbling with the blade.

"Parry! Parry!" Flinn shouted. "Quit using the sword as just a shield!"

"You told me to use it as a shield!" Jo retorted.

"Never mind what I told you! Parry the stroke, don't just meet it!" Flinn shouted in return.

Spurred on by his words, Jo stepped forward, forcing his blows back rather than merely blocking them. She successfully turned six strokes in a row. Astonished, she smiled.

Suddenly she was lying on her back with Flinn's sword at her waist again and her own beyond reach. Flinn shook his head at her, clicking his tongue. He pulled her to her feet.

"You got cocky, girl," he said. "Worse thing that can happen to a fighter—think the fight's over and gloat. You had a couple of nice moves, but don't let those go to your head. That's why you're in the snow again." He gestured toward her sword and shook his head. "Never, never lose your sword, Jo, no matter what the cost of keeping it in your hand." His dark eyes were serious as he peered into hers. "Losing your sword will cost you your life."

"But I was afraid you were going to break my arm. I had to drop the sword."

He shook his head. "No, you only thought that. Human bone is strong, Jo, particularly with a little armor." He rolled up the left sleeve of his woolen tunic and traced the deep scar in the middle of his forearm.

"I lost my shield once in a fight. The next blow struck my left arm. The blade bit through my armor, gouged out some flesh, and broke the bone in two places. I survived and lived to win the fight." Sighing, he continued, "The point is, don't be afraid to suffer some pain in the short run if it can save your life in the long run."

Johauna hesitated, then reached out and lightly traced the ridged scar. "I'll remember, Flinn."

"Now," Flinn said briskly as he rolled down the tunic's sleeve, "do you want to continue or are you tired?"

Jo knew she was tired. She also knew Flinn enjoyed these practice bouts, particularly because she became a more worthy adversary daily. "Continue," she said, retrieving her sword and returning to her starting stance.

This time Jo concentrated on parrying each of Flinn's moves without trying to anticipate them. She carefully avoided being maneuvered next to the buildings or the fence, where she might be trapped. At one point, Flinn drove her toward the corral's gate. Jo dropped and rolled toward Flinn, bringing her wooden sword upward in a thrusting stroke inches from his gut. Flinn leaped neatly aside.

"Good move!" he cried.

Jo rolled to her feet and took the offensive, slashing enthusiastically with her blade, forcing Flinn toward the barn wall. Flinn laughed, the first genuine laughter Johauna had ever heard from him. The sound spurred her on. Each stroke fell with greater force, sharper precision. Even so, Flinn stepped back, parrying the blows easily.

At last Jo cried, "Enough!" She released her sword and dropped to the ground. Her nearly healed shoulder throbbed with the exertion. Flinn plopped down beside her on the packed snow.

"Well done, Jo, well done!" Flinn proclaimed and began massaging her sword arm. He had stressed the importance of stretching her muscles before any exercise bout and chasing away any knots in her muscles afterward.

Jo's heart pounded loudly in her ears. Her lips parted and her breath became shallow.

Flinn was still speaking. "You've improved quite a lot since we first began practicing. Anyone who can keep showing progress will . . ." Flinn's words trailed off as he gazed into her face. His lips pursed and his eyes darkened.

She wondered if he thought she was trying to seduce him. She abruptly pulled her arm from his hands and leaned away. "Thanks, Flinn. My arm's fine now."

Flinn stood, picking up the weapons and taking a few brisk strides about the yard. "You're progressing very well, Jo. I'm pleased." He paused to look down at her. "I think you should spend the rest of the day practicing with the bow. The target's still set up by the barn."

The warrior extended his hand and pulled Jo to her feet. "You want me to practice target shooting?" Jo asked, "Or should I do the run–and–shoot maneuvers?"

"Target shooting," Flinn said, smiling. "Your archery isn't nearly as advanced as your swordplay. We need to fix that."

"Will you watch and tell me again what I'm doing wrong?" Jo asked, moving to the barn where Flinn kept his bow and arrows.

"No, Jo, you'll do fine without me," Flinn answered, then

paused. Jo turned around in the silence. Shaking his head, Flinn spoke again. "I'm going inside to work on restoring my armor."

"I can do that this evening. It's part of my job as a squire."

Flinn held up a hand to forestall her. "I know, I know, Jo. But there's a lot of work to be done, and you can't do it all."

". . . A lot of work to be done?" An odd chill ran down her back.

Flinn only nodded. "Yes," he said curtly, his eyes glinting. "We're going after the abelaat."

Jo felt as though her throat was closing in on itself. "When?" was all she could say.

Flinn's eyes were dark with compassion. "This week, depending on the weather. When I think you've advanced a little more and I get the armor back in order, we'll head out. I'm tired of keeping Ariac and Fernlover here in the corral. And I want us to be able to gather firewood without looking over our shoulders every minute.

"We're going to kill the abelaat—before it kills us."

Chapter IV

ir Brisbois yawned. The council meeting had dragged on for nearly three hours now. He gazed restlessly at the fourteen lords and knights who lined the small meeting room—the small prison, he thought. Brisbois closed his mind to the discussion surrounding him, his attention wandering to the stone ceiling some thirty feet above. A vague dizziness flushed through him as his eyes traced the intricately carved bosses and the pale murals on the ceiling. Brisbois's eyes shifted to the huge tapestries that hung from three of the walls. Then his gaze turned toward the fourth wall, which held arching windows filled with leaded glass. He had watched the early winter sun set almost an hour ago through those windows. The brass lanterns throughout the room had magically lit at sunset, their blue-white glow casting harsh shadows across the people's faces. Brisbois squinted. He had drunk too much last night.

He sat in an unupholstered, ornately carved chair that was distinctly uncomfortable for his angular, lanky frame. Before him was a U-shaped table, its top so perfectly joined that the seams were invisible to all but a master carpenter. Excepting me, of course, Brisbois thought wryly. If I sit here any longer, I'll have every dust mote in this room catalogued. Beneath his feet stretched a green marble floor lined with gold. It was beautiful and cold and practical—just like the baroness herself, Brisbois mused.

Brisbois stared at the young matriarch, sitting at the center of the table. She was as tall as many of the men there, Baroness Arteris Penhaligon. Her blue and silver raiment set off her chestnut hair and eyes. To many of the older knights, she was the youthful image of her father, Baron Arturus Penhaligon. They revered her because the likeness was not simply physical; honor ran deep in the daughter of the baron. Other courtiers though—mostly younger knights who had never met the old baron—murmured against giving allegiance to a woman. She didn't even have a husband, they argued. She should provide not only an heir but a husband as well— a proper lord to rule. Brisbois chuckled inwardly; his age placed him among the baroness's supporters, but his views placed him among her adversaries.

Baroness Penhaligon continued to drone on about lifting the peasantry's tax burden, and Brisbois, a leer coming to his lips, let his thoughts slip back to the maid he had cornered last night. He closed his ears to the discussion surrounding him.

". . . Sir Brisbois? Would you be willing?" The baroness's voice broke through Brisbois's reverie. Her brown eyes, hard as agates, bored into him. He was sure she had called upon him deliberately, and his dislike for the daughter of Arturus Penhaligon deepened. She's got her father's eyes, he thought waspishly. I remember the old man looking at me in just the same way.

Sir Brisbois hurried to his feet. He bowed toward Arteris. "Of course, Your Ladyship. I should be delighted to handle the matter for you," Brisbois said smoothly. He held one hand on the silky blue tunic that covered his chain mail and used the other to hold back the ceremonial sword hanging at his side.

"Wonderful," was Arteris's sour reply. "Who will you appoint to the committee?" she added.

Brisbois flashed his most disarming smile. "After I've given the matter some consideration, Your Ladyship, I'll report back to you. I have some ideas of my own I need to take under advisement." He nodded gracefully.

"Good sir knight," Arteris said with asperity, "we have spent the last several hours 'considering' the matter. Enough is enough. Please make your selection now."

Out of the corner of his eye, Brisbois spotted a furtive gesture from one of the council members. Three seats away from the baroness, Lord Maldrake nodded slightly. Brisbois smiled. Maldrake was Arteris's cousin-by-marriage and Brisbois's cohort. "Why, Your Ladyship, I'd like to appoint Lord Maldrake, with your permission." Brisbois held out his hand toward the blond knight, a younger man clearly entering the prime of his life. Lord Maldrake was considered something of a rake, for he charmed women easily. Most men respected and feared him, and he had the reputation of being ruthless if crossed—a reputation not undeserved.

The baroness glanced toward Maldrake and nodded with icy civility. "If Lord Maldrake accepts—"

"I do, my baroness, with alacrity." Lord Maldrake, who didn't rise in deference, was equally icy, his tongue caressing the term "my baroness." His thickly hooded green eyes glinted darkly. "I'm delighted to attend Sir Brisbois in this matter. I have many excellent ideas for easing the peasants' burdens."

The baroness responded, "Splendid, Lord Maldrake." She turned to Sir Brisbois but touched the arm of the graying gentleman to her left. "And I think I shall appoint our good castellan to the committee as well. Doubtless Sir Graybow's wisdom and experience will . . . add to the originality of your plans." She smiled once again at Sir Brisbois, a smile that showed she would brook no argument. He shot a glance at Sir Graybow, but the old knight's head was lowered. The baroness stood.

Arteris closed her eyes and lifted her hands toward the vault above. "We thank the Immortals for blessing us with the outcome of this meeting and this day." Then she lowered her arms, clasped her hands together, and gazed steadily at the council members. "And thank you for joining me today, good friends. Fare-thee-well." The baroness took the castellan's proffered arm and left the room. The other members of the council, a number of them grumbling quietly, followed after.

Only Sir Brisbois and Maldrake remained seated. Casually, Brisbois stood and sauntered over to Maldrake. The blond lord tilted the heavy chair back on two legs—no mean feat—and propped his spurred boots on the elegantly carved cherry table. His hard-edged boot marked the table as he tapped his foot distractedly.

Brisbois leaned against the table and peered at his long-time friend. "Thanks for stepping in. I'm afraid I was thinking of other things—"

"The wench I sent you last night?" Maldrake grinned wickedly.

Brisbois felt a momentary shudder; his friend was sometimes so clearly malevolent. Slowly, Brisbois also grinned. "Yes. Thank you for her, by the way. She was a treat—I may even ask for her again." He shifted his weight to his other foot. "But I missed what Arteris was talking about. What's she snagged us for this time?"

Maldrake's chair crashed forward to the floor, and he

clapped his hands together. "Hah!" he cried. "This'll be great fun! We're supposed to come up with ways to *decrease* the tax burden on the peasants!"

Brisbois frowned. "That doesn't sound very exciting."

Maldrake's green eyes turned malicious. He stood and leaned toward Brisbois. "See, we tell the peasants we're instituting new tax plans that will *help* them, but in reality we'll tax them harder in ways that can't be traced. I'll work on that. We'll pocket the difference. Brisbois, the baroness's practically begging us to commit larceny!" His green eyes glinted in the lantern light.

Brisbois felt again a stirring of admiration for his friend. "I see, I see!" he said excitedly. "But what about Graybow? How do we get around him?"

Maldrake waved his hand. "Leave him to me. Graybow's old and starting to dodder. He won't be hard to handle." He clasped a hand on the taller man's shoulder and said, "Yvaughan has dinner waiting in our quarters. Why don't you join us?" He added spitefully, "She'd be glad of the company."

Brisbois grimaced. "Is tonight a good night? Your wife waxes cold and warm toward me, Maldrake. I've never understood her or her moods."

"Perhaps she secretly resents you, Brisbois," the younger knight replied. "Perhaps she resents you for destroying her former husband." Maldrake's heavy-lidded eyes gleamed.

"Why should she? I did everything as she requested— everything," Brisbois countered hotly. "Without me, she couldn't have divorced Flinn to marry you. I deserve praise, not blame." The two walked across the marble floor and through the fifteen-foot-high double doors.

"And I'm glad you did it, Brisbois," Maldrake rejoined. "Make no doubt about that." He stopped walking and turned to the knight, his face alight with new thoughts. "Have you made arrangements for our . . . friend?" Lord Maldrake's look was maliciously inquisitive.

"The, er, watcher—" Brisbois lowered his voice as a page hurried by "—is in place, if that's what you mean. It's unfortunate that it misunderstood my directions before."

"That's what has me concerned," Maldrake put his hand on Brisbois's arm. "I want you there next time, to make sure everything goes as planned."

"What?" Brisbois exclaimed. "What if it fails and comes after me? What if I'm seen?"

"It won't, and you won't be," Maldrake leaned closer and lowered his voice to a whisper as two pages and a squire walked down the wide hall. "Teryl has something that will see to that. I'll give it to you tonight. Besides, you won't get close enough to be seen. Just make sure it follows orders this time."

The knight nodded, though his face had darkened perceptibly at the mention of Teryl Auroch, Maldrake's mage. "All right, Maldrake. However you want it. I just wish you'd hurry this up and get it over with."

The blond lord smiled toothsomely. "If you take care of our little problem next week, all will run smoothly. It's as simple as that." Maldrake smiled again. "Why don't you come to my quarters in, say, half an hour or so? I've got a few orders to leave with the captain of the town guard."

"Like what?"

Again he flashed the smile. "Like having fifty horses 'taxed' from the peasants and delivered to that abandoned logging camp in the Wulfholdes. Horses we can sell to a merchant—a very reliable merchant—arriving next week from Specularum."

"How are you going to explain this if anyone asks?"

Brisbois said, admiring the younger man's temerity.

"Easy!" Maldrake crowed. "Without horses, the peasants won't have to pay taxes for traveling our roads. Therefore, their taxes will be reduced."

"Brilliant!" Brisbois said. "But what if the baroness hears of this?"

"She won't. Besides," Maldrake shrugged nonchalantly, "if she does, I'll just tell her I'm new to this taxation business and didn't know any better. After all, what will she do to her crazy cousin's husband?" Maldrake's face crinkled into laughter. "See you for dinner!" The lord sauntered down the wide, majestic hallway, laughter bubbling from him.

Brisbois called after his friend, "Is Teryl Auroch going to be there?" He detested the mage and might avoid the dinner if the old conjuror was planning to attend.

"Of course!" cried Lord Maldrake, walking backward. "Yvaughan doesn't take a step without her advisor. She's given him permanent quarters in our tower, by the way, so he's there all the time. Come anyway, you old spoilsport! We have fortunes to build!" The lord turned and continued his way down the immense hall.

Brisbois nodded curtly. He would have dinner with Maldrake and his wife, but only because Maldrake insisted on it. And he would watch Teryl Auroch very, very carefully. That mage had plans—plans Brisbois intended to uncover.

ra ra ra ra ra

Yvaughan leaned forward, a thin sliver of sweetmeat between her fingers. She dangled it in front of the large bird before her. It was an elegant, lovely bird, and Yvaughan never tired of watching its long and graceful form. The bird's tail coverts were nearly twice as long as its body, the plumage fine, almost hairy. Its white tail was laced with emerald green plumes. The rest of the bird's feathers were pure, blazing white, save for an iridescent green crest upon its head.

The bird was a finicky eater, and Yvaughan had spent the last hour coaxing it into eating various goodies. Finally it pecked delicately at the proffered sweet and then greedily ate it all. Yvaughan sighed in relief. The bird's shy mate, a dove-brown creature that was no less stunning, jumped from its perch to join the cock. In the potted trees dotting the large tower room, dozens of smaller birds roosted and preened. Others took wing, flitting this way and that, filling the room with chirps and exotic calls.

Yvaughan turned around, sighing at the beauty of the place: the rosy marble floor, the white pillars, the tapestries gracing both floors and walls—all kept meticulous by a troop of servants. Potted plants of all sorts provided perches and nesting sites for the birds. From a tiny, well-hidden pool, the noise of falling water filled the air. The furniture in the tower was elegant, yet comfortable and inviting. Even the bars on the windows soothed Yvaughan's troubled heart. She and her birds lived safe in their tower hideaway, safe from the world and its dangers. Yvaughan never felt alone in this chamber, not like she did in the bedroom at night with her young husband. Strangely enough, only the white bird and his mate ever entered the bedchamber, but even these two beloved pets couldn't provide the comforting sound that a thousand birds could. The pair roosted at night on the rail above her head, sending Yvaughan to sleep with their cooing.

Seated on a divan before her was her advisor, Teryl Auroch. He was a tiny, wizened man, apparently ancient, though none but he knew his actual age. He sported a mousy brown goatee, currently in vogue at the castle, and a moustache that was so nearly the color of his skin that it was often not seen. His hands, which were white and shapely, moved constantly, as though he suffered from some inner agitation. In contrast to his withered body and jittering hands, the man's eyes were the brilliant, youthful blue of a summer sky. They inspired trust in Yvaughan.

"Today it is sweets, Teryl," Yvaughan complained to the man sitting before her. "Yesterday it was grain, the day before it was meat. Will I never know what to feed my lovely pets?" She placed a shallow, gilded container on the granite floor, clucking in sympathy. The two birds milled about and then began eating the sweets it contained. The remaining birds, creatures of lesser glory, fluttered near. The moment the pair had had their fill, the others would swoop down and eat.

Yvaughan rose unsteadily to her feet, her pregnant bulk upsetting her balance. She put a hand to her rounded stomach, said a silent prayer to comfort the child within, and moved slowly to the barred windows. The winter sun had already set, so she could see little outside the tower window save for a few lights being lit in the country houses. Her husband should arrive soon. Yvaughan was glad Baroness Arteris no longer insisted that they join the other nobles and knights for the evening meal. The public meals made only for political posturing and simpering.

Yvaughan leaned against the damask drapes that outlined the tall window before her. She was nearing forty and late to childbearing, but her figure was still strong and graceful, her golden hair still untouched by gray. Although her cornflower-blue eyes were generally untroubled, today they stared emptily. She reached a pale hand out to touch the delicate, wrought-iron bars she had installed on the windows of the tower to prevent her beloved birds' escape.

Baron Arturus, her uncle, had granted her the tower on her wedding day. He and she had spent many happy times together in the tower conservatory, one floor above. The conservatory's plants and birds had inspired Yvaughan to begin the slow transformation of the rest of the tower. Soon all four floors would harbor birds and plants and pools of water. Yvaughan smiled. Her uncle would have been proud of all she had accomplished.

Then she frowned. Her happy childhood had ended when Arturus gained a daughter of his own and had no time for his young niece. *How happy I was before Arteris,* the woman thought, *when my uncle loved me best of all.* Yvaughan's parents had died from plague shortly after her birth, and her uncle had raised her as his own. As his wife seemed unable to bear children, Yvaughan had been brought up as his only heir. But the birth of Arteris had spoiled all that.

Yvaughan sat on the divan next to the mage. "You've been very good to me, Teryl," she smiled. "I'm so glad I could persuade you to leave your studies and join me here at the castle. I don't know what I would have done without you the last two years."

"I am also glad, lady," Teryl said in his high-pitched voice. "Though your husband had a hand in the persuading, too, I might add."

"Fain?" Yvaughan's voice was tinged with hysteria. "Have you seen him? Fain Flinn is returning? Where is he?" A familiar terror welled up in her, and she put one jeweled hand to her throat.

"Calm yourself, my lady," Teryl responded, his hand fluttering on her arm. "I was speaking of Lord Maldrake, your second husband." The mage stood and went to a sideboard. There he poured a little wine and mixed it with the contents of a stoppered vial he produced from his voluminous robes. He handed the glass to Yvaughan and said, "Here, my lady. A glass of claret before dinner will soothe your nerves. Drink."

She looked at the glass wildly, then glanced up at the wizard's smiling face. She trusted Teryl. He was her only friend at the Castle of the Three Suns . . . besides my husband, of course, she dutifully added. Whatever Teryl has put in the glass is for my betterment. She downed the wine with one swallow and handed the glass back. Teryl replaced it on the sideboard, taking care to wipe it dry.

"You're right, of course, Teryl," Yvaughan said a moment later, her tongue feeling thick. "How foolish of me to mix up my first and second husbands." She turned at the sound of footsteps. "Ah, I believe my love is here now." She gazed toward the door as Lord Maldrake strode forward, her face lit with an uneasy smile.

"Yvaughan!" Maldrake cried, placing his hands on her shoulders and kissing her cheek. "And how are you today?" he asked her, glancing at Teryl Auroch who stood nearby. The mage shook his head slightly.

"Maldrake, I'm fine!" Yvaughan cried. "Teryl's just being a worrywart. Come, sit beside me and tell me about your day."

"With pleasure, love," the young lord said. "By the way, Brisbois is joining us. I hope that won't be a problem." He sat down and mussed Yvaughan's hair. Teryl sat down on a nearby chair and fidgeted.

"Certainly not!" She returned the kiss shyly, then rose slowly with her husband's help. "Let me check with the kitchen, and I'll have an extra place s-set," Yvaughan slurred.

"Let the servants do it," Maldrake said, holding Yvaughan's hand.

"I'm up already," she replied, stroking her pregnant abdomen. "It would be more work to call a servant than to do it myself." Slowly she made her way across the cluttered room toward the hall that led to their private kitchens.

As she walked from the hall, she heard, faintly in the background, her husband and Teryl talking about her. Their apparent concern for her health made her face flush. Everything was going as planned, Teryl was saying. That can only mean the baby, thought Yvaughan. Maldrake responded with a hearty laugh—the proud and happy cry of a man expecting his first child.

As she pushed open the kitchen door, a tiny fear rose inside her. She touched her throat again. "I must learn to be less afraid."

🐚 🐚 🐚 🐚 🐚

Verdilith drank deeply from the underground stream in his cavern. The icy water sluiced through his spearlike teeth and dripped, glistening, from his cruel lips. He swallowed, and the man-sized gulp of water rolled down his long, slender neck. Seventeen dorsal plates, each the size of a small shield, shifted gently as the gulp passed by. He sighed. Golden-green scales rippled in pleasure from the peak of his massive shoulders to the tip of his long, supple tail. He stretched, spreading leathery wings nearly to the ceiling, one hundred feet above. His eyes glowed with orange fire, scanning the treasure-strewn lair around him. He rumbled to himself, the shaft of air in his throat whistling heavily as he spoke, "I've had enough of gold and silver—for the moment. What I want is flesh and blood."

The pangs of hunger had started. Verdilith rolled to one side, his mountainous bulk settling against a cluster of stalagmites. He scratched the coppery scales of his belly, his vision clouding with images of something fresh and fat and swollen. He chopped his jaws in anticipation, then rolled to his feet and stomped off toward the gold and silver hoard where he nested.

Above his bed, the vault of the cave was higher, rising fully three hundred feet. The cave was twice that distance wide. Despite occasional dampness from the spring rains, the ground generally remained dry and cool and comfortable. The underground stream provided fresh water, and air circulated in from a number of tiny, almost invisible cracks in the cavern's walls. Reaching the gold pile, Verdilith rolled onto his back and gazed up at the ceiling. The magical crystals he had imbedded in the vault still glowed, filling the cavern with their shimmering light. Ruby, emerald, and sapphire rays of light leaped furtively from crystal to crystal, casting a twinkling light over the treasure horde. Verdilith was glad, for he couldn't bear absolute darkness in his lair.

A thunderous groan echoed through the cavern, and Verdilith stroked his rumbling stomach. The bloodlust time was upon him. It filled his eyes with a crimson haze and made his enormous heart pound heavily. The desire for blood would only deepen in the coming months. Perhaps he should sate his hunger a bit now so that he could give his undivided attention to furthering his plans. Yes, his thoughts whispered, draw blood first. Then think of Penhaligon and what the future holds.

The dragon shifted his great bulk, his hind leg kicking aside an offending crown. Life is good, he thought complacently, though there is much yet to be done. What should we do to slake our thirst for blood? Attack the castle itself? No, too many paltry humans live there. We would be overcome by their hordes. The orcs east of here? No, we may need them intact for later. The little village south of here? Ah, now there's a thought! Or perhaps one of the logging camps nearby . . . ?

The dragon smiled and his eyes clouded over with dreams of blood and heat and rending flesh. Rising to his feet, he leaped once into the air. With a sudden roar of wind through the cracked walls, the massive dragon disappeared, and in his place floated a tiny bat. His eyes glowed red with hunger, and his leathery wings bore him to the ceiling. Squeaking once, the bat flapped into a hole in the cave vault. The papery noise of his wings filled the narrow tunnel beyond as he flapped and crawled toward the surface. Within moments, the tiny bat emerged from the hole into the chill air of late afternoon.

Instantly Verdilith reverted to his true form. He had learned early on to shapechange as fast as possible, for once a sharp-eyed sparrow hawk had almost eaten him before he transformed. He surveyed the snow-covered knoll above his lair and the surrounding jagged hills. No tracks showed in the snow, and nothing moved upon the hills.

The great green sat back on his haunches and scented the air, his tongue flicking in and out, tasting the winter afternoon. Horseflesh! And a scent of pine! With a single bound he leaped into the air. His great leathery wings beat once, twice, a third time before they finally lifted the weight of the dragon. Powerful wing strokes hurtled him into the silver sky, over the hilltops and the twisted copses of the ravines. Rising to a comfortable height, Verdilith turned and soared southward, following the smell of horseflesh. Below him, the treacherous hills of the Wulfholdes whirled past. A small herd of deer froze as the dragon's shadow flashed overhead, then scattered into a deep patch of woods nearby. Verdilith dived after them, but pulled up short. Why hunt deer one by one in the forest? he asked himself. I can eat horses by the tens in their corral. The sweet scent of horseflesh grew stronger on the wind, intoxicating his already excited senses.

Verdilith screamed his hunger. Blood would soon be his! His heart pounded in time with the surge of his awesome wings. The scent filled his scaled nostrils. Verdilith extended his wings and soared silently, outracing the clouds.

In time, the dragon's eyes glazed over. The setting sun cast a red pall over the trees below. His excitement grew. His breath became fast and shallow. His wings turned effortlessly, dropping him low above the ground. A hideous anticipation pounded in his heart. The desire to rend flesh flooded through him.

It had been so long since he had eaten.

Then, below, the dragon spied a small loggers' camp. Only one tiny light glimmered inside the wooden structure. Out back, in a large corral, horses stood, champing nervously. The dragon circled once, then screamed again and plunged earthward.

The terrified horses below neighed shrilly in return. Verdilith descended on them. He swooped low, his talons clamping around three of the beasts. He rose into the air, his laden claws smashing into the side of the stable. The wood splintered, and the dragon dropped the broken beasts at the base of the barn.

Verdilith rose on the wind, wheeling around in the blood-red sky. Again he fell on the corral. The horses reared and kicked, trying to avoid the sudden claws that raked their backs, the wicked teeth that snapped mercilessly around them. They galloped along the fence, their eyes white with fear. Foam hung from their gaping muzzles. The horses' screams rent the air, but no one came to save them.

The dragon ripped great chunks of flesh from the beasts,

not heeding the few hooves and teeth that found their marks. Verdilith left the flesh; he was bent on carnage first, not feeding. He would not eat until all lay dead. Only one beast escaped: a bay mare. Her lathered skin shuddering in fear, the mare somehow clambered over the corral's high walls. The horse ran blindly into the woods, and night swallowed her up.

Verdilith slaughtered the remaining horses, delighting in the blood and the dung and the flesh. It was a beautiful carnage, worthy of a dragon such as he. The blood was hot and charged with fear, and it slaked his thirst.

Chapter V

linn had found abelaat tracks in the deep snow during his latest check of the trap line, and he and Jo now rode the griffon to the spot. A light dusting of snow had fallen since Flinn had found the tracks, but he had notched a tree so as to find the area again. Flinn searched the ground for fresh tracks, hoping the abelaat was a creature of habit.

"Two of my traps were damaged," Flinn said in the silence as Ariac waded through the deep snow, his crippled wings fluttering now and then to maintain balance. Ariac wasn't accustomed to carrying double weight. The trail they followed was an old and familiar one, however, and the beast moved ahead with confidence.

"Do you think the creature got caught in the traps and escaped?" Johauna asked. She shifted in her seat behind the saddle, trying to get comfortable with Flinn's bow and quiver and her sword strapped to her back. Jo rubbed her nose, then returned her hands to Flinn's waist.

"No, I think it's too smart for that," Flinn replied. "More likely it tried to eat whatever was in the trap. I think it succeeded, too. The two traps wouldn't have been so badly damaged otherwise. There was blood around each."

Rounding a break in the woods, the trail curved down

around the side of a large, frozen pond. The sky was gray and laden with snow. Flinn felt the girl shudder behind him. "Cold?" he asked, a grim smile forming on his lips.

"Scared," she replied quietly.

The warrior stroked her hand at his waist. "We'll get the beast, Jo, have no fear," he said gruffly, his voice low with emotion. "If not for your sake, then for mine. I'll get more sleep once you stop waking up screaming."

The girl turned aside, then said, "I am not the only one who wakes up screaming, Fain Flinn."

Flinn drew in a breath and released it slowly. The old nightmares still dogged him, but over the years he had learned to accept them, albeit reluctantly. "But your nightmares can be dispelled, Jo." He nodded once and then clasped her hand. "We'll kill the beast today."

Unexpectedly, Jo leaned forward and embraced him. "Flinn," she said, "you are a good man." Just as quickly, however, she leaned away.

Flinn cocked an eyebrow and looked ahead along the trail. He said nothing and gave Ariac a little squeeze of his legs. The griffon continued at a walk.

The former knight and the would-be squire continued their trek in silence, Flinn pointing now and then to a few landmarks. When they reached the spot where Flinn had seen the creature's tracks, he didn't bother to dismount. His keen eyes traced the remains of some creature's trail. The abelaat's? Flinn wondered. The outline of the tracks was too decayed to tell for sure.

Ariac clicked his beak, sending a small puff of breath into the breeze. Flinn shushed the griffon immediately, then turned the beast up the incline to their left, following the line of tracks. He patted the sword strapped onto the saddle's pommel, secure in the knowledge that it was close at hand.

It had been impossible to wear it with the girl riding behind him.

"Be quiet," Flinn said softly to Johauna. "I think we may be in the abelaat's territory now." He fidgeted a little in the saddle, shifting the breastplate on his chest. He had grown accustomed to not wearing armor over the years, and he'd forgotten how cumbersome it was.

The girl nodded, checking the weapons strapped to her back.

They climbed slowly through the rugged, wooded terrain. The brush grew thicker and the trail grew more obliterated. Ariac slowed. Flinn began to wish he had left both the griffon and the girl behind. But Jo needed this kind of experience to prove herself to the council. The woods deepened. Flinn gazed dubiously at the trail. Is it a false track? he wondered. Or perhaps a trap?

The trail led him to a tiny valley, no more than three hundred paces long by fifty wide. There the trail ended, leading into a small stream—not yet frozen over—which ran swiftly through the bottom of the valley. Animal tracks of all sizes and shapes littered the snow-covered ground of the valley's bottomland. Flinn dismounted and Jo did the same.

"Well," said Flinn, "we've lost the trail. I won't be able to pick up the abelaat's tracks through all this. If, indeed, we've been following the abelaat. Those tracks were pretty obscure." He knelt and studied the hopeless muddle of tracks on the ground. Looking up at Jo, he sighed, his breath curling away in white tendrils. "We'll water Ariac, rest a bit, then make our way back up to that ridge—" he pointed to the northwest "—where we'll find a little higher ground and maybe easier going."

"Do you think we'll find the creature today, Flinn?" Johauna asked, her voice edgy.

Flinn glanced up at the clouds. The breeze had grown stronger and had shifted behind them. A heavy storm was moving in from the southwest.

He shrugged, the breastplate rising up, "Maybe, maybe not. I'm going to water Ariac. Stay here."

"I'd rather follow, if you don't mind," Jo said nervously.

Flinn nodded and led the griffon over the stony ground to the open water. On the bank of the stream, caps of untouched snow marked the presence of boulders, the largest of which was half the height of a man. Flinn gazed toward the swift water that lay just beyond that rock. The warrior stepped cautiously forward, leading Ariac among the large, snow-covered mounds. After passing the first few, the griffon stopped and lowered his beak, his nostrils blowing puffs of white. He sniffed at the path Flinn had made.

Flinn, annoyed, turned to face the griffon. Tugging on the bridle rein, he called sharply, "Ariac!"

Suddenly, the rock behind Flinn moved. The bird-lion reared and screeched in fear. Ariac's buff-colored wings flapped awkwardly, the tips stretched wide as though to bat back some unseen assailant. Flinn's scabbard and sword, fouled by the flailing wings, flew to the rocky shore. The braided leather rein broke near the metal bit.

Flinn wheeled about. The "rock" rose up, its scabrous surface unfolding into a towering beast. Thin, almost skeletal arms swung out to its sides as razor-tipped fingers slowly unfurled. Snow dropped in clumps from its knobby back, and its eyes fastened on Flinn.

Flinn dived to one side between adjacent boulders. The corner of his breastplate caught upon one rock, somersaulting him forward. The abelaat lunged, its claws snagging the warrior's pant leg. Flinn's boots followed through above his head, striking the beast's face and driving it back. The warrior rolled to his feet. The creature dived again, its claws arcing toward Flinn's neck. Flinn fell back against a rock, unable to avoid the blow. The claws stopped short, however, and a blood-chilling howl erupted from the beast. Ariac had reared and sunk his claws into the monster's shoulders, the leather balls dangled from the cuffs. The abelaat turned, its talons closing around the feathered forequarters of the bird-lion.

For the second time that day Ariac screeched, but this time the sound was terrible to hear. The griffon tore loose from the monster and then stumbled backward, shrill squeals filling the air. Ariac fell thrashing into the shallow stream, the pain in his forequarters driving him into a frenzy. He beat the rocks and water with his crippled wings and clawed at the snowy riverbed. Lunging frantically, he cleared the water and crashed away into the brush.

The abelaat turned and faced Flinn. Slowly it rose to its full height, baring its teeth and as if testing the air. The eight prominent canines dripped rust-colored saliva as the creature hissed.

Flinn eyed his sword, lying two paces beyond the monster. He side-stepped quickly, positioning himself behind one of the boulders. Whichever route the creature took around the large rock, Flinn would run the opposite way and retrieve his sword. Then he saw Jo, stealthily approaching behind the beast, her wooden sword gripped at both the pommel and the center. Flinn grimaced. She doesn't even remember how to hold a sword! he thought.

Jo shouted "Flinn!" and threw her sword. The abelaat leaped to scramble over the rock. The wooden blade arced over the beast's head as the first claw sank into Flinn's left arm. In the breadth of a heartbeat, Flinn snatched the wooden sword from the air and battered back the bloody talons. Flinn stepped back from the beast. The monster lunged forward, but Flinn cautiously backed into the rocky streambed. The abelaat paused, then lunged again. Flinn pulled back once more, his eyes shifting from Jo to the sword she was searching for in the streambed.

"Hurry, Jo," he muttered under his breath. The abelaat leaped onto the slippery rocks, its sickle-shaped claws scraping across Flinn's breastplate. He spun, knocking the claws away, and brought the blade smashing down upon the beast's arm. The creature pulled back, though its arm showed no injury. So much for ironwood, thought Flinn.

The abelaat roared, hurtling itself at Flinn. Tightening his grip upon the hilt, Flinn leaned into the attack, swinging the blade in wide swipes before him. The wooden edge struck the beast's talons, and a line of blood started down its arms. Still it pushed forward, its claws slashing the side of Flinn's head. The warrior staggered back, blood running warm down his neck. Apparently smelling the blood, the beast leaped onto the warrior and seized Flinn by the shoulders. The claws sunk in and Flinn shouted in pain. The bony arms lifted him from the ground. Flinn wedged his sword in the creature's gut and thrust upon it, but it bit shallowly.

Suddenly the creature dropped Flinn, who fell, splashing into the streambed. The abelaat arched its spine and hissed, its claws scraping at its back. Flinn struggled to his feet in time to hear the twang of an arrow. The abelaat fell to one knee. The warrior leaped toward Jo, catching a glimpse of two arrows in the abelaat—one in its shoulder, the other in its thigh.

"Good girl!" he managed to call out as he caught the other sword she threw. He dropped her wooden blade and whirled to meet the abelaat. His arm and the side of his face had gone numb. For the first time, he felt fear. The creature was back on its feet and rushing toward him. Was it unstoppable? Flinn gritted his teeth and raised the steel blade before him.

The warrior met the abelaat's charge with a flashing flurry of sword strokes, his blade clashing fiercely with the creature's wicked claws. Flinn drove forward, seeking firmer ground. He entrenched his feet in the rocky streambed, blood dripping into the water around him. The creature swiped at his chest, its claws leaving deep marks in the breastplate. Flinn held his footing, then continued to press forward.

He lunged with a pointed thrust to the abelaat's chest, which he knew the creature would brush aside. He followed up with an overhead arcing swing, trying to beat past the bony arm and hit the vulnerable neck area. The abelaat deflected the stroke, flinging the blade to its side. Flinn allowed the heavy sword to continue on its new course, and the momentum swung him around. He spun into a crouch and then extended his arm. The stroke arced back, slicing deep into the abelaat's knobbed knees.

The monster roared in pain as Flinn drew back his blade. The fetid stench coming from the creature's mouth nearly overcame Flinn, but he stood his ground. Clutching its bloodied legs, the creature snarled, its tiny eyes glinting. Rusty spittle fell from its mouth, dropping into the running water beneath. As Flinn drew back slowly, the creature lunged. Flinn leaped sideways and ducked. An arrow flew at the abelaat, sinking with a solid thud into its bony back.

The creature roared, then advanced on Flinn, its claws whirling within inches of the warrior's face. Flinn reluctantly backed into deeper water. His feet were numb from the icy water, and now the stream engulfed his calves as well. But he could feel his second wind coming, and his breath came in sure measures. The warrior laughed aloud—a deep, grim laugh that chilled the girl loading her bow with her last arrow. Flinn once again tried to press the attack; with two hands on his sword, he began a series of taxing, brutal blows.

The blade's bite was keen, and the snow-capped rocks ran red. Yet the monster was drawing blood, too. It caught hold of Flinn's breastplate and tore it loose. The claws raked across his bare chest, and Flinn's blood commingled with the abelaat's. The cold water, the loss of blood, and the fatigue of battle began to take their toll. Bit by bit Flinn felt his strength waning, his reflexes failing. The abelaat, though bloodied, didn't appear weakened. They circled each other. "Keep the arrows coming, Jo," Flinn murmured as a shaft narrowly missed the beast.

The words had hardly left Flinn's mouth when the creature lunged again. With a surge of reckless abandon, Flinn leaped onward to meet it. His sword tip found the beast's belly and cut through the papery skin. Flinn drove forward, into the the creature's vicious embrace. He thrust his sword through the abelaat's stomach and up into its chest. Hot blood poured out over his hand. The abelaat released a gurgling roar, its claws raking furrows in Flinn's back. Flinn gritted his teeth. He twisted the blade, seeking the creature's heart. The monster's arms locked about Flinn and pulled him tight.

Blood sprayed between them, gushing into Flinn's face. Blinking, Flinn saw Jo on the creature's back. Her short knife shone in her hand as she dragged it across the creature's neck. Shuddering violently, the creature tottered and staggered deeper into the stream. Its limbs spasmed with convulsions, and it toppled into the shallow water, taking Jo and Flinn with it. Gasping from loss of breath and the icy cold, Flinn and Jo struggled to untangle themselves from the feebly moving monster. Blood filled the water, streaming like crimson banners from the creature's body. Its eyes grew glassy, and the jittering paroxysms of its limbs stilled.

Jo and Flinn stood and looked down at it, Flinn's breath coming in great, ragged gulps. In death the beast seemed to have shrunk, and the cruel contortions of its face had eased. The cold water masked the beast's foul odor and cast a sheen over its mottled skin. The maw lay open, and water circulated gently among the eight fangs.

Flinn knelt by the body. Taking his knife, he used it to maneuver the abelaat's jaw so that he could see the canines more clearly. As he had suspected, each fang had a hollow tip. The creature's poison came through tiny tubes in the teeth and mixed with saliva inside the creature's mouth. It was likely the monster only produced the poison when it was preparing to bite.

Only then did Flinn notice the wind whistling into the valley. Both the warrior and the girl shuddered in their wet clothes. "We've got to get back to the cabin," Flinn said. He moved away slowly, picking his way through the rocky streambed. Jo did not follow, her eyes fixed on the beast.

Flinn turned, approaching Jo from behind. He placed his hands on her shoulders, compassion running through him. "Is this the first time you've seen something die?"

"No," she replied, "but it's the first time I've ever really killed anything. The wharf rats were always dead by the time I collected them. The traps killed them—not me." She rubbed the beaded handle to her blink dog's tail nervously. "I ran out of arrows and had to use my knife."

"You did well, Jo," he replied, smiling grimly. "Not an arrow left, eh?"

She nodded, her eyes still fixed on the dead abelaat. "Sorry about that. I think I can retrieve some of them—not all of them broke on the rocks I hit."

Flinn pointed to the tail at her waist. "Good thing you had

that, by the way. Proved useful. Your father gave that to you, didn't he?"

"Yes, he did." The girl's eyes didn't waver. "A mage made it for my father. I don't know why he made it, or else I've forgotten. The magic's beginning to fade though; I can't blink nearly as far as I used to." With another shudder, she turned to Flinn. He was glad to see that she had recovered her nerves. "Are you hurt bad?" she asked. "Did it bite you?"

"No, I don't think so anyway. I can wait until we get back to the cabin." He wiped at the blood on his face and neck. "Much of this is from the abelaat."

"If its teeth didn't pierce you, maybe you didn't get any of its spittle. It was drooling quite a bit, though," she added matter-of-factly.

Flinn turned, his eyes scanning the ground. "Perhaps some of the abelaat's saliva mixed with the blood and formed more crystals." He began backtracking the fight's route, following the tracks of blood in the snow. He also picked up the undamaged arrows he came across.

"Flinn?" the girl asked, concern in her voice. "Why don't we just leave? I'm cold." She, too, began retrieving arrows.

"It was about here," he mumbled under his breath. He searched several more steps, bending low and coursing back and forth. A few moments later, he stopped. "Ahhh," the warrior murmured and knelt in the trampled snow and mud. His fingers brushed aside slush and debris, and he picked up six crystalline rocks.

Flinn said slowly, his eyes never leaving the stones in the palm of his hand, "These are like the eight crystals I withdrew from your wounds, only not so dark." He studied the newly formed rocks for a moment, then looked up at the girl.

Her eyes met his, their expression intense. "What're they for? If there were eight in me, why are there only six? The abelaat had eight fangs," Jo asked.

"I'm not sure what they're for, but we'll find out. As to there being only six, I'd guess that only six measures of poisoned spittle found blood," answered Flinn, his eyes returning to the crystals.

Jo shivered again from the cold. The wind was picking up, and the two of them were soaked.

Flinn stood and scanned the hills around them. His face grew pale. "Did you see which way Ariac headed? If he could make his way out of this valley, I'm guessing he's not too badly injured. He's quick to panic once he's hurt."

Jo pointed northward. "He went that way; you can see his trail. He was bleeding quite a bit. . . ."

A deafening roar swelled strangely inside Flinn's head, drowning out Jo's voice. He shook his head, tapping his ear. Then he spotted a mounted horseman, watching from the southern crest of the valley. The figure wore armor and a midnight-blue tunic. Flinn turned toward it, squinting, but it melted into the forest. Snow began cascading down, and the moan of the wind deepened.

"Come," he said abruptly, scooping the crystals up and placing them in his belt pouch. He considered whether to tell Jo about the figure he'd seen. The wind howled again. "We've got to go, Johauna, or the storm will trap us here." Already the sky was growing dark.

"Let me at least stop the bleeding here in your side—and your head, and your shoulders."

He shook his head. "There isn't time. Gather the things—and hurry! We're both wet and chilled to the bone, and we won't last long out here if we don't move."

Flinn's dark eyes scanned the area where he had seen the mounted knight. The snow had begun to fall fast. "We'd die before catching him on foot," Flinn murmured to himself.

Just why was a knight from the Castle of the Three Suns watching him? And why did the knight let him and Jo fight the abelaat unaided? Why?

"Flinn?" Jo called, breaking his reverie. "Is something wrong? I've gathered our things. Shall we go?"

He looked at the girl again, wondering again if he should tell her of the figure he had seen, but he decided against it. Until he could discern why they had been watched, he wouldn't frighten her. He took his sword and breastplate from her, and then they began following the griffon's trail out the valley.

"Ariac hasn't lost his sense of direction—he's heading for home—which means he'll be all right. We'll follow his trail while we can," he added, flashing a concerned look at the thickly falling snow. The mounting wind promised a terrible storm. Flinn tried to hurry his pace, but felt a sudden pain rip through his side. The abelaat's claws had done more damage than he had thought.

"Here, let me help," Jo said. She pulled his free arm over her shoulders, her right arm going around his back. Flinn lurched forward and almost fell.

"Take it easy, Flinn. We'll get there . . . we'll get there," the girl struggled to hold up his weight. "Let's just make it up the hill."

Flinn focused his remaining energy on the task the girl had set him. "I'll make it, Jo." His tired eyes looked around the valley once more, both fearing and hoping to see the mailed horseman.

&a &a &a &a &a

Jo feared they would never top that first hill, or the second, or the third. Snow piled deep in the protected, wooded spaces, impeding their progress. They floundered through the thigh-high snow, uncertain of the footing. The undergrowth tore at them, raking their exposed hands and faces.

Jo and Flinn were both freezing, their clothes drenched from the stream and the snow. Only the struggle of moving forward kept their joints from stiffening and their limbs from going numb. But their strength was waning rapidly. Night loomed in the east, swallowing the thick clouds. The falling snow darkened the sky even more. Jo's lips drew into a tight line as she studied the snow-choked woods. At least the trees cut the wind, she thought. And though Ariac's tracks were being covered by the snow, Jo could still make out the depressions and broken branches marking his passage.

"Take another step, Flinn," she mumbled, hardly aware of the words. "We'll be home soon. To the top of this hill, Flinn, to the top."

She tried not to think about how far they had come, for she knew the path ahead was much longer than that behind. The swirling snow and the dark sky confused her sense of direction. Although she was sure they were lost, remaining still meant only freezing death. She gritted her teeth, determined to press on to the cabin or die of exhaustion.

"Another step, Flinn, another step," she murmured. "One more hill to go."

A familiar screech broke through the surrounding wind, and Jo stopped. Ariac? she wondered. Could the griffon be coming back to us? She searched the gloom ahead of her, her eyes so tired she could only focus on passing flakes of snow and not beyond.

Jo saw the griffon led by the wildboy, Dayin, appear through the gloom. Seeing them, the boy hurried forward with the steed. Exhausted, Jo leaned against Flinn, hoping he wouldn't fall. She was certain she would crumple if he did and that neither would rise again. Brushing aside a frozen tendril of hair from her eyes, she pulled her wet vest closer.

The boy halted beside them, and Ariac bent his head to gently nibble at his master. The griffon squealed in distress. His forequarters where the creature had raked him had stopped bleeding, though the wounds had not been dressed.

"Jo," Flinn said hoarsely, "climb into the saddle. We're almost home."

"You're hurt, Flinn." Jo's whispered words emerged from lips so numb she doubted she really said them. "You get on Ariac; I'll lead."

The warrior gave her a push. "No, Ariac's too injured to bear my weight," he said weakly.

"Then we'll all three walk."

"Fine. You get on the other side and loop your hand through the stirrup," Flinn responded mechanically. He gestured to the boy. "Dayin, lead us home."

The rest of that trip was lost to Jo's memory. She knew only that she clung to the griffon's saddle and that she found a little warmth from his body. The snow fell relentlessly. The wind howled overhead, and dead branches rained down on them. Darkness fell, too, the true blackness of a night let loose to the elements. Jo's wet garments clung to her coldly. She wanted only to lie down in the white, white snow.

Then, somehow, they found themselves standing before the barn. Johauna fell to the ground, her legs numb from the hips down. A strange haze was engulfing her, and she wanted to sleep. The wind had begun to sing to her.

Someone was shaking her, forcing her to stand again. It was Flinn. "Dayin," she heard the warrior say, "the lantern's inside and to the right. Take Jo inside and light a fire. Make sure she doesn't sleep! I have to tend Ariac."

The boy led her inside the cabin, quickly lit the lamp, and

helped Jo to the chair before the hearth. He removed her icy outer garments and threw one of the bed's furs around her. The wildboy removed her shoes and briskly rubbed her feet until the white glow had turned pink. Then Jo felt a pewter tankard against her lips, and a little water wet her mouth. Jo could only stare glassily back at Dayin, her thanks mute on lips too cold to even murmur.

"It'll be warm soon, pretty one," the boy was saying.

The numbness in her limbs gave way to a painful prickle, like a thousand needles. The pain cut through the fuzziness of Jo's mind. She wanted nothing more than to crawl to the bed, but that seemed too great an effort. Her bloodshot eyes mechanically followed Dayin's movements, and a sensation of warmth began to wrap her skin. Instinctively, she turned toward the hearth, cheered by the glow of yellow flames and the smell of smoke. She held out her hands eagerly. Dayin, sitting at the hearth, smiled and did the same.

Flinn entered the cabin with a gust of snow. He closed and barred the door wearily, then leaned against it. Jo watched him look about the room, fatigue lining his face and making him suddenly look old. She stood and helped him with his wet clothing, piling it beside the door with her own. The warrior sank into the chair, and she covered his shoulders with a fur.

"How's Ariac?" Jo asked, her own strength slowly returning to her. The painful tingle grew stronger across her body. She took some bandages from the cupboard and with slow, measured movements began dressing Flinn's injuries. Fortunately, most of them weren't severe, though the one puncturing his arm was still bleeding.

"He'll live, though it's going to be the better part of a week before he can be ridden. He's had a bad scare. Griffons are flighty beasts," Flinn said heavily, then turned to the boy at his feet. "Dayin, there's some bread and dried meat in the cupboard. Fetch some, will you?"

Dayin gathered together the simple meal. Flinn, Jo, and the boy huddled around the fire, too tired to move or eat much. They nibbled their cold food in silence.

"You two can take the bed, Jo," Flinn said when he had finished his last bite. He looked at Dayin and said, with a touch of his old asperity, "Unless you'd prefer to go back to the woods tonight, boy?"

Dayin vigorously shook his head. "No, please."

"Flinn, you're injured," began Jo. "You take the bed."

The warrior waved a hand. "Actually, Jo, the bed's bad for my back. I'll be all the better for not sleeping in it." He stood, shoved the chair to the side, and grabbed an extra fur from the bed. After Jo and Dayin moved out of the way, he spread out one fur and gingerly lay down on the floor. "Good night," he groaned.

Jo blew out the lantern, and by firelight she and Dayin crawled into the bed. She rolled over once to find a better position, then fell asleep listening to the warrior's heavy breathing.

2a 2a 2a 2a 2a

Flinn awoke to a noise behind him, by the fireplace. He grew suddenly still. Who—? What—? The morning's disorientation left him when he recognized the low tune Jo sometimes hummed. Slowly he turned over, his muscles protesting, and sat up. Jo smiled at him, then turned back to the porridge she was trying to stir while straddling his legs. Looking toward the cupboard, Flinn spied the boy, who sat on the table's edge, his feet swinging back and forth. Dayin smiled also.

"Time to get up!" Jo said cheerily. "Are you feeling better today? I am, though my legs are still sore. Quite a walk back last night. The storm's still raging. It doesn't look like it's going to let up anytime soon."

Flinn was irritated by her talkative good humor so early in the morning, but the smell of a warm breakfast appeased him. Jo was a good cook, and even the inevitable porridge was appetizing when she made it. He arched his back and groaned, the bones shifting into place. Then he stood and began stretching his tight muscles.

Jo busied herself at the table, scrubbing it clean and trying to set it with the ill-sorted dishes. The usual braid down her back was replaced with a riotous length of unbound reddish tresses. She was wearing her leather shift and breeches and had cinched her waist with a wide belt.

Flinn was suddenly struck by how different this day would be if she weren't here in his cabin.

"Quite a walk, indeed," he agreed, "and quite a fight. It was like the old days—tracking, doing battle, returning to camp frozen and wounded . . . and happy." Jo glanced quickly at him, her cheeks flushing and a smile spreading across her face.

Flinn turned away, replacing the fur on the bed and reaching for his dried clothes. Can I do it? he asked himself. Can I return to those days of glory? In that moment, he acknowledged the secret desire that had germinated the day Johauna Menhir entered his life: to be worthy again of the faith and belief she had in him, that other people once had. The Quadrivial is a long and treacherous road to walk, he thought. I'd have to regain each of the four corners as though I were a squire again. And even if I completed the four corners, the Order of the Three Suns would rather spit on me than readmit me.

"Few knights are worthy of the legends told of them," Jo said quietly as she stirred the porridge. "You proved yesterday that your courage still remains."

Flinn winced, then looked into her hopeful eyes. I am nothing now, he thought. I have nothing to lose and everything to gain. If only I had her faith in me. But I cannot disappoint that faith.

"Jo, I—" Flinn said haltingly "—I've a question for you, about . . . about your petition to the council to become a squire."

Jo whirled around, her eyes wide with alarm. Without a word, she gestured for him to sit down. When he did, she did the same. Dayin watched them intently. "Is . . . something wrong, Flinn? Did I do something wrong when we fought the abelaat?"

Flinn shook his head. "No, Jo, it's not that—not that at all. You were wonderful in the fight. I doubt I would have survived without you." He played with his food, then said slowly, "I was hoping you might consider something . . . else." He took a deep breath and caught her gray eyes. "You see, I've decided to petition the council myself, to try to reinstate my knighthood. I want you by my side as my squire. Of course, since I'm technically no longer a knight, you wouldn't technically be a squire. Whatever—I'd like you there with me."

"Flinn . . ." the girl whispered, blood draining from her face.

"Of course," he said nervously, "if—if they refuse to review my case, I will gladly recommend that the council take you on as a new squire for some other knight."

He held up his hands, cutting her short when she tried to speak. "Know this, Jo: the decision is yours. I have no right to ask you to become my squire; in fact, I'd caution you

against doing so. If the council members refuse my petition—
if they refuse to even see me—they may look with less favor
on your petition. It's a risk, Jo, and one you'd probably better
not take."

"Oh, Flinn," the girl's voice was tight, fighting back tears.
"I'd do anything to be your squire. Even at the risks you
mention." She swallowed convulsively. "When do we
leave?"

Jo's eyes were shining, and Flinn found himself swimming
in their gray purity. He looked away.

"As soon as Ariac's well enough to travel," he said. "Now,
let's eat before the oatmeal gets cold."

Chapter VI

linn, Jo, and Dayin stared at the crystals spread across the table in the cabin. Flinn had grouped them by type: the eight he had pulled from Johauna's shoulder and the six that had been formed with the creature's blood at the stream. Several candles added their glow to the lantern light and the wan beams of the winter sun. The inside of the cabin shone brightly.

The stones from Jo's shoulder were the color of clear red wine. They were about an inch long and spindle shaped, with six lateral edges that slanted to a point at each end. Those from the abelaat's blood were rougher in line and form, as though shaped too hastily. They were nearly an amber hue, and they were eight-sided.

Flinn picked up one of the crystals he had pulled from Jo's shoulder, his dark eyes glinting in the bright light. He twirled the stone between his long, scarred fingers, his moustache twitching as he frowned.

"My guess," he said at last, "is that the ones I removed from you, Jo, are better formed because the creature's poison was in you longer." He cocked an eyebrow. "I think the extra time allowed the crystals to draw more blood."

"Draw blood?" Johauna's eyes grew wide in sudden

horror. "Flinn—Flinn," she stammered. "Could these things be *alive*?" Dayin's eyes also opened wide.

"No, I don't think so." He shook his head, his black hair grazing the collar of his tunic. "I'm no sage, but I think the crystals need blood to form, not to eat."

Cautiously Jo picked up one of the wine-red crystals and peered at it. "It is kind of pretty," she said after a moment, "though I still think it's pretty gruesome how it was formed."

"I wonder what purpose these crystals serve," Flinn mused, rubbing his neck. "Perhaps they poison the victim."

"Or maybe they preserve the body," Jo added with a grimace.

"My father used to put them in fire," Dayin piped up.

Flinn and Jo stared at each other, then at Dayin.

"Used to put them in fire? Just what did your father do, boy?" Flinn asked, setting the stone aside. "And what happened to him?"

Dayin shivered, and his eyes grew wide. But Jo put a gentle arm around the child and stroked his shaggy hair, saying, "It's all right, Dayin. Flinn and I are your friends."

"My—my father died almost two years ago. We . . . our home was near here, about four days' walk north, I'd guess. We lived in a tower." The boy paused for breath.

"Near the River Highreach?" Flinn asked. When the boy nodded, Flinn went on, "I think I saw the tower about a year back when I ran trap lines north. A three-story tower? Red granite?"

The boy nodded again. Jo looked at Flinn questioningly.

The warrior gestured with his hand, his eyes troubled. "Almost half of the tower had been destroyed in some sort of explosion. It was obviously abandoned, so I went in and investigated, thinking I might move there. The damage was too great to fix, though. What's more," Flinn paused and his keen eyes turned to Dayin, "the place smacked of wizardry."

The boy's face blanched, and then he hid in Jo's arms. She gently pushed him away after only a moment's comfort. "Was your father a wizard, Dayin?" she asked, her tone serious, though her face was kind.

The boy could only nod, then added slowly, "My father was Maloch Kine, a great and kind mage. I—I wanted to be just like him when I grew up. I was just starting to learn from him."

Dayin flung his hands into the air and murmured a quick, unintelligible word. A burst of bright red light flashed above the table and was replaced almost immediately by an aromatic, though faintly acrid, smell of roses. There, on the table before the astonished Flinn and Jo, lay dozens of fresh red rose petals. They touched the fragile pieces delicately.

"Dayin, did you do this?" Jo asked. She sniffed the handful of petals she held and smiled.

The boy was despondent. "It didn't work, Jo. You were supposed to get *whole* roses—not just petals." Dayin looked from Flinn to Jo and shrugged his narrow shoulders. "I guess I'm out of practice."

Flinn laughed and clapped the boy's back. "Are you interested in coming with us to Bywater, Dayin, when Jo and I leave for the castle? There's a mage there who's been looking for an apprentice for some time now. But all the children in Bywater are too stupid to even be considered. What do you say?"

Dayin looked from Jo to Flinn and back again, his eyes wide with fear. The boy turned to the warrior. "I'd rather go with you, Master Flinn, all the way to the castle. There's bound to be a wizard there who could use me."

Flinn's eyes darkened. "We'll see, Dayin, we'll see. I'm

not sure I want to be responsible for you that long." He noticed Jo's disapproving gaze, and his mouth grew grim. Then he looked away; he couldn't refuse Dayin, not with Jo championing the boy's cause. "All right, Dayin. If you'd rather come to the castle, then do so." He glanced at Jo and then turned to the boy. "But that's the end of the tether for you. I have no need of a wizard apprentice—a would-be squire's all I can handle." Flinn smiled, then laughed aloud. "Maybe I should leave Dayin with Karleah Kunzay. She's batty enough to take on a boy like you."

To Flinn's surprise, the boy's face lit up. "Would you really take me to Karleah? Really?"

"You know the old wizardess?" Flinn asked, incredulous. The boy nodded. "She used to visit us a lot."

"That's . . . interesting," Flinn said noncommittally. Jo looked at him sharply, a question knotting her brow.

"You said your father used fire on the abelaat crystals?" Flinn asked Dayin in the pause that followed.

"Yes, I think so," Dayin responded. "At least, I remember him holding a stone in a flame and saying, 'Ah, this is good.' He always said that when he was excited. Why it was good, I don't know."

Flinn fished out the eight-sided crystal from the mug and stared at it, bemusement written on his face. "Let's try holding it in the candle flame, then. Jo, hand me my gauntlets, will you?" Jo retrieved the gloves from the cupboard and silently handed them to the warrior, who put them on.

He held the stone lengthwise a finger's width away from the flame and stared at it, waiting for something to happen. Silence fell. Their heartbeats marked the passage of time. Flinn, impatient at the delay, began to wonder if the boy had mixed up the abelaat stone with some other kind. Slowly the crystal warmed, and he could feel the heat even through his heavy leather and metal gloves.

Then something *moved* inside the crystal. Flinn hissed, and Jo crowded to his side, leaning over his shoulder. He focused minutely on the plane of the crystal facing him.

A shape was forming within the crystal. The lines around the shape slowly resolved, and the colors grew clearer. Vaguely Flinn realized he was pushing the crystal closer and closer to the open flame. That seemed to clarify the murkiness inside the crystal, though he wondered how long his gloves could protect him.

Flinn's eyes adjusted to the minuteness of what he was viewing: a scene in exquisite miniature played inside the shell of the crystal. Flinn gasped. "This—this is astonishing," he muttered aloud. The stone seemed almost like a stage on which tiny actors could walk. Jo leaned on Flinn to get a better view, and Dayin crowded closer.

The scene within the stone sharpened into recognition. It was the conservatory at the Castle of the Three Suns. The colors were muted and the shapes of the walls and furnishings were distorted. Otherwise, the conservatory looked much like Flinn remembered it from seven years before. Is this a memory? A dream? A prophecy? he wondered. The arrangement of the plants and furnishings were slightly different than he remembered them. "It must be the garden room as it stands now, this very moment," he murmured excitedly.

Sunlight streamed through the glass ceiling panels in the room and filtered past the leaves of exotic plants that had been transplanted there throughout the centuries. Some ancestor of old Baron Arturus's had decided to make this room into a conservatory, and the room had been steadily added to and renovated until it had become the pride and glory of the castle. Even in the coldest winter this room retained its tropical heat, allowing the delicate plants and trees inside the chamber to thrive.

Several decades ago, a great mage had populated the conservatory with gold- and jewel-encrusted magical birds that flitted about and sang. They were wonderful to behold, and the old baron swelled their ranks with real birds—native and exotic. Arturus called the magical birds the gold of his crown and the living birds the jewels.

Flinn moved the crystal almost into the candle's flame, and the scene focused more sharply. The intricately carved stone bench came into view as did the pond beside it, filled with brilliant-hued fish. Sunlight glinted off their purple and blue and scarlet backs as the fish occasionally surfaced. Flinn fancied for a moment that he even heard water splash and trickle.

From a door at the back of the scene, a woman entered the room. She walked slowly, her hand rubbing her pregnant midsection. Reaching the bench, she slowly sat down, her bulk making her movements less than graceful. She began crumbling bread into the pond, leaning toward where the fish frenziedly leaped to the surface. Her pale face, so perfectly composed in miniature, was blank and listless.

"Yvaughan," Flinn whispered. Jo gasped.

The woman in the crystal looked up expectantly, as if she had heard something, and turned the way she had come. Then, very distinctly, Flinn heard a tiny voice say, "Is someone calling me?"

Yvaughan could hear him through the stone!

"Yvaughan! It's me—Flinn!" the warrior cried.

The crystal popped and shattered, little pieces of it flying from between Flinn's fingers and falling to the table. The warrior stood abruptly, his shocked expression tense. His eyes sought Jo's.

"I—I saw my wife, Jo, in the crystal," he said, his gauntleted hand trembling. "Or, rather, my former wife. She—she divorced me after . . . after . . . Did you see—"

"Flinn!" The girl grabbed his hands. "Calm yourself." She nodded. "Yes, Dayin and I saw the image, too."

Flinn's moustache quivered. He nodded abruptly and squared his shoulders. He sat down again, one hand stroking his chin. "I don't know what to do now, Jo. She seemed . . . unhappy. Should I try to see her through the crystal again?" Flinn looked aside. "She's also with child."

Jo and Dayin gazed intently at the warrior. "I take it . . . she's remarried?" Jo asked.

"I assume so," Flinn responded, still not looking her way. "I—we never had children." Flinn found his thoughts skirting that particular hurt. He blinked, shaking the memory from his head. Taking a deep breath, he said, "Let's test a different stone. The one we used was one of the abelaat's, I believe." He handed Jo the gauntlets and a six-sided crystal. "Here, Jo. This stone came from your blood, so you do the honors."

Jo heated the stone as she had seen Flinn do. The former knight and the wildboy peered over her shoulders into the wine-red depths of the crystal. Flinn expected to see a continuation of the scene they had previously witnessed. But when the scene finally coalesced, it was not the conservatory they saw. Rather, they peered into a dim cavern, a cavern that twinkled with small lights. In the center of the cave lay a dragon, staring intently at his claws—a green dragon in perfect miniature. Flinn hissed, and Jo dropped the crystal, which fell to the table and bounced unharmed.

Jo's eyes were wide with shock. "I've never seen a dragon before, even in miniature," she said. "Was that Verdilith?"

He nodded once, abruptly. "Continue," he prompted, pushing the stone toward Jo. She picked it up and again held it to the candlelight. After a moment or two, the image of the cavern came into focus.

Inside the tiny scene, the dragon lifted his head. He began looking about, his tongue flickering between his teeth. It was almost as if the creature sensed he was being watched. Johauna shivered but this time did not drop the stone. Flinn sucked in his breath.

The dragon moved his head sharply back and forth. He rolled off his pile of coins and began lumbering about the cavern. His golden eyes whirled feverishly about, and his tongue continued to test the air.

"Flinn!" came a quiet, powerful rumble from within the stone. All three felt a chill cross their bones. The call had come from the dragon.

The crystal shattered. Jo jumped as the pieces of the stone dropped to the table. Flinn and Dayin sat down in silence.

"That dragon knew we were watching it!" Jo cried.

Flinn nodded. "It would seem so."

Johauna frowned. "I understand how your former wife heard us, because you called out to her, but we didn't say anything to Verdilith. He couldn't have heard us after I dropped the stone. Could he?"

"He . . . may have. That wyrm has some . . . extraordinary perceptions. I rather wish we had tried to call his name, but we might have courted disaster doing that," Flinn finished.

Jo looked at Dayin. "Do you remember anything else about these stones?"

The boy's blue eyes looked off into space while he chewed a fingernail. His eyes narrowed. Finally he said, "Sorry, I don't remember."

Jo turned to Flinn. "What about the mage in Bywater you

mentioned? Can we bring the stones to him and find out what they're good for? Or crazy Karleah?"

"Esald?" Flinn named the village wizard, then shook his head. "He's quite a run-of-the-mill, garden-variety mage. Doesn't deal in anything too exotic—or dangerous. No, Karleah's the only person I'd trust with these."

"Where is she?" asked Jo.

"She lives near the Castle of the Three Suns, though some distance north. A little northeast, if I remember correctly. She'd know about the crystals, plus no one would believe her if she mentioned I had them. She's got quite a reputation for eccentricity," Flinn answered.

"Should we take these stones to her, Flinn?" Jo asked.

Flinn frowned. "Probably. I'm leery about testing them again when we don't really understand how to use them. Obviously, they could prove extremely useful, and I'd rather not waste any more experimenting." Flinn frowned again. "I think we will visit Karleah, and I think we'd better do it before we get to the castle."

"Why?" Jo and Dayin asked simultaneously.

"If the stones can be made to show past events, then that will be all the proof I need to present to the council," Flinn replied. Besides, he added privately, I may be able to check on a certain Sir Brisbois with Karleah's help. We'll see if he's been haunting my woods on horseback. Flinn added, "I think I could have conversed with Yvaughan if the stone hadn't burst. As to the ones made from your blood, Jo, I think they might be longer lasting and perhaps give a better image."

Jo looked at Dayin, as if seeking some answer in the boy's serene gaze. "Why do you suppose we saw those two images? I mean, why didn't you see Bywater, and why didn't I see Specularum?"

Flinn shrugged. "I don't know."

"I do," Dayin piped. "I remember that much now. Dada said you had to concentrate on what you wanted to see or who you wanted to contact."

Johauna looked at Flinn closely. "Were you thinking of your former wife before, Flinn?"

"Actually, no. But I was daydreaming about the conservatory at the castle—it's quite a sight. How about you? Were you thinking of Verdilith?" Flinn queried.

Frowning, Jo tried to remember exactly what she had been thinking. "No, no, I don't think so, not consciously anyway. But . . . I was scared for some reason, and I was thinking about danger and the people in Bywater. It was all very jumbled."

Coincidence? Flinn wondered. Danger for the town, or danger for us? What is that wyrm up to, anyway? He sighed heavily and said, "Well, whatever the case, next time we try the stones, we concentrate on a subject. We'll do that with Karleah's help. As to Verdilith, when we get to the Castle of the Three Suns, we'll find out what plans they have for killing the dragon. They should have something in the works for dealing with Verdilith."

"What happens if your petition goes as planned?" Jo asked.

The warrior smiled. "Then we join the others in the hunt for a great green." His eyebrows rose in anticipation.

🐾 🐾 🐾 🐾 🐾

Five days later, Jo and Dayin carried large, willow-handled baskets down the path to the stream. Their eyes searched the underbrush for redberries. The tart, juicy clusters of fruit kept well all through winter and only fell from the bush come spring. It was one of the few foods that could be harvested in wintertime, and Flinn had suggested they gather the berries in preparation for leaving. They had left Flinn exercising Ariac in the corral. The warrior thought Ariac was coming along well and should be ready again for travel in another day or two.

After a short walk, Jo and Dayin discovered a large break of redberry bushes. Picking the berries was easy because they grew in thick clusters that readily broke from the branches. Redberries liked lowlands, however, which meant that the terrain surrounding the bushes was rough and difficult to traverse. Jo resorted to using her blink dog's tail to reach some of the more inaccessible bushes, even crossing the stream via the tail. She told Dayin to pick the berries on the outskirts of the marshy area that bordered the stream.

Jo's thoughts turned inward. She was worried about Flinn. She applauded his desire to confront the council and seek reinstatement as a knight, but she also knew that he was not the man he had been seven years ago. He had become a recluse, a man unused to the ways of men and women. She wondered if he would regret losing his solitude once he became a knight again. Jo smiled. She had absolutely no doubt that the council would reinstate Flinn. None whatsoever.

Jo looked up, seeking the boy. "Are you finished, Dayin?" she called. "My basket's full."

"Mine, too, Jo!" the boy answered.

Jo used her tail to blink back across the stream and handed Dayin her basket. She had prudently thought to conserve trips, bringing along the buckets and the ash yoke to gather water. Jo decided against using the tail to blink to the center of the stream; she had used it several times this morning, and she felt the familiar fatigue she always did when she overworked the magic. She filled the buckets with water as quickly as she could, then hooked them to the yoke and settled it on her shoulders.

"Can you carry both baskets, Dayin?" she asked. At his nod, she gestured for him to start up the steep hill.

The pair made the return trip slowly, for the path was icy in some spots and filled with snow in others. They kept their eyes on the trail, trying to find the best footholds. Johauna grunted under her load, but she was unwilling to leave a bucket and have to return for it. Dayin, meanwhile, was struggling with the two large baskets of berries. They were breathing hard and making so much noise that they didn't hear the sounds coming from the encampment until they crested the hill.

They were unprepared for the sight that met their eyes: the cabin was in blazes. Before they could even take in the devastation of their home, they saw Flinn being strangled by a knight clad in armor and a dark blue tunic. Flinn gasped for air, his face turning purple as he tried to pull the mailed grip from his throat.

୨ଈ ୨ଈ ୨ଈ ୨ଈ ୨ଈ

Flinn had breathed a sigh of relief when Jo and the boy left to pick redberries. He had found himself tongue-tied around the two of them, growing more taciturn than even his usual wont. But Johauna, too, had been strangely silent the past few days. Dayin, surprisingly, had not. He had talked about the nearly two years he had spent alone in the woods, telling of his animal friends, his daily forages for food, and his many brushes with death.

But now the talkative child was gone, and Jo with him. Flinn sighed again, planting his feet in the center of the corral

and leaning back upon the lunge rein. At the other end of the
rein, Ariac trotted, the scars on his chest rippling as he did.
Flinn turned slowly, letting Ariac move in a large circle
around him. The griffon's muscles seemed to be healing
well, and his old fighting spirit had returned.

Ah, Ariac! he thought, a little wistfully. How sad it is that
you have never flown, and how sad that I haven't either. He
remembered finding the ungainly little fledgling at the
bottom of a cliff. It was half-starved and its wings broken
beyond repair. Even the griffon's parents had given Ariac up
for dead, an atypical act for griffons. Flinn had carried the
feebly squawking creature home strapped to the back of
Fernlover.

Flinn smiled, remembering when Ariac, then a little
older, had tried to attack Fernlover. The old mule soundly
kicked him. To Flinn's knowledge, Ariac had never tried to
attack Fernlover again. Flinn was pleased with the griffon's
restraint, but he still muzzled the bird-lion when approaching
horses or their kin.

Flinn whistled to the winged creature, and Ariac pranced
toward his master eagerly. The leather balls beneath the
griffon's front claws produced puffing sounds against the
packed snow. Ariac squealed and nibbled at the warrior's
pockets, seeking a tidbit of dried meat. Flinn fished it out for
him and then left the corral for the barn, where he had left
his sword and whetstone. He intended to spend some time
now sharpening the blade. He also grabbed a piece of elkhide to rewrap the blade's hilt—the grip was beginning to
fray. Flinn retrieved the items, then started walking back
across the yard toward the cabin. Idly he rubbed the stone
against the edge of his blade, whistling some half-forgotten
court tune. Ariac screeched and Flinn looked up.

A fully armored knight leading a stout warhorse barred

Flinn's way. The man wore a midnight-blue tunic emblazoned with three golden suns. Instantly Flinn was certain it was the same man he had seen watching the battle with the abelaat. He dropped the whetstone and elkhide and readied his sword.

The knight removed the covered helmet from his head, and looped it over the pommel of his saddle.

"Brisbois!" Flinn gasped.

"One and the same, Flinn, old man," Brisbois rejoined, an insincere smile gracing his thin lips.

"What are you doing here?" Flinn raised his sword slightly, determined to keep up his guard. As well as instigating the treachery that brought Flinn's downfall, Brisbois had equalled Flinn at swordplay. Flinn had no doubt that the man could defeat him now, for Brisbois doubtless practiced daily against the other knights. Flinn's only challenge recently had been Jo.

Brisbois spread his hands expansively, as if making a friendly gesture, but Flinn noted that the knight's scabbard tab was undone. His sword could be drawn in an instant. "Now, Flinn, is that any way to treat an old—" Brisbois smiled, his pointed canines gleaming "—*comrade*? I was in the region and thought I'd drop in."

"Have your say, Brisbois, and let's be done with it," Flinn shot back.

Brisbois bowed stiffly. "If that's the way you feel about it, Flinn, so be it. I bid you good day." The knight casually put his helmet back on, moved to the left side of his roan horse, and climbed into the saddle.

Flinn looked past Brisbois and stiffened. His cabin door stood open. Flinn hadn't left the cabin door opened, and Jo and Dayin left before him. Then Flinn saw a wisp of smoke come through the open doorway, followed by a lick of flame.

"You bastard," Flinn said through clenched teeth. He leaped toward Brisbois just as the knight applied his spurs to the horse. Flinn reached up, curled his fingers around the armor's neck opening, and pulled savagely.

Flinn and Brisbois fell to the ground heavily, the horse cantering off toward the barn. Flinn rolled lightly to his feet. Holding his sword before him, he waited for Brisbois to stand. A snarl spread across Flinn's lips, and his heart pounded angrily. Twice his hunger for revenge drove him forward to attack before Brisbois had risen, and twice he backed away.

The knight rose to his feet, limping and holding his back. "You barbaric imbecile—pulling me from my horse! What has come over you?" The knight hobbled slowly toward the horse, casting a fleeting glance toward Flinn.

"Trying to see if the audience is watching, eh?" Flinn asked, sliding sideways until he was between Brisbois and his mount. Flinn's eyes narrowed and the humor left his gravelly voice, "You'll pay for burning my home—you and whoever sent you."

Warily the knight drew his own sword. "Why, so there is a fire! So quick to blame, are we? Perhaps a log rolled from the hearth." The two men began circling each other slowly, some ten feet apart.

"Who sent you?" Flinn growled. He leaped forward and swung his sword in a warning gesture. Brisbois flinched and raised his sword to block the move. Flinn smiled wickedly.

Brisbois circled slowly, his limp conspicuously diminished. "I'm here on behalf of Lady Yvaughan. She's asked me to invite you to the christening of her child. A son."

Flinn studied the knight's eyes. Brisbois stared unblinkingly at him, as though daring him to disbelieve the story. The warrior smiled cynically, then raised his sword and charged. The blade met solid metal and not the flesh its wielder had sought. Flinn whirled, swinging his sword behind him in a wide cutting arc. Again Brisbois met the blow. Flinn would have to increase his speed to gain any advantage that way.

Brisbois lifted his own sword and struck for Flinn. The warrior easily avoided the blade. He and Brisbois went into a crouch and began moving in a steadily decreasing circle. Flinn edged away from the corral and barn, careful not to be run up against the wall. He shifted his sword higher, waiting for Brisbois's next move.

Brisbois smiled evilly. "My dear Flinn," he said sarcastically, "I'm going to enjoy this so much. I've wanted to give you your comeuppance for a long, long time."

"Go ahead and try, Brisbois," Flinn rejoined. "Your treachery was never a match for my skill."

Brisbois leaped at Flinn, his sword singing as it whirled. Flinn blocked the blade, holding his own sword barlike before him. The force of the knight's blow drove Flinn to one knee, his arms and shoulders aching. But Flinn rose instantly and delivered his own blow.

The two began to parry, each delivering a sword stroke and blocking the other's in return. Occasionally a stroke would slip past an opponent's guard. Flinn couldn't see any harm done yet to Brisbois, for his strikes were only denting the man's armor. Some of Brisbois's hits, however, were finding flesh. So far they had only been glancing ones, but Flinn was bloodied in a number of places.

A sudden blast of smoke surrounded the two men as the wind shifted. Flinn coughed and saw that the cabin was now engulfed in flames. The fire had lapped through the log walls and was rapidly licking away at the outside. Ariac screeched in alarm, and even Fernlover brayed at the smell of smoke.

Flinn jumped forward, his anger fueled by the destruction of his home. He swung his blade with reckless fury, battering

Brisbois as though his sword were a club. Brisbois deflected the blows, turning each with the flat of his blade, but the volley of steel did not stop. Flinn pressed forward, the tip of his sword striking ever nearer the man's neck. Flinn's eyes shone with rage and a strange, savage joy. His wild, reckless onslaught forced Brisbois back.

"My cabin will be your pyre, Brisbois!" Flinn shouted.

The knight's hands shook as he turned his sword, blocking Flinn's strokes. Beneath the dark helmet, his eyes showed fear. Flinn growled, slashing in a mighty arc that battered back the knight's blade. Flinn's sword sliced through the gap between the breastplate and shoulder-guard. A spray of blood spotted the knight's armor. The sight spurred Flinn's anger. His strokes forced Brisbois back against the side of the barn, but there the knight let his armor take the force of some of Flinn's blows. Flinn smirked in disdain.

Abruptly, Brisbois leaped forward with his own savage blow. With a resounding clang, the knight's blade bit into Flinn's, notching it. Flinn wrenched his sword, pulling Brisbois's weapon from his hand. The knight leaped upon Flinn, toppling him to the ground. Flinn's sword tumbled loose. The armored weight of Brisbois knocked Flinn's breath away, but Flinn pushed against Brisbois and twisted out from beneath the knight. Brisbois's mailed hands seized Flinn's unprotected throat and clamped tight. Flinn pried at the cold gauntlets, but could not pull them loose. He grew dizzy, and the strength left his hands.

Suddenly, water and hard pellets rained down on them. Flinn and Brisbois sprang apart, shocked by the cold dousing. Flinn lunged for his sword, coughing as he did. He rolled to his feet and turned in time to see Jo swing the ash yoke and bash the knight's helmeted head. Brisbois staggered backward, one hand pulling an amulet from around his throat. Then the knight leaped for his blade lying in the snow.

Jo swung again, but Brisbois dodged the yoke and dissolved into a thin, wispy mist. The vapor disappeared even as Flinn swung at it with his sword.

"Coward! Coward!" he roared, his dark eyes searching the air above them. "Return and face me, Brisbois!" Rage had revived Flinn's energy. He stomped about the yard looking for any sign of the knight. The warrior shouted curses for a few minutes more, then drew a deep breath. He turned his attention toward the blazing cabin, now an inferno.

Jo came and stood by him. She put her hand on his arm. "Your home, Flinn, your home. I wish Dayin and I had come back earlier. We might have been able to stop it, or at least salvage something."

Flinn shook his head. "It's not your fault, Jo," he said quietly. "I have the crystals in my belt pouch, so they're not lost. My breastplate's in the barn, where I was going to fix it, so that's at least a little armor. And as to food . . . well, there's a bag of oats in the barn and some dried meat I had intended to feed Ariac—and all the berries you and Dayin picked." Flinn's eyes grew brighter, for he was very fond of the tart fruit.

"The, ah, redberries were part of our attack, Flinn," Jo said apologetically and pointed to the smashed red fruit at their feet. "Dayin threw the berries while I splashed the water." She shrugged. "It seemed like a good idea at the time."

Flinn laughed, albeit ruefully. "It was, Jo, it was." He gave her a quick hug and turned to the barn. "Now, let's see what we can do about making this place habitable for the night. We need to salvage what we can because tomorrow we have to go into Bywater. We need supplies, first and foremost. We won't make it to the castle otherwise." Flinn cocked an eyebrow. "It's a good thing I hid my gold in the barn and not the cabin. I haven't got much, but it'll get us some things."

"And then, we go to the castle?" Jo asked, her voice and eyes expectant.

"And then we go to the Castle of the Three Suns—" he paused for wry effect "—and beat Sir Brisbois into smithereens *before* we become knight and squire. There are rules against knights fighting each other, you know."

Jo laughed, a happy sound in an otherwise dark moment.

Fernlover brayed then, and Brisbois's horse nickered in response. Jo looked toward the corral. "It looks like we won't have to ride double on Ariac."

Chapter VII

vaughan pulled back the blanket and bit her lip. Her brutally deformed infant son lay there in the white-and-gold crib. Four nights ago, after a long and difficult delivery, Yvaughan had given birth to the child. She had screamed upon first seeing her son—one half of his head missing along with one eye, the hands twisted and corrupted with lesions, and the stump of a third leg forming out of his back, almost as if it were a tail. His bluish skin indicated he had stopped breathing, and for one hope-filled moment she thought the baby was stillborn. But Maldrake roared, pushed through the healers, and grabbed his infant boy. He shook the baby, screaming that he must live. The infant gasped and drew his first breath, and Yvaughan sank into a miasma of pain and horror.

Still recovering from her ordeal, Yvaughan stood now before the crib, clutching the rail for support. Her eyes fastened on the thing before her, the thing called her son. Even after four days he hadn't died, though Teryl and the castle's clerics had all sworn the child wouldn't live, that he would die and be at peace.

These predictions brought curses from Lord Maldrake, who insisted that they give the infant the best care and magical healing possible. For three days and nights he haunted the nursery, making certain no one spoke of his son in any way that displeased him. Yvaughan meanwhile kept to her bed, unable and unwilling to see the creature called her son. Maldrake cursed her, too, and called in a wet nurse to feed the child. Only the direst threats to her family kept the woman with them after seeing the infant. But when Brisbois had returned earlier today, Maldrake had left immediately on an urgent matter. He'd commanded his son's nurse to keep the boy alive.

Tonight, in the darkest hour, Yvaughan slipped from her bed, secure in the knowledge that Maldrake wasn't at the castle. She faltered coming into the room, but then her resolve hardened, and she made her way to the beribboned bassinet.

It still hasn't died, Yvaughan thought as she looked down on the baby, refusing to think of it as her son. It must die. I must kill it, for I gave it life. Weakly she picked up a tiny white pillow, one she had lovingly embroidered herself, and looked again at the hideously contorted mouth of her son. Give me strength, she prayed as a wave of wracking pain flowed through her. She steadied herself against the crib. Give me the strength to kill this monster. He's evil, he's evil. I know he's evil. With one hand she held out the pillow and placed it on her son's mouth. She pressed down. A tear formed on her cheek.

"My lady!" Teryl stood in the nursery's doorway. "You are awake at this hour!" He advanced into the room, his eyes on Yvaughan, her hand holding the pillow over the child's mouth. "Is there something wrong?"

Yvaughan stared uneasily at the aged mage. His withered form looked dark in the moonlight, like a living shadow. Suddenly she felt unsure of Teryl Auroch, the man whom she called friend. "Teryl," she whispered, taking the pillow away from the baby. She covered her eyes with her hands, for she couldn't bear to look at the infant any more. "The child—he's dead. . . ."

"Let me check, lady. Sometimes infants breathe irregularly," Teryl soothed. The mage came to the crib and looked down at the deformed baby.

Yvaughan could bear it no more, and she took a few faltering steps away, clutching at the little pillow. Teryl reached down into the crib with his right hand and said, "Poor, poor little baby." His left hand fluttered convulsively, and he murmured words she didn't understand. She thought she heard the child gasp and her own breath faltered. Fervently she hoped the mage wouldn't cast a spell to keep the child alive.

The mage walked over to Yvaughan's side and put his hand on her arm. The hand did not shake. Teryl looked at Yvaughan, his face swathed in dark shadows. His teeth flashed coldly, though his voice was warm with concern. "Lady, we knew it would happen sooner or later. Do not grieve. The child's death was all for the better; he's at peace now." He put an arm around Yvaughan. "Come. Let me return you to your chamber."

Stumbling out of the nursery, Yvaughan allowed herself to be led back to her room. She was numb with emotion. "How . . . how will I tell Maldrake?" she whispered. Her eyes were wide and unblinking.

"Leave that to me, my lady," soothed Teryl. "When Lord Maldrake returns in the morning, I will tell him the tragic news. Now, lie down and rest, lady. I will send someone to tend you."

Yvaughan's blue eyes were glazed. "Thank you, Teryl. A cup of warm tea would be delightful." The white and green bird hopped to her pillow, rested its bill next to Yvaughan's ear, and cooed.

☙ ☙ ☙ ☙ ☙

As night settled on the little village of Bywater, a dark, menacing shape glided in broad circles above its single street. The creature's wings of leather whispered on the evening breeze. He watched as townsfolk closed their shops and walked quietly to their houses. Not one of them looked to the sky. Even the lamplighters did not look beyond the glow of their lanterns.

But then a horse neighed shrilly, and others took up the cry. They tugged at their hitching rings. A few lucky ones pulled free. They raced toward the forest east of Bywater, leaving their mates behind. The remaining horses pulled fearfully against the reins, rearing to break free.

The dragon descended. He hovered above the struggling horses, his golden eyes malevolently studying their fear. Lower the dragon came, its massive talons sinking into view from the lamplight. One claw-tipped hand seized a piebald pony as a child might grasp a toy. The pony bucked and kicked to keep the fearsome claws at bay, but to no avail. The talon wrenched the pony from the ground, snapping its haltered neck. The dragon flung the limp body across the road, where it smashed through the window of the abandoned winery. The remaining horses screamed. Lunging into the pack, the great wyrm set both claws to the slaughter. In moments seven horses lay dying, their death rattles rising into the air as their blood sank to the ground.

Townspeople rushed out, a few with swords in hand, but most with bows or axes. Baildon threw open his mercantile, arming the farmers with his most powerful weapons and giving the bowyers all the arrows he possessed. The people had known the dragon was back in the Wulfholdes, but they never dreamed the wyrm would come so far south to their little village. They were not cowards, however, and they would defend what was rightly theirs.

The townspeople rushed from the mercantile, shouting angrily and brandishing picks and flails. As they approached the gruesome carnage, however, their courage melted. They halted, their angry words dying in the sounds of the horses' screams. Dropping their makeshift weapons, some of the villagers turned and fled.

The dragon stomped past the scattered bodies of the horses. He turned to the townspeople, and his golden eyes positively glowed. The remaining folk fell back as sudden fear gripped their hearts. A lucky handful of villagers ran in stunned terror, leaving the doomed village behind. The others were too stricken to move. The dragon hissed, and a large green cloud spewed from his maw. The vapor covered the throng of remaining defenders, and they began to cough and wheeze at the choking cloud. Many fell to the muddy snow, their limbs writhing with deadly spasms. The dragon advanced.

It was a brutal massacre, according to the accounts of those few who survived. The great wyrm simply advanced and slew all those who stood before him. His wings beat down and buffeted those his arms couldn't reach to rend. His tail lashed out behind and battered those few who tried to stand after his initial attack. But most horrible of all was his mouth, with its rows of wicked, pointed teeth that snapped constantly. That maw delivered death and dismemberment left and right.

The carnage did not end when the folk lay dead; it continued throughout that long, terrifying night. The beast couldn't be stopped. The archers shot arrow after arrow, but they could not penetrate the dragon's hide. They shot at the leathery wings, the glassy eyes, and the blood-gorged mouth. These attacks only infuriated the beast to a greater rage.

Bywater's only wizard, who had prudently waited for the initial attack to subside before he appeared, had prepared all his best spells in defense of the village. By relaying messages through archers and runners, the villagers planned their next move. The archers would let loose a barrage of arrows. Under that cover, four or five of the most skilled men would attack the dragon's rear flanks, using the merchant's magical weapons. Then, while the dragon was being distracted on all sides, the mage would launch his spells.

All worked as planned. The arrows whistled toward the beast's eyes and mouth and wings, the weapons bit into his flanks, and lightning streaked through the air toward the creature's massive heart. But the dragon ignored the raining missiles, flicked his tail and took out the rear guard, and launched his own spell at the mage who challenged him. The dragon's ball of fire engulfed the mage and all the farmers surrounding him. The fire exploded backward and onto the blacksmith's shop. Before long, the south side of the street was in flames.

The horses on the street were dead, many of them disemboweled. Two-thirds of the townsmen lay dead as well. The people of Bywater were shattered—their last hope had died with the mage. Those few who still had their wits about them turned and fled the town.

But Verdilith was still not finished. The glow in his eyes grew red, and his teeth gleamed evilly. The light of a few remaining lanterns cast a faint glow on the gleaming green hide of the beast as he coursed the street. He sniffed the smoke-filled air, and a line of saliva fell hissing from his mouth. He reached toward the front of a house. The wooden doors groaned as he ripped them from their hinges. Next came the screams of women and children hidden inside.

Bywater rang with the cries of the dying that night, and the cries of the living on every night thereafter.

ٷ ٷ ٷ ٷ ٷ

The dragon winged his way north and to the east after ravaging Bywater. The town had sated his blood and appeased his cruel appetites, but the night wasn't finished. He slowed his flight once he crossed the fork of the river and entered the hills surrounded on either side by the Castellan and the Highreach rivers. Greasetongue's orc tribe claimed this treacherous land for its own. The dragon would call on the Rooster's tribe located farther west after his work here was done.

Verdilith scented the air carefully, changed his direction, and flew another thirty wingspans before spying the light of a fire well hidden in the rugged hills. He went into a slow spiral to give himself time to take in the temperament of the camp before the orcs could discover his presence.

Gliding in lower, the wyrm laughed, a low rumble that started at the base of his long neck and worked its way out of his mouth as a roar. Shrieks filled the air, and Verdilith was pleased by the pleasant sound of his prey. He was going to enjoy this.

ٷ ٷ ٷ ٷ ٷ

Maldrake stared at the white pillow Teryl Auroch had just handed him. The blond lord didn't move, and Brisbois was moved to compassion for his friend. He said as gently as he could, "Yvaughan's young yet, Maldrake. There'll be other children."

Maldrake burst into movement. He threw the pillow at Teryl's feet and rounded on Brisbois. "She killed my son! Didn't you hear Teryl? There will be no more children!" The noble threw up his hands and began circling the small chamber in the tower that the three of them used for meetings. "The plan's ruined! Completely ruined!"

"The plan?" Brisbois asked, puzzled.

"The, ah, plan to have his son inherit the estates of Penhaligon, should the baroness not take a husband," Teryl rejoined smoothly as Maldrake paced the room.

"Arteris is still young! What's Maldrake thinking of?" Brisbois asked the mage. The knight stared at Teryl Auroch and wondered just what had happened last night. Today the wizard had lost much of his nervousness, as well as his obsequiousness. He'd even lost the habit of shaking, which had always annoyed Brisbois enormously. Teryl's new steadiness, however, annoyed Brisbois even more.

Maldrake whirled on the two men. "You!" he pointed to Teryl. "Get back to Yvaughan's side. You failed me by not keeping my son alive last night, by not watching that woman. Fail me again, Teryl Auroch, and you won't like the consequences!" Maldrake's green eyes glittered with wrath in the sunlight, but Teryl merely bowed calmly and left without a word.

The blond lord turned on Brisbois and grabbed his blue tunic. Maldrake stared up at Brisbois and growled, "I blame you for the death of my son, Brisbois."

Brisbois's eyes grew wide with innocent fear. "Me? Maldrake, why me? I left last night only to attend to another crisis. I suppose you blame me for the dragon's slaughter at the stable, too!"

"That's not it," Maldrake hissed, giving the knight a contemptuous push and turning away. The lord paced the room twice before turning on Brisbois again. "If you had killed Flinn and not just destroyed his home, I wouldn't have had to go out last night. I could have protected my son from that woman."

Brisbois snapped, "Flinn had too much help for me to take them all on, and he was never alone long enough for me to finish the deed. Besides, does Flinn really have to die? Isn't burning his house enough?"

Maldrake screamed. "No, it's not! He's the one who's made Yvaughan what she is, Brisbois! Can't you see that? Yvaughan's been hearing his voice—what other evidence do you want? He's trying to get her back! He knows I have her, and now he wants her back."

Brisbois shook his head. "Now wait a minute, Maldrake," he said sternly. "Flinn didn't even know you and Yvaughan were in love when the council stripped him of knighthood, unless you told him and didn't tell me. It's possible Flinn doesn't even know you married her—I certainly didn't tell him." Brisbois hit his fist on the lacquered table, an inspired light entering his eyes. "Maldrake! Did you notice how Teryl acted? Something strange has happened to him—he's not his usual kowtowing self. Maybe *he* killed your son! I don't trust him, and I never have!"

Maldrake peered at Brisbois from beneath his heavy-lidded eyes. "Brisbois, my dear Brisbois, Teryl would *never* harm my son," the young lord said, his lips curling into a sneer of a smile. Maldrake extended a chair for the knight. "I think it's time I tell you a thing or two. . . ."

Chapter VIII

linn looked down from his vantage point on a small crest overlooking the road to Bywater. The little town was less than an hour's easy ride away. Although the barren forests still obscured his view, Flinn saw smoke trickle into the air from where Bywater was situated. The cloud looked blacker and more pervasive than the smoke of chimneys. Flinn looked up uneasily at the ravens circling overhead. Their ominous croaks in the winter air grew louder as Flinn, Jo, and Dayin approached the small town. The presence of the birds boded ill. Flinn spurred on Ariac, followed by Johauna on Brisbois's horse and Dayin on Fernlover. Both the young woman and the boy had noticed the same omens as Flinn, and all three were grimly quiet as they traveled the road.

As they topped the final rise before Bywater, the ruin opened up before them. Flinn's breath caught short. The once-lovely village of Bywater lay like a festering scar upon the land. Half the town was nothing more than a charred skeleton. Fire had ravaged the buildings, and thick timbers still smoldered. Bits of stone masonry remained, as did a portion of the second floor of the inn. Ash stirred in the light wind and swirled into the midafternoon sun.

The other half of Bywater hadn't been touched by fire.
Flinn at first hoped those buildings had been spared the
destruction. But, passing the outskirts and entering the
village proper, Flinn saw that he was wrong. Doors had been
ripped from their hinges, windows had been smashed, and
shutters torn away. Bodies draped the wreckage or lay in the
road. An unearthly pall hung over the town. Flinn rode
forward, and a lone dog ran barking across the street and
disappeared into the remains of the blacksmith's shop.

"Isn't anyone left alive?" he mrumured.

Stopping, Flinn tied Ariac's rein to the ring in front of
Baildon's Mercantile. Only then did Flinn notice the long
claw mark of a dragon. The gouge ran across the front of the
mercantile and must have taken out the double doors, for
burlap bags covered the opening now. It had shattered one
of the windows, too, and bits of glass lay scattered about.

Verdilith! Flinn's mind shouted. He bounded up the steps
in front of the shop and burst past the cloth partition.

Baildon was inside, trying to restock the wares that had
been scattered about in the attack. He looked up when Flinn
entered. The merchant's expression was stupid with fatigue
and terror.

"So it's Flinn the Fallen come to rescue us at last," Baildon
said. His voice was filled with scorn.

Jo and the boy crowded in behind Flinn. Dayin tried to
say something, but Jo clasped a warning hand on his
shoulder. Flinn threw her a grateful glance and then stepped
forward.

"Verdilith?"

"Aye," Baildon said softly, then sank to the floor. Slowly
Flinn sat down beside him. The shopkeeper's eyes disappeared
into the folds of his face, and he began to cry. "He came last
night, just at sunset. Nothing stopped him, Flinn. I doubt

even you could have. I passed out every arrow and enchanted blade I owned. Esald—" the merchant's face crumpled at some memory "—Esald attacked with his magic, too, but nothing halted the dragon. Nothing. He killed the horses first, and they screamed and screamed, but we couldn't stop him. We thought he'd be satisfied with the horses, but he wasn't. We tried . . . but . . . everything failed. Even after most of our men were dead, the wyrm wouldn't cease his bloodletting. He went after the women and children we'd hidden in our homes and shops."

The merchant shook with remembered terror, and Flinn saw that the man was near collapse. Flinn touched Baildon's shoulder in compassion, but Baildon angrily shrugged the gesture away.

"Where were you, O Flinn the Mighty? Where?" Baildon yelled, his voice cracking. "You could have saved us if you'd wanted to, like I asked you to, if you hadn't been such a coward! I knew you were afraid of the prophecy. I knew you were!"

"Baildon," Flinn said quietly, "I'm sorry the dragon attacked Bywater. I can't tell you how much I grieve for you—"

"Better yet," the man continued as if he hadn't heard Flinn, "why didn't you kill the dragon when you had the chance all those years ago? Why'd you let him go? My town lies destroyed because of you. My daughters lie dead because of you." The shopkeeper crumpled against Flinn. Wracking sobs shook Baildon's large frame. Awkwardly Flinn tried to comfort his friend. Jo and Dayin stood a respectful distance away, trying not to intrude on the shopkeeper's sorrow. They began clearing away the damaged goods and straightening the rest.

"What can I do to help, Baildon?" Flinn asked when the

man's cries began to subside and Baildon pulled away. Flinn put his hand on the merchant's shoulder and looked him in the eye. "Let me spend a few days here with you, and I will help you put the mercantile back to rights."

Baildon grabbed Flinn's elbow. A strange energy pulsed through him. "Flinn!" he shouted. "Flinn! *You* can avenge my daughters' deaths!" The man's eyes fixed on Flinn.

The warrior leaned back. "Take it easy, Baildon. You've had a bad shock. Let me help you put your store back to rights, and we'll discuss vengeance later."

Baildon stood abruptly, and Flinn followed, though more slowly. "No, no. The best and only way you can help me is to leave now, and hunt the wyrm."

"But the town . . ."

"There isn't a man in Bywater other than me who ever gave you a kind word," Baildon stated. His color was returning, and a fevered light shone in his eyes. "I'm asking you to do this for me, Flinn, though the town would ask the same of you if they only dared to speak to your face instead of behind your back."

Flinn was reminded of all the whispered words of spite he'd heard in the past and the ringing taunts that had greeted him on his last trip. He gritted his teeth. To be a good and honorable man, he should stay here and help these people who had scorned him throughout the years. But even the jeering survivors would prefer him to win their vengeance rather than help rebuild their homes. The pain of past humiliations stung. Baildon's plea was almost enough to tip the scales in favor of leaving Bywater.

"No, I can't, Baildon," he said slowly. "I must stay here and help you. It's what I should do."

Baildon looked aside. "It's not quite that simple. Some survivors blame you for their troubles, Flinn. They need a scapegoat. You aren't welcome in Bywater any more. Ever. If you don't leave now, they may kill you." He looked back at Flinn. "And I cannot stop them."

Flinn ground his teeth. "As you wish," he said abruptly, giving in despite his better intents. Baildon clapped the warrior's shoulders and smiled grimly, but Flinn held up his hand warningly and said, "I'll go, but first I'll need some supplies. And I have to go to the Castle of the Three Suns and become reinstated as a knight again, Baildon. Vengeance may take a little time."

"Take all you want, Flinn. I knew you wouldn't let me down," Baildon said brusquely. "What do you need?"

"Only enough food for about a week, Baildon. I don't want the townspeople to go hungry because of us," Flinn began. "I have money, too."

The merchant stared back at Flinn, his eyes colored with pain again. "There are so few of us left. The food'll go bad before we can eat it all. And I know it'll take you more than a week to get to the castle and then find Verdilith's lair. Besides, this is for my daughters."

Baildon began gathering up the supplies Flinn requested: flour, salt, sugar, grainmeal, jerky, salt pork, dried fruits, and twice-baked bread, all packed inside two burlap bags that would straddle Fernlover. At the last moment Baildon insisted on adding a pot of honey, a fresh haunch of venison, and a flagon of mead.

While Baildon gathered the supplies, Flinn looked over the few remaining short swords, none of which were magical. He checked the blades for balance and keenness of edge. Finding one to his liking, he threw it to Johauna, who promptly checked the blade for herself. She nodded her approval to Flinn. The former knight turned to the shopkeeper.

"I've only thirty-five goldens, Baildon," Flinn said and pointed to the blade. "Can I afford the sword, too?"

Baildon gazed intently at the well-wrought blade in Jo's hands. "Give me thirty for the food and the sword, Flinn, and we'll call it even," Baildon said finally. "You're getting the best deal I've ever made, but I wouldn't want to take the last gold from the man who's going to lay my girls' spirits to rest." The large man finished packaging the supplies and handed them to Flinn, who put his coins on the counter. The two men clasped wrists.

"My thanks, Fain Flinn," Baildon said steadily, his eyes bright with tears.

"I will bring you the head of Verdilith himself," Flinn promised. "You can mount him over your doors."

"Once they're in place again," Baildon managed to say with something of a smile. "I'll see you to the edge of town. Go out the way you came in. The others are burying their dead out on the knoll to the east, and the sight of you would be enough to start a lynch mob. I buried Enyd and Naura there this morning," he added in a strangely calm voice.

Flinn called to Jo and Dayin, who joined the warrior and the merchant outside. Flinn put the supplies on Fernlover. Leading their respective mounts, Flinn, Jo, and Dayin all followed Baildon as they walked back the way they had come. Flinn gritted his teeth. By rights he should pay his respects and then leave Bywater. Instead he was slinking through town hoping not to be seen!

They saw no one as they left the ruined village. Baildon and Flinn clasped wrists one last time, then parted company without saying anything. Flinn gave the signal, and he and Jo and the boy mounted up.

➷ ➷ ➷ ➷ ➷

"Shouldn't we be heading west for the castle by now, Flinn? Or are we headed somewhere else first?" Johauna asked after Flinn signaled a quick halt. They were less than an hour's ride north of Bywater, and the crippled village lay out of sight behind the winter forests. The sojourn in town had been painful to Jo, though she had seen worse destruction done to parts of Specularum when the lords had decided to "clean up" the slum quarters. But the poor folk of Specularum had learned of the coming disaster and fled. The people in Bywater had had no such warning.

"To keep my word to Baildon and avenge Bywater, I must see if I can locate my sword before I do anything else," Flinn said slowly. His moustache twitched a little, and he leaned against Ariac as he looked at Jo and Dayin. "I lost Wyrmblight deliberately—I won't tell you why—in a game of bones to a dwarf. His name is Braddoc Briarblood, and a finer man I never knew. He lives somewhere north of Bywater and to the west of the Castellan River."

"Somewhere? Don't you know where he lives?" Jo asked.

"No. I've never visited his home. You see," the warrior hesitated, "we were mercenaries together for a while before I began trapping." Flinn shrugged. "It was a living."

"You lost Wyrmblight—the most fabulous sword in history—to a *mercenary*?" Jo's voice rose. "Of all the—! What makes you think this—this paid raider still has Wyrmblight?"

Flinn shook his head. "I don't think he has it. In fact, I'm sure he doesn't. But I've got to find Braddoc to see if he knows where the sword is. The dwarf is notoriously well informed. He should also know the news of the castle—why the order hasn't killed or banished Verdilith, who Yvaughan married, and whether she had her baby like Brisbois said."

Jo stiffened. "So we're going to run around the Wulfholdes

in the middle of winter until we find this dwarf?" she asked sarcastically.

"Yes, we are. I know how to find his place, and it's not that far out of our way," he answered, growling slightly. "We head north along the Castellan, then turn west at a rock formation called the Broken Arch. That'll bring us to Braddoc's and head us back toward the castle."

"What about Karleah?" Dayin asked quietly. Jo and Flinn glanced questioningly toward him.

"Karleah?" Jo asked.

"You said Karleah was northeast of the castle," the child said to Flinn. "Couldn't we stop to see Karleah on the way to the castle?"

"It's a possibility I considered, but the decision's Jo's," Flinn said heavily, then looked at Jo. "I know how eager you are to get to the castle, Jo."

"Aren't you eager, too?" she retorted.

Flinn cocked an eyebrow. "I've waited seven years; I can wait another few days." He put his hand on Jo's shoulder. "Jo, we can head straight for the castle if you want. I know time is precious to the young. I only wanted to go to Braddoc's so I can find my sword, because I won't be able to defeat Verdilith without Wyrmblight." The warrior shook his head. "And if there's trouble at the castle . . . if Brisbois and his cohorts are waiting for me, as they likely will be, I'd feel better with Wyrmblight in my hands. That's assuming I can retrieve it between Braddoc's and the castle, of course."

Jo paused to consider the options. "You still think Karleah might show us how to use the abelaat stones to see past events?"

"Yes, I do," Flinn nodded.

"Then, let's do it," Jo said agreeably. "Braddoc's first, crazy Karleah's second, and the castle's third. If we can use the crystals at the council, we'll be sworn in as knight and squire that much quicker." Jo smiled wistfully at the warrior and the boy.

"Good girl," Flinn said briskly. "Mount up! I want to be north of the river before we set up camp."

≈ ≈ ≈ ≈ ≈

Nightfall found them north of the Castellan. They had located the wide river's shallow ford just before the Castellan branched off into the upper Castellan and the Highreach. Flinn had not traversed the Wulfholde Hills in a long while, and he felt uneasy. The Wulfholdes were a rugged, treacherous range, home to ogres, bugbears, orcs, and other humanoids. The Order of the Three Suns had often tested its mettle in these hills. Flinn set the boy the task of rubbing down and feeding the animals, while he and Jo set up the tarpaulin and the rest of camp. He scanned the sky nervously.

"Is something wrong, Flinn?" the girl asked.

"Something *feels* wrong," he answered. "Don't start a fire just yet. I want to check around a little before true night falls."

She nodded, and Flinn slipped away from camp. His sword drawn, he began a systematic search of the half-mile or so of surrounding hillside. Their position by the riverside allowed the water to protect their backs. Few creatures would cross the river before morning, and by then they would have already broken camp. The hills surrounding him now were another matter. They seemed too quiet, as if something was on the march and silencing the lands as it went. Flinn cursed himself for not asking Baildon about activity north of Bywater. As a rule, none of the humanoid tribes moved in winter, for the Wulfholdes were too wild and treacherous even for them. Still, a small band of orc hunters or scouts might be on the move.

The warrior scanned the terrain as well as he could in the fast fading light. The wind blew from the south and the air was moist. They'd have snow on the morrow. He frowned. The Wulfholdes were no place to get caught in a blizzard. He could only hope he was overestimating the strength of the coming storm. At last, satisfied that nothing imminently threatened their camp, Flinn returned to the river.

"Did you see anything?" Jo asked, handing Flinn a bit of smoked pork on bread. She added by way of explaining the cold meal, "I figured we weren't having a fire." She and Dayin turned to their own food.

"Thanks," Flinn said. "No, I didn't see anything. Something still doesn't feel right, though maybe it's the weather. We're in for a storm tomorrow. I think we'd best break camp before first light," Flinn added, wolfing his food. "You two turn in after you're finished eating. I'm going to stand watch for a while."

"Wake me at midnight for the next watch," Jo said. She and Dayin disappeared into the tiny tent.

"If it's necessary," Flinn called after them. He made a tour of the campsite one more time while he finished his meal. Then he checked Ariac, Fernlover, and Jo's horse. She had named the roan gelding Carsig, though why she wouldn't say.

Flinn stood watch for the next several hours, restlessly roaming the camp's perimeter. His thoughts were occupied by the bloody massacre of Bywater. The carnage there had forcibly reminded Flinn of the unspeakable evil of the dragon. Somehow he'd forgotten that evil in the last seven years. Verdilith was a threat to the entire region, and Flinn had to address that threat. At the least he should discover why

the order hadn't hunted the dragon. By rights, the Order of
the Three Suns was supposed to protect all the citizens of this
region. That right had been stripped of Flinn upon his
dismissal as a knight. He had been strictly forbidden to act in
any manner as a knight for fear his actions would mock the
sanctity of the order. If my petition to be reinstated is denied,
he thought, perhaps they will at least let me help track
Verdilith. I know Verdilith's mind better than anyone else.

At midnight he checked the perimeter one last time, but
only a few wolves were moving in the hills. Flinn quietly
entered the tent. He decided against sending Jo out on
watch.

Flinn crawled to one side of the tent, Jo to the other, and
Dayin took the middle. Flinn had instructed the child to
sleep between the two adults. The warrior slid between the
furs and knew immediately that it wasn't the boy's slim form
next to him.

"Dayin? Dayin?" Flinn whispered, his voice cracking.

The child responded only with rhythmic breathing. Jo,
however, said sleepily, "The boy's asleep, Flinn, and so was
I until you came in."

"What are you doing in the middle?" Flinn asked, trying
to relax his suddenly tense muscles.

"I told Dayin I was often cold in the morning, and he
offered to trade places with me. I accepted. Am I supposed
to stand watch now?"

"No, you don't have to. Things are quiet out there."
Flinn shifted his position, wondering why he wasn't
comfortable.

"Good," the young woman murmured. Then she rolled
over, her head unexpectedly finding the hollow of his
shoulder and her arm resting on his chest. He wondered if
she could feel the rapid beating of his heart through all the

clothing he wore. Flinn found himself putting his arms around her.

"Tell me about your days as a mercenary, Flinn. There aren't any tales about that," Jo mumbled sleepily, her breath warming his body.

"There's not much to tell, really," he said quietly. Lost in thought, he began rubbing his thumb back and forth where it rested on Jo's arm. "I was dismissed from the castle with literally only the clothes on my back. I had no money, and only a little food. I quickly became impoverished. There's not much call for a former knight."

"Save as a sell-sword," Jo added. One of her fingers kept curling and uncurling a leather thong on his shirt.

"Exactly," Flinn sighed. "I met Braddoc in a tavern in Rifllian, over by the Radlebb Woods. We . . . we hit it off, though not immediately. He didn't care about my fall as a knight, though he'd certainly heard all about it." Flinn's voice grew bitter. The months following his dismissal from the order had been the hardest ones of all to live through. Every town, every village tavern, had heard the tale of his supposed disgrace, and many people greeted him with jeers and even rotten fish or vegetables. His humiliation had been complete by the time he reached the town of Rifllian.

"Go on," whispered Jo. Flinn wondered if the young woman was falling asleep, though he detected a certain tenseness in her back.

"I entered the Flickertail Inn that night in a foul mood." Flinn gave a snort. "I was spoiling for a fight, and Braddoc and his cronies knew it. They knew who I was, of course, and that only made them all the more eager. Anyway, I insulted them—they were obviously mercenaries by the looks of them. I told them that even I wouldn't stoop so low as to take up their profession." The last words rolled out bitterly.

In the darkness he felt Jo turn to look at him, but the tent was swathed in blackness and he couldn't see her eyes. She kept her hand on his chest, and Flinn found himself wanting to touch it. Biting his lip, he took hold of her hand.

"Go on," Jo whispered.

"Braddoc and the others beat me up. Worse thrashing I'd ever had, too," Flinn added. "But after it was over, Braddoc reached down and gave me a hand standing up. He offered to buy me a meal and a mug of ale, and I accepted. I was starving, and I think he knew that. Over our food he told me about himself and why he had joined the others. He asked me to join him, and I did. That was the beginning of my days as a mercenary."

Jo snuggled against his chest again, sleep overtaking her. "Why'd Braddoc become a sell-sword?" she mumbled.

Flinn stroked her hair and said, "Another time, Jo. It's time to sleep."

Her only response was light breathing.

ಸಿ ಸಿ ಸಿ ಸಿ ಸಿ

Flinn had always had the innate ability to awaken whenever he chose, be it dawn, the middle of the night, or a half hour after closing his eyes. He opened his eyes now at early dawn. The shelter was still dark with night, but the time had come to break camp. Slowly he eased his way out of the furs to give Jo and Dayin a few more precious moments of sleep. He left the shelter and walked about, stretching his muscles.

Dawn approached slowly; darkness still lay heavily on the valley by the river and the surrounding Wulfholdes. The warrior arched his back, feeling the bones slip into place. The hills were silent—strangely silent. Flinn scanned the land, west, south, east, and north.

The hairs on the back of his neck rose.

More than a dozen shapes—each darker than the hills surrounding them—were moving toward the encampment. Flinn's senses newly aroused, he heard the rustle and clink of chain mail on leather as the shapes shifted position. They were slowly advancing, though their movements were still cautious. Good, thought Flinn. They aren't sure of us. We can still escape this situation. He was acutely conscious of the ford behind him, and he cursed himself for not having pushed farther inland last night. Whatever was coming at him wanted to cross the Castellan, and this was the only ford for miles around.

The slowly dawning sunlight glinted off metal axes and spearheads. The shapes trudged nearer, their faces forming in the darkness. Their teeth jutted forward from protruding lower jaws, and their snouts were pushed back and flattened.

Flinn slowly reached out and pulled back the tent flap. "Break camp—now!"

Chapter IX

 war-drum sounded from a distance, its single beat reverberating through the early morning air. Its tone left no doubt that tribe approached from the north, on the near side of the river. The drum sounded a second time, then a third. Each successive beat was louder than the one before, and the third beat was answered by a single piercing tone from a horn to the northwest. Two factions will soon join at the ford, thought Flinn. Jo and Dayin scrambled out of the tent and joined Flinn where he stood. All three gazed northward at the Wulfholdes.

"Orcs!" Flinn hissed, a shiver passing through him. "From the sounds of the drums, two tribes are on the move!" He jerked his thumb behind him and added, "Jo, get the animals ready." As he and Dayin began tearing down the tent, Flinn kept a sharp eye to the north. If the orcs attacked, he'd give the command to mount up and race back to Bywater. Even without saddles and bridles, Flinn and his friends should still be able to escape with the griffon, the horse, and the mule. He considered leaving behind the shelter and the other supplies and fleeing the moment Johauna had the animals ready, but the orcs' march seemed unnatural. Why haven't they attacked? Flinn asked himself anxiously. Breaking camp

152

gave him an excuse to find that answer.

Dawn was breaking, but the overcast sky still revealed little light. Anxiously Flinn eyed the orcs surrounding them to the north and the river that lay to the south. The orcs were agitated. One orc warrior pointed his spear toward the camp. Another orc held up a staff tipped with a tattered red rag. "Banner of the Rooster," Flinn muttered. The orc with the Rooster staff hit the gesturing orc and shouted something. The scant Orcish he knew told him the orcs were bickering over what to do. "Why are they hesitating?" Flinn wondered aloud. "They could easily overrun us." He turned and quickly began loading Fernlover. Then Flinn made out the words ". . . only south of, not north." The orc clearly spoke of the Castellan, but why? Were they awed by the sight of humans entering the Wulfholdes in winter? Did their orders forbid a fight north of the river? If so, why?

In a sudden flash of intuition, Flinn decided not to break for the ford and return to Bywater. He had already failed to avert the dragon attack—he would not bring two tribes of orcs down upon the beleaguered folk of Bywater. Besides, if Flinn, Jo, and Dayin continued south, the orcs would only dog their heels. By traveling north, they might elude the orcs in the wild roughness of the Wulfholdes. If they kept the Castellan to their right, the river could guard their flank from the tribe to the east. The only orcs that could harry them would be those from the northwest—the Rooster's tribe. "One orc tribe is better than two," Flinn observed as he shifted a bundle on Fernlover's back, "Especially if the northeastern tribe is Greasetongue's." They would get no quarter if they met up with Greasetongue.

Flinn tied the last knot and secured the tent on Fernlover's back. He'd thought again about leaving behind their supplies and racing away to elude the orcs, perhaps to the west. But he had no clue as to what might be coming from that direction. Better to face the known threat than the unknown, he thought. He grimaced. Even if we manage to evade the scouts here at the river and those in the surrounding hills, we're likely to die in the Wulfholdes, he thought. The hills are treacherous enough at any time of the year, and doubly so during the cruel winter months. "I was stupid to bring Jo and the boy," Flinn muttered savagely to himself.

Flinn tightened Ariac's girth strap, hoping they could get moving before the orcs' argument ended. But then the orcs bunched together and began to move again. Are they clearing a route for us to leave—or preparing a mass attack? Flinn asked himself caustically.

Another drumbeat echoed through the hills, coming from farther west than had the first drum sounds. This drum was answered from the east by three beats in quick succession. Hastily Flinn mounted up.

"Follow me without fail!" he hissed, his eyes flashing at Jo and Dayin. "Don't show any fear, and whatever you do, don't break from my side!" Flinn dug his heels into Ariac's flanks, and the griffon bolted northward. Jo and Dayin followed immediately, though Flinn fancied Jo looked surprised by their heading.

These creatures respect offense more than defense, Flinn thought as he and Jo and the boy galloped past the orc scouts. A number of them brandished their spears, snarling and gesturing to attack, but the leader threatened them with his staff. The orcs cowered and lowered their weapons. Why aren't they attacking us? Flinn couldn't fathom the answer, and he wondered how long the creatures would hold off.

Flinn led Jo and Dayin north along the Castellan, proceeding as quickly as the mounts could over the rocky ground. The river guarded their right flank. Nothing could attack them from that direction without their knowledge. The river was wide and running fast, and its banks—relatively clear of snow—were smooth enough for Flinn, Jo, and Dayin to make good time. To the west, a perimeter guard of Rooster's orcs kept a keen eye upon them, dispatching runners to stay abreast of them and watch their maneuvers.

"Why are orcs on the move in winter?" Jo called out as she spurred her horse next to Ariac. "Is war afoot?"

Flinn shook his head. "I'm not sure. There're two tribes, one to the north and west of us and another to the east across the Castellan. If they are massing for war, maybe they're gathering at the river so they have room to fight."

"Do you think that's the reason?" Jo pressed.

"Orcs are a lazy lot. They wouldn't go to war in the dead of winter without good cause," Flinn answered back. "The winter's been a tough one so far, and maybe they're just joining up to gather food."

"Why did you turn us north instead of going back to Bywater?" Jo asked.

"I'll tell you my reasons when we have a chance to stop. Let's just hope I made the right choice," Flinn said. "Right now, it's time to move—and no more talking." He tapped Ariac's flanks with his heels, and the griffon responded with a surge of speed. Flinn could still hear, albeit faintly, the drums that the orcs used to convey messages as the tribes converged. Yet what the chieftains had planned, Flinn couldn't guess.

The warrior watched an orc run north along the line of hills to Flinn's west. The runner kept the trio in sight until he met up with another orc. The second orc took up the post until he met a third runner. Flinn won-

dered how long the orcs would keep up their surveillance. He suspected the Rooster's tribe was moving
south somewhere through the hills to their west, while
he, Jo, and Dayin rode north. He also suspected the
perimeter guard set up by the runners wouldn't cease
until the tribe had passed south of the former knight
and his two comrades. Before that happened, however,
the orcs would surely send out a patrol to hunt them
down. Flinn grimaced. He was surprised they had held
off this long.

The hours wore on, and still Flinn maintained the
grueling pace he had set in the beginning. Ariac's
feathered chest was wet with sweat, despite the cold,
and the bird-lion's breath came in sharp whistles. The
griffon wasn't suited for cantering, and certainly not
for a pace that required both speed and endurance.
Flinn glanced back and saw that Jo's horse was in good
shape and that Fernlover, though laboring, was also
keeping up. A game creature, Ariac was nevertheless
unaccustomed to such prolonged speed. Flinn spurred
the lagging griffon forward.

Suddenly, the cloud-laden sky let loose the snow
Flinn had predicted the night before. Wave after wave
of white flakes fell, dropping from the sky with silent
fury. Then the wind picked up, especially along the
unprotected riverbanks, hurling the snow horizontally
across their path. It whipped through the fur cape
Flinn wore and took away his breath, and it smothered
sound with its dull roar. Shielding his eyes, Flinn
looked at the sides of the river. The rugged bottomland
was giving way to steeper hills. Ahead, the Castellan
sluiced fast and wild. The river's embankments would
be too treacherous to follow in the growing storm.

Soon Flinn, Jo, and Dayin would be forced into the surrounding Wulfholdes.

Flinn eyed the few orcs he could still see off to the west. Trees, rocks, and snow blurred his view. He had hoped to have reached the end of the orcs' exodus by now. But the current runner was the seventeenth. "Do these orcs stretch all the way to Duke's Road Keep?" he asked himself.

Although Ariac strained to maintain the pace, his strength was clearly flagging. The riverbank was growing too steep to negotiate; Flinn turned Ariac toward the hills and slowed the party to a walk. Inland, the winds grew even stronger than at the river. "Certain death on the sheer bank and certain death with the orc tribe," Flinn said, shaking his head. He wondered briefly just how far north he would have to travel before striking west to find Braddoc Briarblood's house. He knew that to turn west now with the orcs at hand was suicidal. If the orcs forced him past the Broken Arch, he would simply have to double back after shaking them.

The warrior slowed their pace still further. The stony, snow-covered ground and the obscured vision made any faster pace impossible. Flinn lost sight of the orc runners in the blowing snow. Certain they remained, he didn't dare relax his guard. Keeping an uneasy watch to the west, Flinn stretched in the saddle.

Then, just above the roar of the wind, Flinn heard the sharp, extended blast of a horn some distance west. Immediately he halted Ariac, and Jo pulled up beside him. Her eyes hung wide as she caught her breath. Flinn held up his hand for silence, then cocked his ears for the response he was sure would come. A single shrill bleat answered back. The echoing hills and muffling snowfall distorted the sound's origin; Flinn couldn't discern its direction. But the origin was near.

Too close, in fact. The orcs had gained ground on them and were closer than Flinn had feared.

"Does that mean what I think it means?" Jo asked just above the sound of the storm. "They're coming after us?"

"Yes," Flinn nodded. "The tribe to our west is led by an orc named the Rooster. His people are safely south of us by now, and he's sending out a patrol after us." Dayin pulled up beside them, the child all but hidden by the supplies and Flinn's shaggy fur vest.

"Flinn, can we take much more of this?" Jo gestured at the storm overhead and then pointed to the griffon. "Ariac's about to burst from the strain."

The griffon dripped with frothy sweat, and his footing had grown less sure with each passing hour. Ariac was trembling with fatigue. Flinn considered his options. The orc patrol would be actively hunting them now, and the storm was fast turning into a blizzard. Night would fall in less than two hours, and they would be unable to see anything then. They had to make a stand or they would never survive.

"The orcs are too close for us to outrun them, at least not in the condition Ariac's in. Follow me closely, and be prepared for whatever happens," the warrior said suddenly. Jo drew her sword and rested it on her lap. Flinn nodded his approval. "Jo, don't use your blink dog's tail to attack; use it only if you have to retreat. You've said the magic is beginning to fade, and I'd rather you learn to trust only yourself and your sword in a fight."

Jo nodded and then asked, "Do you think they'll find us in this storm?" Her voice trembled a little but her gaze was determined.

Flinn smiled grimly. "Not if we find them first." He gave her and the boy a quick nod of reassurance, then dismounted.

Flinn took the griffon's lead and turned Ariac around. He headed back across the hill the way they had come. In silence, Jo and Dayin followed him.

The warrior drew his sword silently. He patted Ariac's neck and hoped the griffon's strength wouldn't give way. Then Flinn prayed to Tarastia for the opportunity to avenge himself against the orcs who followed him. As a knight in the Order of the Three Suns, he and his men had tangled often with both the Rooster's tribe and Greasetongue's. He could right a few wrongs today if the Immortal Tarastia was so inclined.

Though his sense of time was hampered by the ceaseless snowstorm and the incessant roar of the wind, Flinn came upon the orcs far sooner than he had thought he might. Barely twenty minutes after they had turned around, Ariac nibbled his master's shoulder. Instantly, Flinn spun about and gestured for Jo and Dayin to dismount. He gave Ariac's rein to the boy and pointed for Dayin to lead the animals off the hill and out of the way. Without a word the child disappeared into the snow. Flinn stepped off the trail, pulling Jo down beside him near a rocky outcropping. If Ariac's senses were right, they would soon see the orc patrol following their trail in the storm.

Flinn whispered in Jo's ear, "Wait for them to get by us before we attack. We will surprise them from behind, and with any luck we'll get most of them right away. There shouldn't be more than five or six of them. Make your strokes count, and remember what I said about not losing your sword."

The young woman nodded. Flinn saw that she was shaking, but her eyes were bright and clear. Good—that's the way to feel, Flinn thought just before one orc, then a second and a third came into view through the swirling snow. They were humanlike—as tall as Flinn, though considerably broader of girth, and clad in misshapen armor. They wore boiled leather helmets, from which their flattened jowls protruded. Stained tusks and beady eyes lay in the shadow of the helmets. The orcs appeared completely oblivious to anything but the trail they followed. The snow and wind were fast obscuring the tracks Flinn's animals had made only a short time ago, and the three orcs bent over the trail and argued which way to continue.

The largest orc sniffed the snow. Flinn stiffened. This beast was a tracker, an orc who could follow a trail by scent alone. Some trackers could pick up a trail even through rain or snow, or after days or weeks had passed. Flinn bit the inside of his cheek. Here was his first target.

Jo tensed beside the warrior, and Flinn put his hand on her shoulder. Two more orcs came into view. They stopped by the first three orcs, who were kneeling and bickering loudly. Flinn caught the gist of their words: the orcs had come upon the place where he and Jo had parted from Dayin.

Flinn whispered, "The ones on the right are mine; the others are yours." He tightened his hand upon the hilt of his sword, waiting until the orcs' argument reached its peak.

"Now!" the warrior hissed, springing forward. His sword sang to the right, and he heard Jo's on the left connect with orc armor. Flinn's blow came arcing down on the back of the tracker's neck. The monster never knew what cleaved his spine. The orc crumpled where he stood, blood staining the snow beneath him.

The remaining orcs cried in anger and surprise. Flinn caught sight of one of them leaping toward Jo, but he had no time to call out. The other three orcs rushed him with their spears. Deftly he dodged their attack and swung his heavy blade, managing to break one spear as he parried the other two. The orc with the broken spear whirled in his charge and jumped on Flinn, a jagged knife in the creature's gnarled hands.

Flinn tumbled backward. He and the orc rolled into the snow. Flinn grabbed the orc's dagger hand. He twisted the rubbery wrist until the blade sunk into the monster's back. The orc cried out in pain. With a roar the other two orcs charged again with their spears. Flinn rolled onto his back, pulling the orc on top of him as he did so. The other orcs' spearheads sank into the chest of their comrade. Flinn scurried from beneath the dead orc, barely escaping the spears pulled from the new-fallen body. The warrior sprang backward, his sword held before him.

Jo backed up to him. He was glad to see she hadn't been injured. "There're two more lurking in the shadows," she shouted.

Flinn grunted. "They'll attack, don't worry." The rest of his words were cut short, however, because one of the spear-bearing orcs charged Jo. She ducked beneath the thrust and came up with her own attack. Just then, another orc charged Flinn. He leaped forward, grabbing the orc's spear handle and pulling. The beast stumbled forward into Flinn's waiting sword. With one quick thrust Flinn dispatched the monster.

From out of the swirling snow, two more orcs leaped toward him. They wielded battle axes, and their heavy blows rained down on Flinn. He parried them, straining to meet the weight of the axes. Jo was busy with her own orc, and Flinn couldn't expect any help from her. The two who attacked had obviously fought together before, for they timed their attacks well. One swung his blow, and the other would immediately follow that blow with his own. Flinn gritted his teeth and smiled. The fight warmed his blood. He parried both axes and tried to snake his way past the orcs' defenses.

A ball of bright orange light suddenly burst in the space between Flinn and the two axe-wielding orcs. The monsters' tiny eyes opened wide at the sudden light. The orcs stammered in fear. The fiery ball hung in the air for a few moments, and then collapsed in on itself, changing into three white doves. The birds dived at the orcs, befuddling the monsters. Dayin! Flinn thought, and from the corner of his eye, he caught sight of the boy with his hands spread toward the orcs. The warrior jumped forward, swinging his blade in a shining horizontal arc. One orc fell instantly, his head almost severed from his body. Flinn continued his sword's swing, but twisted the blade so that the flat hit the second orc. The monster dropped his axe and then collapsed into the snow.

Flinn turned to help Jo with the remaining orc, only to see her draw her sword from her opponent's belly. A brutal smile hung on her face, a smile uncommon to so inexperienced a squire. The girl had enjoyed this bout. Jo wiped her blade on the orc's padded leather armor and approached Flinn, her step sure and sound. The young woman had killed two orcs and not been injured. Flinn was pleased. Dayin, too, joined Flinn by the fallen orc.

"Why didn't you kill him?" Jo poked the orc with her foot when she saw the monster move his head.

"I want to question him as to why the orcs are on the move," Flinn answered. "Dayin, get some rope, will you? And bring the animals back with you; we're going to have to find shelter soon. I don't want to chance questioning him here in the open at the risk of our not finding shelter." The boy nodded and disappeared into the falling snow.

"But after we question him, he'll know where our camp

is," Jo protested. "Or will we just have to kill him after questioning him?"

"No, we'll tie him up and keep watch over him. In the morning we'll leave him tied to a tree. He'll escape by next sundown, but we'll be long gone." Flinn turned toward the orc. "Jo, watch him—if he looks like he's coming to, hit him on the head with your sword's pommel."

"Where are you going?" Jo asked as Flinn moved away.

"I'm going to hide the dead. My guess is that these orcs won't be missed, but if they are, I don't want them found. We'll have to trust the storm to cover our tracks." Flinn finished, dragging the first dead orc off the hill. He deposited the body in a deep gully and returned for the next ones. Meanwhile, Dayin brought the animals to the hilltop. When Flinn finished hiding the dead, he returned to Jo. She was holding her blade to the orc's chest, and she had bound and gagged the now-conscious monster.

"Good job, Jo." Flinn nodded. "We've got to find shelter quickly, but we also have to put as much distance as possible between us and this place. I don't know if any more orcs remain in the hills, and I doubt this one would tell us one way or the other—" Flinn glowered at the orc "—so we've got to get out of here. We'll question him later when we're in a safer place. Jo, lead Ariac. I'll walk. You and Dayin follow close. Night's falling, and we could lose each other easily otherwise."

Flinn pulled the orc to his feet and held onto the length of rope left over from binding the creature's arms. He pushed the orc toward what he believed to be north and mumbled "Go!" in orcish. After Jo mounted the horse and Dayin the mule, they both followed Flinn as he led the way. A short distance after they set out, Flinn directed them off the hilltop to escape the snow and wind. His arms, which once tingled with the heat of battle, were now cold and numb.

The landscape of snowdrifts and frozen trees seemed something from a dream. In the vale curving between the hills, the wind didn't whistle so strongly—didn't wrap them in violent noise and motion. Snow still fell, but less heavily, and the winds bore it in a billowing arc overhead. Flinn felt as though he were leading the party through a dim cave of snow and ice. Light filtered meekly through the storm that raged above the protecting hillsides. Flinn hoped the light would see them to shelter.

As the group wound its way through the gully, the snow grew deeper and footing became treacherous. The blizzard might protect them from the orcs, but it might kill them in the process. Flinn's lungs began to ache with the cold air, and his eyes grew weary from squinting. They needed shelter to survive. The orc also appeared to sense their danger, for it moved along with little prodding.

Just as night was beginning to fall, Flinn happened upon a deep, narrow ravine. The roaring wind and falling snow relented in this sheltered area. All noise faded away, and the silence left their ears ringing. The cold, too, seemed not quite so biting. Jo and Dayin both sat up; they had been lying on their mounts for additional warmth. Flinn led the group farther into the ravine, seeking a suitable outcropping of rocks for shelter. When he found such a spot, he halted the orc and tied him quickly to a short, stubby tree. Jo and Dayin gratefully slid off their animals and stretched their legs.

Flinn turned to the young woman and the boy. Snow and ice clung to the long strands of his hair, his moustache, and the fur cape he wore. "I think it's safe enough to have a small fire here," he said. "We've traveled quite a distance away from the orcs—or at least I think we have—and the ravine should hide the flames from view in this storm. We'll set up the shelter, warm ourselves, and eat a bit of food. Then I want to ask the orc some questions."

"Like why the orcs are gathering?" Jo asked between teeth that chattered.

"Exactly," Flinn answered. "Dayin, you gather some firewood. I'm trusting to your woods' sense not to get lost. Jo, you take care of the animals, and I'll set up the shelter. Nobody get too close to the orc. I don't want him to escape." Jo and Dayin moved away, eager to finish their tasks and warm themselves. Flinn, too, hurried. None of them had eaten that day, and suddenly Flinn was famished.

Flinn poked the orc once with his foot. The orc's eyes shone at him, but it did not respond. It was gagged and bound tightly to the tree. As Flinn began setting up the tent, he hoped the creature would be able to answer his questions. If the orc responded well, he'd live until the sunrise. If not, a quick, merciful death was the best Flinn could offer.

🐸 🐸 🐸 🐸 🐸

Jo sat warming her hands before the small but hot fire. Dayin had gathered elm, a wood that gave off a strong, steady heat with minimal flame. She, Flinn, and Dayin had just finished their meal. Jo wanted nothing more than to curl up and sleep, but she knew she should wait. Flinn was holding a strip of heated dried meat before the orc, trying to tempt him. The monster's gag had been removed, but not the bindings.

"Do you speak Common?" Flinn asked slowly in a clear voice. He held up the piece of meat again. "I will give you this if you can speak Common."

The orc looked from Flinn to the meat and back again. His eyes were bright and tiny and almost obliterated by the folds of fat wrinkling his face. His nose was flattened and pushed back, the bridge of it ridged. Two long, lower canines jutted from his bottom jaw and rested against his upper lip. He had pasty white skin, unlike the ruddy orc captives Jo had seen in Specularum. This particular orc wore rough furs and padded leather armor. Flinn had searched him earlier and piled his belongings to the side. The warrior had found three knives, an assortment of crude orc coins, a bag containing bright pebbles, and a chunk of stale bread.

Jo studied the orc's crafty expression again. She was certain he understood everything Flinn had said. The warrior waved the piece of meat closer to the orc's face. The orc snapped at it, straining his jaw as far forward as possible. Flinn easily pulled the meat out of reach.

"Answer the question!" Flinn shouted angrily. "Do you speak Common?" The shout made Dayin shudder and he huddled closer to Jo. She put her arm around the boy's thin shoulders, not wanting to admit that Flinn's voice scared her, too. *Flinn is just trying to browbeat the orc,* she told herself.

Slowly, grudgingly, the orc spoke. "I . . . speak Common, human pig." His voice was thick with orcish accents.

Flinn proffered a mouth-size piece of meat on the end of his knife and leaned toward the orc. The monster greedily bit at the meat, but Flinn didn't stop moving his hand. Only after the knife was mostly in the orc's mouth and the orc's eyes were wide with terror did Flinn stop. He drawled, "Watch your tongue, orc, and I may let you keep it to taste another piece of meat." As if to emphasize his point, Flinn pulled out the knife and lightly drew it across the lips of the orc, though he didn't draw blood.

The warrior rested on his heels before the orc and slowly, teasingly, cut the remaining meat into bite-size pieces.

"Why did the Rooster's tribe and Greasetongue's tribe meet at the river ford?" Flinn cocked an eyebrow and held up a tidbit.

The orc's eyes fixed on the meat and glistened. His mouth drooled. With thick, almost indecipherable, accents he answered, "To join and go south." His long white tongue licked his lips in anticipation, and he opened his mouth.

"Why?" Flinn flicked the piece of meat. It landed on the orc's neck, just beneath the chin, and stuck there. Jo watched the orc twist to reach the meat, and she was suddenly sure Flinn had deliberately missed the orc's mouth. She wondered when he had learned his interrogation skills: as a knight in the Order of the Three Suns or as a mercenary with Braddoc Briarblood?

The orc squealed in disgust. He couldn't reach the meat, and his bright, tiny eyes glared at Flinn. "Won't tell. Not allowed tell," he hissed.

"Tell me," Flinn rejoined calmly. He flicked another small piece of meat at the orc. This tidbit landed in the creature's lanky hair by his ear. Jo watched the orc's snout wrinkle, and the monster suddenly writhed in his bindings.

The orc hissed, and his tiny eyes darted above him. "To attack village-by-the-water."

"By-the-water?" Jo exclaimed, leaning forward. "Flinn, the orcs are attacking Bywater!"

"*Fliiiin?*" the orc hissed again, this time with evident terror. "Flinn has caught Kushik! Flinn will kill Kushik!" The orc tried to bite the cords surrounding him, and he twisted and heaved against the ropes. Unexpectedly, a key cord snapped, and the orc reached out with one long arm. Flinn was on him instantly, and man and orc tumbled backward. Before Jo and Dayin could act, Flinn was withdrawing his knife from the crumpled form of the orc.

Flinn looked at Jo, his eyes narrow with anger. "Damn his hide!" he swore. He looked down at the orc and then dropped his knife in disgust. Shaking his head angrily, the warrior took hold of Kushik's legs and dragged him off into the darkness.

When Flinn returned to the fire, Jo handed him a cup and looked at him. "You did what you had to do, Flinn," she said calmly. The former knight looked at her and nodded once, curtly. They sat down on spare furs, and Jo shook Dayin's thin frame. "Dayin," she called gently, "you're falling asleep. Why don't you turn in?" The boy nodded sleepily and crawled into the tent, while Jo picked up her mug of mead and leaned closer to the small fire. Overhead, the blizzard still raged, but only a few snowflakes drifted down into the sheltered ravine.

"The orcs are attacking Bywater, Flinn," Jo said. "Is there anything we can do?"

Flinn grimly clenched his jaw. "I have failed them twice in as many days." He turned his gaze toward the dark, stormy sky and slowly shook his head. "There's no way to help them now. We could never overtake the tribes, and we certainly can't stop them." He hung his head, rubbing his temples painfully.

"Flinn, we have to do something! We must warn them. Baildon and the others—they've been through too much already," Jo cried. "First Verdilith and now orcs!"

"Calm down, Jo," Flinn said gently. He put his arm around her briefly. Jo leaned against him, feeling the warm strength of his large frame. "There is something we can do, but it could be dangerous," Flinn said.

"The . . . crystals?" Jo asked in a quieter voice.

Flinn pulled out his little pouch that held the stones. "Yes, the crystals. We can try to contact Baildon through one of the stones and warn him that the orcs are coming."

"What if they're already there?" Jo asked. "What if we're too late?"

"If that's the case, then," Flinn said heavily, "we'll at least know we tried." He pulled out two stones, one a dark red crystal made with Jo's blood and the other a light amber crystal of the abelaat's. "Which should we use?" Flinn stared at the two stones he held up to the light of the fire.

"Yvaughan heard you using the abelaat's crystal, Flinn, didn't she?" Jo asked. "I know we have fewer of them, but that's the one I think we should use."

Flinn nodded slowly. "I think so, too, but . . . I mistrust the power inherent in the crystals. I think, somewhere, something *knows* when we use the stones." Flinn shook his head. "I wish the orc hadn't died. I wanted to find out why the tribes are bent on attacking Bywater." He held out his hand. "Give me your knife, Jo. If I put the stone between two knives, I should be able to hold the stone in the fire long enough to heat it without burning myself."

Jo handed him her knife. "Isn't it obvious why the orcs are attacking Bywater? I mean, they must be starving here in the hills. You yourself said it was a bad winter already, and it's only half over. Aren't the orcs attacking Bywater for food?"

Flinn shook his head and practiced positioning the crystal between the two blades. "Two orc tribes wouldn't gather together to attack Bywater—maybe each tribe individually, but not the two of them together. No, someone or something is behind this attack, and I wish we had found out before the orc died." He leaned toward the fire. "Now, let's both concentrate on Baildon in Bywater."

Jo leaned next to Flinn, and the two of them watched the amber crystal the warrior was slowly heating. She concentrated on Baildon and wondering what was happening to him now.

The moments crawled by. This stone seemed more resistant to heat than the other two had been. As Jo's thoughts centered upon Baildon, she counted forty-seven strokes of her heart. Finally the crystal began to glow. Flinn caught his breath, and Jo leaned closer to the fire. A miniature scene began to form inside the amber stone.

It was indeed Bywater, or what was left of Bywater. Several buildings were in flames, and the streets writhed with hordes of orcs. Jo moved closer to the crystal. Literally hundreds of the creatures filled the icy lane, dancing in a ghastly revelry.

"We're too late," Jo whispered, her chin quivering. The villagers who had survived Verdilith couldn't survive two tribes of orcs.

"Baildon?" Flinn whispered. The scene shifted a little, though only slightly. At the edge of town, two orcs stood over the body of a stout, bloodied man who still carried a cleaver in his hand. Although the man was lying face down in the muddy snow, they knew it was Baildon. A spear stood upright in his back.

The two orcs squabbled, one of them putting his foot on Baildon and pointing at the man. The orcs savagely shoved each other and bickered loudly. One wore a red-plumed helmet, and Jo figured he must be the Rooster. The other was probably Greasetongue. She wanted to ask Flinn if he understood anything they said, but his face was so intent that she didn't dare distract him.

The crystal shattered. Jo had expected that to happen, but it startled her nonetheless. Silence fell on the little camp, broken only by the quiet snapping of the fire. Jo and Flinn both stared blankly into the flame's depths.

"I should have been there, Jo. I should have been there," Flinn said at last. "I shouldn't have let Baildon talk me into leaving. He needed my help. I knew he needed my help."

"Flinn, don't talk like that!" Jo turned to him and gripped his arm. "Flinn, look at me! Look at me!"

Jo sensed the effort it took the warrior to turn from the flames and look at his squire. When he did, she grabbed his other arm and locked eyes with him. "Flinn, do you honestly think that you alone—that you, me, and Dayin—could have saved Bywater from all those orcs? Do you?" Her eyes flashed.

The man's dark gaze narrowed, and his eyes glistened wetly. He reached out and gripped Jo's arms, his touch painful. "I could have warned them somehow, could have held off the hordes while they escaped," Flinn said raggedly.

She leaned nearer. "Flinn, what do you mean?"

Flinn ground his teeth and glanced to the side. His grip on her arms remained tight. Jo hoped he drew some strength from her in that moment. At last he turned back to her. "That was the Rooster and Greasetongue standing over Baildon's body," he said slowly. "I know a little orcish—enough to get the gist of what they were talking about."

Jo tightened her hands. "What did they say, Flinn?" His face flushed and he swallowed hard. "Tell me what's wrong, Flinn," she said. "Whatever it is, tell me."

When he spoke, his voice was hoarse and choked. "The orcs were . . . sent to Bywater. They were supposed to sack the village."

"Why?"

"They were arguing because they couldn't find my body. One said that the man beneath his feet—Baildon—was me; the other disagreed. I was supposed to be there—they'd been told that I would be there, Jo," Flinn's hands fell from Jo's arms.

"Who told the orcs you'd be there?"

Flinn hung his head for a moment, then turned back to Jo. His eyes had grown hard as nails. "Verdilith," he said, licking his dry lips. "Verdilith sent the orcs to Bywater and told them I would be there. Verdilith promised them the town to sack as well as my hide. The orcs agreed readily enough, since they have no love of me and they were in need of food. But they didn't find me, and they found only a portion of the town left for them to savage. Verdilith hadn't told them what he'd done to Bywater only a few nights before." Flinn spat into the fire. "The orcs were supposed to find and kill me."

"But why would Verdilith think you'd be in Bywater?" Jo asked, removing her own hands from Flinn. "That doesn't make sense."

"It does if you know that my home was destroyed the day before," Flinn answered through clenched teeth. "It makes perfect sense if you know I have no supplies and have to head for the nearest town to get them."

Jo shook her head. "I don't understand. How would Verdilith . . . ?" Her voice trailed off as dread welled up within her.

Flinn nodded. "Sir Brisbois." Jo caught Flinn's expression in the light of the campfire, and she shivered in fear. The man continued, "The death of Bywater is on my hands now, Jo." He shook his head when she protested. "They were killed because of me."

Jo watched Flinn's face in the firelight, then took his hands in hers and waited for him to look at her. "Flinn, your death would have meant nothing to the people of Bywater. With you still alive there is the chance for goodness to redeem itself. There is the chance of vengeance," she said slowly, her eyes locked on his. "It's the only thing I can offer you. Their deaths will not be in vain if you slay Verdilith."

Flinn pulled her to him and wrapped his arms about her,

but Jo knew he wasn't aware of what he was doing. He stroked her braid and whispered, "Verdilith and Brisbois will both pay for the death of Bywater, Jo—and for the death of my honor."

Chapter X

he storm broke by morning. The trio left the ravine, heading once more for higher ground. Ariac had recovered from the grueling pace they had maintained yesterday, though Flinn had to fashion new leather pads to cushion the griffon's claws. The additional snow from last night's storm made travel slow and tiresome, even in the windswept, rocky barrens they now traversed. All the while, they scanned the western hills, neither seeing nor hearing any orcs.

The weather turned cold and clear. The sun, glittering brightly off the snow, did little to warm the travelers. The wind had stopped howling and the chill air was sharp and silent. Flinn found no trace of the orcs' passing in the deep snow. Flinn, Jo, and Dayin struck northward, glad the Castellan was still in sight and that the orcs were not.

"We travel north," Flinn said when they stopped at the top of a large hill, "until we see the Broken Arch. It's a rock formation near the Castellan. There we head west to find Braddoc's home."

"If we head west, Flinn, do you think we'll run into any of the Rooster's tribe returning home?" Jo asked.

Flinn shrugged. "That's a chance we'll have to take, but

I think it's an unlikely one. I think they're all still in Bywater. Verdilith probably had to threaten them severely to get them down to the village so quickly. They'll take their time coming back, I'm sure."

Jo was puzzled. "Just why didn't they attack us at the ford?"

"My guess is Verdilith told them to move—and move fast. I think he told the orcs not to bother attacking anything north of the river because that would slow them down. Rooster only sent the patrol after his tribe was south of us," Flinn said, then squinted up at the sun. "Time to move out. If we're lucky, we'll be to Braddoc's by evening." He gave Ariac a light tap, and they continued down the hill. Both Flinn and Jo kept the western hills under surveillance.

The hours yielded no sign of orcs. Jo felt her guard relax a little, then chided herself. A squire is always on guard to protect her master, she told herself sternly.

The three of them kept up the fastest pace Flinn dared set for Ariac. They reached the Broken Arch at midmorning, and Flinn turned the group west. He led them through the rough countryside, trying to find the easiest path between the twisted hills. At midday, they halted for a brief respite. Jo brought out the dry trail rations and passed them out.

"How much farther, Flinn?" Jo asked. She stood behind him as he checked Ariac's front claws.

"Another three, maybe four hours," Flinn grunted, then stood up, rubbing his hands.

"Is Ariac going to make it?" She stroked the griffon's feathered neck.

Flinn nodded. "Yes, I think so. He'll have to." His eyes restlessly roamed the hillsides. "It's time to go."

Once again the trio mounted up and continued through the silent, barren Wulfholdes. Johauna realized she hadn't seen anything moving the entire day. The lack of birds and animals began to worry her, and she wondered if she was the only one who felt that way. Dayin was preoccupied with his own thoughts, and Flinn seemed unconcerned. Jo stilled the feelings inside her. The trio continued to ride, halting only once for a brief stop when Jo's horse Carsig picked up a rock in his hoof.

Just as twilight fell, they found a stone house sheltered at the base of a craggy cliff. Beside it stood a number of huge red pines, embracing the house with their branches. The pattern of the bark was still visible in the fading light. Smoke curled lazily from the chimney, and a cheery light glowed from the windows. Jo thought she had never seen a more welcoming sight, for she was frozen to her very bones. Her legs were stiff and saddle-sore.

Carsig neighed abruptly at the sight of the corral and the familiar odor of a barn. Two shaggy shapes in the corral looked up with interest and whinnied in response. Jo saw they were large ponies. Ariac squealed, and the ponies nervously shifted to one side of their large corral.

The top half of the door to the stone house swung open. Jo heard the faint click of a trigger mechanism. In the faint light of dusk, she could just barely discern the forward curve of a crossbow.

"Halt!" bellowed someone from the house. "Who or what goes there?"

Flinn pulled Ariac to a stop, and Jo reined in Carsig. Dayin also halted.

"An eye for a brain, a tooth for a mole, and a dwarf for a friend!" Flinn shouted cryptically in return. Flinn dismounted, and Jo and Dayin followed suit.

The person inside the house paused. Then came a huge roar of laughter, which Jo found almost more alarming than the crossbow.

"Flinn!" The bottom half of the door swung inward and a dwarf emerged, his man-sized body swaying above the stocky legs that carried him sturdily up the path.

"Fain Flinn! Flinn the Fallen! By Kagyar, it's the Fool Flinn!" the dwarf shouted. Jo felt her ire rise at the taunts she was hearing, but Flinn's laugh set her at ease. He grabbed the dwarf in his arms and then swung him about.

"Braddoc!" Flinn was shouting. "Braddoc of the Cloven Eye! Braddoc, you sorry dwarf!" Flinn laughed again, and Jo and Dayin looked at each other. Neither had ever seen this side of Flinn before.

The man and dwarf continued to chuckle, clasping hands in greeting. Jo studied Braddoc Briarblood, the mercenary who had cajoled Flinn into joining his less-than-honorable lifestyle. Specularum had seen its share of dwarves, and so had Jo. They were far less colorful than elves and, on the whole, a surly lot in Johauna's opinion. But Braddoc was different: colorful, friendly, and boisterous. A thick scar cut across one eye from the dwarf's forehead to his smiling cheek—apparently the mark that won him the name "cloven eye." The eye was milky with the fog of blindness. Much of the rest of his face was hidden by his beard, which was neatly styled into a single braid tucked into the dwarf's belt. His long hair was braided, too, though in two plaits. He wore a softened leather jerkin belted at the waist with wide, studded leather. Hammered copper cuffs ringed his wrists, making his hands look extraordinarily large. He wore sturdy bearhide boots, which covered half of his short legs. Jo smiled; she was determined to like this dwarf.

Flinn gestured toward Johauna, and she stepped forward. The dwarf's intense, almost avaricious scrutiny fell on her, and she was suddenly aware of the dirt and blood on her clothes and the tangled mess her hair had become. How interesting that Braddoc has that effect on me and Flinn doesn't, she thought quickly.

"This is Johauna Menhir, my squire," Flinn was saying with surprising warmth. "Jo, this is my old friend, Braddoc Briarblood." Flinn smiled broadly.

"Salutations, Braddoc Briarblood." Jo nodded stiffly. She met the dwarf's eyes, but he stared silently back. Feeling compelled to fill the silence, she added, "Are you any relation to the dwarven King Aedelfed Briarblood? I heard stories of him while I lived in Specularum."

The dwarf's intense expression didn't fade, though he did lose eye contact when he bowed rigidly. "I'm a poor relation of sorts, but, then, so are many," he answered. He added formally, "And greetings to you, Johauna Menhir."

Flinn's eyebrow rose. "You never told me you were related to the king."

"You never asked," Braddoc retorted.

Flinn, glancing at the animals and the darkening sky, hastily pointed out the boy. Braddoc led the three riders into the snug barn, where he lit a lantern.

"You're looking as fit as ever, Flinn," the dwarf said, gazing intently at his guest, "though a bit grayer than when I last saw you!" Flinn only snorted as he led Ariac into a stall. He began removing the griffon's tack.

The dwarf turned to Dayin, and this time Braddoc snorted. "You smell of magic, boy," he said, suspicion edging his voice. He jerked a large thumb toward a second stall. "Take the mule in there and care for him. We'll be eating soon." Dayin did as he was bid, his shy blue eyes wide with curiosity.

Braddoc turned to Jo then, the light swinging and shining fully on his face as he held up the lantern. The dwarf's blind eye added to the intensity his stare. He scrutinized her from the top of her disheveled hair to the bottom of her muddied boots. Then, nodding, he gestured for her to put the gelding into the third stall.

Keeping his gaze still on Johauna, the dwarf called out to Flinn, "I've finished with my washing ritual for the day, Flinn. The girl wishes to bathe now. Do you and the boy want to go before her?"

Flinn turned toward the dwarf. "You know I'm not bound by the old customs, Braddoc. Quit trying to unsettle Jo; she has a perfect right to bathe where men do. Show her the lodge. Dayin and I will bathe after we've seen to the animals." He turned back to the griffon.

The dwarf hung the lantern on a peg, lit another one, and silently led Jo out of the barn. She wondered how such a seemingly friendly person could become so taciturn. She wondered, too, just what taboo she was breaking by bathing before Flinn. They walked past the corral, behind the house, and out to a small building about the size Flinn's cabin had been.

Braddoc entered the lodge and gestured for Jo to follow. She did so reluctantly, stooping under the short doorway. The unexpectedly warm room inside centered around a large pool glazed over with ice. Benches lined the walls, and a huge brazier stood in one corner. Braddoc hung his lantern on the wall, picked up the wood axe standing near the door, and chopped at the pool. He threw the chunks of ice onto some stones contained in the brazier.

Jo was startled by the sudden hiss of steam rising from the stones. Smoke and steam mixed and swirled throughout the room. The odor was strangely appealing, and Jo guessed Braddoc used a sweet-smelling wood for the fire. She sat down on a low bench in the room and waited for the dwarf to finish.

Braddoc threw one last piece of ice on the hot stones and then walked to the door, obviously intending to leave. Jo called out nervously.

"I—I beg your pardon," she stammered, "but I've never been in a sweat lodge before. . . ." Her words trailed off as the dwarf turned to stare at her.

"That's like as not," he said gruffly. "It's usually a rite reserved for men, but you are Flinn's squire—" the dwarf's stare grew more piercing "—and as such you've a right to the ritual."

Jo crossed her arms and forced herself to say, "Will you show me the ritual?"

Braddoc gestured to the pool of water, a bar of soap, and a nearby brush. "You bathe in the spring there, but be careful. The water has magical properties—"

"Magic? But you distrust magic—"

"Aye," the dwarf interjected, his good eye sharp in the lantern light. "But the magic here is a natural thing, not crafted by humans. It is a magic of the earth, of the waters that lace the rocks beneath your feet, Johauna Menhir. Only those who are pure of heart may bathe in this water—all others are rejected by the spirit of the spring. You will know immediately if you are worthy of her gifts, for if you can't stand the cold, then your heart isn't pure enough to receive the sending."

"The sending?" queried Jo.

"Aye, the sending—the vision the waters may grant you. They grant a vision only once per day, and the waters denied me earlier. That's why you should've waited until after Flinn had bathed. The knight deserves the vision and not the squire," he said. "But perhaps the waters will deny you, too, and wait for Flinn." He crossed his arms.

Jo caught herself mimicking the dwarf.

"After you have bathed," Braddoc continued sternly, "lie on the bench and cleanse your mind and body of all thoughts, all desires, all hopes." He pointed to the bucket. "Pour water on the stones when you are ready to be purified, and the steam will prepare your soul. If the spirit of the pool so grants it, you will see a vision of the future in the steam."

Braddoc paused, as if he were about to say something but then shook his head. He muttered, "When you're through, come into the house. You can help me prepare the meal while the men have their turn in the lodge."

Johauna was glad to see the strange dwarf turn and leave. She gazed at the pool. "Superstition," she muttered. The lodge appeared to be nothing more than a purification sauna, something she had heard about in Specularum. "Sweating cleans the skin, not the soul."

Jo discarded her clothes and frowned at the thought of putting them on again after she bathed. Perhaps when she reached the Castle of the Three Suns, Flinn could outfit her in better clothes, as befitted a squire. Naked, she looked at the water. Taking a deep breath, she stepped into the pool.

The water was breathtakingly cold. For a moment she wondered if she could bear it. But she wanted to prove to Braddoc that she was "pure of heart." She gritted her teeth and washed as quickly as she could. The thought of plunging underwater to wash her hair made her heart skip a beat, but she longed to be rid of the tangles. Strangely, she felt her skin grow warmer each time she ducked under water. By the time she had finished washing her hair, she felt as though she could stay in the pool forever. But she knew she should finish the ritual so that Flinn and Dayin could bathe. Languorously, she left the pool and poured a bucket of water on the hot stones. She sat down on the bench.

The tension began to leave her body, and Jo felt wonderful. Her eyes began to flutter, and her head fell to her chest. She jerked upright, afraid of falling asleep in the lodge. There, in the swirling steam before her, she saw a faint image of herself. Jo blinked. The image remained, the vapors inside the lodge still swirling around and through the vision. She was standing before a forge, waiting for a smith to pull something from the fire. Her stance was strangely expectant, and Jo felt that same emotion course through her now. What was she so eagerly awaiting? Oddly enough, Braddoc stood beside her. Flinn was nowhere in sight. Then, as abruptly as the image had appeared, it vanished. The steam in the lodge was nothing but steam again. Jo waited for the vision to return, her eyes searching the swirling mists. But the vision was gone.

She dressed again in her now-damp clothing and tied a thong around her hair to hold it out of the way. Jo left the lodge, closing the door behind her. Flinn and Dayin were coming up the path.

The tall warrior stopped in front of her and asked teasingly, "Any visions?"

"Visions?" Jo repeated tentatively. She felt uncertain about telling Flinn about her sending because it hadn't included him.

"Yes," Flinn laughed. "Braddoc claims the pool grants visions. None of Braddoc's mercenary cohorts ever had a vision there. They thought Braddoc touched in the head."

"Perhaps they weren't pure of heart," Jo responded lightly.

Flinn looked at her with a strange expression. "No, perhaps they weren't," he said slowly. "Are you going in to help Braddoc?"

Johauna nodded, blushing as she thought of her own

vision. I probably just imagined it, she told herself un-convincingly.

"Braddoc can be a . . . difficult sort to know," Flinn was saying, "but he's a good dwarf. Forgive him, if only for my sake." Flinn touched her arm, and then he and Dayin entered the sweat lodge.

Jo walked down the path to Braddoc's house. She stooped through the back entry and found she was in the kitchen. The house was substantially larger than Flinn's cabin had been. Through the short hall straight ahead of her lay the front door and the main room. To her right, two doors opened, one to a supply room and the other to the dwarf's bedroom. To her left lay the kitchen, which she now entered.

Braddoc was stirring something in a large pot hanging over the fire in the kitchen's hearth. He looked up as Jo entered, then silently gestured for her to sit at the large wooden table at the center of the room. Two benches flanked either side. She considered sitting on the bench farthest from the dwarf, but decided against it. Like as not, he would think she was being impolite—which she would have been. Besides, the warm fire is inviting, she thought as she sat down on the sturdy wooden bench. It had been sanded smooth and painted a pale green, though the paint was old and wearing thin.

The dwarf turned toward her, his eyes level with hers. In the ample light of the kitchen his hair looked richly russet, a shade redder than her own. The few strands of gray indicated that he was fairly young in dwarf years, but Jo couldn't guess his age. He had rebraided his beard and hair, for golden threads now intertwined with the plaits. The braids began and ended in elaborate clasps. Braddoc wore a golden yellow tunic of finely woven cloth; the edges were embroidered in a colorful, repeating pattern of graceful curves. A copper torque circled his neck, fashioned in the same style as the cuffs on his wrists.

All in all, the dwarf was a splendid sight. Jo, accustomed only to squalor and poverty for most of her life, felt awed. She had seen such finery only from a distance in Specularum, and then only rarely. She didn't immediately notice that the tunic was nearly threadbare, or that the clasps and the torque had been stripped of gems.

The dwarf wrinkled his nose and sniffed the air. "Flinn told me about the fire," Braddoc said at last. "You truly have no other clothes?"

Jo crossed her arms irritably and shook her head. "I only had the ones I wore on the day I met Flinn. They were ruined by a creature Flinn calls an abelaat. Flinn made me these, and what I am wearing is all I possess." Jo rested her hand on the pommel of her sword, deriving some confidence from the weapon she had learned to carry always at her side. The dwarf's refined ways left her feeling boorish, which annoyed her.

Braddoc wrinkled his nose again. "They will have to do, then." He looked at her clumsily bound hair. "We can do something about your hair, however."

"My hair?" Jo repeated.

The dwarf left the room without responding. He returned almost immediately. "Turn around," Braddoc said.

Jo looked at him, still unsure of what he wanted.

"Turn around," Braddoc repeated, "and I will braid your hair. Long hair such as yours should be properly bound, as is mine."

Johauna saw that he held a comb in one hand and a silver clasp in the other. Slowly she pulled off the leather thong that had gathered her hair.

Braddoc came and stood behind her. He paused for a moment, as if to gather his bearings, and then he began combing out Johauna's still-wet hair. His strokes were gentle, and he worked out every tangle without unduly pulling at her scalp. Jo found herself relaxing in the silence that followed. The careful actions of Braddoc's fingers felt almost pleasurable.

"You had a sending?" Braddoc asked quietly.

"Y-yes, I did," Jo answered. "How did—?"

"Tell me about it," the dwarf interjected.

Something about the tone in his voice and the gentleness in his hands inspired Jo to trust him. "I was standing near a forge," she said, seeking to find the words. "You were beside me, and we were waiting for the smith to pull something from the fire."

"Could you see what it was?" Braddoc asked.

"No. It was in the fire—I saw nothing of it. But you and I, and even the smith . . . we were all filled with expectation," Jo said suddenly, her mind whirling with the emotion she was trying to describe. "It is the strangest feeling. The image of the vision is leaving me, but the feeling isn't."

The dwarf finished Jo's long braid and attached the silver clasp. He turned Jo around and pulled the plait to her front, letting it fall to the hollow of her arm. Jo watched his brown eye travel from her rough boots, linger at the calloused hand on her sword, and then continue to her eyes. Then Braddoc smiled, a smile of genuine warmth.

"Your vision was a true one—you didn't make it up. I would have known if you had, and it's good that you didn't lie to me," he said. "I see now why Flinn chose you to be his squire."

Jo stared back at him, glad that the dwarf had warmed to her. "Thank you," she said simply.

"Wait here and close your eyes," Braddoc said suddenly. "I have something to show you." Without waiting for her response, the dwarf left the kitchen.

Obediently Jo shut her eyes, keeping them closed even when she heard Braddoc return. He placed something on the table before her, and then she heard a little click, as if a catch was sprung. She felt the faintest touch on her arm and opened her eyes.

&a &a &a &a &a

Flinn opened the door. Dayin followed close behind. It feels good to be clean again, Flinn thought, and he looked forward to the meal his friend was preparing. Braddoc had always been a stickler for the finer things in life, like good food and cleanliness. Flinn had benefited from the dwarf's predilections more than once.

Flinn entered the kitchen and was unprepared for the tableau that met him. Jo's face was flushed, and her eyes were bright. Braddoc was standing beside her, and they both turned at Flinn's entrance.

Jo stood up. "Flinn!" she cried. "Look!" She pointed to a case resting on the table.

Flinn saw a case crafted of hammered gold, the corners reinforced with chased silver. Gems of brilliant color and clarity encrusted the case's open top. The case was more than six feet long, and only two hands' width wide. A case like that could hold—

"Wyrmblight," Flinn breathed. The warrior moved to the other side of the table and looked inside the case. There, on a bed of midnight-blue velvet, lay his sword, its gray-black blade shining dully in the lantern light. Tentatively Flinn touched the cloth, unable to touch the blade just yet.

How long has it been? he thought, suddenly humbled. And why, oh why, did my friend keep you even when I told him you were evil? But Flinn knew the answer to that question even as he asked it: because Braddoc Briarblood was his friend. The dwarf had known, somehow, that Flinn would return for the sword someday. Flinn's fingers lightly stroked the shining edge of the blade. The blackness still clung to it, though Flinn fancied the taint had faded with the years. Perhaps he had misremembered how much of the sword had been stained.

"Aye, Flinn, the blackness is leaving it," Braddoc broke the silence that had fallen on the kitchen. Flinn looked at his friend, wondering how the dwarf had read his thoughts.

Braddoc withdrew the sword from the golden case and handed it to Flinn, the dwarf's good eye glinting in the light. "I saved it for you, Flinn, for its rightful owner. It'll rest no more in that case," the dwarf said respectfully. Jo and Dayin crowded around on either side of Flinn as he held the blade in his hands.

"How—why—" Flinn fumbled for the words "—what is happening to the blackness? Have you done something to Wyrmblight? No matter how hard I tried, I couldn't clean it. . . ."

The dwarf frowned. "I've done nothing but store it in the case, Flinn. It's been brightening all on its own this past winter, particularly during the last week." Braddoc's good eye caught and held Flinn's. "I had a pretty good idea you might be stopping in. And I think you know why the sword is brightening."

Jo reached out and touched the flat of the blade, her fingers lingering over the runes marking the Quadrivial. Flinn had taught her the images of the Four Paths to Righteousness, and she touched them now one by one. Two of the runes shone with silvern clarity. "You've regained your honor and your courage, Flinn," she said slowly, her gray eyes watching him intently. "And so has Wyrmblight."

Flinn's eyebrow rose, but he said nothing. He gazed at the sword, his eyes clearing. The sword *was* overcoming its taint, its evil. To Flinn it appeared to grow even brighter as he held it. With Wyrmblight once more in his hands, he stood a chance. With Wyrmblight he could defeat Verdilith, avenge the town of Bywater, and regain his good name. He could regain his knighthood and his pride.

"Thank you, Braddoc," he said humbly. "You are a true friend indeed. I . . . I am astounded." He shook his head, looking down at the dwarf. Then Flinn turned his attention back to the beautiful blade. Memories crowded into his mind.

Wyrmblight had been wrought many years ago, when Flinn first became a knight of the Three Suns. It was given to Flinn by old Baron Arturus Penhaligon. Though many folk marveled at the man's generosity, all knew that Flinn was beloved by the baron. And the gift matched Flinn's goodness and nobility.

The sword was a greatsword, nearly as long as Flinn was tall, and Flinn stood over six feet. A goodly portion of its length was given over to the hilt and pommel, its grip designed for two-handed use. Although Flinn could let loose an arcing stroke with but one hand on the blade, the sword was simply too heavy to maneuver without using both hands.

The metal used in the forging of the weapon had been the finest silver Penhaligon's armorer could find, for he, too, had a soft heart for the young and valiant Flinn. In fact, the metal was dwarven steel chased with elven silver, and the combination had lent the sword a particular strength, grace, and hue. The blade was extraordinarily attuned to Flinn's movements, seeming to respond to the very will of its wielder.

The old baron had said a knight as valiant as Flinn needed no magic to help him in his quests, and Arturus asked that no enchantments be placed upon the blade. Instead, he had taken the partially forged weapon to the church one day. There the baron himself had stood at the altar with the sword and sought the blessings and good wishes of all who would honor Flinn the Mighty. Many folk entered the church that day to give the blade the honor its bearer deserved, and not one befouled the blade with unkind words. The old baron was well pleased with his people, and with a glad heart he returned the half-forged sword to his master armorer and weaponsmith.

The smith labored tirelessly for a fortnight before the blade was perfect. When finished, its edges gleamed with a sharpness that seemed to never dull. The flat of the blade was ornamented with ancient runes depicting honor, courage, faith, and glory—the Quadrivial of Knighthood. Although gracefully wrought, the quillons were solid and functional and would stop an opponent's blow. The pommel, too, was fully functional, and would provide a nasty blow of its own if so used. Finally, the grip had been wrapped in steel chain of the finest size.

The old baron presented the sword the day Flinn was formally initiated into the Order of the Three Suns. From that day forward, Flinn and the silver-white blade were inseparable. Together they purged the countryside of vile monsters and the foes of the land Flinn swore to protect. They banished strife from the estates of Penhaligon. No matter what evil they fought, the sword retained its gleaming whiteness, as if it were newly pulled from the forge. Nothing tarnished that sword—nothing until the day Flinn left the Castle of the Three Suns in shame.

Flinn joined Braddoc's mercenaries, his sword for hire. He was no longer Flinn the Mighty, but Flinn the Fallen, Flinn the Fool. Flinn's fall from grace was bitterly reflected in Wyrmblight, too. No matter how hard he tried to polish the blade, a taint of blackness clung to it and grew greater day by day. Flinn believed that somehow the sword had turned against him and become evil. He despaired at the blackening of his sword, not realizing that his very despair deepened its taint. He believed that when the sword became utterly black, he would die. With fearful deliberation, he gambled the blade away.

Braddoc Briarblood won the prize. Flinn tried to warn his friend of its evil, but Braddoc would not listen. The warrior's shame was complete. He left Braddoc's band that night and became a hermit and a trapper.

Now Flinn stood in Braddoc's kitchen, holding Wyrmblight in his hands. He blinked, his eyes suddenly moist. The sword wasn't evil as he had supposed, only a reflection of his own soul. Flinn's heart pumped unevenly. He would overcome his fears and the ghosts that dogged his every step. He would regain the rest of the Four Corners of Righteousness and become again the knight he had once been.

And Wyrmblight, too, would return to its former glory.

Chapter XI

"S it and eat," the dwarf said, breaking the silence that Wyrmblight had cast over the room. He pulled the kettle off the fire and quickly dished up four plates of steaming stew. Then he pulled out a small keg, unstopped it, and began to fill tankards for everyone. His good eye twinkled suddenly at Flinn. "Maybe I should draw you a second mug and a third, as long as I'm at it, old friend," he said.

"Trying to get me to blather in my cups, eh, Braddoc?" Flinn rejoined. He took a sip of the ale the dwarf had poured and nodded his appreciation.

"That's not hard to do, as you well know," Braddoc retorted as he handed a cup to Jo.

"Hah!" Flinn shot back. "You're the one who can't hold your ale, Braddoc, not me!"

"Oh? And just who is it who's always under the table by cock's crow?" Braddoc hooted.

"I might be under the table, friend—" Flinn slapped Braddoc's shoulder "—but there's a dwarf under me!"

Braddoc broke into laughter, and Flinn, Jo, and Dayin joined in. It is good to laugh again, Flinn thought, after the horrors of the last few days. And it is good to be warm and safe, with a hot meal and a decent cup of ale. His fingers stroked the blade resting beside him. And most of all, he added, it is good to have you back again.

"Tell me more of your travels," Braddoc said as he passed around a small pot of honey to garnish the little loaves of bread he had given everyone.

Sighing and downing a large swig of ale, Flinn settled back to recount all that had happened to them that strange winter, omitting nothing—not even the creation of the crystals or what they had revealed. He ended his tale with the revelation of Bywater's destruction and Verdilith's orders to the orcs.

Braddoc shook his head. "I first heard the orc drums three nights ago, which must have been just after Verdilith attacked Bywater," he said. "They were quite a distance away, but I could make out enough of the beat to learn they were going on the move immediately—straight south through the hills where I was hunting."

"What did you do, Braddoc?" Jo asked. "It's strange to think you were in the same situation as we were."

"I hid the ponies in a cave nearby, hoping the orcs wouldn't find them by accident. Thank Kagyar they didn't," Braddoc said in an aside to the ceiling. "Then I hurried home as fast as I could, trying like you to slip past them as they went on the march. Unlike you, I had the benefit of their never having seen me."

"I take it the Rooster's tribe dwells south of here, then?" Flinn asked.

"More or less." Braddoc laughed grimly. "I, too, had to cut my way through their lines. The Rooster was missing a few orcs after passing me." He grinned at Flinn. "When you rode up this evening, I was sure you were orcs sent back to check on missing patrols."

They all laughed, and a companionable silence fell as the four of them finished their meal. Braddoc's eye wandered to Dayin. The boy was too busy eating to notice the attention.

Flinn noted Braddoc's interest. "There's not a great deal to tell you about Dayin," he said. "He spent the last two years haunting my woods, but I only really met him after Jo came along."

"You said he knows magic, eh?" Braddoc murmured, taking another sip of ale.

"That's right," Jo answered. "He made rose petals appear out of nowhere at the cabin. And during the orcs' attack, he distracted two of them with doves." She smiled at Dayin, who smiled back. "They were beautiful."

Flinn cocked an eyebrow, then turned to Braddoc. "The boy's father was a mage, and he taught Dayin some spells before he died."

"What was the mage's name?" Braddoc asked off-handedly. "Maybe I knew him."

"Maloch Kine," Flinn answered, his attention drawn to the boy. Dayin listened closely.

"Maloch Kine, eh?" Braddoc rejoined. "Doesn't ring a bell. Though the castle's got a new mage—fellow named Auroch. Hmmm," he said, stroking his braided beard. "In the old tongue, both Kine and Auroch mean cattle. Was your father some kind of magical herder?"

Dayin shook his head and said, "No, he was a mage."

The dwarf stood and gestured toward the hall. "Let's adjourn to the great room. I've some dried apples the boy can heat in the fire." He smiled at Jo. "Flinn says you're quite a storyteller. I'd like to hear a tale tonight, unless someone has a lute in his pack and would care to sing?" He looked at the others and then shook his head. "I thought not. Well, I'm providing the food, so you'll have to provide the entertainment. My singing would drive you all away. Jo, have you a tale for us?"

Jo laughed. "All I know are the tales of Flinn that my father used to tell me. Surely you've heard all those."

Braddoc nodded. "Yes, I have. And most of them are full of audacious lies about Flinn's courage and skill," the dwarf said with a wink. "Still, tell us the story where Flinn meets up with Verdilith. Perhaps we'll learn some long-forgotten weakness of the wyrm."

Shaking his head grimly, Flinn led the companions into the great room. Its walls were fashioned of rough-hewn granite and its ceiling supported by dark oak timbers. It was comfortably furnished with low upholstered benches, a few small tables, and a single human-sized chair. Braddoc went to the hearth and stoked the fire banked there. He gestured to the chair behind Flinn. "Sit, and let's hear the tale Johauna has to tell. Then we'll discuss plans for the morrow. Dayin, you can warm the apples on this poker." Braddoc pulled a small barrel from a corner of the room and presented it to Dayin, who sat on a short stool before the hearth.

The dwarf sat on a bench opposite Flinn, and Jo took a place across from Dayin. Jo smiled shyly, then let her gaze rest on Flinn. As always, he felt uncomfortable being the center of attention, but he knew that Jo would tell no other tales.

"There is a tale," Jo began, "a tale told in taverns near and far, in castles high and low, in hamlets humble and dear. This is the tale of the Mighty Flinn and the good blade Wyrmblight. This is the tale of Verdilith, the Great Green, scourge of Traladara, now Karameikos. Listen to the tale I tell you now, and listen you well."

Johauna stopped and coughed. "I'm not a bard, but that's how my father always started this story," she said nervously.

"It had quite an effect on a six-year-old in front of a campfire." Her eyes flicked from Flinn to Braddoc.

"Tell the tale, Johauna," the dwarf said patiently, then smiled. "It's the price of your dinner."

Guessing the girl felt uneasy under Braddoc's piercing gaze, Flinn gave her a reassuring smile. Dayin began quietly handing out the warmed rings of dried apple.

Jo continued, "A fierce and terrible dragon saw the lands of Penhaligon one day as he flew, and he coveted the lands beneath his wings. The hills and trees were bountiful, and water, too, was in plenty. Nearby, in the wild barren hills of the Wulfholdes, he could hide. Aye, he could hide from those whom he taunted . . . those whom he killed. He could bring his treasures from far and wide to secrete away. He could sleep on his bed of gold in peace.

"Or so the wyrm thought.

"Verdilith was the great green's name, a name that means 'green stone' in the ancient tongue. Verdilith, in his debaucheries of blood, hadn't reckoned on the knights of Penhaligon. Most noble of all these knights was Fain Flinn. He was not called 'the Mighty' for naught, and many was the monster that had fallen beneath his blade, the good sword Wyrmblight. The sword was well named, for it devoured dragon blood with glee. The Mighty Flinn learned the art of tracking dragon with the help of his wondrous blade, and he became legend."

Flinn snickered. Immediately he was sorry he had, for three sets of eyes fastened accusingly on him. He held up his hands in appeasement and leaned farther back into the chair. He would interrupt the story no more.

With a warning look at Flinn, Jo continued. "The Mighty Flinn became legend, but Verdilith was filled with overweening pride. He did not believe the tales of Flinn, nor did he believe the power of Wyrmblight. Or, if he did fear Flinn and his blade, he coveted the lands of Penhaligon still more.

"Verdilith invaded the hills of Wulfholde, spreading terror in his wake. The good Baron Arturus of Penhaligon sent five of his finest knights to rid the land of the great wyrm. At their head rode Flinn, the bravest of all. His armor gleamed in the bright spring sun; the light glinted off his sword. His charger pranced sideways, eager for the hunt. . . ."

Flinn found his mind drifting off in the memories Jo's words stirred. The sound of her voice receded away. He remembered the day Baron Arturus had sent him after Verdilith: It was late winter, not early spring, and the weather was miserable. Rain and sleet pelted him and the two squires who accompanied him. Disputes with giants along the western borders of Penhaligon had escalated, and most of the knights and their squires were serving there. Flinn had just returned from a mission and was preparing to rejoin the fight to the west, but the old baron had other plans. As always, Flinn did as his lord commanded.

He and the two squires, who were both quite new and really little more than stablehands, headed northeast to the spot where the dragon had last appeared. There, Flinn drew Wyrmblight and held it before him; he concentrated on the image of the green dragon. The blade, forged to slay dragons, scented the dragon's essence and turned toward it, leading Flinn through the forest. In time, he found tracks and broken branches that marked Verdilith's occasional landings.

Flinn continued on, Wyrmblight ever before him. If he encountered Verdilith, the blade would prove his greatest weapon and his best defense. Earlier, the blade had turned the fiery breath of a young red dragon and the lightning strike of an older, white dragon. Wyrmblight faithfully led Flinn toward Verdilith. Flinn and his squires traversed the woods and rocky hills, then returned again to the forests before they discovered the creature in a tiny glade. Verdilith was sunning himself on a rock. He seemed sublimely confident of his powers and not the least bit afraid of the three humans who interrupted his rest. The dragon roared when Flinn approached, and the two squires fled in terror. They never returned to the Castle of the Three Suns.

"So you are the Flinn I have heard about," the dragon rumbled. "And that is the sword I am supposed to fear."

Disregarding Verdilith's taunts, Flinn shouted in return, "By the order of good Baron Arturus Penhaligon, I charge you to leave these lands willingly and never return, wyrm, or I shall drive you from them!"

The dragon responded by stretching wide his fang-studded mouth and blasting Flinn with a choking green cloud. Although Flinn coughed a little at the noxious fumes, he suffered no ill effects. He strode forward and attacked. Through glade, through forest, and on into the Wulfholdes their battle raged. Twice more the dragon let loose his foul breath, but each time Wyrmblight drew the poison into itself, protecting its master.

Wielding Wyrmblight foremost, Flinn drove Verdilith toward a dark pine forest. Only there could he stand a chance of defeating the dragon single-handedly—by out-stepping the ungainly beast. But the dragon only smiled his toothy grin and retreated into the open. Flinn was forced to follow. There, in the rocky outcroppings of the Wulfholdes, Flinn at last met his match. Although he was a powerful knight, a man renowned for strength and stamina, the dragon's strength waxed beyond measure that day. For the first time ever, the knight knew fear—fear so great he wanted to run as the squires had.

The barren hills offered Flinn no cover. Verdilith buffeted him with his great wings and knocked him aside with his tail. The dragon raked the knight with his claws and snapped teasingly at him with fangs of ivory. When Flinn's strength was finally spent, the dragon lost interest in playing with his foe. Deep and true was the wyrm's next bite, piercing nearly through the knight. Flinn still bore the scars of those ugly wounds. But deep and true, too, was the bite of Flinn's sword that day in the dragon's side. Dragon blood cascaded to the rocky ground. Both seriously wounded, the dragon and the warrior gave and took a series of blows so great that Flinn thought they would die together. But then the huge green dragon took to the skies and fled.

Flinn fell to his knees, almost mortally injured. Four knights of Penhaligon, returning home from the war with the giants, came upon Flinn. They had heard the battle raging from afar and arrived with swords drawn, but they saw only their fallen comrade and the dragon winging away.

". . . with cries of dismay," Jo was saying, her words returning Flinn's thoughts to the present. "They carried their brave leader back to the Castle of the Three Suns, tears falling every step of the way. But at the castle the great baron called for his finest healers and clerics. In time, the brave knight mended, becoming whole and strong again.

"Shamed, the wyrm fled the lands of Penhaligon in defeat. Thus ends the tale of the Mighty Flinn, his sword Wyrmblight, and Verdilith the Great Green." Jo's eyes flashed. "But I won't add the ending I was taught, for Verdilith has returned, and that rather spoils it."

Braddoc and Dayin enthusiastically voiced their appreciation for the tale, and Dayin handed Jo some apple rings he had saved for her. Flinn, too, expressed his pleasure, and Jo's face lit up at his praise. How good it is to have someone believe in me again, really believe, he thought suddenly. His smile turned rueful.

Dayin yawned suddenly, and Braddoc put his hand on the boy's shoulder. The dwarf said, "It's late, and I think the child should get some sleep while the rest of us discuss what tomorrow may bring." He looked at Jo. "I've put your things in my room, Johauna. There are advantages to being a woman, like a comfortable bed rather than a hard floor. I hope the bed's not too short for you. Flinn, your bedroll's here by the hearth. Dayin and I will bed down in the kitchen."

Dayin yawned widely, but tried to mask it with his small hands. "No, please. I'm not sleepy, just tired."

Jo mussed his hair and said, "All right, Dayin, you can stay up. But the moment you fall asleep, Braddoc will take you to the kitchen." She smiled at the boy, who sleepily nodded in return.

Flinn put his elbows on his knees, leaned forward, and sighed. The last few days had been long and grueling ones, and for a moment a part of him didn't want to contemplate what the morrow might hold. But he knew he must, and with another sigh he looked at Jo and then Braddoc.

"Well, my friends," the warrior said, "it's time to make some decisions. I've promised to take Dayin to Karleah Kunzay to see if she would like to take him on as an apprentice. That errand will delay my return to the Castle of the Three Suns by no more than half a day, so to Karleah's I'm headed."

"When?" Braddoc asked.

"The day after tomorrow," Flinn replied readily. "The animals—not to mention the riders—have been through much the last two days. We need to rest, but for one day only."

"Will Ariac be fully recovered, do you think?" Jo asked. Her hands were clasped before her and she seemed calm, but Flinn saw that her knuckles were turning white.

"Yes, I think so. There are easier paths to follow to the west, and there won't be a blizzard and an entire orc tribe trailing us. At least, I hope not," Flinn added wryly. "It will probably take a day and a half to get to Karleah's, but after that I head straight to the Castle of the Three Suns." He took a deep breath.

"Between now and then, Jo, you need to make a decision," he continued. "Do you want to petition the council for squiredom on your own—or do you want to stand at my side while I petition for reinstatement as a knight? You should know that I think your skills have improved enough that they would accept you as a squire. Furthermore—" he looked at the young woman keenly, and she grew nervous under his gaze "—I think you do have the dedication and commitment necessary to become a knight, even without me."

"Oh, Flinn," Jo cried softly. Her gray eyes were luminous in the light of the dying fire. The faith and devotion he saw there touched him deeply. He remembered he had once slapped her because of that shining belief. "I don't need a day and a half to make a decision," she said, shaking her head. "The decision I made when you first asked me that question still holds: I will be your squire no matter what. I don't need to think on that."

Flinn looked at her closely, trying to determine whether she knew what lay in store for them. Although she'd been a flighty girl in the past, in the last few months she had developed into a courageous young woman. He nodded toward her, then said, "That's settled then. After we bring

Dayin to Karleah's, we go on to the castle. There I settle a score with Sir Brisbois, and then I petition the council for reinstatement as a knight. If all goes well, Jo, you and I will leave the castle as members of the Order of the Three Suns." He smiled and Jo did the same.

"And your plans for Verdilith?" Braddoc asked, thoughtfully stroking the plait in his beard.

Flinn sat back in the chair and drew Wyrmblight onto his knees. "Once I'm a knight again, my rights as a knight will be restored. Only then will I be a match for the dragon, and only then will Wyrmblight shine in full glory. I'll avenge the town of Bywater and my friend Baildon the Merchant. I will hunt down that wyrm and, as Thor is my witness, I will kill him." Flinn's teeth clenched involuntarily, and his hands tightened on the sword.

"Would you like another comrade?" Braddoc asked casually.

Flinn looked at the dwarf in surprise. "You?" he asked. "But, Braddoc, what of your mercenary duties? Don't you have any contracts pending?"

"I disbanded the group shortly after you left, Flinn," the dwarf said slowly.

"Why?" Flinn and Jo asked simultaneously.

"Because, like you, I wanted something better for myself. I wasn't going to find it as a mercenary. I took up goldsmithing; the case I made for Wyrmblight was the first thing I made." Braddoc held up his braids and smiled ruefully. "I stripped the gems from my hair clasps—not to mention my goblets, my daggers, rings, and everything else I could find—to ornament that case."

"The case is lovely, especially now that we know what you sacrificed to make it. What made you become a goldsmith?" Jo asked politely.

Braddoc shrugged. "You might say I wanted to return to my dwarven heritage." He turned his good eye toward Flinn. "You haven't said whether you'd like my company."

Flinn held out his hand. "I would be grateful, friend, if you'd join me."

The dwarf extended his hand, too, and the two men clasped wrists. Braddoc nodded and said, "It'll be good to be on the trail again with you, Fain Flinn." He stood and looked down at the sleeping Dayin. "And now, if you'll excuse me, the boy's got a good idea. I'm off to bed. Good night." Braddoc picked up Dayin and carried him from the room. Just before entering the kitchen, Braddoc flashed Flinn a thoughtful look. The warrior looked away.

Jo quietly looked at the fire for a few moments, then turned to Flinn. "I had best be going to bed, too." She made as if to stand, but Flinn caught her arm. She settled back in her seat.

Flinn looked at Jo, taking in the curve of her neatly braided hair and her high, intelligent brow beneath. He noted her firm chin, sensitive lips, and compassionate eyes. He touched her hand.

"Stay and talk awhile?" he asked quietly. He'd never actually asked her to converse with him before, and for a moment he wondered if she would misinterpret his desire.

"Certainly," Jo said with alacrity. "What would you like to talk about?" Her eyes watched him intently.

"Tell me what you think will happen when we reach the castle," he suggested.

Jo smiled. "That's easy. I know what will happen. You will present your case, exposing the lies of your accusers, and not one person there will vote against you. Everyone will know that you were unjustly accused and that you deserve to become a knight again. Your knighthood will be reinstated."

Flinn looked at her, baffled at how she could have so much faith. "You can't really believe that, can you? There are people who don't think of me as you do, you know," he added with asperity.

"Yes, I know," Jo said, then smiled solemnly. "Your petition isn't likely to go that smoothly. But I do know you will regain your knighthood. Have no fear."

Flinn looked at her questioningly. "Do you have any fears, Johauna?"

She looked away for a moment, then turned back to him. Her eyes were clear and steady. "I fear that perhaps you may find it difficult adjusting to a life with people again. You've lived outside society for the last seven years, and been a recluse for the last three."

"What makes you think I'll have trouble getting used to people again?"

She shrugged. "Only that I had trouble adjusting to a life without people. You might have the same problem, but in reverse."

"Do you miss Specularum?" Flinn asked suddenly. It had never occurred to him that Jo might be homesick.

"I did, but not any more."

"And you don't think I'll adjust as easily as you did?" Flinn asked laughingly.

"I didn't say that," she responded. "I only wanted you to be aware of my thoughts. My only fear is that you will think things would be the way they used to be, and then discover that they're not. You'll need to readjust, that's all."

"And is that really your only fear?" Flinn asked slowly. He leaned near her. He wanted to make sure Jo harbored no lingering doubts about becoming his squire.

The girl looked at him sharply. Her hands were tightly

clasped again. "No . . . there is one other fear I have." Her voice was barely a whisper.

Flinn's peered into her eyes. "And what is that?" He lowered his voice, too, though he didn't know why.

Jo didn't look away. "My last fear is that Yvaughan will plead for your forgiveness."

Flinn's eyebrows knit. "Why should you fear that?"

"Because I'm afraid you will forgive her, and that she will once again mean to you what she used to," Jo said in a small, tight voice. "Because, if that happens, you won't need me to—to love you." The last words were spoken in a broken whisper.

Flinn reached out and took both her hands in his. He gripped them hard. "Jo, Jo," he murmured. "My feelings for . . . Yvaughan died a long time ago. My forgiving her—if indeed I do forgive her—won't change how I feel about her now."

Jo hung her head. "I think it might."

Flinn touched her chin and tilted her face upward, but her eyes remained averted. Flinn waited. Finally she looked back at him. Her eyes were clouded, and he couldn't discern her emotions. He moved as if to hold her, but something held him back. "Jo, dear," he said, unaware that the endearment slipped out, "you are right. My feelings for Yvaughan might change, but too much time and pain have passed. I will never love her again."

Jo bit her bottom lip. Flinn felt her hands tremble within his. He could only imagine what it cost her to say her next words. "Do you . . . do you think you could . . . love me—someday?" Her voice cracked.

Flinn tightened his grip even more and smiled wistfully. "Jo, my . . . my feelings for you are too new for me to understand just yet. I must regain my life—my soul—before I can have anything to offer you, or anyone else." He released one hand and permitted himself to touch her cheek. "It's not that I'm not tempted. . . ." He shook his head. "It's that I'm not sure I should."

Jo took the hand touching her cheek and turned her head so that her lips rested against his palm. She kissed the inside of his hand, and he felt her tremble. She released his hand and nearly ran across the floor to the bedroom door. "Good night, Flinn," she called over her shoulder without looking back.

Flinn stared at the dying fire. The girl worshiped him. She had from the very beginning, that much Flinn had known. But her feelings had escalated into something much deeper, and he wondered why he hadn't stopped it. He should never have allowed that. A glowing log shifted position in the hearth, and Flinn used the poker to push it back in place. The fire snapped and hissed in return. "Would I have quelled Jo's feelings if I had known?" he asked himself. His gaze darkened.

Johauna Menhir had turned his life completely around. She had believed in him wholeheartedly, despite his fall from grace as a knight. She had believed him a man worthy of knighthood; she had believed him honorable and courageous and good. He smiled grimly, shaking his head. Her faith was so groundless, and yet it was her faith alone that nourished his soul.

As the midnight hours slipped slowly by and the fire died completely, Flinn realized that he couldn't have faced his past disgrace were it not for Jo. She had inspired him to look beyond his misery and petty spite to see that he was still, at heart, a good and honorable man.

Flinn sighed, scanning the elaborate runes that chased the flat of Wyrmblight. He had regained his honor and his courage, and he touched those two shining runes of the

Quadrivial. His fingers slipped slowly past to the points of faith and glory. Jo had faith in him. Jo had complete and absolute faith in him. But he needed more than that. He needed to find his own faith in himself, and he needed the faith of the people, too. Confronting those who had wronged him seven years ago and righting that wrong would restore that faith, he was sure.

He picked up Wyrmblight and pointed the tip of it toward the ceiling. He stared down at the last stained sigil and said aloud, "Slaying Verdilith will bring me the fourth point of the Quadrivial: glory."

The warrior returned the sword to his side and looked about the room, his eyes filled with a restless hunger. "And on that day, I shall once again be a true knight."

Chapter XII

he crystal shattered, and Verdilith roared in frustration. The shards fell to the sandy floor, adding to the layer of crystalline fragments from other abelaat stones. The dragon flicked his tail angrily. A gold-spangled crown and an emerald scepter flew against the far wall of the lair. The crown crumpled on impact, and the scepter smashed a crack in the rock wall. Verdilith snorted, green fumes roiling from his nose.

The abelaat stones had grown unpredictable in their duration, fouling the dragon's plans. "Worthless lackeys," Verdilith growled, his voice rattling hollowly through the lair. He scratched one scaly cheek. "These stones are flawed! They should last hours, not minutes!" He punctuated the words with a thunderous slap of his tail and the cave rumbled like a great drum. The dragon hissed. Once he had watched Flinn for an entire night and day, whispering his magic words of despair over and over and filling Flinn with impotent rage. Previously, Verdilith could use the stones to plant evil thoughts and emotions into Flinn's mind. The dragon's seeds of fear and self-loathing had taken root and nearly turned Flinn's soul black. "Now I can hardly even see him!" Verdilith roared, the sound reverberating through the cavern.

The dragon looked up at the twinkling ceiling far above. If only the woman hadn't happened by. "Who is she?" he wondered to himself. "Who is this disruptor?" The abelaat's attack on her had been most untimely—the tiny traces of spittle remaining in her system rendered her nearly impossible to observe through the crystals. And where Flinn was, she was nearby. Since the arrival of the woman, Verdilith had gained only brief, tantalizing glimpses of his most hated enemy. Now only one unshattered crystal remained in Verdilith's hoard.

The wyrm shifted on his bed of gold and silver. Absently, he licked the coins and gems slipping through his front claws. One claw grasped a single large amethyst and squeezed. The gem shattered and Verdilith smiled hugely. He would be able to crush diamonds in not so many more years.

The dragon let his thoughts drift away to the latest, most disturbing glimpse he had seen through the crystal: Flinn held aloft a greatsword and spoke of slaying Verdilith to regain glory.

"He evaded my trap," the dragon seethed darkly, his sibilant voice echoing over the stone. "Those stupid orcs. I'll have my revenge on them." Thoughts of the orcs dispersed when Verdilith remembered Flinn's shining sword. "Wyrmblight!" Verdilith seethed, a green cloud issuing between his teeth.

Something dug unpleasantly into the dragon's side. He shifted his bulk on the treasure hoard and pulled out a silver urn. A leer of satisfaction flashed across his spearlike teeth as he looked at the now-crumpled item. Then, flicking the scrap away, he returned to his musings. "I should have killed Flinn the first time," he roared. The old witch's prophecy surfaced in his mind—*One of you will die when next you meet.* "Yes—and that one will be Flinn."

But he had wanted Flinn's death to be more than merely physical—he had wanted to kill the man's very soul. How delicious it has been to corrupt Flinn's honor from afar rather than simply bite him in two, Verdilith thought. He smiled. And how satisfying the man's suicide would have been. The dragon slowly licked one claw. "But revenge takes many forms."

Verdilith looked down at his last remaining abelaat crystal. He needed more. He slid to one corner of his lair, pulling his massive bulk up before a large brazier. Reaching into a deep alcove, he pulled forth some aromatic herbs and flowers and placed them in the brass basin. Then he raked his claws along the rugged cave wall, sending a shower of sparks down onto the herbs. In moments, a fire flared to life. The sweetly scented smoke rose to the dragon's vapor-scored nostrils, soothing his senses. Drawing a deep breath, the dragon began to speak, the sounds rumbling low in his long neck. The ancient command words rolled out into the smoke and mingled with it.

The miasma above the brazier began to thicken and swirl. Strange, bright colors glimmered through a veil of misty ash, like lightning bolts dancing behind summer storm clouds. But at last the colors coalesced, and the smoke took on the vague shape of a human's face.

"Your bidding is all, Master," came a disembodied voice as indistinct as the face in the smoke.

"Bring me more abelaat crystals," the dragon rumbled. "Good ones this time. Make them if you must."

"Is that all, Great One?" the voice droned.

"No!" The single word was nearly a roar, sharply contrasting to the servant's voice. "Have you done the penance I set for you?"

A brief silence hung in the air, then the words "No, I

have not."

"Do so!" Verdilith hissed. "Do not try my patience!"

"Yes, Master," came the barely audible reply. The image wavered and disappear. Another shadowy face formed in the smoke, as indistinct as the first. It spoke.

"I understand Flinn has regained Wyrmblight." The words were smooth, without any detectable malice. Verdilith bared his teeth anyway.

"Yes," the dragon hissed.

"Don't fail in your revenge, Verdilith. Your domination of Penhaligon is critical to our plans. And, I must ask—" the speaker paused "—is that item I entrusted to you still safe?"

Verdilith smiled uneasily and said, "Yes. It is where you left it." His eyes wandered over to the one-foot–square box resting in a corner of his cave. It was a simple box, iron reinforced with steel. Not a single gem or rune graced it. Even the lock was inauspicious—a simple clasp. Its looks were deceiving, however. Verdilith had spent more than a month trying to open the box, but to no avail. The clasp simply would not be undone, despite the dragon's best magical and physical efforts. And neither would the box break. Verdilith had carried the box to the loftiest height he could climb and then dropped it on the rocky Wulfholdes far below. A tiny, one-inch scratch was his reward.

"Good," the voice replied. "When you are finished with your business with Flinn and I have things settled here, I will take the box from you. Do you need anything?"

"Only the abelaat crystals, but the other one is taking care of those." Verdilith needn't have bothered with his response, for the swirling image had dissolved into simple smoke. The dragon turned away and hissed in annoyance. He lumbered over to the precious box and picked it up.

It fit easily into Verdilith's palm and was inexplicably

heavy. Nothing rattled inside. He tried the lock again, and as usual it wouldn't budge. The dragon put the box down and returned to his bed.

"Vengeance," the dragon rumbled, a green cloud swirling like a dark halo about his head. "First, death to Flinn, then to the orcs . . . and then to you, my fine friend."

🙚 🙚 🙚 🙚 🙚

Yvaughan whimpered in her sleep. A voice tolled incessantly in her mind, like a death knell, but she couldn't understand the words. Her dream was starting again, and a part of her was aware of it and feared it. She rolled over, seeking her husband's warmth, but her arms remained empty. Maldrake was away tending other matters. Silent, bitter tears fell from her eyes to the silken pillow. Her two pet birds cooed and fluttered to her side. One nestled at her ear; the second cooed again, then flew to a dark corner of the bedchamber.

Her dreams grew more frightening. The dark, many-fanged creature entered them as he had so many times before. He was moving toward her, a man-shaped beast with brutal claws. A tiny groan escaped her lips. She knew of the dream and what was to come. She struggled to control her thouhgts, to force the monster from her mind, but the angular creature continued toward her. She covered her face with her arm, trying to bar the vision from her mind.

Still it came.

The thing with the shining claws came to her bedside and bent over her. She couldn't breathe. She couldn't scream—only whimper. Drawing her arms from beneath the covers, the monster stroked them lightly over and over. His claws raked her skin just hard enough for the flesh to open and

ripple with pain. Then he bit her at the tender joint of one
elbow. She almost welcomed the pain, for it meant her
dream was almost done.

But something inside her fought back tonight, something
that was suffocating. Her breath was being pulled from her
body in wave after wave. Yvaughan panicked and fought her
way toward consciousness, thrashing in the bed. She had to
awaken, she had to, or else she would surely die. With a
sudden, strangled gasp for air, the woman sat up.

Darkness surrounded her, the familiar darkness of her
bedchamber. Beside her, a bird cheeped a complaint at
having its rest disturbed. Automatically she soothed her pet,
petting and stroking its downy buff feathers. Then something
flew at her from the corner of the room, and she threw her
hands around her head and gave a tiny shriek. But it was only
her other bird, jealous for attention. She took it in her arms
and lay back down. It cheeped plaintively.

She noticed then how weak her arms felt, how cold and
drained of life. She rubbed her hands across them. They felt
wet and slippery. Am I still dreaming? she thought. This has
never happened before. Concerned, she reached out to the
table beside her and touched the lantern. Instantly, it sprang
into magical light.

Yvaughan extended her arms before her and looked at
them. Blood and jagged lacerations laced her white skin. She
screamed. "Teryl! Teryl!" she cried for her advisor, her only
friend with Maldrake away. "Teryl!"

The doors to her chamber flew open, and the mage ran
toward her. "Lady Yvaughan!" he called. "Is something
wrong? Has someone disturbed your rest?" In the room
beyond, her other birds fluttered and cried out in alarm.
How wonderful that they care for me, she thought suddenly.

Teryl tottered to the bed and sat on its edge. Tearfully,

Yvaughan stretched out her arms to him. The mage's eyes grew wide. "Oh, lady," he whispered. "What have you done? What have you done to yourself?"

Yvaughan shook her head in growing horror. He thinks I did this! she thought wildly. She shook her head again, desperate that he understand. "Teryl, this is not what it seems! I didn't—"

The advisor put his hand on her shoulder and pressed her back into the waiting pillows. "Calm yourself, my lady. I will fetch bandages and a cool drink for you."

"Teryl, you don't understand!" Yvaughan cried as the man walked away. "I didn't do this! There was a monster, and he—"

"The monster of your dreams?" Teryl inquired as he reached the door. "Come, come, lady. We all know dreams cannot hurt us." The mage left the room, and Yvaughan pounded her fists impotently on the silk coverlet beneath her hands. Why doesn't he believe me? she asked herself. He is my friend! More hot tears fell from her eyes.

"Here we are, lady," Teryl said, coming back quickly. He held up a goblet of wine and pressed it to her lips.

Yvaughan choked on the pungent bitterness. "What is this?" she asked.

"Something to help you sleep peacefully through the rest of the night. Didn't you take the draught I made you earlier?" Teryl asked accusingly.

Between swallows Yvaughan replied, "No, I didn't drink it. I didn't think I would need it, Teryl."

"But you always sleep so poorly when Lord Maldrake is away, lady," Teryl chided. He set aside the chalice and began applying salve to her injuries.

"That's true, but . . . tonight was no different from the other nights I've had this dream, Teryl," Yvaughan responded slowly, her tongue suddenly thick. "Except that tonight I fought back."

The mage pursed his lips. "And that, my lady, is obviously how you hurt yourself."

"But I've dreamed the attack before, and there were never any marks on me then."

"Ah, but you didn't wake up those times, did you? That's because you never hurt yourself before tonight, which is why you woke up this time," Teryl said sagely.

Yvaughan tried to clear her muddled mind. "What . . . what are you saying, Teryl? That I *deliberately* hurt myself?"

The man nodded, a twitch gripping his shoulders. "I'm afraid so, lady." He applied one last dab of salve and a bandage. "There, that's the last of it."

"But I don't understand, Teryl," Yvaughan's voice dropped to a whisper. She could barely keep her eyes open. "I don't understand. Why would I want to hurt myself. Why?"

Teryl gathered his things together and looked down at her. Her cloudy mind thought it heard the words, "You'll find out soon enough, lady. Soon enough." The mage turned on his heel and left the room.

☙ ☙ ☙ ☙ ☙

Sir Brisbois nervously paced the flagstone bridle path leading to the back of the stables. White puffs of breath escaped his lips in the cold, biting air. "It's just like Maldrake to make me wait," the knight muttered as he paced up and down the winding path, blowing on his hands to warm them. A few knights galloped past. Brisbois looked up for a moment, then turned away immediately when he didn't see Maldrake. The knights merely nodded and continued down the path.

On their heels came another knight, who halted his steed beside the pacing man. Brisbois sighed inwardly, then gazed with irritation at the rider. It was Sir Lile Graybow, the castellan of the castle.

"Good morning, Sir Brisbois," Graybow said affably, his gravelly voice cheerful and sincere. He was seated on a golden mare and bedecked in his finest armor.

"Good morning to you, Sir Graybow," Brisbois said brusquely. When Graybow made no move to continue down the path, Brisbois was forced to add, out of deference, "And where are you off to this morning?"

"I'm visiting some of the villages of Penhaligon today," Graybow said smoothly. After a pause, he continued, "I'm going to institute some of the peasantry tax relief measures Lord Maldrake and I devised."

"Tax relief . . . measures?" Brisbois asked slowly. He and Maldrake hadn't made any plans since the deal with the horses had fallen through.

"Yes," Graybow said archly. "I was surprised you didn't want to meet with us, Brisbois, but Lord Maldrake told me you no longer wanted to be a part of the committee. Of course, when we presented our plans to Baroness Arteris, we had to tell her of your decision. She was quite distressed. A shame, really."

Brisbois put his gloved hands behind his back and clenched them. He smiled civilly. Collect yourself, Brisbois thought. Graybow could be trying to rile me for all I know. Maldrake's in for quite a conversation, if he ever arrives. "Ah, thank you, Sir Graybow," Brisbois said formally and gave a little bow. "You've been most . . . informative." The castellan nodded and then moved his horse off at a trot.

Many long minutes passed before Maldrake came down the bridle path. His horse was cantering sideways in a highly stylized and controlled parade march. All Maldrake's concentration seemed centered on making the horse take deliberate, measured steps. Brisbois was freshly irritated. He took off his gloves and slapped them into one hand. His friend had made this appointment seem urgent. Apparently equestrian practice was more important. Brisbois wouldn't put up with such insults.

With a flourish, Lord Maldrake dismounted from his horse and bowed elaborately before the knight. "Brisbois!" he shouted with great affection. "Have you been waiting long?"

"Maldrake," Brisbois growled. "You were supposed to be here an hour ago."

"Oh, please, Brisbois," Maldrake looked pained. "Isn't there something else we can talk about?"

"Yes, there is," retorted Brisbois. "We can discuss just exactly what you're doing with Graybow, or we can discuss what happened to Yvaughan!"

"Oh, that," Maldrake scowled. "Nothing more than she deserved."

"Maldrake!" Brisbois shouted. "She's your wife! Don't you care about her?"

The young lord crossed his arms and looked both bored and annoyed at the same time. "Look, Brisbois, there's something you should know. I was never in love with Yvaughan—not even in the beginning. Our feelings were all one-sided—hers. I only wanted to marry her because she was a Penhaligon and Arteris is far too icy for my tastes. Marrying Yvaughan was a good move for me, and I'm grateful for your discrediting her previous husband."

"Maldrake—!"

The blond lord held up his hand. "As to Yvaughan's deserving anything, the only thing she deserves is to be thrown from the highest tower!" Maldrake's green eyes flashed, and his pale skin turned red. "That woman killed my son, Brisbois, and you want me to be worried about her? Those little scratches she gave herself are nothing! I wish she'd clawed out her jugular—"

Brisbois shook his friend. "Stop it, man! Can't you see? Yvaughan's innocent! She didn't kill that pitiful being you called your son! And she didn't wound herself. It's that damned wizard who did both!"

Maldrake knocked away Brisbois's hands. "Never touch me again!" he hissed through clenched teeth, his canines shining in the bright morning sun. Brisbois stepped back involuntarily.

"Maldrake . . ." he whispered.

The lord stabbed his finger against the knight's chest. "I told you about Teryl Auroch. He didn't kill my son or injure my wife. And even if you are right about his harming Yvaughan, he did it to please me. *He* succeeded—" Maldrake's eyes flashed "—where *you* failed."

Brisbois stared unblinking at his friend. He had always tried to do his best for Maldrake; how could he be faulted for trying? Brisbois held out his hands. "All right, Maldrake," he said in a subdued voice. "Whatever you wish. You asked to see me. What did you want?"

Maldrake smiled. It was a thin, reptilian smile, and it chilled Brisbois. "Flinn is on his way to the castle."

"When?" Brisbois felt fear trickle into his heart. He had done more than enough to earn Flinn's wrath.

"Soon," answered Maldrake. "In the next few days."

"What are you going to do?" Brisbois asked.

"What am *I* going to do, Sir Brisbois?" Maldrake responded coyly, then shook his head. "You have it all wrong, my friend. All wrong, indeed." He put his arm around Brisbois's shoulder. The knight stiffened and Maldrake shook him, smiling all the while. "Relax, Brisbois, relax." They began walking toward the stables, the trampled snow crunching beneath their boots.

"What do you have planned?" Brisbois insisted, knots forming in the muscles across his shoulders and back.

Maldrake laughed and looked at Brisbois. "Listen, and I'll tell you." He shook his head, his green eyes wide. "The best part is, neither you nor I will have to do a thing." Maldrake's laughter filled the morning air.

Chapter XIII

he setting sun touched the top of the trees as Flinn and his friends overlooked the valley leading to Karleah Kunzay's home. Snow blanketed the forest and the rugged hills beyond, and rays of fading sunlight sparkled off the unblemished white. The slopes of the valley were lined with pale aspens and dark green spruces. A few birds circled lazily in the air, and Flinn eyed them warily. Spies of Karleah's, he thought. A blue jay cackled, its voice reminiscent of the old woman's laugh. The warrior grimaced. So much for my plan to surprise the wizardess, he thought. We'll have to enter the valley on her terms. He nudged Ariac into a slow walk, and the others fell in behind. Jo followed on her horse Carsig, and Braddoc and Dayin rode the dwarf's long-legged ponies. Braddoc used a lead rein to tow Fernlover, who took up the rear carrying supplies.

Flinn frowned as they descended into the valley. No tracks appeared in the snow, which had fallen at least three days ago. Along the line of trees, a deer spooked suddenly, her eyes wide and unblinking. She flicked her tail, bounded across the open valley floor, and disappeared into the forest. Immediately after the doe's passing, the snow closed over the tracks.

219

Flinn smiled grimly. He raised an eyebrow and wondered what other surprises Karleah's valley held in store. "Keep your eyes open," he said as Jo and Braddoc came to flank him.

"I don't like the idea of calling on crazy Karleah," Braddoc grumbled once again. He'd voiced his misgivings once or twice before on the trip, but to no avail. "Seems we're just asking for trouble," he added.

Flinn pulled Ariac to a halt and looked at the dwarf. "What do you expect me to do? I promised Dayin I'd bring him to Karleah Kunzay because he knows her and doesn't want to go to the castle." Flinn waved his hand. "I can't just leave Dayin here by himself!"

The dwarf said stubbornly, "Why not? He survived the last couple of winters just fine without you."

"We've come this far, Braddoc," Jo noted. She added sensibly, "It can't be much farther."

The dwarf looked uneasily from Jo to Flinn and then to Dayin. His eyes roamed the trees around him. "There's something about . . . about this place that's giving me the willies. The—the . . . trees want us to leave. Can't you hear their whispers?" Braddoc's voice cracked, and Jo looked at Flinn in sudden alarm.

The warrior moved next to Braddoc and gripped the dwarf's arm. "Braddoc!" he said in a low, authoritative voice. "Calm yourself! The whispers—"

"There're so many, so many!" Braddoc's eyes darted to the woods again.

Flinn slapped the dwarf. "The whispers are just Karleah's wards trying to drive you away! She doesn't like dwarves, but fight against the charm and it'll stop."

Braddoc's eyes dimmed, and he tugged nervously at his beard. The dwarf coughed suddenly and looked up at Flinn, his eyes clearer. His expression was grim. "I knew there was a reason why I hate wizards." He laughed wryly, and the others joined in.

"Flinn," Jo asked when the laughter subsided, "how did you know about the ward against dwarves?" She spurred her horse next to Flinn's griffon. They continued slowly down to the center of the snow-filled valley. The cold wind was dying down.

Flinn found his thoughts slipping nearly fifteen years into the past as he told Jo, Dayin, and Braddoc the story of how he had met crazy Karleah Kunzay. He'd been recovering in the castle's rose gardens one day after his battle with Verdilith when, unexpectedly, an old crone approached him. She was dressed in filthy rags and smelled of dust, and Flinn had sneezed three times during his greeting.

The old hag had come straight to the point. She told Flinn that she had dreamed of the battle between him and the dragon. On three nights afterward she'd had a dream of a second battle between them. In the first, Flinn had died while the dragon won. In the second, the reverse had occurred. In the third dream, both man and dragon died. Karleah told Flinn that, for a small fee, she would dream a fourth time and divine the true future for the next battle. Flinn laughed, handed the old woman a coin, and told her that he knew who would die: Verdilith.

Flinn chuckled as he relived the incident. "Although I saw Karleah Kunzay after that, she never did tell me if she'd had a fourth dream or not. And I never asked her," Flinn finished his tale as they reached the valley floor.

"Why didn't you ask?" Jo asked curiously. Dayin echoed the question. Braddoc was still eyeing the woods suspiciously and paid little attention to Flinn's story.

The warrior shrugged. "I prefer not to know my fate."

Flinn lapsed into silence, his thoughts returning to the strange wizardess.

Once, in the middle of the night, he had walked onto the parapets of the castle and found Karleah there. She told him she was settling in the hills northeast of the castle and that she wanted advice on how to protect her home. Flinn readily complied, telling her the kinds of defenses he would create. Snow that could conceal tracks after their creation had been one of his suggestions, and he was flattered she'd taken it.

Abruptly, as though he hadn't interrupted his tale earlier, the warrior stated, "Unfortunately, word got out about Karleah's 'prophecy.' First it was rumored that Verdilith would die." Flinn shook his head. "People actually prayed for the dragon's return so I could kill it."

"When did the prophecy change?" Jo asked.

"After my fall from grace. People said then that I would die if I was to meet up with Verdilith. The same ones who prayed for the dragon's return so I could kill it now prayed for its return so it could kill me."

Suddenly the animals jerked to an abrupt halt. Ariac squealed and flapped his stubby wings, and Carsig and the ponies whinnied. Dayin and Jo were thrown from their mounts, while Flinn and Braddoc had to fight to keep their seats. Fernlover panicked, fell to his knees, and then was still. Flinn lightly heeled Ariac in the flanks. The griffon quivered and tried his best to take a step forward, but he couldn't move. Flinn looked back at Jo, who was kneeling by Carsig and pushing the snow from the horse's hoof.

"Can you see anything?" he asked the young woman. He and Braddoc were still mounted, and each had drawn his weapon. This defense of Karleah's certainly seemed effective, thought Flinn.

Johauna dug out a large ring of snow from her horse's foot

and called out, "Carsig's hobbled by vines, lots of them. There must be something growing underne—ohhh!" Jo's cry cut through the air, and Flinn saw dark, shiny green vines snake up around her legs and arms. He could hear the sudden rustle of greenery moving beneath the blanket of snow, and he saw the top of the snow quiver. I applaud your defenses, Karleah Kunzay, Flinn thought.

"Jo!" he shouted. "Are you all right?" He turned sideways in the saddle and prepared to leap toward her.

"Y–yes," Jo said, tugging on the vines. "I'm not hurt, but I sure can't move. How about you, Dayin?"

The boy stood beside his pony. Dayin struggled to lift his left foot and then his right, but could not. He shook his head and answered, "I'm fine, but I can't move, either."

Braddoc called out, "Can you reach your knife and cut the weeds, Johauna?"

"Cut my pets and I'll cut you off at your knees," a querulous voice shouted from the spruces behind them. Flinn and the others whirled in that direction, but they could see nothing in the dense underbrush.

"Come out and show yourself!" Flinn challenged.

"And why should I?"

Flinn was startled. The second call had come from immediately behind him, in a grouping of large stones.

"I only want to speak to you. We wish you no harm—" Flinn began.

"Spare me the details. Everyone who goes through my valley wishes me no harm. But they always do something, like cut my vines." This time the voice came from behind Braddoc.

"We were only going to cut the vines because they trapped us," Flinn said crossly. "If you will make the vines release us, we'll harm nothing in your valley, Karleah Kunzay."

"Humph," said the voice again, only this time it came from a body. The wizardess stood halfway between Flinn and Johauna.

Karleah Kunzay looked exactly as Flinn had remembered her: a wizened old woman, so ancient her body was nothing more than dry leather over bones. She had bowed shoulders, lank gray hair, and an ashen face creased with myriad wrinkles. She wore gray sackcloth ornamented with gray basswood twigs. Thin green vines held the dress together. A faint, shimmering aura surrounded her, blurring the outline of her body. She carried a rough wooden staff, which she now leaned against for support.

"Humph," the ancient woman said again. "So you know my name, which is more than I can say for most, but knowing my name doesn't mean you'll not attack my pets. Without assurances, why should I let you go?"

Flinn sighed, realizing she had forgotten their acquaintance. "Because I'm—"

"Because it's vail vine," Dayin interjected suddenly, and all eyes turned to him, "and it won't hurt us if we give it a few coins to buy passage over it." The boy smiled sweetly.

The old woman's eyebrows disappeared into her hairline, and she harrumphed a third time. She pushed her staff before her, and the blanket of snow parted just enough for her to pass through it; it closed immediately after her. She walked stiffly over to Dayin. She was very short, standing only slightly taller than the boy before her. She reached out with a bony finger and jabbed Dayin in the chest.

"I know you," she said crisply. "Follow me." The ancient wizardess tapped the boy's feet and turned around. She began walking back the way she had come, Dayin studiously following her.

Next to Flinn the woman stopped and peered up at the

still–mounted warrior. "Seems like I know you, too." Karleah looked Flinn up and down and then smiled a large, toothy grin. Her teeth, though crooked, were extraordinarily white. "Yes, I remember you. You fought a green dragon once; I saw it in a dream. You can come, too. The others will have to stay where they are, or they can pay the toll and make camp outside my valley. The vail vine needs to be fed, you know." She turned and began moving leisurely away.

Dayin looked up at Flinn and whispered, "Throw down a coin for Jo and one for each animal, too, or the vine won't let them go." The boy scurried after the old wizardess.

Flinn pulled out six silvers from his purse, throwing one in front of the animals and another at Jo's feet. A distinct slithering noise followed and Jo hurriedly mounted up on her horse. "You and Braddoc make camp where we entered the valley," Flinn said to Jo, "and I'll be back soon."

"I don't like your going off with her," Jo warned.

"I know you don't, Jo, but that's just Karleah's way," the warrior responded as he dismounted. "Try not to worry. We'll be safe. Take Dayin's pony and Ariac with you." He handed Jo the reins.

Jo nodded and turned her horse around. Braddoc, with one disgruntled look, followed. Flinn joined the slow-moving wizardess and Dayin.

"So you know about vail vine, do you, son?" Karleah Kunzay was saying with a certain admiration. She gave a laugh that was just short of a cackle. Flinn was reminded of the blue jay. We didn't stand a chance of quietly riding into Karleah's valley, he thought. "It's not many that do," Karleah added. Flinn raised an eyebrow and wondered whether Karleah was responding to his thoughts or making a comment to Dayin about the vail vine.

Dayin quietly agreed with her.

"Your father teach you about the vine? Did you ever make one?" The old woman was obviously prying for information, and Flinn thought to interject but decided not to. Dayin would likely tell Karleah whatever she wanted to know since he wanted to become her apprentice. Besides, the wizardess was quite capable of magically extracting the truth, if the tales about her were to be believed.

"My father made one and I helped, too, so that sort of counts." The boy laughed shyly. "I got to hold the coins of greed he used to feed the vine."

"Is that so?" the old woman responded.

"Oh, yes. It took a long time before Father taught the plant to prefer gold coins over earth and water, and I always helped with feedings. The coins always squawked about not wanting to be eaten by the plant. They wanted me to run away with them, but I didn't," Dayin gushed.

"Doesn't look like your father's with you, son," the old woman peered over her shoulder toward Flinn. "I don't remember him looking like that."

"Father's dead—been gone two years now," the boy responded easily, without any grief. He turned and pointed at Flinn. "You know Flinn. He's a knight of Penhaligon. And we left behind Jo, his squire, and our friend Braddoc."

"Flinn, eh? Yes, that was the name. The Mighty Flinn," the old woman murmured. When the boy opened his mouth to elaborate, the crone touched his shoulder and pointed to a tiny path entering a thick copse of evergreens.

"There's my home, right through those trees," Karleah said proudly as they approached. "I built it myself." Her crooked white teeth gleamed in the dusk. "Follow me." Without further word, Karleah stepped into the trees, Dayin immediately behind her.

Flinn hesitated, harboring deep misgivings about the

wards Karleah must have set around her home. "I can't leave Dayin in there all alone." Taking a deep breath, he stepped into the copse. Silence. He could still see the spruces and smell the pines, but all sound ceased. Nothing moved inside the still woods, and the magical blanket of snow had already erased the tracks of the wizardess and the boy.

Flinn continued forward, expecting to see Karleah's house. Abruptly, darkness fell, black and unnatural. "Now I am deaf and blind," he whispered, though he couldn't even hear his own words. "Still smells like a forest, though." Stretching out his hands, he stumbled through the trees. The branches bit at him with their brittle winter boughs. A twig jabbed his forehead and he cried out in annoyance, but the woods consumed the sound immediately. Panic threatened to rise in him, but he fought the feeling down.

"Karleah? Dayin?" he said, tentatively. This time, the names sounded muffled in the unnatural stillness. He tried calling as loudly as he could, "Karleah? Where are you?"

He thought he heard the old woman's cackling response, "You are almost there. You're almost through the wards," but the words may have come from his own mind. Running his hand through his hair, Flinn pressed forward. How long he walked in that sightless, soundless void, he didn't know. Only the scent of pine seemed real, tangible, solid. His relief at the sight of light coming from two windows ahead was almost overwhelming.

In a clearing ahead stood a hut, roughly the size of his cabin. A little light still remained in the sky above. The dark spruces that ringed the cabin seemed familiar once again and not darkly magical. The cottage's walls of rough-hewn rock were topped with a pine-bough-thatched roof. The two windows were covered with thin animal hides that had been oiled and waxed so often they were semitranslucent. The light that emanated from behind the skins was golden. Flinn opened the door, which was made of planks bound together by vines, and stepped inside.

Warmth and light and an indefinable, almost palpable, peace engulfed him. Karleah and Dayin were nowhere to be seen in the opulent room he entered. Tapestries covered the walls, ornate furniture beckoned him to sit, and hundreds of candles cast their glow about the room—all only serving to highlight the loveliest woman Flinn had ever seen. In front of the fireplace sat a maiden, her skin pale and clear, her hair the color of sable fur, her eyes green as spring grass. She was framed by the light of the welcoming fire. At her feet lay a sleeping cat.

The woman stood and smiled, holding out her hands. The gesture was so beguiling in its innocence that Flinn stepped forward and grasped those hands without question. As he gazed into the woman's eyes of green, he found himself struggling to remember why he was here and whom he was looking for.

The maiden smiled up at him, her gentle beauty shining in the light. "Kiss me," she said simply.

Flinn almost complied. He leaned toward her, his eyes intent upon her perfect lips. But he stopped; the image of Johauna Menhir rose unbidden in his mind, and with it came the knowledge of what he was seeking.

"I—I cannot, lady," he said as graciously as he could, releasing her hands. "I lost my way in the woods, and I am looking for an old woman and a young boy. Have you seen them?" Flinn cocked his head suddenly and looked sharply at the maiden before him. "Or are you . . . ?"

Flinn felt, rather than saw, the radiant image before him shimmer. The dazzling candles disappeared one by one until only two remained, one on a suddenly plain wooden table and the other on the equally rough mantle. Gone, too, were the tapestries and furniture, replaced by homely counterparts. The cat became Dayin, who blinked rapidly and said not a word. Last to shimmer away was the beautiful maiden, and in her place stood Karleah Kunzay, in all her wizened glory. The magnificent room became simply a stone hut, cluttered with bottles and cups and canisters. Herbs hung from the rafters, lending an unpleasant smell to the stifling room. A brisk fire burned in the hearth, adding its pungent odor of smoke.

"Karleah Kunzay. As I thought," Flinn said slowly.

"Yes, it is me," Karleah said. She gestured toward a bench while she slowly sat in a rocker opposite it. Flinn lowered himself to the seat and drew Dayin to his side. "I sometimes test those I allow to enter my valley," she explained. "Amusement, you know. It makes the days pass. I keep a tally, too; you're only the second person to resist that particular illusion. I must be losing my touch." The old woman winked and tapped Flinn's knee. "'Course, I might have preferred it if you had failed." The old wizardess stared at Flinn with avidity. Her eyes, sunk into her flesh, glistened with greed. "Why have you come, Fain Flinn? Are you here to discover the true foretelling?"

Flinn put his hand on Dayin's shoulder. "The boy here is Dayin Kine. He says he knows you," Flinn began, ignoring Karleah's question.

"That is so," Karleah nodded serenely. "I knew his father, too. What has Dayin's fate to do with yours?"

Flinn shook his head and said, "Dayin asked to come here—"

"I told Flinn and Jo that you'd take me in," Dayin said in a breathless rush. "I said you'd want me to come to you instead of anyone else, mostly because there isn't anyone else. You meant what you said, didn't you?" The boy's sky-blue eyes grew wide with fear, and Flinn suddenly remembered how young the child was.

Karleah Kunzay cracked a smile and said, "Yes, Dayin, I meant it when I said you'd make a fine apprentice. I also meant it when I said I'd take you on someday. Since it looks like the day is here, here is where you'll stay."

Dayin impulsively hugged the old crone, who looked surprised at the display of affection. "Well," she said, smiling and pushing the boy away, "that's enough of that." One of Karleah's bent and bony hands patted the boy, and then the wizardess pushed him toward the door. "Go back to your friends for tonight, Dayin. Flinn and I have things to discuss."

"Will he be all right?" Flinn asked with concern.

"Pshaw!" cackled Karleah. "The boy is safer in my valley than he was in his mother's womb!" Dayin called good night and left the cabin. Karleah watched him go, then busied herself by putting a log on the fire. In silence she sat back in her rocker and eyed Flinn.

Flinn gazed back at her and said, "It's good to see you again, Karleah. I wondered how you were faring."

"Hah!" Karleah chortled. "Had you really been concerned about me, you would have come to see me." She tapped his knee again, suddenly serious. "Why are you here, Flinn?" She gestured toward the door with her staff. "I appreciate your bringing the boy to me, for I am fond of him. But you could have let him make his way here on his own. He would have found me. You came for another reason."

Flinn nodded. "Yes. I . . . need answers."

"To . . . ?" Karleah queried.

Flinn pulled out his pouch of abelaat stones and spilled the crystals into his hand. "To these—and more." He looked at the wizardess and then asked calmly, "What do you take in payment?"

The old woman's eyes were lost in the wrinkles of her face. Flinn grew increasingly uncomfortable in the silence. "The payment is usually in blood, Fain Flinn, for answers like those you seek," she said slowly. "But from you I want something else. Give me four of the crystals made with Johauna Menhir's blood."

Flinn looked at her curiously. "Granted, provided you tell me why you want those stones in particular. And further, how did you know that some of these stones were made with Jo's blood?" he asked.

"The vail vine is more than a toll. It also 'reads' a person's history so that I know who enters my valley. But the vine couldn't read much of your squire's life, save that she'd been bitten by an abelaat." Karleah warmed to the subject. "There's something about abelaat spittle that defies detection. It's very difficult to spy on someone like Jo, even using crystals made with the abelaat's own blood."

Karleah reached over and took four of the dark red crystals from Flinn's hand. "These were inside your squire a long time. They are well made and probably more powerful than most other human-blood crystals I've seen. Johauna nearly lost her life in making these. Although these stones won't allow communication like those made of the abelaat's blood—"

"But we heard Verdilith through one of Jo's crystals when she saw him in his lair," Flinn interjected.

"So the vines told me," the old woman nodded. "The vision was too tiny for you to see in the stone, but I believe Verdilith was using a crystal to spy on you at the same time. If two stones are used simultaneously between two parties, communication is possible." Karleah paused. "However, there is a second explanation for your hearing the dragon through the stone."

"What is the second? And is this the reason why you want Jo's crystals as opposed to the abelaat's?" Flinn held up the remaining amber crystals.

The old woman sighed and looked at the crystals she held. "The stones made from Johauna's blood may be used only to communicate with Johauna, or for her to communicate with someone else—which is what she did with Verdilith." Karleah paused unexpectedly, then chewed her lower lip. "Furthermore," she continued slowly, "there is a possibility—however slight—of using these crystals to communicate *whenever* you choose."

"*Whenever* I choose?" Flinn asked sharply. "What do you mean, Karleah? I don't understand."

The old woman was quiet, as if weighing her words. Flinn moved to speak, but she held up a hand warningly. "Do not hurry me, Fain Flinn," Karleah said. She pursed her lips, blowing air through them in a soundless whistle. At last she spoke. "It is true that *some* crystals can cut across not only the barriers of space but those of time as well. They allow communication across the years," she said slowly, "even with someone who is dead. . . . Yes, some of the stones are that powerful. But the effort to make such contact is immense and requires much skill."

Flinn stared at the crystals in his hand. "Tomorrow I am going to the Castle of the Three Suns to right a wrong done to me seven years ago. Can the crystals be used to see an event that happened in the past?" Slowly he looked over to the wizardess.

"You wish to prove your innocence, is that it?" Karleah asked sharply. Flinn only nodded, and the old woman shook her head in response. "Flinn, look to your heart when you confront those who wronged you. You don't need magic when you have truth," she said solemnly.

Flinn continued to gaze at her. He sighed lightly. "You're right, Karleah Kunzay, and I thank you for that. Truth is on my side, and with words I will make the council see that truth." He tucked the remaining crystals back into his purse. "You have the gift of second sight, don't you?" he asked quietly a moment later.

Karleah nodded. "It's true I have the gift—or the curse, as the case may be. It has become a fickle one of late." She paused and then continued, her eyes intent on the warrior. "However, it would be a simple matter to see what lies in your future, for it is a short one, Fain Flinn." Her expression didn't change.

Flinn's brows drew together in a knot. He had expected nothing else. He shoved the thought aside for now and looked down at his hands. "And . . . and the girl's future?" he asked tightly.

The old woman's eyes glazed over. She spoke a moment later, her voice low and deep. "You meet your doom, Fain Flinn, the day you join Verdilith in battle. If your friends are with you, they will share your fate." Karleah's tiny eyes focused again on Flinn.

The warrior rubbed a callus on his left hand. "Your prophecies of doom interest me little, old woman," he said, his voice deliberately distant. "If I must fight the wyrm, I must fight it."

"Yes, but must your comrades?" she rejoined.

Flinn knew the answer to that question. He couldn't bear to see Johauna die because of him, but neither could he bear to live without her. Not just yet, he thought, then closed his mind to the subject. Flinn considered what other questions he would ask the witch. He opened his mouth, intending to ask whether the slaying of Verdilith would restore Wyrmblight. Somehow the words, "What will happen if I don't seek Verdilith?" came out instead. Flinn hadn't even been aware of the thought, and he was ashamed he had voiced it.

The old woman smiled gently at him. "You know the answer to that question as well as I, Fain Flinn. The question is moot because you *will* hunt the dragon." She shrugged.

Flinn returned her look, and after a while his lips grew rueful. Karleah Kunzay was right. He could no longer live a life without honor, without following the Quadrivial. Slaying Verdilith and avenging both Bywater and himself would ensure that he attained all the points of the Quadrivial.

His thoughts took a different turn. For Jo's sake, he could live without following his knightly code of ethics. They could build another cabin—a larger one. They could forget about vows of honor and live a blissful life, cut off from the troubled world. A blissful life? he thought. I am a fool. A fool and a coward. I cannot turn back from the path now. I cannot betray Johauna's faith and belief in me. I must slay Verdilith.

Karleah Kunzay coughed once, discreetly, to draw his attention. "I think it's time, Flinn, for you to use the abelaat's crystals," the old woman's voice was sharp and high-pitched. Her thin hand trembled before she rested it on her staff.

Flinn stared at her. "For what purpose?" His voice was singularly gruff, and he fixed his gaze on the wizardess.

"To see what you are to face. It's time you take a look at your enemy."

"The dragon will see us as well, Karleah," Flinn argued. "And I won't put you in jeopardy for an action of mine, not as I did the town of Bywater." He shook his head.

The crone held up a hand, halting Flinn's refusal. "The wyrm won't see us, for this valley is protected well from such as he. But we will see what he is planning, and thus you will be forewarned." Karleah brought out a copper brazier and filled it with small embers from the hearth's fire. When the brazier was ready, she asked Flinn for one of the abelaat's stones. She looked at it closely.

"Hastily made. I'd say they won't be good for much. But let's see what we'll find out with this one. Hopefully we'll learn enough so we don't have to use another." She placed the crystal in the brazier, and both she and Flinn peered into the basin. "Concentrate on the dragon, but don't call out his name. We can talk because the dragon won't be able to see or hear us through my wards unless we say his name." After a pause, Karleah said, "It's starting."

The old wizardess drew some powdered quartz from a pouch and sprinkled it over the burning embers, taking care not to scatter any on the crystal itself. "I've enlarged the crystal so we won't have to peer so closely into it. Ahhh, here we are."

Flinn looked at the crystal, which Karleah's magicks had enlarged ten times. As before, he caught the sensation of movement first. Then the images shimmered and coalesced into a coherent vision.

Flinn gave one anguished cry, "No!" and jumped to his feet, knocking over the bench behind him. The warrior leaped across the floor and out the door.

≈ ≈ ≈ ≈ ≈

Jo sat close to the fire, her front too hot and her back too cold, despite the fur wrapped around her shoulders. "I wish you had let us camp in the valley, Braddoc, or at least next to the woods," she said petulantly as the wind howled through their camp again. The dwarf had insisted on camping at the rim of the valley in a stony, barren plain. Although the snow lay shallow on the ground, the wind whistled endlessly and chilled Jo to the bone.

"I told you before, I want to stay as far as possible from that woman, her trees, and her vines!" Braddoc snapped. "At least out here in the open she can't hurt us."

The young woman was too distracted to keep up the argument. Instead, she listlessly stabbed the fire's embers with a stick. Braddoc sat at her side, drinking a cup of mead. Dayin had returned a while ago, eaten his meal, and was already asleep inside the tent Braddoc had supplied for Jo and Dayin to share. Flinn and the dwarf shared the other hastily erected tent.

"What do you suppose is going on down there?" Jo asked for the fourth time that evening.

"Same thing as I told you last time," Braddoc said tersely. "Relax, Johauna. Flinn is with a friend—at least I think she's supposed to be a friend—and he'll return as soon as possible." He sipped his drink and hummed a little beneath his breath. Jo usually found the bass rumble pleasant, but tonight she found it irritating.

"It's just that tomorrow we head out for the Castle of the Three Suns," she said. "What if Flinn doesn't return? What if the witch does something to him?"

"I see it now," the dwarf smiled, though not unkindly. "You're not so much concerned about Flinn as you are about reaching the castle tomorrow. Aren't you?"

Jo rubbed one of her hands. She broke the stick and threw the pieces on the fire. "You're right, Braddoc. I'm worried about nothing. Flinn is with a friend, and they're just talking about old times or whatever. He'll be back soon and tomorrow we'll—" Jo choked on her words, her flesh suddenly crawling. She could feel the hair on her neck stand on end. She looked at Braddoc, who glanced back at her curiously. Then very slowly, very carefully, Braddoc's eyes shifted to the darkness behind Jo, and his eyes went wide.

The would-be squire touched the tail at her side and blinked fifteen paces away. Braddoc rolled aside, but he wasn't quick enough. The space beside the campfire erupted into a flurry of dragon limbs and wings and teeth as Verdilith leaped from the shadows just beyond the fire's flames. Giant jaws snapped where Jo had been only a moment before, but she was now beyond the dragon's reach. A massive and scaly talon fastened around Braddoc, and the claws began to tighten. Struggling within the beast's grip, Braddoc worked his battle-axe loose and ruthlessly hacked away at the claws.

The dragon stretched his neck toward Jo again, and this time he opened wide his jaws and breathed. But the young woman used the blink dog's tail again, and she found herself near the dragon's rear haunches. Immediately she pulled her sword out of its scabbard and began attacking. The tough, leathery scales seemed impervious to her blade, but she continued to attack anyway. She would draw blood. She would. Verdilith turned his head away from Braddoc, whom he had been about to bite, to look at Jo.

"Hah!" she shouted defiantly. "Let go of my friend, and we won't hurt you!" To back up her threat, she drew her sword high overhead. If bravado worked so well for Flinn the Mighty, perhaps it would work for her, she thought.

Noise rumbled in the dragon's throat, but Jo couldn't tell whether the beast was laughing or roaring. Then something crashed into her back and she was thrown to the ground. Somehow, despite the pain, she managed to hang onto her sword and roll over. The dragon's long, supple tail was waving above her.

Jo heard Braddoc cry out. The dwarf swung his axe wildly as the dragon's giant maw descended on him. Verdilith ignored the blade and engulfed the dwarf. Jo rose shakily to her knees and then to her feet. Verdilith's mouth opened slightly and Jo glimpsed Braddoc, hacking at the teeth with his axe. She stumbled forward with her sword straight ahead, like a lance, and stabbed the dragon. The blade tip jabbed between the emerald scales and sunk shallowly into the creature's haunch. Jo pulled the blade forth to stab again.

A sudden burst of color and light appeared in front of the dragon's face. Surprised, Verdilith dropped Braddoc. The dwarf jumped out of the way, although he groaned after the twelve-foot fall. As the spinning sparks whirled before the dragon, Braddoc gestured for Jo and Dayin to come to him. He gripped the boy's shoulder briefly in mute gratitude for his timely spellcasting.

"Do you think we should run?" Jo asked as she arrived.

The dwarf shook his head. "Our only chance is to make a stand and hope Flinn's on his way."

The colorful sparks faded away, and in their place doves and rose petals fluttered on the wind. Blinking, the dragon turned toward Jo, Braddoc, and Dayin. Again came that low rumble Jo now knew was the dragon's laugh. She trembled in fear, certain she was about to die, but she remembered Flinn's words about facing danger even when afraid. She shifted her sword a breadth higher. She couldn't let Flinn down.

A shining burst of light raced toward them along the rim of the valley. The streak came closer. It was Fain Flinn, bathed in such a white, radiant light that he was both beautiful and terrible to behold. He held Wyrmblight high over his head and prepared to charge.

"Remember the prophecy, wyrm!" heckled a crone's voice in the darkness. The words were repeated over and over again, in waves that echoed out from the valley. Jo felt the earth beneath her feet begin to slither toward the dragon. The vail vines crept through the snow and onto the barren ground of the camp. The leaves rustled and took up the chant where the echoes left off.

Flinn halted before the dragon, his sword arced back in a formal invitation to battle. He was still bathed in an eerie, white glow that made him seem twice as tall as normal.

"What say you, Verdilith?" Flinn's voice rang out, deep and penetrating, shaking the ground. Jo felt something akin to awe strike her at the ominous sound. The warrior advanced two steps.

A rumble started in the dragon's throat, and this time it emerged as a full-fledged laugh. "I say that now is not the time for us to meet, Flinn the Fool," Verdilith said in heavy, dragon-accented common. "And as they say, tomorrow is a better day to die!" Verdilith launched himself into the air. Three heavy flaps of his wings saw the dragon aloft and out of sight in the night sky. The blasts of air from the gigantic wings buffeted everyone but Flinn to the cold, stony ground. The warrior staggered backward from the wingbeats, but he remained standing.

Jo and the others ran to Flinn when the dragon was gone. The odd, scintillating light around him was fading. He looked tired and strained, and Jo wondered what spells had been cast upon him. Karleah Kunzay came out of the shadows and joined the group at the campfire.

"What did Verdilith mean about tomorrow being a better day to die?" Jo asked anxiously.

Flinn put his arm around her shoulders and shook his

head. "I don't know, Jo, but your guess is as good as mine." He looked at Jo, then at Bradoc and Dayin and finally Karleah.

"Tomorrow we find out." Flinn's lips tightened, and his expression grew grim.

Chapter XIV

 linn pulled Ariac to a halt and dismounted. The warrior stroked the griffon's neck, nervously plucking out a few stray feathers. Beside him, Jo, Braddoc, Dayin, and Karleah halted their beasts and dismounted, too. Jo strode through the snow to stand beside Flinn, not saying a word. There, on a promontory that overlooked the Penhaligon valley, stood the Castle of the Three Suns. Its limestone walls glittered whitely in the midmorning sun, and the clay tile roof glowed with red splendor. Flinn's eyes tightened to hold back the tears that threatened to fall. It has been so long, he thought, so long.

The castle itself was diamond-shaped, the main approach and angle towers comprising the points. Four other towers supported the outer walls, which presented a formidable barricade to the world. These eight outer structures stood four stories high, and a single tower rose twice that height from the center of the castle. The tall structure was the keep, or donjon as some called it in the old tongue.

The castle of the Penhaligons had no moat; the sheer and rocky slopes around it made assaults nearly impossible. The main thoroughfare leading to the castle was a narrow, winding road; nothing larger than two merchant wagons could pass side by side. Approaching the castle from any other direction involved climbing the steep hill on which the castle stood.

An easy trail led from the Wulfholdes down to the curving castle road. In little more than two hours, Flinn would confront his past and regain the people's faith in him, as well as his faith in himself. He turned to face the others. "Listen to me," he began. "This is something I must do by myself." His dark eyes studied each of their faces.

"If you think you're going alone, forget it. We want to go with you," Johauna said clearly. She gestured at the wizardess, then crossed her arms. "Karleah and Dayin didn't come along for the ride. They came because they want to see you be rightfully reinstated as a knight. We're coming with you; we've come too far to turn back." Her brows knitted stubbornly.

Briefly Flinn wondered why these people should care about him, but he was grateful nonetheless. It had been so long since he'd had friends, true friends. "If you insist. I would be . . . pleased to have you there," Flinn said steadily and then smiled.

Braddoc spoke up. "What else would we do? Besides, what if Verdilith has plans for you? What would you do without us?"

"At the castle?" Flinn was incredulous. "The Castle of the Three Suns is powerful and well armed. Verdilith wouldn't stand a chance attacking there. The castle's inhabitants are also renowned for their purity of heart. No one there would ever have dealings with a beast like Verdilith." Flinn was affronted at the very idea. "I think the dragon was trying to frighten us with his warning. I think he would have attacked us by now if he'd had plans to do so."

Braddoc jerked his thumb toward the castle and said

gruffly, "It's been seven years since you were there, Flinn. You don't know what's happened since you've left, and you have no idea whether the people are still 'pure of heart.' After all, Brisbois is still there, isn't he?" The dwarf's lip curled in a sneer.

Flinn looked away from the dwarf and then back. "One bad apple doesn't always spoil the rest in the barrel, particularly if it's removed. That's what I intend to do with Brisbois." Flinn's voice grew cold. "As to Verdilith, if he fulfills his threat to attack today, he'll do so on the road to the castle—out in the open. If Verdilith is down there waiting for me . . . yes, I'll need your help." Flinn thought of Karleah's prophecy. He knew he was risking his friends' lives by taking them with him, but some instinct told him now was not the time of Verdilith's choosing. His instincts had always been true in the past, and he hoped they would be again.

Jo uncrossed her arms and said, "Then let's get this over with! Enough said." She grabbed the reins to Carsig, mounted the gelding, and smiled down at Flinn.

The warrior cocked an eyebrow. "Remember the protocol I taught you, Jo," he said dryly. "Once we get to the road, ride to the left and behind me by two lengths—no more, no less. And when we go inside, you follow to the left and behind at four paces." Jo nodded coolly, one hand on the pommel of her sword.

Flinn mounted Ariac and called to Braddoc, Dayin, and Karleah, who was riding Fernlover, "The rest of you should follow a little way back. If Verdilith does attack, we don't want to be lumped all together. If you're behind me, that'll give you a chance to rush to my defense." Flinn smiled his lopsided grin.

The dwarf fixed the tall warrior with his good eye and said, "We'll watch your back." Karleah cackled.

Flinn continued, "Once we're safely inside the castle, you three are on your own. There's plenty to see—or you can come to the great hall, which is where Jo and I will be. Today is open court—they hold it the same day of every month—and I will have my chance to speak to Baroness Arteris and the council. Hopefully they will listen to me. If not—" Flinn shrugged "—it would be good to have you on hand." He smiled reassuringly and turned back to face the valley.

Without further ado, the warrior guided Ariac down the path toward the castle road, and the others fell in behind him. The sun shone warmly on the softening snow, and the wind had died down. "Spring's on her way," Flinn murmured to himself. Ariac appeared to feel the same enthusiasm, for he picked up his claws and nearly pranced down the path. Carsig eagerly kept pace, shaking his head and arching his neck in response to Ariac. Jo moved beside Flinn.

"Carsig's a delight to ride. I don't think I've ever ridden a finer animal," Jo said easily. She flashed Flinn a smile, and Flinn suddenly saw that she was beautiful. Without volition, he smiled in return.

They fell into companionable silence for the rest of the short journey down the hill's path. Before long, they could see the winding road leading to the castle. The rumble and clang of a merchant caravan rose in the still air. As Flinn and the others approached the crossroads, the two wagons passed by, heading toward the castle. The noise was coming from the metal pans hanging along the wagons' sides. Other bits of metalwork hung from the wagon: harness rings, axeheads, chisels, and tools.

No one else was in sight, and Flinn held up his hand to Jo and the others to halt. "We'll wait here until they're a little farther up the road. The wagons should be safely to the castle by then, in case the dragon attacks us out here. Remember your protocol, Jo. If anyone from the castle happens to be watching you, proper protocol will commend you to them."

Johauna was looking at him with something akin to compassion. "Are you afraid, Flinn?" she asked softly.

He turned his eyes to the road and said thickly, "Afraid? Of course I'm afraid." The aging warrior urged Ariac into a gentle walk onto the road, his thoughts turning dark and somber.

As Braddoc had said, more than seven years had passed since Flinn last saw the Castle of the Three Suns. He and several other knights had spent the day routing a band of ogres foolish enough to cut across Penhaligon lands. An easy dispatch, the attack was little more than a training exercise for the younger knights. Flinn and Brisbois, being the only senior knights, had led the expedition.

They headed home, meeting up with another group of knights along the way. Both parties had been victorious, and their cries of triumph rang in the air. Flinn was content, for he had done a good day's deed and was returning home to his wife. Only the devotion and loyalty he'd had for old Baron Arturus, his wife's uncle, could compare with what Flinn felt for Yvaughan.

As the knights entered the courtyard, their shouts and laughter died down and were replaced by a growing murmur. Flinn looked over at the other knights curiously, wondering what was wrong. Brisbois had been unexpectedly quiet the entire trip home, but was now whispering to the younger knights in their party. A young blond knight, Lord Maldrake, began jabbing his cohorts and pointing toward Flinn. Flinn was about to question Brisbois and the others when he saw Lady Yvaughan in the courtyard, looking over a peddler's fresh produce. She was surrounded by several of her handmaidens, and she carried her pet bird of the moment, a dazzling white creature with a crest of brilliant green.

Flinn forgot his comrades' actions and called out, "Greetings, dear heart!" He dismounted and strode toward his wife.

"Halt!" Brisbois shouted, maneuvering his horse between Flinn and Yvaughan.

"What is the meaning of this, Sir Brisbois?" Flinn demanded, trying to walk past Brisbois's horse.

The knight spurred his horse forward and shouted, "Do not move! You will not taint your wife with your base dishonor!"

Annoyed and not a little affronted, Flinn put his hands on his hips and demanded hotly, "Dishonor? What have you, Sir Brisbois? Why do you keep me from my wife?" Yvaughan's expression was coolly poised, and he was surprised. His wife was usually volatile, and the slightest incident distressed her. The peddler, a ragged old man who was missing one ear, moved closer to Yvaughan and Flinn. His eyes were alight with overweening interest. Other peasants and servants, hearing the commotion, drew nearer as well.

Brisbois dismounted and signaled for the other knights to do the same. The younger knights, the ones Flinn had seen Brisbois talk to, did so with alacrity. Some of the older knights looked puzzled and frowned at Brisbois, but the younger knights quickly urged their comrades to comply.

Brisbois turned to Flinn and pointed at him. "Knight of the Order of the Three Suns, I accuse you of dishonoring our most sacred code—that of denying mercy," Brisbois declared, his voice ringing out in the courtyard. Servants and peasants pushed closer. Flinn was too stunned to say anything. "Sir Flinn," continued Brisbois, "today an ogre beseeched you for mercy on the battlefield, and you did not grant it. Instead you laughed and slew the creature where he lay!"

"You lie!" Flinn shouted, outraged. He advanced on Brisbois, determined to tear the truth from the man's lips. But at a signal from the knight, two young men interceded and held Flinn at bay. "Why are you lying, Brisbois?" Flinn demanded, trying to pull his arms free. "What foul treachery are you planning?" He managed to free one hand and strike Brisbois with it. The knight staggered back a step.

"It is no lie." The words, softly spoken, came from the ranks of Flinn's comrades. The young blond knight, Lord Maldrake, stepped forward. The man had come to the Castle of the Three Suns and been given knighthood status immediately—something rarely, if ever, done. Flinn had seen very little of the man and had never spoken more than a few cursory words with him.

"It is no lie," the knight repeated again, this time more loudly. He pointed at Flinn and said, "I saw Flinn slay the ogre, too. Sir Brisbois is telling the truth."

"You misunderstand!" Flinn's voice rang out authoritatively. He struggled against the men who held him. "The ogre didn't—" one of the knights holding him punched him beneath his breastplate. Flinn doubled over in pain. He fought for breath and shook his head. When he looked up again, Yvaughan stood in front of him, tears streaming down her cheeks.

"Oh, Flinn, how could you? You have defiled my house and my name," she cried out in sad bitterness. "You have shamed the niece of Arturus Penhaligon, a man you profess to revere. How could you deny an enemy mercy? You have committed an act of absolute shame." Brisbois, Maldrake, and several of the other knights murmured ill-tempered words loudly.

Yvaughan's voice shook and her tears came faster. "You have dishonored the house of Penhaligon, Fain Flinn, and as a Penhaligon I strip you of your knighthood!" She shook her fists at the knights, her tears mingling with her anger and shame. "Cast him down, O true knights! Cast down this aspersion on the conscience of the righteous!" The older knights, who hadn't believed Brisbois's allegation initially, were swayed by loyalty to the house of Penhaligon. Their voices joined the growing roar.

"Yvaughan!" Flinn shouted. "Listen to me!" His words were swallowed up, and Yvaughan never heard them. She picked up a head of lettuce from a nearby peddler's cart near her and threw it at her husband. It hit Flinn squarely in the chest. The old peddler chuckled and feebly tossed a carrot.

What happened next was something Flinn had always carefully blocked from his memory. But now he confronted the thought, his lips curled in a sneer of grim fear and rage and shame. His eyes narrowed to slits, his shoulders slumped forward ever so slightly, and one arm crossed his stomach as he continued to ride toward the castle.

Flinn's fellow knights of the Order of the Three Suns— his friends and cohorts who had often fought by his side and who would gladly have given their lives for their commander—beat the man they hailed as Flinn the Mighty. With the flat of their swords they turned on Flinn, but Flinn refused to draw Wyrmblight. Instead he wielded his shield this way and that, trying to block the blows. He shouted at the men to stop, hoping to seek a council session rather than this mob trial to settle the matter. But Yvaughan's white bird panicked at that moment and fluttered into his face, scratching Flinn with its tiny claws.

Then Flinn caught sight of Yvaughan, her ladies and the young blond knight hurrying to her side. They grabbed the peddler's produce and threw it at Flinn. Peasants, servants, and even a few knights joined in. Vegetables and fruits and bitter taunts battered him from all sides.

In a single afternoon, Flinn the Mighty became Flinn the Fool, the Fallen. The shouts that rang that day mortally wounded his spirit. He leaped onto his horse and fled.

A single groan escaped Flinn's lips, and the sound brought his thoughts back to the present. He looked around warily, fighting back the horror of his memories. He gritted his teeth. I survived being falsely accused, and I will survive whatever pain is to come in overturning that accusation. I will right the wrong done to me, and I will avenge myself of Sir Brisbois.

Flinn sighed and consciously buried the thoughts of his disgrace once again. He sat taller in the saddle and moved his free hand to Wyrmblight's pommel. His lips were once again grimly pulled together, but a new hardness and assurance marked them.

The Castle of the Three Suns lay just ahead.

🙰 🙰 🙰 🙰 🙰

Flinn entered the main approach and pulled Ariac to a stop. He was grateful the wyrm Verdilith hadn't attacked him out on the road; Flinn's instincts had been right. Two guards flanked either side of the entrance, and a handful more stood nearby. "I'm here to seek council with the baroness and her court today," Flinn responded to the guard's inquiry. He jerked his thumb back at Jo and added, "She's with me." The guard waved him through, and Flinn nodded for Jo to follow him.

They crossed through the approach and passed under the guard towers flanking the entrance to the castle. Low buildings lined the perimeter of the castle's grounds. Next came the guards' dormitories, craftsmen's dwellings, shops, stables, and the like. Inside the perimeter stretched a huge courtyard, paved in rose granite, leading to the castle proper.

The metalmaker's wagons were nearby, Flinn noted, and haggling already filled the air around them. Hundreds upon hundreds of people filled the castle's courtyard, moving from stall to shop to wagon. Open council days always drew big crowds, but Flinn had forgotten just how many people the Castle of the Three Suns could hold. The air rang with bickering voices and laughter. Hawkers and merchants milled about, trying to steal each other's customers away. Ragged peasant children ran wild, playing games or begging for food. A pair of mages cast minor spells to amuse a small crowd of onlookers. A number of knights and their squires engaged in practice swordplay. A trio of washerwomen sang a ditty as they did their daily scrubbing. Soon a man joined them, lugging his own bundle of clothing, and added a pleasant baritone.

Flinn and Jo tied their mounts to one of many hitching rings lining the courtyard, and Flinn tossed a peasant girl a coin to keep an eye on the animals. Etiquette demanded that those who dwelt outside the keep tie their mounts here.

Few people appeared to take note of the rough, fur-clad warrior and his young assistant. Flinn's sharp eyes caught sight of a female knight, however, who seemed to find them of particular interest. She had been watching the swordplay practice but not participating in it. With a nod to her comrades, she excused herself and hurried off. Flinn lost sight of the woman far too soon for his liking, but he gave her no further attention. He was intent on reaching the castle's large central tower: the donjon.

Someone caught his arm and stopped him midstride. Flinn's hand flew to Wyrmblight's hilt.

"Did you see—" Jo said, tilting her head in the direction

the knight had gone.

Flinn relaxed his grip on Wyrmblight and nodded curtly. "Yes. I had thought I could get to the keep without being recognized, but apparently I was mistaken. If memory serves me, that was Madam Edwina Astwood. Watch my back!" He continued his way through the crowds, impatiently trying to find the quickest route. Within ten minutes, he stood before the keep.

The donjon was eight stories high, its windows placed at equidistant intervals. The white of the limestone looked grayer, dirtier somehow, than Flinn remembered. He looked at the southern tower and saw that its walls, too, had darkened over the years. Every window of the tower had been fitted with bars of black iron. Behind the bars flitted birds of all colors and sizes. The southern tower had once been Flinn's home.

So Yvaughan did make the rest of our home into an aviary, Flinn thought. He had always liked Yvaughan's birds well enough, but her enthusiasm for them had grown into an obsession. Her passion for two birds in particular had bothered him. She would go nowhere, not even the bed-chamber, unless one of them went with her. Yvaughan favored the white bird and its buff-colored mate above everything—including her husband. Flinn frowned. Just when had she gotten the two birds? Shortly after he had attacked Verdilith? Was it really that long ago? He shook his head and turned his attention to more important matters.

As Flinn and Jo approached the donjon, he noted a new addition to the castle's defenses. A steep-sided, deep canal circled the tower. The channel was fully twenty feet deep and twice that wide, with sides that stood at nearly right angles. The far wall of the canal extended straight up to form the walls of the donjon; no ledge ran between them. At the bottom of the canal, thousands of spearheads gleamed, rising from three-foot shafts. "Quite a deadly fosse," Flinn murmured.

A sturdy wooden and iron bridge spanned the dry moat's gap. The bridge was lowered now because of all the traffic the castle received on its monthly open council sessions. Long ago, Baron Arturus had reinstated the abandoned practice of arbitrating the common people's concerns. On council day, the baron had permitted anyone to appear before him and the council to seek judgment or retribution. Flinn was glad to see that Baroness Arteris had upheld her father's policy.

He turned his attention to a guard standing at the little gatehouse on the near side of the fosse. Flinn and Johauna approached the man.

"I wish to enter the donjon, gatekeeper," Flinn said decisively.

The guard casually looked at Flinn and sighed, indifferent. "State your name and business, ruffian. We don't let just anyone into the keep, you know."

Flinn drew himself to his full height, Wyrmblight resting on the ground between his hands. "I am Flinn, former knight of the Order of the Three Suns," he said. "Today is the open council, and I wish to speak before Baroness Penhaligon."

The young guard's eyes bulged. "I thought you were dead," he said inanely. He opened the gate leading to the drawbridge and beckoned Flinn through.

"Not hardly," Flinn growled between clenched teeth. He'd encountered this sort of response before, and he was in no mood for it today. His palm itched, and he rubbed it against the metal-clad pommel of Wyrmblight. He and Jo stepped onto the bridge, Jo following him at the requisite distance. A pair of guards wielding spears strode forward, and

Flinn saw more lurking in the shadows of the archway. He halted halfway, as did the guards.

"Is something amiss, good sirs?" Flinn called out pleasantly enough, though a thread of irritation laced the words. Madam Astwood had doubtless informed the castle guard of his presence. Flinn prayed Brisbois wouldn't be so cowardly as to flee.

"We have orders to escort you to Lord Maldrake's chambers, peasant," one guard said stiffly. "Will you come with us peaceably?"

Lord Maldrake? Flinn thought quickly. Why Lord Maldrake? To admit he'd misunderstood Flinn's actions regarding the ogre? That seemed highly unlikely. Perhaps Maldrake had been promoted to castellan and was in charge of security. Or perhaps Maldrake was trying to protect Brisbois.

"I am here for the open council," Flinn said as easily as he could. "I will be delighted to meet with Lord Maldrake either at the council hall or later today in his chambers."

"But, sir, we have—" began one knight. She was interrupted by someone walking up behind the two guards.

"I'll handle this, Gerune," an approaching man said gruffly. When the guards hesitated, the man fixed them with an icy stare and said, "You may go now. Lord Maldrake may think this is a peasant matter, but it isn't. This man will answer to me." The guards turned and walked quickly away.

Sir Lile Graybow, castellan of the keep, strode forward and grasped Flinn's wrist in greeting. He wore fine clothes and a gyrfalcon pendant, which signified his office. He had gained an extra chin, Flinn noticed, and his hair was thinner and grayer, but he was still Lile Graybow. Flinn sensed the steel that bound this man's soul. The castellan's position had always been, by tradition, filled by the knight most revered in all Penhaligon, and the rule still held true. Flinn had once hoped to take Graybow's place when the man was ready to step down.

"Fain Flinn. As I live and breathe, I always knew you'd return one day, but events like this are unexpected, nevertheless," Sir Graybow said.

"It's good to see you again, Sir Graybow," Flinn said formally. "I'm on my way to the council to explain the truth about what happened when I left here so many years ago. Aren't you on the council any more?"

"Yes, I am. However, I couldn't pass up welcoming you back personally. I have my spies, and they told me you were here," Graybow added conspiratorially. "It's about time you returned. I wish I'd been around when you were accused. You deserved a fair trial and not a mobbing. I'd have kept the young hotheads in tow if I'd been there, believe me. But today will be your chance to amend old wrongs. Be careful— the same people who wished you ill back then are still here." Sir Graybow gestured toward the donjon, and they began walking into the keep. As they did, the old knight looked over his shoulder at Jo. "See you've found yourself a squire. 'Least she knows protocol. Things have gotten a bit slack around here of late, but the baroness is trying. We make do."

"You mentioned people who wish me no good, Sir Graybow," Flinn said after a moment's silence. "Sir Brisbois, for one, obviously. Is Lord Maldrake another? I barely remember him. Exactly who is he?" Flinn stopped abruptly inside the castle. He'd forgotten how lovely the donjon was, with its soaring stone pillars, patterned granite floors, and magnificent tapestries. Warm light beamed from hosts of magical lanterns.

The castellan came to a halt and turned to Flinn. He said slowly, "You mean you don't know who Lord Maldrake is?"

When Flinn shook his head, Graybow continued, "He's the man who married your wife."

Flinn stared in stunned silence at the castellan.

"Come," Graybow said, nodding toward the council chambers. "Justice is long overdue."

In silence the two men passed through the giant doors into the great hall where the open council was held. The roar inside the hall was almost unbearable, as was the heat. Nearly two thousand men and women crowded into the great hall, all waiting their turn to state their case before the baroness and her council. Many had arrived in the night and waited for the doors to open at cock's crow. At that time, pages and squires had immediately begun collecting names and complaints to give to the junior knights, who in turn filtered the more interesting or faster cases on to Baroness Arteris. The fourteen other council members handled the more mundane cases. Matters were swiftly presented to a council member—and swiftly decided. Although many peasants would have their case resolved that day, still more would be turned away once cock's crow hailed the next morning.

Flinn and Graybow fought their way toward the front of the hall, and the castellan used his office more than once when someone protested their passage. Finally they reached an area that was cordoned off around a long rectangular table on a dais. Only the pages, squires, and knights presenting the commoners' cases were allowed into the cordoned area. At the center of the table sat Baroness Arteris. Around her, the other council members stood or sat. Flinn bit his inner lip when he saw Sir Brisbois at the far end of the table. The knight had been given Flinn's seat on the council! Flinn looked at the rest of the members and recognized only a few of them. His eyes paused at an elegantly dressed, blond man who looked strangely familiar. Then realization dawned:

Lord Maldrake.

Lile Graybow touched Flinn's arm. "Wait here, son. I'm going to have a private word with the baroness. She'll want to try your case herself, I'm sure."

Flinn nodded. Behind him Jo tugged on his sleeve, and he turned to her. She pointed off to their left; Braddoc, Karleah, and Dayin had entered behind them and wormed their through the crowd. Flinn nodded to the dwarf, who returned the gesture. Then Flinn turned back toward the front, where Sir Graybow approached the back of the dais to speak privately with the baroness.

"Why aren't there any guards surrounding the baroness?" Jo asked suddenly. "Does she trust the people that much? Don't they ever get out of hand?" Setting her hand on her sword, she eyed the people jostling for position around her.

"There are guards, but not as many as you think." Flinn pointed to the blue velvet ropes surrounding the dais. "You see how no one is standing anywhere near the ropes? That's because the rope repels people. The cordoned area is laced with magical defenses to keep people out. If you get too close to it, a jolt of fire ripples through you. I hear it's quite painful. Furthermore, no magic can penetrate that area, and weapons such as ours disappear if we enter the cordon uninvited. Don't ask me how that works because I'm not a wizard. Ask Karleah; she could answer that one. The ropes are why the guards don't bother checking weapons at the door."

"Are the defenses foolproof?" Jo asked curiously.

"As far as I know, yes. Even arrows and crossbow bolts disappear once they enter the cordoned area. My guess is there're wards other than just the ropes, but I don't know for sure," answered Flinn absently. Graybow was talking to the baroness now, and Flinn saw the older man gesture toward him. He glanced at Brisbois and Maldrake, noting that only the latter appeared to see him. Then Flinn saw Edwina Astwood leave Maldrake's side.

"But if the baroness unknowingly invited a magical beast into the cordon, it could wreak havoc, couldn't it?" Jo asked, but Flinn shushed her. Sir Graybow was waving him down and would meet him at the entrance to the cordon.

"It's time to go, Johauna," Flinn said hastily.

"Already?" Jo's voice broke, and she coughed. "Already, Flinn?" she said in a lower voice. "I thought we'd have a chance to sit around for a couple of hours and—and get prepared for this!"

"Well, I thought so, too, but Sir Graybow's called in some favors. He wants us down there, now!" Flinn pushed his way through the last of the crowd. Jo followed so closely behind him that she stepped on his heels. Moments later, they stood before the castellan, who put his hand on Flinn's shoulder, then looked at the baroness and nodded.

Baroness Arteris Penhaligon rose, and immediately four dozen trumpets sounded. They continued until the crowd fell silent in the great hall. All eyes turned to the baroness, who spread her hands and spoke before the huge audience.

"My people!" she called loudly, and the words, amplified either by architecture or magic, carried to the farthest corners. "A most extraordinary case is about to be presented to us."

Brisbois cast a vaguely bored expression at the baroness. "He still doesn't know I'm here," Flinn muttered under his breath. Just wait, thought Flinn, that expression of yours will soon change. Flinn turned his attention toward Maldrake, who nodded cordially in response.

"Fain Flinn," the baroness was saying, and the crowd began to murmur at the name, "a man formerly dear to the heart of Penhaligon, is here today to seek justice. Step forward, Master Flinn." Arteris sat down.

As Flinn strode forward, Jo behind him, someone called out, "Look! It's Flinn the Fool!" Others took up the shout, and in less than a minute more than half the people inside the great hall were shouting, "Flinn the Fool! Flinn the Fallen!" The warrior clenched his teeth and entered the cordoned area with Graybow and Johauna.

Arteris let the chant continue for a few minutes more, and Flinn endured it as patiently as he could. He tried to ignore the awful and relentless chant, but could not. Instead he focused on a point just past the baroness, who sat less than twenty feet away. Arteris had a streak of something less than kindness in her, and it was evident now. Only after Flinn's expression had grown dark with anger did she signal the trumpeters to silence the crowd. The mob had become so raucous by this time that the trumpeters played long minutes before the crowd quieted.

The baroness rose again. "Fain Flinn, you stand before us. What justice do you seek resolved?"

"I seek retribution for an injustice committed seven years ago," Flinn called out. The audience quieted still more, straining to hear every word. Grimy peasant faces and clean freemen faces alike shone with hungry interest.

"And what injustice, pray tell, is that?" Arteris asked. Her voice was cool and civil. He wouldn't receive any quarter from her.

"That of my being falsely accused of dishonor on the battlefield, Your Ladyship," Flinn's voice rang out clearly. He pointed to Sir Brisbois. "That man did maliciously and falsely accuse me of denying an enemy mercy!"

"Sir Brisbois!" Baroness Arteris cried, and Flinn saw his enemy's face blanche. "You have been named in this case. Please stand before Master Flinn!" Brisbois slowly stood and walked with measured paces until he stood between Flinn and the council table. Brisbois turned to face Flinn. "And did anyone else accuse you of such a heinous crime, Master Flinn? You have the right to face all your accusers," the baroness continued.

Flinn had been about to point out Lord Maldrake, but he remembered that the man hadn't actually accused him of dishonor. Maldrake had only upheld Brisbois's position—an understandable mistake. But someone else had directly accused him of dishonor. He paused, then said heavily, "The Lady Yvaughan, Your Ladyship."

"Bring the Lady Yvaughan to the hall at once!" the baroness cried. Not more than a minute passed before Flinn's former wife was brought in by a side door and led to stand near Brisbois in front of the council table.

Flinn was saddened at the sight of Yvaughan, for she was obviously ailing. She's given birth to her child, he thought, but she hasn't recovered yet. I should have thought of that and not named Yvaughan in my suit. The woman stumbled a little in her walk, and she cradled a white bird in her arms. Refusing to look at Flinn, Yvaughan nervously petted her bird and mumbled beneath her breath.

The man leading Flinn's former wife was particularly short and particularly nervous. His features were plain— so plain as to be indistinct—save for his eyes, which were a brilliant blue. His hair was a medium brown and modestly cut. His chin was weak, though covered with a tiny goatee, and the flesh beneath it wobbled as the man jerked his head about, which was often. He was dressed in a gray tunic, dark breeches, and a brown cape. Flinn had never seen the man before.

Lord Maldrake stood and addressed the baroness, "Permission to attend my wife, Your Ladyship?"

The baroness said icily, "Permission granted." The blond knight walked over to his wife and put his hands on her shoulders. Yvaughan momentarily cringed away, then leaned against Maldrake. The young lord gestured for the man who had brought Yvaughan into the council area to leave. The gesture awoke in Flinn a memory: sometime before Flinn's fall, Lord Maldrake and Yvaughan had stood in the same stance, and Maldrake had made the same dismissing gesture toward Flinn. *How could I have been so blind?* Flinn thought.

"You may state your case, Fain Flinn, and none may gainsay you until you are through. Speak you now, or the former judgment on you shall stand!" Arteris cried in a voice that carried to the rafters. The people in the great hall rumbled in return, and Flinn fancied he heard some shouts of support.

"I charge you, Sir Brisbois, with falsely accusing me, intending to stain my honor and discredit my reputation as a knight!" Flinn's voice rang out sternly. He turned to his former wife and his voice trembled. "And I charge you, Lady Yvaughan, with falsely accusing me, intending to divorce me and claim a new husband!" Flinn didn't want to believe that Yvaughan had been a willing partner in his scene of shame, but the indications seemed irrefutable.

"How say you, Sir Brisbois?" the baroness cried, and all eyes in the hall turned on the knight. "How say you? Are you innocent of this deed—or are you guilty?"

Sir Brisbois took a step toward the people, addressing them instead of Flinn or the council. "I am—" he said solidly, then paused. Flinn clenched his jaw, resenting the man's dramatic pause. Brisbois repeated, "I am—" The words broke off and doubt edged the man's voice. Flinn looked at the knight closely and saw that he was staring at

Maldrake. Brisbois's face worked, and he clenched and unclenched his hands.

The knight tore his gaze from Maldrake and hurried toward the edge of the blue cordon. "I am—*guilty!*" he shouted to the great hall. The people erupted into a frenzy of emotion. They stomped their feet where they stood, slapped fists into palms, and shouted. The roar was almost unbearable. Brisbois held up his hands and shouted again, though the words were barely audible, "I am guilty—and he is responsible for that!" Brisbois whirled and pointed at Maldrake.

The lord hissed, "Fool!" Maldrake ripped the white bird from his wife's arms and threw it at Flinn's feet. The bird dissolved into a viscous white substance that slowly began to reshape. Jo's words echoed in Flinn's mind, ". . . if the baroness unknowingly invited a magical beast into the cordon . . ." Flinn drew Wyrmblight and rushed Maldrake.

"Draw your sword, Maldrake! I will avenge my honor!" Flinn shouted.

"I think not, Fool!" Maldrake cried. His hand jerked once, and Yvaughan whimpered in pain. Her eyes glazed over and Maldrake pulled a knife out of her back. The young lord pushed Yvaughan toward Flinn, who caught her. Maldrake backed slowly away, brandishing the dagger as Flinn cradled his one-time wife.

"Yvaughan," he murmured. For an instant, her pallid form seemed to transform again into the lively and vibrant woman he had once fallen in love with.

"Fain—" she gasped and then grew still. Her eyes rolled back and her eyelids closed. Flinn smoothed the silken hair on her brow once, then laid Yvaughan on the floor. He advanced on her murderer. Maldrake was slowly backing toward the mass of people in the great hall. He swung his bloody knife at a guard who came near.

"Stand still, Maldrake!" Flinn called out, rage pulsing through him. "Your game is up!" He stepped forward.

Maldrake leaped the blue cordons, and as he did a transformation took place. His neck, arms, and legs sprouted horribly, growing to the size of trees. A great tearing noise filled the hall as his torso lengthened and broadened, stretching into a scaly, reptilian body. Gossamer wings unfurled along his back, then solidified into thin membranes of leather. His head warped horribly, bulging and reshaping into a vast skull lined with spearlike teeth. All this transpired in a heartbeat, and then the wyrm's scream erupted through the hall.

"Verdilith!" Flinn shouted, a thin film of red filling his eyes.

The crowd beneath the dragon broke into shrieks of panic, and the people fell back. Those near the door flooded out in terror, while those trapped within pushed mercilessly to escape.

"Verdilith!" bellowed Flinn again, leaping forward with Wyrmblight overhead. "Turn and face me, wyrm!"

"Another day, Flinn! Face me alone, not with a score of knights at your back!" The dragon shimmered suddenly and then winked out of the air.

"I'll hunt you to your death!" Flinn roared, shaking his clenched fist at the vaulted ceiling. He charged to the spot where the dragon had been. "Come back! Murderer!"

"Flinn!" Jo shouted. "Behind y-"

A snarl interrupted her voice. Flinn wheeled. A humanlike creature with scaly brown skin and wiry hair towered above him. It swung its foot-long claws toward Flinn. He dropped, hearing the claws whirl above his head. Jo leaped behind the beast, wedging her sword into its bony back. It wheeled, smashing her with the back of its hand. Jo fell, sprawling

across the floor, but retaining her sword. Flinn swung
Wyrmblight in a whistling arc toward the creature's overlong
muzzle. The monster spun, deflecting the stroke with its
scaly shoulder. It hissed at Flinn, baring eight glistening
fangs. The monster swung its huge, spidery arm, catching the
edge of Flinn's breastplate with its claws. The blow spun
Flinn about, knocking him to the ground. He rolled over
quickly, expecting the beast to follow with a killing slash.

But the beast paused, sniffing the air. Council members,
their weapons drawn, formed a broad circle to surround the
monster. Slowly, awkwardly, it turned and knelt beside
Yvaughan's crumpled form. It sniffed again. Then, tentatively,
it reached out to touch the woman who had been Flinn's
wife. A little croon escaped the creature's lips, but the sound
was lost to the shouts in the hall.

"Now!" shouted Flinn to the council members. In accord,
the knights of Penhaligon rushed in to attack. Half the
knights slashed first at the monster, then fell back to allow the
others to strike. The second wave of knights hit just after the
first wave. Their onslaught was fierce and mercifully swift.
The creature fell almost immediately.

Flinn stepped back, his heart thundering. He felt saddened
to witness such a slaughter, but the baroness and all the folk
in the chamber had been in danger. Pushing his way through
the crowd of knights, he carefully rolled the creature's
bloodied body off Yvaughan and picked her up. Flinn
carried her limp form to the council table and laid her to rest
there. "She'd been deceived by the dragon all along,"
he murmured with sudden belief. "She didn't willingly
betray me." He stroked her flaxen hair once, then turned
to the baroness.

"My heart goes out to you in your sorrow," Arteris said
formally. She clasped her pale hands together, her eyes

avoiding the body of her cousin.

"And mine goes out to you," Flinn replied equally formally. He looked at Yvaughan once and said a silent goodbye as her soul slipped away. The woman who had died in his arms was not the girl he had loved in his youth. Her death he had mourned seven years before. Shaken, he turned around to face the council members. They were all standing near him quietly, as was Jo. Her wide and somber eyes were filled with emotion. Flinn looked away. The people remaining in the hall had grown strangely quiet. A hushed expectation filled the chamber.

Baroness Arteris stepped forward, her hands spread wide in an embracing gesture. "In the name of all that is holy, Fain Flinn, I rescind the accusations levied against you seven years ago. Only a true and valorous knight could have returned to this hallowed hall and revealed the evil that had come to live among us." The baroness raised her hands and shouted, "People of Penhaligon, what say you?"

Flinn turned around slowly, clutching Wyrmblight tightly against his chest. A chant began—a chant like that which had haunted him for seven years. It spread in a ripple, traveling from one corner of the huge chamber to the other. The chant grew in volume as more and more voices joined. Flinn clenched his jaw, hearing only the remembered taunts of the people:

"Flinn the Fallen! Flinn the Fool!"

He shut his mind to the words the people shouted, unaware that tears were streaming down his face. The people saw those tears and they rose to their feet, their fists pounding their palms with the rhythm of the chant.

Flinn blinked, gripping Wyrmblight more tightly. The pounding of his heart filled his ears, finally drowning out even the remembered taunts of the crowd. Wyrmblight's hilt felt hot in his hand. Flinn peered down, uncertain, at the blade. None of the beast's blood remained on it. Flinn's heart beat faster still, and the people's clapping kept up with the rhythm.

Flinn took Wyrmblight in his hands and looked at the white silver of the sword. No taint of darkness clung to it anywhere. Slowly, slowly, Flinn lifted the blade sideways above his head, gripping the hilt and the center. The crowd's frenzy rose. With a shining Wyrmblight in his hands, Flinn finally heard the crowd's true chant, breaking apart the scars that had festered in his heart for seven years.

Two thousand voices rang as one in the great hall of the Castle of the Three Suns that day. The roar of the people shook the very rafters. They were shouting Flinn's name— shouting it in gladness and joy and not the jeering anger of the past.

"Flinn! Flinn the Mighty! Flinn! Flinn the Mighty!"
Flinn the Fallen was no more.

Chapter XV

ater that day, Arteris raised her hand for silence in the small meeting chamber. The council members, Flinn, and Jo ceased their debate and turned toward the baroness. "We've been here nearly two hours and not even approached a decision regarding Sir Brisbois." Arteris pronounced the defamed knight's name with clipped precision. In the silence that settled, the music of the festival outside the hall intruded. Faint shouts of "Flinn the Mighty!" interspersed themselves with the songs of bards and the sound of lute and pipe. Flinn stifled a smile, hoping that Braddoc, Karleah, and Dayin were enjoying the feast-day Arteris had declared in his honor.

Sir Brisbois certainly was not enjoying the feast-day. He sat in front of the U-shaped council table, his hands resting uncomfortably in his lap. Two guards stood at either side of him.

Flinn smiled wryly. He thought it poetic justice that he had regained his council seat—a spot Brisbois had occupied that very morning. He remembered being in the council sessions many years ago, taking part in the active administration of the estates of Penhaligon. He had believed in justice and goodness then, and he had believed in his ability to help those

less fortunate than he. The beliefs that sustained him so long
ago had returned. Once again, he believed that justice would
prevail and good would defeat evil. This afternoon had
affirmed that.

Flinn's attention returned to the trial at hand. The council
members had split into two factions—those who said that
Brisbois had been under the malevolent influence of the
dragon all along, and those who believed he had willingly
bartered with the wyrm. The debate was growing heated.
Flinn had said next to nothing in the council, letting the
factions wrestle the issue of Brisbois's guilt. He personally
thought Brisbois had willingly sided with Verdilith, but that
was a matter for the council to decide.

Flinn turned and looked at Johauna beside him and
smiled. She was quiet and, he guessed, a little overwhelmed
by all the proceedings. But she was as composed as always;
he feared no discredit from her. This closed council session
would be a good introduction to the less-glorified aspect of
knighthood: political duty. Although protocol stated that no
one who was less than the rank of knight could attend a
closed council, Flinn had insisted on Jo's behalf, stating that
her future was at stake, too. The baroness had graciously
given her consent.

"Sir Flinn," Arteris said loudly, breaking Flinn's train of
thought, "what say you? This man has defiled your honor,
and we may debate the whys of that forever. Although
Penhaligon has suffered a blow to its good name, it is you
who have suffered most at the hands of this knave. The
decision is yours. I repeat, what say you?"

Flinn looked at the baroness, then shifted his gaze to
Brisbois. The man sat in the center of the room before the
council; he was stiff-backed and unmoving. Brisbois's gaze
reluctantly shifted from the baroness to Flinn.

"Sir Brisbois," Flinn began, deliberately using the man's title, "your honor and reputation as a knight are at stake. You must know that for your disreputable actions you are likely to be dismissed as a knight in the Order of the Three Suns." Flinn paused for effect. "I am personally in favor of that, but I would like to know the reasons behind your actions."

Brisbois continued to look at Flinn. "I do not defend myself, Sir Flinn," he said coldly. "I believed Lord Maldrake was my friend, and for him I would do anything—include besmirch your honor. Maldrake told me that Lady Yvaughan was in love with him and that he needed my help in securing a divorce. Accusing you of dishonor on the battlefield and stripping you of your rank as a knight was an easy matter."

"What made you confess your guilt?" Flinn asked equally coldly. "Why today? Why not years before? Or have you developed a conscience after all this time?"

Brisbois flinched, but maintained eye contact. "No. I don't have a conscience. I admitted my guilt and accused Lord Maldrake of his influence on you to get revenge. The man was betraying me—"

"The *dragon*, you mean," Flinn interjected.

"I mean the man. I never knew until today that Maldrake was, in fact, Verdilith. I had been led to believe that the mage Teryl Auroch was the dragon," Brisbois stated. "I betrayed Maldrake's trust in me because I was afraid he and Auroch were setting me up to take the blame for whatever Maldrake had planned for you."

"Would you have continued to act on Maldrake's behalf had you known he was the vile wyrm?" Arteris asked. The council members stared at Brisbois.

For the first time, Brisbois faltered. He looked down at the marbled floor and said, "As long as Lord Maldrake's interests paralleled mine, it . . . it would have made no difference to me had I known he was the dragon."

"Is it possible, man, that you are still enchanted by the dragon?" Sir Graybow asked.

At that, Brisbois's head jerked up, and he glared at the castellan. "I am not now enchanted by the dragon, nor have I ever been enchanted by it. I am a free-willed man, perhaps more so than any of you here. Everything I did, I have done willingly and knowingly."

"Does honor and justice mean nothing to you, Sir Brisbois?" Flinn asked quickly.

Spittle came to the man's lips, but Brisbois quickly wiped it away. "We can't all be knights of renown like you, *Sir* Flinn. Some of us think your quest to attain all four points of the Quadrivial is amusing." He clenched his hands on his knees and added, "I think it's pitiable."

Silence fell in the room, and all eyes were on the unrepentant knight. "Sir Brisbois," the baroness began heavily, "it saddens me to hear you say those words. As such, I have no choice but to—"

Flinn stood suddenly. "Your Ladyship," he bowed in the direction of the baroness in apology for interrupting her, "I have something I would like to say—in defense of Sir Brisbois."

"In defense?" the baroness repeated shrilly. Several others in the room echoed her sentiment, including Jo and Sir Graybow.

Flinn held up his hand and turned to Brisbois, holding the knight's eyes with the intensity of his gaze. "It's true that I returned to the Castle of the Three Suns with the intent to avenge myself on you. I wanted to have you dismissed as a knight, much as I had been. But—" Flinn rubbed his chin, the stubble of a beard itching him. "—stripping away one's rank as a knight would mean nothing to a man like you. I suggest you be censured in other, more appropriate, ways."

"You are saying that I not be dismissed from the order?" Brisbois demanded.

"I am," Flinn nodded. Brisbois put his head in his hands. Flinn turned to the baroness and the council. "That is, of course, if the council has no objections."

The baroness sat back in her chair and looked at Sir Graybow. The castellan nodded curtly to the baroness and then stood. Flinn took his seat.

"We haven't objections, Sir Flinn," Graybow began, "so much as concerns. Your . . . desire to show leniency to Sir Brisbois is commendable, to say the least. I doubt that any other knight here would be quite so willing to do the same." The castellan gestured to either side of the table. "But there are other issues to consider here, such as our faith in this man. If he were to remain a knight, how should we trust him? How can we put our faith in a man who—by his own admission—holds honor so cheaply?" The old knight sighed. "You have spoken on behalf of this man, Sir Flinn. What do you propose the council should do with him?" Graybow sat down.

Flinn stood slowly. "I ask that the council retain Sir Brisbois's stature as knight, but that he be censured by serving as my footman for one year."

Brisbois jumped to his feet. "Your footman? You mean your lackey! You——" The guards pushed him into the chair, and one placed a warning grip on his shoulder to quiet him.

"Am I to understand, Sir Flinn," the baroness asked gravely, "that you believe such service would be punishment enough for all that this man has done to you?"

Flinn bowed low. "I do, Your Ladyship. Sir Brisbois is a skilled and talented knight, but he needs to learn . . . manners. I intend to teach him that." The warrior paused and then added, "And I intend to teach him proper respect for the Quadrivial." Flinn gestured to Jo, who nodded at the baroness when Arteris's eyes flickered to the young woman. "My companion, Johauna Menhir, saw the remnant of honor and courage in me when I was a—a self-centered hermit. She taught me the importance of following the Path of Righteousness, no matter how far one has strayed from it. I would like to teach Sir Brisbois that same truth." Flinn took his seat.

The baroness scanned the council members' faces. They each shook their heads or shrugged their shoulders in abstention. She turned back to Flinn. "I have nothing further to say. As of this day, Sir Flinn, he is yours."

"Your Ladyship!" Brisbois protested again, though this time he remained seated. "This—this is slavery! This is—"

"It is bondage, Sir Brisbois, not slavery. For the next year you are a bondsman to Sir Flinn," Arteris said sternly. She pointed a sharp finger at Brisbois. "And know you this: if you break that bond in any way, do not return to the Castle of the Three Suns. I will have no truck with a man who would bring dishonor on himself twice. Is that understood, Sir Brisbois?" Arteris's voice was icy with disdain. Brisbois pursed his lips and refused to answer. "Is that understood?" the baroness reiterated, sharply.

Brisbois's eyes flashed, then he nodded and replied curtly, "Understood, Your Ladyship. For one year I shall be Sir Flinn's bondsman, and I shall obey his every command." He gestured to the two guards. "Are these necessary any more?"

Arteris glanced at Flinn, who shook his head. She said, "Guards, you may leave. And you, Sir Brisbois, may take your post behind Sir Flinn." The chastised knight stood slowly and then walked stiffly into position behind his new master. Flinn ignored him.

The baroness spoke directly to Flinn. "You have sought justice today, Sir Flinn, to right an old wrong. Certainly you have righted that wrong and will gain that justice in the year to come from Sir Brisbois. But he is not the true culprit, as you well know."

Flinn nodded and stood. "I do, Your Ladyship. I now see that Verdilith engineered my downfall from the very beginning. He transformed himself into Lord Maldrake and entered the estates of Penhaligon, fooling all." Flinn was glad to see several of the council members bow their heads at his mild rebuke. "He used his enchantments on my wife, deceiving her into believing that she loved Lord Maldrake. Then he convinced Sir Brisbois to falsely accuse me. At the open council today he . . . killed my former wife." Flinn sat down.

"What do you intend to do, Sir Flinn?" Arteris asked. "Or are you content with Sir Brisbois's bondage as the extent of your vengeance?"

"No, Your Ladyship, I am not," Flinn said forcefully. "I intend to hunt the dragon until he is dead, and I shall set out tomorrow for just that purpose."

Arteris nodded. "Good Sir Flinn, I had hoped you would say as much. We shall gather together a number of our best knights—"

"I beg pardon, Your Ladyship," Flinn stood and interrupted the baroness again. It was his second such transgression, and several of the council members scowled at him. Sir Graybow shook his head warningly. "Your Ladyship," Flinn said slowly, thinking fast, "I must admit it has been a long time since I have been at court, and I apologize for my less-than-courtly ways." The baroness stared at him coolly and then formally nodded. Flinn continued, "I intend no disrespect, Your Ladyship, but I will be hunting the dragon on my own, with only two comrades and my new bondsman."

"I see now that the knights who had been sent to rout out the dragon were led astray by Lord Maldrake, for he always insisted on joining such ventures," Sir Graybow spoke up. "As castellan of this castle, I think it unwise of you to hunt Verdilith with only yourself and three others. Surely even one knight, such as myself, would help your cause." A little ripple of wonder spread through the room.

Flinn inclined his head in respect toward the older man. "You are quite right, Sir Graybow; a knight such as yourself would help my cause indeed. I thank you for the offer, but I cannot accept it. Should I fail, I will return for that help, do not fear." Flinn suppressed the thought of Karleah Kunzay's prophecy.

Baroness Arteris clasped her hands together before her. "If you ask for help, Sir Flinn, then we shall gladly grant it, for we are in your debt. Is there anything else you would ask the council?"

Flinn nodded, then moved to stand behind Jo. He put his hands on her shoulders. "Yes, Your Ladyship, there is one other matter. I would ask that you accept Johauna Menhir as my squire. She has been a boon to me this winter, and without her I wouldn't be here before you. She has learned the sword and bow, and she rides well and is familiar with animals. Most of all, she has the heart and courage to be a knight in the Order of the Three Suns. She will one day do Penhaligon proud." Flinn's grip tightened on Jo's shoulders and she trembled.

The baroness nodded. "If that is your last request, we shall certainly not refuse it. We will be having the next formal initiation ceremony in a month, this spring, and both you and your squire should attend." She accepted a soft bundle from Sir Graybow and stood. "As for now, please step forward, Sir Flinn and Squire Menhir."

Flinn and Jo moved forward as one. Flinn remembered his first initiation as a knight, more than twenty years ago. That ceremony, too, had been in the spring, just as Jo's initiation as a squire would be. The ceremony was held in the great hall, and all were invited. Throngs of onlookers filled the hall that day, and all had cheered Flinn. Even as a young squire he had distinguished himself, and the people expected great things of him.

Flinn stepped forward now in the castle's meeting chamber. The same pride and excitement that had gripped him upon approaching the great baron came over him as he stopped before Arturus's daughter.

Baroness Arteris held out a midnight-blue tunic embroidered in gold. "Fain Flinn, former knight of the estates of Penhaligon," the baroness intoned, "I do hereby formally reinstate you as a knight of the Order of the Three Suns. Go with grace and glory."

Flinn took the silky swath and bowed deeply. "Thank you, Your Ladyship."

The baroness turned to Jo and held out a golden tunic embroidered in blue. "Johauna Menhir, I do hereby formally instate you as a squire in the Order of the Three Suns. Go with grace and obey your knight, for through him you will learn what you must to become a knight, yourself."

Jo took the tunic and bowed as deeply as Flinn had. "Thank you, Your Ladyship," she said, the words barely above a whisper. Then she looked at Flinn, who had never seen her eyes shine more brightly. "I'm a squire, Flinn. I'm a squire!" she said breathlessly.

Flinn nodded, unaware that his own eyes shone back at hers, equally bright. "You're a squire, Jo. My squire."

ಜಿ ಜಿ ಜಿ ಜಿ ಜಿ

Jo swallowed the last of her wine and then pushed her dishes away, sated. The pigeon pie had been truly excellent. Jo had never eaten a finer dinner in all her life. Flinn, Braddoc, Karleah, and Dayin were just finishing their meal. Brisbois, after having served them as per Flinn's orders, was just now sitting down to eat. The six of them dined in one of the castle's numerous guest suites—a spacious communal room adjoined to a number of bedrooms. Baroness Arteris had insisted on their being her guests tonight before they headed off to hunt Verdilith in the morning.

The young squire looked around the elegant room while the others finished the fine burgundy. The carved and delicately tinted ceiling hovered at least fifteen feet above her. It contained designs that complemented the patterns in the parqueted wooden floor. Years of use had not dulled the floor's smooth, glossy shine. Three tall, narrow windows graced the wall behind Jo's back, and a number of dark, wooden doors in front of her led to the bedrooms and the hall.

Jo smiled. She had a truly beautiful room all to herself, as did everyone but Dayin and Braddoc, who shared a room. Jo couldn't remember ever having a room to herself, except the cellar hole she'd left behind in Specularum. Even that she'd shared with sewer rats and other vermin. Jo looked through the open door that led to her chamber. While the rest of the castle had awed her with its magnificence, nothing she had seen could compare to the friendly elegance of her bedroom. The delicate tapestries, the gilt chairs, the watercolor portraits, the window traceries—everything beckoned to Johauna. She wanted to stay forever in that room, safe and warm and well comforted.

The squire sighed. She could see a corner of the softly inviting bed. After all the nights of sleeping outdoors on a few furs, the bed looked comfortable, indeed. One night of comfort, she thought, and then it's time to start my life as a squire. At least now I have proper squire clothes.

The baroness had been generous to both Flinn and Jo. The castellan outfitted Flinn with a new set of armor, which stood in one corner of the communal room. Brisbois had polished it earlier. Jo now owned two changes of proper clothing. Currently, she wore clean, fresh leggings, a soft undershirt, and the golden tunic. A pair of new boots and a warm woolen cape completed the outfit. Freshly bathed, her hair carefully braided, and clad in her new clothing, Jo had presented quite a different image when she entered the anteroom earlier this evening to join the others for dinner. But it was only Flinn's appreciative eyes that she had noticed. The memory made her smile again at Flinn.

"Glad to be an official squire, Jo?" Flinn guessed her thoughts. His smile in return was every bit as broad as hers.

"Oh, yes! I've never been happier, and I have so much to thank Thor and Tarastia for!" Jo said enthusiastically. "I'm a squire, you're a knight, and Dayin's found a home with Karleah—" Jo ruffled the boy's hair, but Dayin pulled away from her and hunched down in his chair. "Dayin? What's wrong?"

"Nothing," muttered the boy sullenly.

Braddoc gestured toward Dayin with a silver bread knife. The dwarf was cutting a last slice of bread from a still-warm loaf. "He's been acting strange ever since your hearing, Flinn. In fact, if memory serves me right, he started acting this way *during* the session."

"And why shouldn't he be acting the way he is?" Karleah said carelessly. "The boy's father is the one who led the lady into the hall."

"Dayin's *father*?" Three voices choroused.

"Dayin," Jo asked first, "what does Karleah mean? Was that man really your father?"

Dayin nodded, his eyes seeming too large for his head. "Yes," he said, his lower lip trembling but trying not to.

"Karleah?" Flinn turned to the wizardess and asked, "You knew Maloch Kine, didn't you?"

The old woman returned Flinn's look, her tiny dark eyes bright in the light of the candles. "I knew him." She shrugged. "It was Maloch Kine, all right. But he abandoned the boy, and now Dayin's mine."

"Sir Brisbois," Flinn called sharply, "who was that man attending Yvaughan?" His eyes locked on his bondsman, who finished a sip of wine and then spoke.

"I was wondering when you'd get around to him," Brisbois said. "The man's name—at least here in the castle— is Teryl Auroch. He came here about two years ago as an 'advisor' for Yvaughan, courtesy of Maldrake, of course," Brisbois added wryly.

"What do you know about him?" Flinn asked.

"The man's a mage, and a powerful one, too." Brisbois leaned toward Flinn. "I can't prove it, but I think Auroch killed Yvaughan's son—though, if he did, that was really a blessing in disguise now that I think just *what* the father was. Also, I think he was slowly poisoning Yvaughan, but I can't prove that, either. Maldrake—Maldrake refused to listen to me when I tried to warn him about Auroch, but who knows? Maybe they had all this planned from the very beginning."

"Do you know if this Auroch is still here in the castle?" Flinn asked.

Brisbois stood and smiled blackly. "Yes. What's more, I'll bring him to you. It'll be my pleasure, Flinn. I'll return as soon as possible." Brisbois went to the door, then hesitated. "The . . . interment for Yvaughan is taking place this evening. The baroness said she would hold a brief ceremony." He left the room.

Flinn nodded, his eyes distant and unseeing. Jo reached over and covered his hand with hers. "I'm sorry about Yvaughan," she said quietly.

The knight turned to her and clasped her hand in his. "Thank you, Johauna. I . . . appreciate your concern, more than I can tell you." Then Flinn withdrew his hands and rested his chin on them. "If Maloch Kine—or this Teryl Auroch—really are one and the same, what do you suppose that means?" Flinn shook his head and turned to the boy. "Dayin? Are you *certain* that man was your father?"

Dayin's lips quivered, and tears touched his eyes. "It was him," he whispered. He leaned against Karleah for comfort, the old woman putting her bony arm around the boy's slender shoulders.

Jo asked, "Why would your father abandon you like that, Dayin? Did something happen to him? Did he think you were dead?"

The boy's face worked. "He—he just disappeared. I don't know. It was a long time ago. I thought . . . it seemed like he died."

"The explosion?" Flinn asked.

The boy nodded. "There was an explosion in the tower, and that's when my father disappeared. I stayed there, waiting for him to come home, but he never did. I—I thought he was dead." A tear trickled down his cheek. "He wouldn't just leave me, would he? My father was a good man." Karleah patted the boy awkwardly, then gave him a little shake.

Braddoc spoke up. "Remember, Auroch and Kine are

both old terms for cattle. That seemed a bit odd to me."

"What gets me," Flinn mused, rubbing his shaved chin and smoothing his trimmed moustache, "what gets me, is just what this mage was doing with Verdilith as Lord Maldrake. What could he gain? Did he know—"

Brisbois opened the door then, accompanied by a short, nervous man—the man who had led Yvaughan into the council area earlier that day. He carried a buff-colored bird in the crook of his arm. Flinn stood slowly, pushing his chair back as he did. Jo followed his example, one hand resting on her sword, and moved into position next to Flinn. She pulled on her blade, letting it rest an inch or two out of the scabbard's top. The man might be a powerful mage, but she would protect Flinn regardless of what happened, even at the cost of her life. Dayin huddled in Karleah's arms, and the dwarf stood near the two protectively. Braddoc fingered his battle-axe.

"Sir Flinn," Brisbois was saying, his voice heavy with irony, "may I introduce you to Teryl Auroch? He was just leaving the castle, but some guards helped me 'persuade' him to call on you first." He nodded his thanks to three or four men standing in the hall and then closed the door.

The mage stepped farther into the room, his brilliant blue eyes averted. In one hand, he nervously held the bird, while the other hand carried a valise. He was wearing a fur-lined traveler's cape. Jo counted it fortunate that Brisbois had caught the man in time. "You wished to see me, Master—er—Sir Flinn?" Teryl Auroch asked. His words were smoothly polished, without inflection, but to Jo they sounded disdainful.

"Yes, *Master* Auroch," Flinn added his own emphasis to the man's lesser title. "I will be hunting Verdilith in the morning, and I want to know the extent of your involvement with the dragon as Lord Maldrake."

The short man shrugged nonchalantly, and then shook as if suddenly cold. "Like Sir Brisbois, I was enchanted—"

"You were not!" Brisbois yelled hotly.

"Brisbois!" Flinn shouted. "Mind your place!" Brisbois glowered at Flinn but then stepped away. Flinn turned back to the mage. "Continue, please."

"I was enchanted by the dragon," Auroch said. "Now that Lord Maldrake has disappeared, I am once more in command of myself. I am traveling south to Specularum to find a position there."

Flinn gestured at Dayin. "And what of your son here?" he asked. Dayin stepped next to Flinn and looked at the mage, tears and hope in his eyes.

A spasm shook Teryl Auroch's body again, then passed. His brilliant eyes darted more nervously than ever. Jo was convinced he hadn't even looked at the boy. "My son? I have no idea what you are talking about. I have no son."

Flinn eyed the mage with distaste, then turned to the boy and touched his arm. "Dayin," Flinn asked gently, "is this man your father? Think carefully. It has been two years since you saw him."

Dayin's blue eyes perused the man who stood before him, silently beseeching the mage to look at him. When the nervous man still didn't, the boy lowered his head, one quick tear escaping his eyes. "No," Dayin said in a small voice some moments later, "no, he isn't my father."

Jo thought she heard him mutter "any more" under his breath as he turned back to the comfort of Karleah's arms. The old woman was watching Auroch with an intensity that would have unnerved many. Auroch, however, seemed oblivious to the wizardess's scrutiny.

Flinn pointed to the bird Auroch carried. "That bird is the mate to the creature we killed in the great hall today. Why do you have it?"

"How observant you are." The mage smiled jerkily. "Yes, it is the mate to the other, but far less dangerous, even in its true form. I am taking it with me so that I can dispose of the creature properly. I hope you have no objections?" He gave a tiny, mocking bow.

"Yes, I do," Flinn responded suddenly. He took a step toward the mage. "As Lady Yvaughan's former husband, I claim her 'beloved pet' as my own. Please give it to me at once."

The mage pulled the bird tighter to his chest. "This is an evil creature, Sir Flinn, one from a dimension beyond our own world. What could you, a mere knight, do against such a creature should it revert to true form?"

"You said it was less powerful than its mate, which was dispatched easily enough," Flinn reminded Auroch. He held out his hand. "That bird, and its mate, were gifts from someone years ago. I now believe that person must have been Verdilith in disguise, and for years his pets whispered words of corruption to Yvaughan. She lies in state tonight," Flinn paused. "I will slay her other nemesis and offer it to her spirit as it departs." Flinn took another step forward, and Jo followed him. Braddoc circled around the other side of the table, and Brisbois blocked the mage's exit. Karleah stayed where she was seated, but she pushed Dayin under the table and began muttering under her breath.

Teryl Auroch's eyes glittered angrily, and his weak chin quivered with rage. "I don't fear you, Fain Flinn—precious knight of Penhaligon! And unlike Brisbois, I shall not fail my orders!" the mage shouted. One hand shot upward, and he yelled two words of power in an ancient language. *Fwoomp!* A swirling column of flame appeared between the mage and Flinn. Jo stepped to the knight's side, her sword drawn.

Wyrmblight lay poised in Flinn's hands, and Braddoc's battle-axe gleamed dully in the fiery light.

Auroch's upheld hand clenched into a fist, and he slowly pushed his fist toward Flinn. The whirling flame began to grow. Slowly it advanced on Flinn. A low, almost inaudible roar began to fill the room. As the whirling column of flame rose and broadened, the roar doubled and redoubled until it sounded like a thousand fires blazing through a forest.

Flinn held Wyrmblight higher and shouted to Braddoc, "Now!" The dwarf threw his axe squarely at the mage. The sharp blade whirled through the air, its keen edge seeking Auroch. Suddenly, the blade struck an aura surrounding the wizard and fell, marring the polished wooden floor. Auroch, oblivious to the attack, began moving the fiery cyclone closer to Flinn.

"Brisbois!" Flinn shouted. "Attack Auroch's back! Jo, skirt around and join Braddoc. Try to distract the mage!" Flinn cautiously sidestepped to evade the blazing pillar of flame. Ignoring everyone else in the room, Auroch followed the knight's move, and the whirlwind slowly drove Flinn into a corner.

Jo and Braddoc warily approached the mage. Why isn't Brisbois attacking? Jo wondered, then signaled to the man when she caught his eye. But Brisbois, his hands trembling with fear, only waved her on. The bondsman held his quivering sword in readiness, but he wouldn't leave the door. Jo turned to Braddoc. The dwarf gestured toward Brisbois, glowered with his good eye, and then shook his head. Retrieving his battle-axe from the floor, Braddoc positioned himself further to one side of the mage and nodded at Jo. This is it! Jo thought quickly, the excitement of impending battle rushing through her. She ran forward at the same time as the dwarf and swung her sword, aiming for

he mage's knees. Braddoc's battle-axe sought Auroch's
hest.

An incredible jolt of pain ripped through Jo's fingers,
preading inside her hands and into her arms. The pommel
f her sword felt as though a thousand hot needles protruded
rom it, and each one seared into her hands. Jo gasped aloud
n pain. Her fingers wanted to uncurl and drop the sword,
ut she forced herself to remember Flinn's maxim: Keep
our blade at all costs, or else you die. Though the pain drove
o to her knees, she drew her sword back for another stroke.
Braddoc was also on his knees; he was struggling to regain the
xe he had dropped.

The mage lowered his fist and slowly, carefully, uncurled
nis fingers, forming his hand into a crescent shape. The fiery
column leaped toward Flinn. It arched high above the
knight's head, grazing the wooden rafters. It swelled,
becoming as wide as Flinn was tall and then growing wider
still. The flames swirled violently, the roar of the fire was
deafening. Dishes rattled, drifting off the table and breaking
as they met the floor. One window's panes of glass refused
to bear the pressure any more, and the glass exploded
outward.

The heat was growing intense; the candles in the room
melted. An unreal, shimmering aura hung in the air, distorting
Jo's vision. The spinning column of fire grew more intense,
its color shifting from blazing yellow to lightning white. Jo
squinted, her hands still numb from the sword. She climbed
shakily to her feet and Braddoc did the same, his battle-axe
in hand again. Jo nodded at the dwarf, and they prepared
themselves for one more attack. Somewhere behind that
wall of flame stood Flinn, trapped.

"Stand back!" shouted the old wizardess above the crackling
of the flames. Karleah Kunzay jumped onto the table,

suddenly spry for such an ancient woman, and more dishes
scattered onto the floor. She stretched out her hands toward
the fiery tornado. Blue flames streamed from her fingers,
their paths fluctuating wildly but seeking the white flames of
Auroch's conjuration.

Incredibly, Jo watched the blue flames circle and entwine
the white tornado. Wind rushed in from the broken window
and flung small objects into the air. The intense heat began
to subside and was replaced by a strange, growing coldness.
Jo stared at the blue flames snaking around the tornado of
fire. Was that a wall of ice forming at the base of the tornado?
She blinked to clear her eyes and looked more closely. Yes!
she thought. Karleah's doing it!

The circle of ice climbed higher. Auroch clenched his fist
and goaded on the fiery tornado, but the wall of ice securely
trapped the flame. Then, with horror, Jo saw the mage
suddenly, chillingly, smile. The man's evil grimace grew as
the wall climbed higher and the flames of fire disappeared
inside. He lifted both hands slowly into the hair, one hand
wrapped around the buff-colored bird.

Jo bit back the pain as she lifted her sword once again. Her
palms felt as though they had been sliced open and salt
poured into the wounds. Tears rained across her hot cheeks.
Whatever the mage was about to do, whatever treacherous
new spell he was about to unleash, she had to stop him.
Perhaps his aura would fail him soon, and she and Braddoc
could strike a blow against the man.

From the corner of Jo's eye, she saw Dayin stumble out
from beneath the heavy table. The child raised his hands, and
his lips moved. Incredibly, a tiny ball of light brighter than
the tornado flashed directly in front of Auroch. An instant
later, a pair of doves fluttered in the man's face. At the same
time, the wall of ice came to a peak, the tornado of fire

contained within. Karleah laughed her old crone's cackle.

It was the moment Jo had been waiting for. Without hesitation, she and Braddoc stepped forward, weapons raised. Jo brought her sword down against the arm of the mage. Her blade sank into the man's thin shoulder, and again the jolting pain of a thousand needles ripped through her. Involuntarily, her fingers dropped the sword. Nearby, Braddoc fell. Suddenly the wall of ice exploded, and chunks of ice and bits of fiery coal flew through the room. Jo fell to her knees, hiding her face with her crippled hands and huddling to the floor. The roar crested in one final boom.

Silence.

The young squire dropped her hands from her face and looked around, stupefied. Flinn stood in the far corner, Wyrmblight held before him. Braddoc lay on the floor near his battle-axe, and Dayin huddled next to the dwarf. Karleah stood on the table, her hands still held before her in midmotion.

Teryl Auroch and Sir Brisbois were gone.

Jo shook her head and blinked. Other than a few dishes that had fallen from the table, nothing was broken. The window was intact, the candles were still lit. For a single instant, Johauna questioned whether Teryl Auroch had ever been in the room.

But the remains of a buff-colored bird with brilliant green markings lay on the floor in a pool of melted ice.

Chapter XVI

linn nodded to the castellan and grabbed the man's wrist in a final greeting. "Thank you, Sir Graybow, for the provisions, and for your help in regaining my honor."

The old castellan nodded and smiled.

"You'd better be off before dawn breaks. The courtyard's full of well-wishers who'll be waking up any moment."

Flinn turned to Jo, Braddoc, Dayin, and Karleah, who were leading their various steeds out from one of the castle's minor stables. "Are your mounts prepared?" Flinn asked. They nodded, white breath whirling from their mouths in the predawn air. The lack of morning light lent a sinister feeling to the early departure, but Flinn knew secrecy was necessary. He and his friends had to leave the Castle of the Three Suns without being seen—and without being attacked by Teryl Auroch or Sir Brisbois if either were still around. Karleah Kunzay thought the two men had been consumed by the magicks, but Flinn wasn't as easily convinced.

"You're sure no one saw sign of them?" Flinn asked the castellan once more. "I'd rather hunt their master, but if Brisbois and Auroch are still here . . ."

The older man sighed and said patiently, "No sign, Sir

Flinn. None of my guards saw either the knight or the mage. If they *are* gone, good riddance, I say." He touched Flinn's arm briefly. "I'm in charge of the baroness's safety, Sir Flinn. Tell me truly: have I anything to fear from Teryl Auroch? Or from Sir Brisbois?"

Flinn grunted. "Karleah Kunzay insists Auroch's magic was weak—that the illusion came from Verdilith through the bird. But, if the mage is still around, he could be anywhere—and he could be dangerous."

"And Brisbois?" the castellan asked.

Flinn shrugged. "I think he has enough sense not to come back to the castle. From him you won't have anything to worry about, but Auroch . . . perhaps yes. Take care, Sir Graybow."

The older knight gripped Flinn's wrist again. "I wish you good hunting, my friend. Hurry back, and we'll teach that squire of yours a few tricks." He smiled at Jo, then stepped back and waved as Flinn and the others mounted.

"May Thor and his warrior's honor remain with you always, Sir Graybow," Flinn said formally, then touched his heels to Ariac's flanks. The griffon responded immediately and entered the long, winding tunnel that led to one of the minor exits from the castle. Graybow had taken the precaution of dousing nearly all the lights along the route Flinn would take to leave the castle, but the knight trusted his mount's night vision. Ariac moved forward unerringly, his peculiar-sounding stride marking time. The soft *thump* from the pads gripped by his front claws alternated with the harder *thud* of his hind lion's feet.

Just as the sun was beginning to rise, Flinn's party exited the tunnel onto the long sloping approach leading from the castle. Flinn pulled Ariac to a halt, the dawning light just touching his face. He turned and gestured for Jo to join him, and she moved Carsig to his side.

"Look, Jo," he breathed, joy in his voice, as he pointed to the hills to the east. "There is the reason why we are here, why this castle was built, and why we are tied to this land. Look!"

Jo's gray eyes turned to where Flinn pointed. A moment later exaltation lit her face. She gave Flinn one shy, beatific smile, then turned back to the view.

There, between the two hills known as the Craven Sisters, rose the sun. It was cloven in three. Great, crescent wedges of brilliant red shimmered upward through the hills, and in another moment the disks would join and become one.

Flinn sighed with bittersweet joy. "It is said that as long as the three suns rise and become one, then the lands of Penhaligon will stand. If the three suns fail, so too will Penhaligon," Flinn said softly. The three segments burst across the horizon and melded into one glowing orb.

It was the dawn of a new day, but they couldn't linger to admire the sunrise. The time for hard riding had come. The morning shone cold and clear, without a hint of snow— perfect weather for a winter hunt. Flinn gave the signal and Ariac leaped forward.

≈ ≈ ≈ ≈ ≈

Braddoc stomped into camp and fell to the ground beside Dayin. Jo, equally dejected, followed the dwarf at a slower pace. She sat down next to Karleah on a fallen log that lay at the center of their camp. Jo moaned a little as her sore muscles hit the hard wood, and she grabbed a nearby fur to provide extra padding. She stretched her long, cold legs toward the fire.

"I'm disgusted with us!" Braddoc was ranting. "Eight days

in the wilderness and not so much as a dragon's whisker!"
The dwarf's face was turning as red as his beard. "Why, if I
had my band of mercenaries, we'd have found Verdilith by
now!"

"Wasn't Flinn your tracker?" Jo asked, rubbing one knee
and grunting. "Your sell-swords wouldn't be helping us any,
Braddoc, and you know it. Besides, mercenaries are too
cowardly to track dragons." Tensions were running high in
the camp. Jo and Braddoc snapped at each other almost
constantly, the cantankerous Karleah pounced on anyone
with no provocation, and even the shy Dayin had learned
how to retort. Only Flinn has remained calm and collected,
a far cry from the man I once knew, Jo thought. How can
he be so . . . so stoic? For five days we've been in these hills,
searching for more evidence of the dragon's passage. I'm
beginning to think Flinn must have been mistaken about
seeing signs of the dragon.

For three days after leaving the castle, the knight had kept
the five of them on the move until Flinn spotted evidence of
the dragon's passage. He instructed the others to set up camp
in a sheltered location. Flinn said that from here they could
make forays into the surrounding Wulfholdes. For the last
five days, Flinn had sent Jo and Braddoc off into the hills
together with strict instructions to return to camp the
moment they found anything. Sometimes Flinn sent Dayin
with them, and once Flinn took the boy with him. Most
often, however, the knight left at sunrise to roam the hills
alone in search of Verdilith and then returned at sunset. He
was always as exhausted and hungry as the rest of them, but
his spirit had never wavered. Jo admired his resolve; despite
the grueling, tedious work, Flinn's spirit was thriving. He
was a knight of the Order of the Three Suns, doing his duty
to avenge the villagers' deaths and prevent further destruction

at the dragon's hand. Jo, too, felt proud of her work, but the daily grind was beginning to wear on her. Braddoc, in particular, tested her nerves. But she wouldn't give in, not while she was a squire in the Order of the Three Suns.

Jo gratefully accepted the plate of stew and bread Karleah handed her. She ate a quick mouthful, then nudged the dwarf with the tip of her cold, dirty boot. "Mercenaries don't ever hunt dragons, Braddoc, so how can you say you wish we had any here? If we were after treasure, that would be one thing, but—"

"Oh, cut it out, Johauna!" the dwarf said irritably. "It was only a suggestion, that's all. Thank you," he said to Karleah when she handed him a plate, who mumbled her response. Braddoc turned back to Jo. "I don't understand why Flinn has us combing these hills. We've been over them five times now, and there's nothing out there!"

"Flinn thinks there is," Jo said before she bit into her bread. She caught Dayin's eye and ruffled his hair. The boy smiled back, his eyes bright. Jo swore he had grown during the last week, though that seemed unlikely with Karleah's uninspired cooking.

"Have you seen any sign of the dragon? Have I?" Braddoc asked, affronted. "Where does Flinn go? What does he hope to find? Why aren't we searching a different part of the Wulfholdes?"

"You have questions, Braddoc?" a voice interrupted from the dark just beyond the light of the campfire. Flinn came into view, then sank onto the log beside Jo. He smiled at her and accepted a plate from Karleah.

"Humph, does he have questions!" Karleah snorted. "Nothing but!" The old woman laid a horse blanket on the packed snow and sat next to Dayin and Braddoc.

"Did you see anything today, Flinn?" Jo asked, her good

humor restored as always when Flinn joined the group. "Braddoc and I searched the entire northern quarter again like you asked, but saw nothing. We don't understand—"

"Just what it is we're supposed to find, Flinn!" Braddoc threw out his hands. "I know I used to be a mercenary and that I used to rough it now and then, but this is ridiculous! It's been eight days, and we've seen no sign of the dragon *or* sign of civilization! When I was a mercenary, at least there were towns—"

Flinn held up his hand and broke into the dwarf's tirade. "I know, Braddoc, I know. Believe me, we could all use a rest, a soft bed, and—for some of us—a decent shave." Flinn rubbed his hairy chin and laughed ruefully. "But we've supplies enough to last another week, and I'm going to stay out here at least that long." The knight shook his head. "As always, you're welcome to go back. I won't begrudge you your right to a bath."

Braddoc rumbled beneath his breath and then shook his head. "Nay, Flinn, I won't do that. I'm in this with you, all the way."

Flinn quickly bit into his food before it grew cold and then gestured with his bread toward Jo and Braddoc. "Like you, I found nothing. I can't tell you why, but I'm convinced Verdilith is around here somewhere. I can feel his presence, as if the wyrm were watching us."

"Through the crystals?" Jo asked.

"Does that matter?" Karleah interrupted. "If Verdilith is here, he knows we are, too. So, use a crystal to locate the dragon's lair. You don't need to hide from him any more. Find his lair and then catch him there." The others turned to stare at her and the old woman cackled. "Good idea, yes? Knew there was some reason I came along."

"Why didn't you suggest that days ago, old woman?"

Braddoc snapped.

"Keep a civil tongue, dwarf, or you won't *want* to bathe!" The wizardess glowered. "I reveal my own counsel at my own time." Karleah looked suddenly chagrined and added, "Besides, I only now thought of it."

"Jo?" Flinn asked, looking at his squire.

Jo returned his look, flattered at his attention. He'd been asking her opinion lately as a way of instructing her. He always applauded her when her suggestions were sound, and he gently pointed out errors when her judgment was not. So now she asked herself the questions the knight had taught her: What would viewing through a crystal accomplish? Would it gain more good than harm? Would it harm others? Yes, Jo thought, but the dragon was certain to do harm regardless of the action they took.

The squire nodded her head and said, "Yes, I think we should do it. We have nothing much to lose, and quite a lot to gain."

Flinn nodded and turned to the wizardess. "An abelaat stone, then, Karleah?" At her nod, he pulled one from his pouch and handed it to her. "You do the honors, Karleah. We'll concentrate on Verdilith's lair to focus the stone."

Karleah's skinny arms emerged from her shapeless robe, one hand holding a tiny brass brazier. She took an ember from the fire and put it in the brazier, then added the abelaat crystal. Finally, she sprinkled on crushed quartz and muttered something under her breath. She gestured for everyone to gather round the brazier, her bony fingers seeming to be twice as long as everyone else's.

"Concentrate on the *location*, not the lair itself," Karleah said. "You've already seen the inside of the lair, so think about the outside instead. Remember: silence. We don't want the dragon to know where we are."

Jo and the others leaned closer. She tried to concentrate on what Karleah asked for, though her weary mind wandered. Then, as before, an image slowly appeared, enlarged by Karleah's magicks. Jo held her breath and leaned closer to the tiny brazier.

A rounded slope came into view, and behind it the interminable and rocky Wulfholdes. A single stunted pine stood to the left. The scene was virtually identical to every hill Jo had seen during the last five days.

"Is that it?" she whispered, before she could stop herself. The crystal shattered. She looked from Flinn to Karleah and shook her head. "I'm sorry—I didn't mean—"

"Don't worry about it, Jo," Flinn said and touched her arm. "We all saw enough."

"Enough to know that finding that particular hill is nigh impossible!" Braddoc snapped. He turned irately on the wizardess. "Wonderful idea! Are you sure you had the right place?"

Dayin threw his arms around Karleah. "Turn him into a butterfly and let him freeze here in the cold!" he yelled. The boy flashed an angry look at Braddoc; the dwarf shrugged and turned away.

"Enough," said Flinn, nearly shouting. The knight's smile was testy. "I'm convinced the vision was a true one. Now, has anyone seen that hill? It has a rounded curve to it, fairly unusual for the Wulfholdes, and there's a stunted pine to the side. Anyone seen it?"

"Are you kidding, Flinn?" Braddoc bellowed. The dwarf jumped to his feet. "We've been up and down so many rounded hills with stunted pines the last five days I'd be surprised if we *hadn't* seen it!" He crossed his arms and sunk his chin into his beard.

"I'm afraid Braddoc's right, Flinn," Jo added more calmly.

"We've seen so many hills that I certainly don't recall seeing that one in particular. But at least we know what it looks like when we go out tomorrow." She pointed to Dayin and Flinn. "What of you? Have either of you seen the hill?"

Dayin simply shook his head, but Flinn lowered his head and picked at a loose tuft of leather on his boot's heel before replying. Is he gritting his teeth? Jo wondered as the knight's cheek muscle rippled. "I may have seen the hill," he said, still not looking at Johauna, "but like you I don't remember it." Flinn stood suddenly and looked at the people around the campfire. "I think it's time to sleep. We've a long day again tomorrow. I'll take watch first. Jo, I'll wake you about midnight." Before Jo could question him, he had turned and left the camp.

"Well, that's a fine how-do-you-do!" Braddoc sputtered in the silence that followed. He shook his head and turned to Dayin. "Come along, son. Let's leave the womenfolk to their duties." He stood and put his hand on the boy's shoulder.

"Karleah?" Whether Dayin was asking permission to leave or to stay and help, Jo didn't know.

Karleah patted Dayin's head with her bony hand and said, "You run along, boy. I'll take care of things here. I want to talk to Johauna, anyway." Dayin nodded and then went off to the tent he shared with Braddoc and Flinn. Jo and Karleah had the smaller tent to themselves.

Jo began gathering the dishes together. "You want to talk about something?" she asked casually.

The wizardess put out her old hand and touched Johauna's young one. Her tiny dark eyes regarded Jo even more intently than usual, and the squire felt a little chill run down her spine. Her initial impression of crazy old Karleah Kunzay returned—the impression that she might be dangerous. Still,

Jo trusted the old woman, despite her odd ways. "I want to tell you that the moon is full, and that I'm going to spend the night meeting with an old friend," Karleah said.

"Old friend?" Jo asked, confused.

As if on cue, the loan, mournful sound of a wolf howl rose up in the distant forest. Karleah nodded and said dreamily, "That's him. It's been a long time. Don't be afraid, dear. I won't hurt you." Jo watched in shocked fascination as dark, bristly fur began sprouting from the wizardess's face and hands. "One more thing," Karleah said huskily, her voice deepening. "Tonight might be the night for . . . truth." She jerked her head toward the direction Flinn had taken. "He needs you, girl." The last words were contorted almost beyond human speech as Karleah's head lengthened into a wolf's muzzle. Her reshaping hands fastened on the gray robes she wore and pulled them off.

Jo nodded slowly at the old woman, her eyes held fast by Karleah's transformation. Jo felt no fear, only an unexpected sense of wonder as a huge, hairy gray wolf slowly emerged before her. The creature sniffed Jo's outstretched hand, gazing steadily at the young woman. Then the animal bounded silently into the snow-covered hills. Jo sighed, wishing she could transform herself into a wolf and roam the countryside on such a cold, beautiful night.

Without a word, the squire stood and began walking toward the animals. Jo and Braddoc had staked the horse, mule, and ponies to one side of the camp, with Ariac a little farther away. Flinn always started his watches by checking on the animals, and Jo was sure she would find him there. Beyond the light of the campfire, moonlight guided Jo's steps. She spotted Flinn standing next to the horse Carsig.

"Hello," Jo said simply, stepping up beside the knight. Flinn released the horse's hoof he'd been holding and straightened. "Anything wrong with Carsig?" Jo asked.

Flinn shook his head. "No, just checking." In the moonlight his wry grimace was eerie. "You know me, check and double-check."

"It's the only way to be prepared," Jo responded. "You taught me that." She smiled up at the tall knight. Then, slowly, Jo reached out and took his hand in hers. She covered his larger hand with her two smaller ones. Again she smiled up at him.

Flinn brought her hands to his lips and kissed each, once. "Maybe it is time to talk, Jo. Maybe tonight is the night, and saving this for another time isn't right."

"Braddoc and Dayin are in their tent," Jo said, "and Karleah's gone off for the evening. The fire's still going. Shall we talk there?"

Flinn nodded, then put his arm about her shoulders as they walked back to the fire in silence. Once there, the knight retrieved a fur from Jo's tent and wrapped it around them as they sat on the log. Overhead, the white moon and a thousand stars shone. This is a moment I am going to remember forever, Jo thought suddenly. The squire added another branch to the fire, then looked at Flinn.

"I'm guessing you have a lot of things to say, Flinn," Johauna said softly, her voice trembling.

Flinn took her hand and stroked it for several long moments, staring at its paleness. Then he began haltingly, "All my life I have struggled to uphold the ideals of truth and goodness, of honor and integrity." He paused to look at Jo, his expression intent. "All my life I have believed in the sanctity of rightness." The words stumbled from his lips, as if they were long unfamiliar to him. Jo guessed he had seldom put voice to the ideals he held dear. Flinn did so now, and as he spoke, conviction grew in his voice.

"I told myself I had always led a life that was true to my principles—even when I lived as a mercenary. I even told myself that although I had fallen in the eyes of my wife and fellow knights, I still remained true to my ideals." Flinn paused and gripped Jo's hand more firmly. His voice was low and firm when he continued. "For a while, at least, I was wrong. You see, I lied to myself. The old ideals were simply that: *old* ideals—not something needed by me. I never thought of them, and I certainly didn't follow them. That was a wrong I committed, and I have righted that one. But . . . there is another wrong I have made that I have yet to right." Flinn released her hand and put his face in his hands.

Jo touched the crook of his arm and leaned against him. "Go on," she whispered.

"Oh, Jo," Flinn cried suddenly and pulled her into his arms. "Don't you see? I hid my heart from you. That was the second wrong I committed." For long moments Flinn was silent, and Jo could hear the pounding of his heart beneath the heavy clothing he wore. "You scared me, Jo. You awoke all those old impulses of goodness and nobility—impulses that showed what a lie I had been living the last seven years. You tore through my life like a summer storm through a forest. You invaded my thoughts and challenged my very existence, the very meaning of my life.

"Jo, I lived a life of mindless rote, and I was happy. At least I thought I was happy. I tended my trap lines, I skinned my pelts, I brought them to town twice a year. I was content; I was safe from prying eyes, and I was safe from emotions. But you showed me there was still goodness within me if I would only acknowledge it, if I would only let myself hope. With you I could no longer be the man I had become. With you I was forced to see that my flame of honor still burned. You showed me I was still a good man." Flinn stopped again and swallowed hard, then continued.

"Jo, you also made me see how far I had fallen from the ideals and beliefs of a knight of Penhaligon." Flinn stopped again abruptly, and Jo caught the sheen of tears in his eyes. He said huskily, "You will never know how much your image of me meant to me. I cursed you for that image—and sometimes I still do." Flinn turned his head away, and Jo felt as though someone had stolen her breath.

"Oh, Flinn," the words escaped her lips. Her voice caught short as she spoke his name.

Flinn wiped the tears from his eyes and looked at the young woman. "You see, I care for you, Johauna Menhir, and deeply. But I shouldn't and I can't because of what I am to you: a hero."

"Oh, Flinn," Jo repeated softly. "Don't you understand? I didn't just worship you. I loved you, too. And I still do." The knight's lips moved, but he said nothing. Jo did the only thing she could. She took his face in her hands and kissed him. "I love you," she said slowly, "but don't ask me to stop worshiping you, for that came first and will always be there."

Closing his eyes, Flinn took her in his arms.

🍂 🍂 🍂 🍂 🍂

Fain Flinn awoke at midnight inside Jo's tent, his eyes opening and his senses instantly alert. He was supposed to be out on watch, and by rights Jo should be taking over. But this was the night for him to leave, and he wouldn't awaken Jo. Carefully he rolled onto his side, glad that sometime in the night she had moved from his arms.

The moon lit up Jo's outline quite well under the tarpaulin. She was sleeping on her side, her back to him, huddled beneath the furs. He wanted to reach out and touch the silken hair that had come unbound earlier in their passion, but he knew he didn't dare. If he did, he might never leave.

Flinn sighed. Oh, Jo, he thought, I do love you. I wish I could give you more than this one night of love, but I can't. You have put me on the path to honor and integrity. It's time I fulfill my destiny. I know where Verdilith is now, and if I don't go and kill him soon, he will attack us—and you will die, my love. So far the dragon's held off because he's afraid of attacking all five of us. But now, now the time has come for me to leave you. I only hope that Karleah is wrong in her prophecy.

Cautiously Flinn slipped from beneath the covers and out of the shelter. Jo was sleeping soundly, and only once did she stir as he left the warmth of their bed.

Outside, Flinn's eyes adjusted quickly. After the darkness in the tent, the moon seemed as bright as daylight. He located the hobbled mounts and then made a hissing noise to warn Ariac not to squeal his usual high-pitched greeting. Fortunately the other mounts were familiar enough with him that they didn't whinny or bray.

Flinn loosely laid Ariac's blanket and saddle across the bird–lion's back. He strung Wyrmblight across the pommel. Then he picked up the bridle, which he carried separately, using his fingers to dampen the metal bit and chin strap. He would saddle the griffon only after he had put some distance between him and the camp.

After a suitable interval, Flinn halted Ariac to put on the griffon's tackle; some of the knight's muscles stretched a little too far and he flinched. His body bore testament to the fury of Verdilith's first attack, and the scars across his chest sometimes troubled him. Ignoring the pain, he tightened the saddle's girth strap and mounted up. Flinn had quite a distance to travel before he could meet up with Verdilith, and the knight was glad for the full moon and clear, windless sky. He would make good time.

The knight smiled grimly, the scar across his cheek tightening as had the others. It is fitting, he thought, that Verdilith returned to this region. He dismissed the vision of the dragon's lair. He had no doubts that Verdilith was waiting for him in the glade where they first fought. With Wyrmblight I will face the dragon, Flinn thought, and we shall have our last battle. What was begun there shall end there. The knight ground his teeth, then deliberately stopped himself. "Only this time there will be a victor," he said aloud.

Flinn dug his heels into Ariac's flanks, and the griffon leaped forward. The bird-lion snapped at his bit, eager to be moving. Flinn headed north, choosing as easy and straight a trail as possible through the rocky Wulfholdes. Although he had slept little, Flinn was tensed and keyed for the fight to come.

Wyrmblight hung by his side, shiny and warm. Since the day the people's faith in him had returned, the heat had not left the sword. It's funny, Flinn mused, how when I first wielded Wyrmblight, the hilt grew warm so gradually that I never noticed it. After my fall, the sword grew cold, and I never noticed that change either. Now, however, Flinn was aware of the slightest fluctuation of warmth every time he touched Wyrmblight. The man smiled. The blade had only grown warmer with each passing day. It was a wonderful advantage in winter.

Flinn urged Ariac into a faster trot. The griffon responded admirably and soon settled into a ground-eating pace. Dawn found the knight and Ariac entering a small, dark forest in a secluded portion of the Wulfholdes. Flinn pulled the griffon to a halt and looked around, noting nothing suspicious in sight. These are the woods, he thought, the scene of what I hope will be Verdilith's death. He dismounted and pulled free a bundle tied to Ariac's saddle. Opening the wrapping, the knight began putting on the armor Sir Graybow had given him at the castle. The familiar weight of a breastplate settled on his shoulders. Flinn struggled to attach the remaining pieces of armor; he found himself wishing for his squire since many of the buckles and straps were in places difficult for him to reach. The frigid winter air stiffened his fingers. It took him twice as long to dress as it should have, but finally he was finished. Flinn pulled out the midnight-blue tunic of the Order of the Three Suns. Reverently he touched the silken threads entwined with the gold. He drew the shirt over his head.

Flinn tried to mount the griffon, but failed. "I've forgotten how to mount up in full armor," he muttered to Ariac. The bird-lion squealed. After several clumsy attempts, the knight finally settled into the saddle. He urged Ariac forward in a slow walk through the deep snow. The conifers were as thick as he remembered them so many years ago, and he almost expected to hear two squires chatter away behind him. The dark forest closed about him.

Flinn continued deeper into the woods until, at last, he saw sunlight streaming into the forest ahead of him. He moved forward cautiously until he was at the edge of a small glade. He dismounted. The glade where he had first fought Verdilith fifteen years ago stretched before him. And there lay Verdilith himself, sunning the rippling expanse of emerald green skin.

The dragon had grown, Flinn noted. He was larger than Flinn remembered, and he took up nearly a fourth of the small glade. His green scales glistened in the sun, and the bright copper plates protecting his chest and neck also gleamed. His claws, of burnished ivory, looked recently sharpened. Scattered about the dragon's body were rods, staves, and other probably magical devices. Some lay half-buried in the snow. Flinn braced himself mentally and thought, I will not turn around. Not now. The knight loosely tied Ariac to a branch and then stepped through the treeline and into the open. The dragon turned his massive head and opened his jaws in something resembling a smile. Flinn could see row after row of sharp, pointed spikes.

"It is about time, old nemesis," Verdilith rumbled loudly, then laughed. "I wait fifteen years, and you make me wait eight days more while you stumble about the hills."

Flinn advanced slowly, his sword held cautiously before him. "It makes no difference how long the wait, Verdilith," Flinn said strongly. "I am here, and today is the day you die."

"Let us speak about that, Sir Flinn," the dragon smiled toothily, and suddenly Flinn was reminded of Lord Maldrake. "You and I both know the prophecy the crazy woman Kunzay has foretold."

"Yes," answered Flinn briskly. "The prophecy says I will win."

The dragon wasn't disconcerted. "Perhaps that is what she told you. I heard a different prophecy." Verdilith lowered his head to Flinn's eye level. "Whoever wins doesn't matter. What does matter is that one of us might die—and neither of us knows which. And so, I propose that we part company here and now, and that we never seek one another again. That way the old woman's prophecy need never come to pass."

Flinn took another step forward and shook his head. "No, Verdilith, I cannot. You destroyed my marriage and my name seven years ago. You slaughtered the town of Bywater, and you murdered my former wife at the council. For these and all your other atrocities, you must die." The knight took yet another step toward the dragon.

The dragon sighed, a strange wheezing noise that sounded more like a cough. He picked up one of the rods in the snow, licked it appreciatively, and then said, "As you wish, Flinn. But I warn you: I've tired of baiting you, so your end is at hand. Your death will be over so quickly as to be ludicrous. Ready yourself; you're about to die!" He aimed the rod at Flinn, who steeled himself and prepared to dodge the coming assault. One hand touched a furry tail dangling from his waist. The dragon, in a most bored tone, spoke the command word necessary to activate the magic in the rod.

Nothing happened.

Flinn heard no noise, saw no flash, felt no different. He spared a quick glance at himself and Wyrmblight. He looked exactly as he had a moment earlier. The dragon stared at Flinn, then repeated the procedure. Again nothing happened; Verdilith picked up a staff lying at his feet. He pointed the staff directly at Flinn and forcefully spoke the command word.

Still nothing happened. A tendril of fear curled through the dragon's golden eyes. Flinn wondered suddenly whether Karleah Kunzay's prophecy were false. The knight, wondering if this was all a trap on the dragon's part, nevertheless began to slowly advance toward Verdilith. "Is something wrong?" he taunted the dragon. "Your fancy gadgets not working today? A shame, indeed. Perhaps you'll care to fight me the old tooth-and-nail, sword-and-hand way? That might prove best for both concerned. . . ." Flinn grew bolder as each item Verdilith tried failed.

The dragon threw one more wand into the snow and gnashed his teeth. Suddenly he cocked his head and looked eastward. "The box," Verdilith mumbled. "That accursed box." The dragon's eyes grew feral in the winter light. He raised one clawed appendage and murmured three words of an incantation. Flinn held Wyrmblight before him and tensed, one hand again on the blink dog's tail at his waist. The ancient stream of words finished, clipped off by the dragon's teeth. Silence. The dragon blinked, then smiled evilly. "You have me at a disadvantage, Sir Flinn, for I've been robbed of my magical powers—at least for now. However, it shall be as you wish—a duel of physical strength without aid of magicks. I shall win no matter what, Flinn the Fool."

In answer, Flinn growled low and stroked the furry tail. He'd heard Jo use the blink dog's tail often enough that he hoped he would get the tone and pitch right in one try. Suddenly, he blinked. Flinn stood a step away from the dragon's right side; he swung Wyrmblight immediately. Using two hands, the blade came down in a shining arc and cut deeply into Verdilith's side. The dragon's scales would have prevented a lesser blow, but so sharp was the edge of Wyrmblight that the blade bit in by nearly a foot. Blood gushed from the wound.

The dragon shrieked in pain and anger. Flinn pushed the blade into the wound he had made and twisted, seeking a vital organ to rupture. From the corner of his eye, Flinn saw a giant, serpentine whip swing at him. The tail! He growled the command word and blinked away. For an instant he had the impression that the tail passed through him. Flinn reappeared in front of the dragon. He jumped forward, holding Wyrmblight like a lance, and stabbed the dragon's chest. Deflected by the impenetrable copper scales, the sword bit into the trampled snow instead. Verdilith hissed, and a noxious cloud of chlorine gas enveloped Flinn. The knight only coughed a little and thanked Tarastia he had Wyrmblight to protect him.

Flinn swung his sword in a series of short, tightly controlled strokes, seeking a way past the dragon's foreclaws. Verdilith raked back and tried to grab the blade from Flinn. But Wyrmblight's edge was too sharp to grasp, and the dragon screamed in pain as the sword sliced into his sensitive palms. He reared back onto his haunches, rising to his full height, and then came back down, both foreclaws reaching for Flinn.

The knight didn't flinch. Instead of retreating, he took a step closer and held Wyrmblight straight up as the claws came slashing down. Verdilith snagged his left claw on the sharp tip of Flinn's sword, and the knight thrust upward, twisting as he did. Wyrmblight sliced through the dragon's palm and into his forearm. Tendons snapped audibly.

Verdilith bellowed in pain. He clawed at Flinn with both front talons, despite the sword still thrust through one. Flinn fought to keep hold of Wyrmblight; the violent thrashing almost tore the sword from his hands. The moment Verdilith paused, Flinn twisted and yanked on the sword as he pulled it out. The knight smiled brutally at Verdilith's ravaged claw.

The dragon screamed, and the sound buffeted the evergreens surrounding the glade. Verdilith raked Flinn again, and this time the claws caught hold of Flinn's breastplate. The links holding the chest and back plates together snapped, and both pieces fell to the bloodied snow. The midnight-blue tunic floated to the ground. Flinn was virtually armorless above his waist. He pulled his sword up as a shield, thinking the dragon would attack with his claws again. Instead, Verdilith opened his mouth and snapped his jaws together suddenly. Flinn jumped back and reached for the blink dog's tail, but Verdilith anticipated the knight's move. With astounding speed, the dragon snapped his jaws a second time, and this time Flinn's chest was caught between the pointed fangs. The growled command word emerged garbled and unintelligible. Flinn dropped the tail. The dragon lifted his head and shook his prey.

Flinn screamed. The ivory daggers lacing the behemoth's jaws pierced Flinn's undershirt and the arm cuffs he wore. Through a haze of pain, Flinn smelled the stench of chlorine and the dragon's bile. The knight had a sudden vision of the animals he had hunted, writhing in his traps, and he knew exactly how they felt. Then the dragon ground his teeth together, and Flinn felt something inside him burst. A wave of blackness threatened to swallow him whole. "No!" he shouted. He fought for consciousness; he didn't stand a chance if he blacked out now.

Below, something streaked into Flinn's vision. A shrill squeal reached his ears. Ariac! He'd bit through his rein. The griffon attacked, his keen claws and beak scraping the gaping wound along the dragon's right side. The bird-lion fluttered his stunted wings as his sharp beak buried deep in the ragged flesh. Suddenly Flinn felt the dragon's jaws open. He fell heavily to the ground and lay in the snow, unable to move. His hand still curled around Wyrmblight, though how he'd managed to hold onto the sword he didn't know.

Flinn lifted his head, and through glazed eyes he saw his griffon charge the dragon. It was a hopeless match from the start, made more so by Ariac's inability to fly. The griffon screeched, his wicked beak piercing the dragon's wounded side, but Verdilith caught Ariac between his good claw and his injured one. "I've killed your master, feeble creature, and it will be a pleasure to kill you!" Verdilith snarled. Gripping the bird-lion, he bit Ariac's neck, tearing almost all of it away. The griffon gurgled one last scream and lay still. Flinn closed his eyes and gritted his teeth, somehow managing to stand. He stumbled toward Verdilith just as the dragon pitched Ariac's broken body away from him.

Flinn lifted Wyrmblight above his head, his arms and chest protesting. His heart labored to pump blood, and he then felt one lung collapse. For a moment he couldn't breathe. He gasped for air. "It is you who will die, Verdilith," Flinn shouted hoarsely as the dragon turned back, "just as the prophecy foretold!" Flinn stepped forward suddenly and, with the last of his strength, brought Wyrmblight down upon the dragon. The blade bit deep into Verdilith's left shoulder, almost to the hilt, and the dragon reared in pain and clawed the blade loose. Wyrmblight fell to the trampled snow. Verdilith shrieked again, and this time the sound of fear tainted the cry. The beast's blood poured in steaming rivulets from his side, his shoulder, and his mangled claw. He backed away from the tottering man, then turned and crashed into the forest. The dragon's leathery wings flapped as he ran, unable to lift the beast from the small clearing.

The knight feebly tried to wipe the blood from his eyes and then stumbled toward the shining silver blade lying in the red snow. Flinn paused by Ariac's body—and fell to one knee. He stroked the silken feathers one last time in farewell. He tried to speak, but nothing emerged from the bruised lips except a bubble of blood. Flinn's eyes clouded over, then turned toward his sword. By supreme effort, Flinn stood and haltingly limped over to the blade. Somehow he picked up Wyrmblight. Never had the sword felt heavier, and never had it felt warmer. Flinn welcomed the warmth, for he was suddenly cold, so cold.

Flinn lifted his glazed, bloodied eyes to the forest and then slowly, slowly began to walk in the direction the dragon had gone. "He is mortally wounded," Flinn said dazedly. He coughed twice, his collapsed lung rattling, "but I must be sure he will die."

He stepped heavily forward, jags of pain racing like lightning through his torso. Broken ribs stabbed into his failing lungs, and his heart beat frantically. A rushing noise grew in his ears. He walked twenty, thirty steps through the snow, leaving a crimson trail behind him.

He fell.

Flinn lay for a moment, fighting back the dizzy blackness that edged his vision. He closed his eyes. The image of Jo rose to his mind, and with it the image of Verdilith. Flinn gripped Wyrmblight in his hands, then opened his eyes and began dragging his beaten body through the brush, still following the trail left by Verdilith. Willpower had failed him. Now heart alone kept him moving.

"Karleah . . ." he gasped through broken teeth, " . . . damn your prophecy."

ða ða ða ða ða

Braddoc Briarblood, Karleah Kunzay, and Dayin Kine halted their mounts and began discussing the tracks before them.

Johauna Menhir heard none of the conversation. The words were drowned out by the litany that had filled her mind since morning: Flinn—where are you? Why didn't I awake when you left? Why? I could have stopped you, or I could have gone with you! The words had echoed in her mind during the entire four-hour ride. Her three companions pointed toward a dark wood before them and turned their mounts to enter it. Jo followed mechanically.

The trail ahead of them stopped, and Jo and the others saw where Flinn must have dismounted—probably to don his armor. We must be close to the dragon, Jo thought, and close to Flinn. She only prayed that they had arrived in time to help him, but something in her heavy heart told her otherwise. Shaking the doubts from her mind, she drew her sword, jumped off Carsig, and raced into the woods. The dwarf, wizardess, and boy followed more slowly.

Giant pines and a few scattered spruces crowded the forest. The silence was palpable, and it frightened Jo. Woodlore stated that such absolute silence meant only one thing: a fight to the death had taken place. Only her fearful breaths disturbed the awful hush as she plunged forward.

Moments later, Jo broke through a line of trees and entered a small glade, a tiny meadow hidden in the woods. The snow-covered ground was trampled and stained. Blood and upturned earth marred the former whiteness. Shining bits of metal gleamed, half-buried in the snow. A tattered piece of midnight-blue cloth waved in the wind, snagged on a broken staff.

Jo halted. The huddled corpse of a griffon lay in the center of the glade. Ariac was sprawled on his back, his eagle's head nearly severed from his body.

"Oh, Ariac," Jo whispered, running toward the fallen beast. Her eyes were wide with grief and pain. She heard the others come up behind her, but she couldn't bear that they see her grief—not yet. She fled forward, seeking Flinn, praying. Praying.

Jo ran for twenty, thirty, forty more paces, across the glade and into the forest again. She felt bile rise in her throat when she saw the bloody path Flinn had left behind. It was fully three feet wide—and crimson. Jo prayed some of the blood was the dragon's. Twigs and chunks of soil had been churned up on the ground ahead, mixing foully with the snow and blood.

Finally, in a glade even smaller than the last, Jo found him. She stumbled toward the still form of Flinn lying on his side, one arm outstretched, his hand poised to claw at the trampled snow. As each step drew her closer, Jo's legs grew leaden. She dropped her sword and one hand cradled her stomach, but somehow she stumbled forward. Reaching his body, Johauna Menhir fell to her knees in the snow by Flinn's side. Wyrmblight lay next to him, the silver of its bright blade shining in the sun. She pushed the cold hilt into the outstretched hand, but there was no response. She clasped her own hand around his.

His face was turned away from her, and she saw only his iron-streaked black hair and blood. His chest and back plate were gone, and the gray woolen tunic he wore underneath was now red. Blood still ran from large puncture wounds that marked both his back and his chest. Jo choked on a sob, then gently rolled the knight onto his back so that she could see him.

"Flinn—" his name escaped her throat. She touched the bloodied, battered face of the man she loved and bit the insides of her cheeks to keep from crying. Through tears that she refused to let fall, she gently pushed aside his tangled locks and wiped the blood from his eyes and mouth. Jo leaned over and kissed him, unaware that Braddoc, Karleah, and Dayin stood silently behind her.

"Flinn—" Jo pleaded in a voice as hoarse as before. She was beyond the ability to pray coherently to her Immortals, but she silently beseeched them for Flinn's life.

His eyelids fluttered open. They closed once, then opened again, and Jo saw that they were filled with inexpressible pain. He blinked a second time, then a third, and she cradled his head to her breast. The tears she had tried not to shed were running silently down her cheeks, landing on Flinn's chest and mingling with his blood.

"Jo," Flinn's voice wasn't even a whisper, "I love you. . . ."

Blood trickled from Flinn's lips. His eyes glazed over completely and rolled upward. The faintest tremor went through his body, and then his neck stiffened.

Fain Flinn was dead.

Jo threw back her head, her hands clutching the body in her arms, a cry in her throat. But the cry wouldn't emerge, and she doubled over in mute pain.

❧ ❧ ❧ ❧ ❧

For four days and four nights Johauna Menhir stood alone before the funeral pyre of Flinn the Mighty. She had requested that her companions stay away during her time of grief, and they respected her wishes. For four days and nights Jo guarded Flinn's body from the ravages of wolves, but no other creatures came to the glade that witnessed the warrior's death. And for four days and nights, Johauna prayed hopelessly that Flinn would rise from his pallet.

He did not.

On the fourth day, three riders joined Jo: Braddoc, Karleah, and Dayin. They handed Jo a torch and moved to different sides of the pyre, each carrying his or her own torch. Jo stood at the front, unwilling to send Flinn's spirit to rest but knowing she must. Her eyes were dark from sorrow and sleeplessness, and she nodded to Dayin to begin.

The boy intoned, "For Flinn the Mighty, there was the first point of the Quadrivial: Honor." He threw his torch at the pile of wood before him. Dayin sat down in the snow, dazed. Ariac's body rested within the pyre, for Jo had decreed that so faithful a mount should join his master in whatever life awaited them after death.

Jo nodded to Karleah, who said in a voice more subdued than any had ever heard from her, "For Flinn the Mighty, there was the second point of the Quadrivial: Courage. None had greater than he." The wizardess added her torch to the pile, and the flames began to lap at the dry wood.

Braddoc looked Jo's way, and at her assent he began to speak. His voice was gruff, and tears ran unashamedly down his face, wetting his beard. "For Flinn the Mighty, there was the third point of the Quadrivial: Faith, for the people in all Penhaligon believed in him." Braddoc's voice broke on the last words. He tossed his torch onto the pile and turned away. Sobs shook the dwarf's broad shoulders, and he buried his face in his hands.

Jo tried to see through the mist of tears in her eyes, but could not. The flames flickered before her, demanding her attention. Then a sudden gust of wind picked up a corner of Flinn's tunic, and she focused on the midnight blue. Holding up her torch, she called out in a voice that rang with a strength laced with sorrow, "For Flinn the Mighty, there was the fourth and final point of the Quadrivial: Glory."

She stopped, unable to speak. She swallowed once, twice, and continued, her voice raw with restraint. "Glory," she repeated and gripped Wyrmblight so tightly her hands bled. "And the people in all lands, not just Penhaligon, will know of the Mighty Flinn, and the glory in which he died, and the glory in which he lived." The words sank to a whisper, and then Jo threw the last torch onto Flinn's funeral pyre.

The patch of midnight blue disappeared in the flames of death.